Disney Fairies

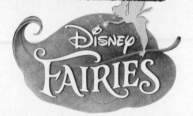

Rani and the Mermaid Lagoon

By Haruhi Kato

TOKYOPOP®

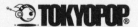

HAMBURG // HONG KONG // LOS ANGELES // TOKYO

All About Fairies

IF YOU HEAD TOWARD THE SECOND STAR TO YOUR
RIGHT AND FLY STRAIGHT ON 'TIL MORNING, YOU'LL
COME TO NEVER LAND, A MAGICAL ISLAND WHERE
MERMAIDS PLAY AND CHILDREN NEVER GROW UP.

WHEN YOU ARRIVE, YOU MIGHT HEAR SOMETHING LIKE THE
TINKLING OF LITTLE BELLS. FOLLOW THAT SOUND AND YOU'LL
FIND PIXIE HOLLOW, THE SECRET HEART OF NEVER LAND.
A GREAT OLD MAPLE TREE GROWS IN PIXIE HOLLOW, AND
IN IT LIVES HUNDREDS OF FAIRIES AND SPARROW MEN.

SOME OF THEM CAN DO WATER MAGIC, OTHERS CAN FLY LIKE
THE WIND, AND STILL OTHERS CAN SPEAK TO ANIMALS. YOU SEE,
PIXIE HOLLOW IS THE NEVER FAIRIES' KINGDOM, AND EACH FAIRY
WHO LIVES THERE HAS A SPECIAL, EXTRAORDINARY TALENT.

NOT FAR FROM THE HOME TREE, NESTLED IN THE
BRANCHES OF A HAWTHORN, IS MOTHER DOVE,
THE MOST MAGICAL CREATURE OF ALL.

SHE SITS ON HER EGG, WATCHING OVER THE FAIRIES, WHO IN TURN
WATCH OVER HER. FOR AS LONG AS MOTHER DOVE'S EGG STAYS WELL
AND WHOLE, NO ONE IN NEVER LAND WILL EVER GROW OLD. ONCE,
MOTHER DOVE'S EGG WAS BROKEN. BUT WE ARE NOT TELLING THE
STORY OF THE EGG HERE. NOW IT'S TIME FOR RANI'S TALE...

Believing is just the beginning

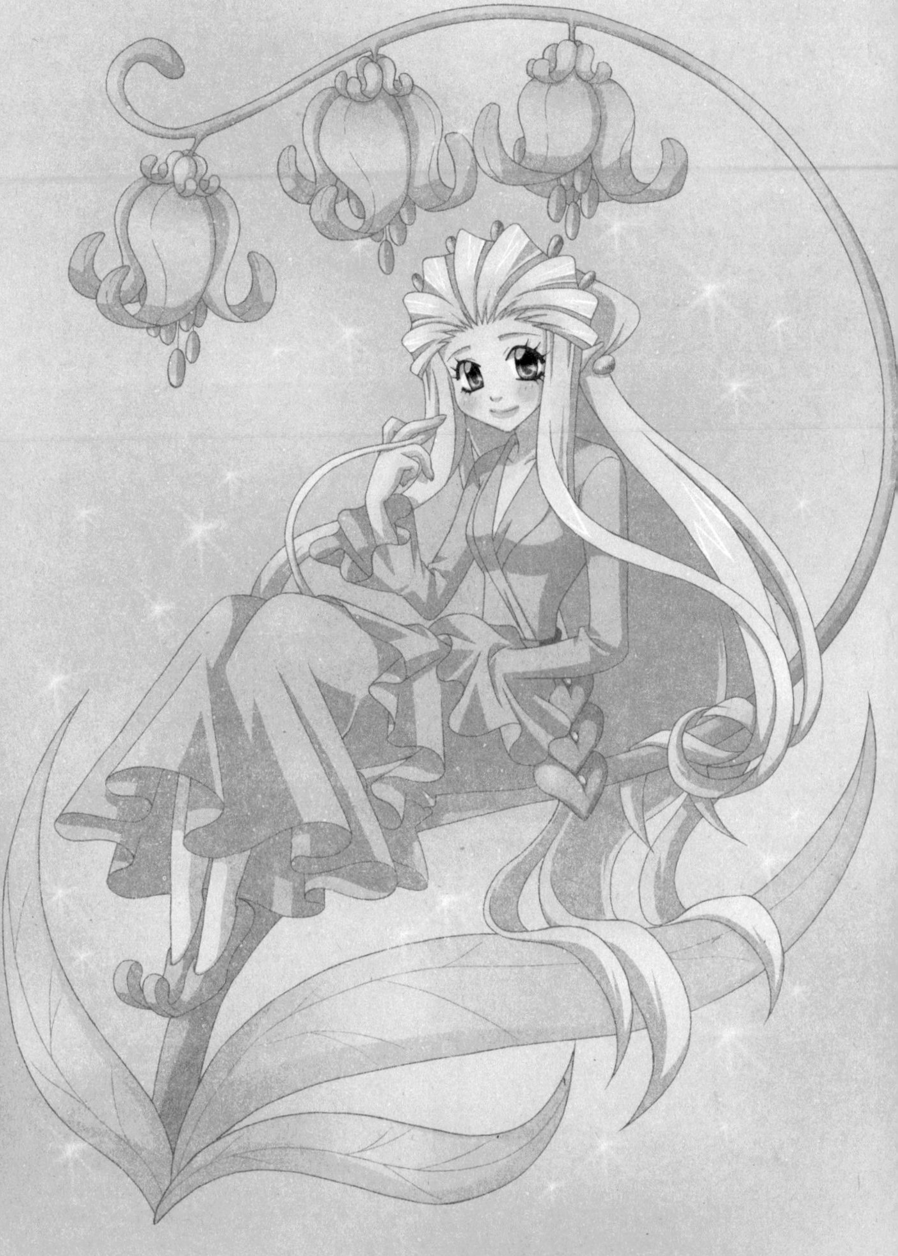

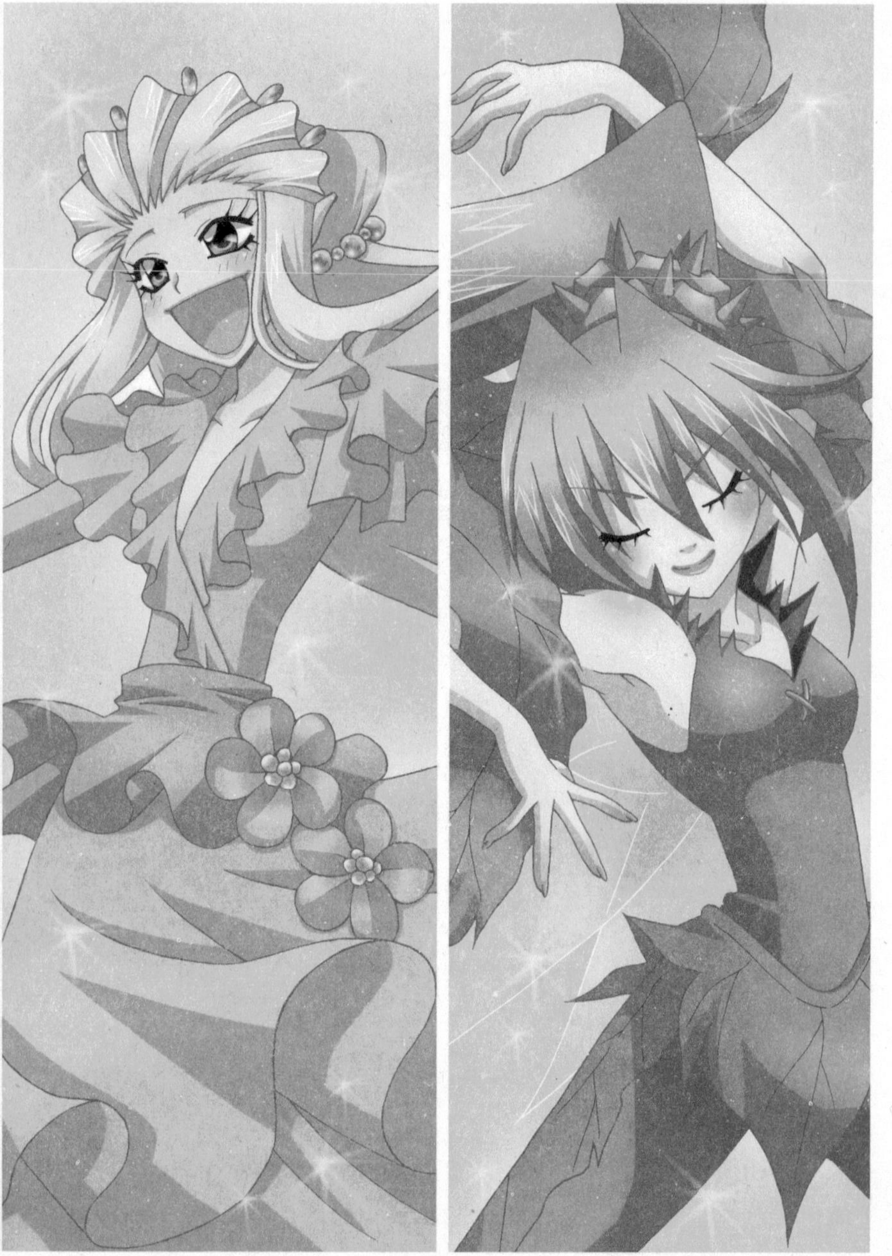

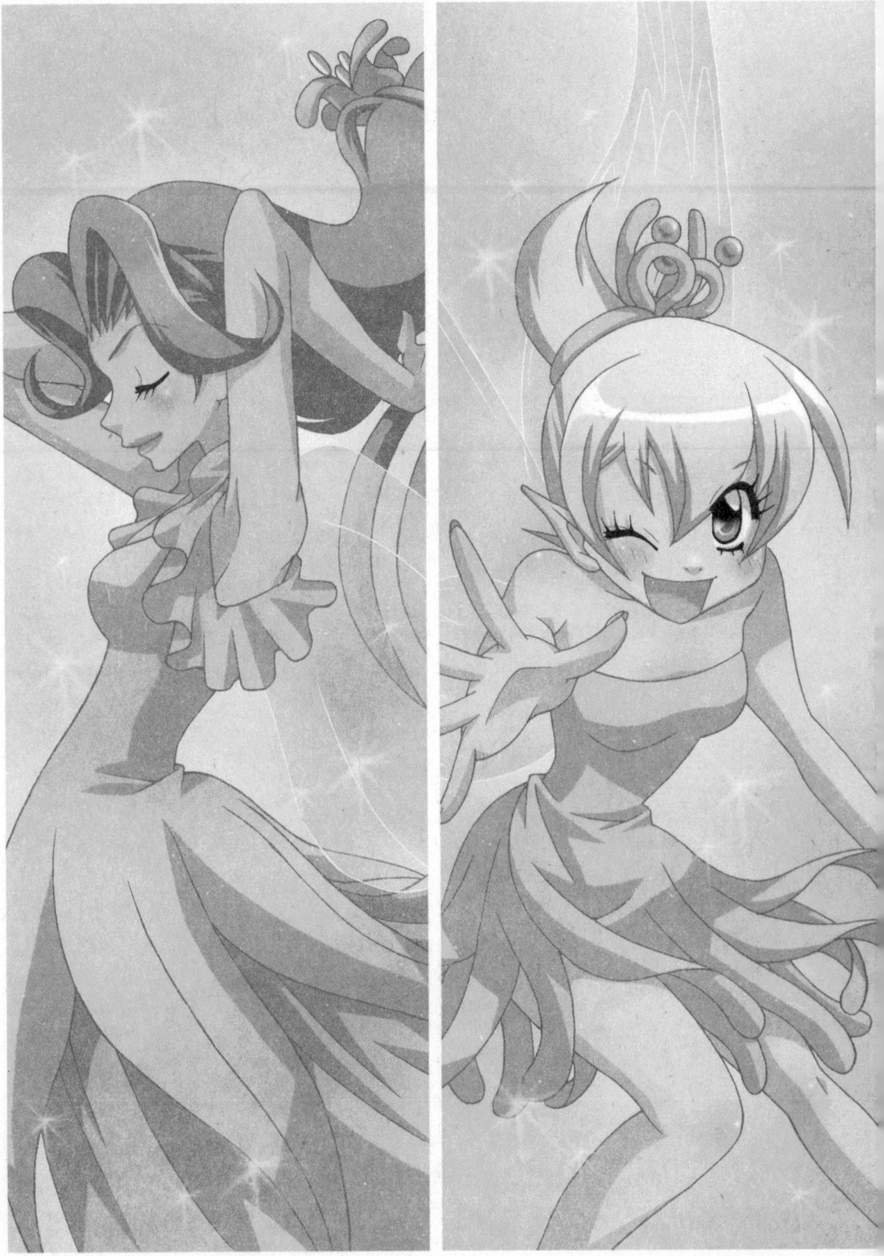

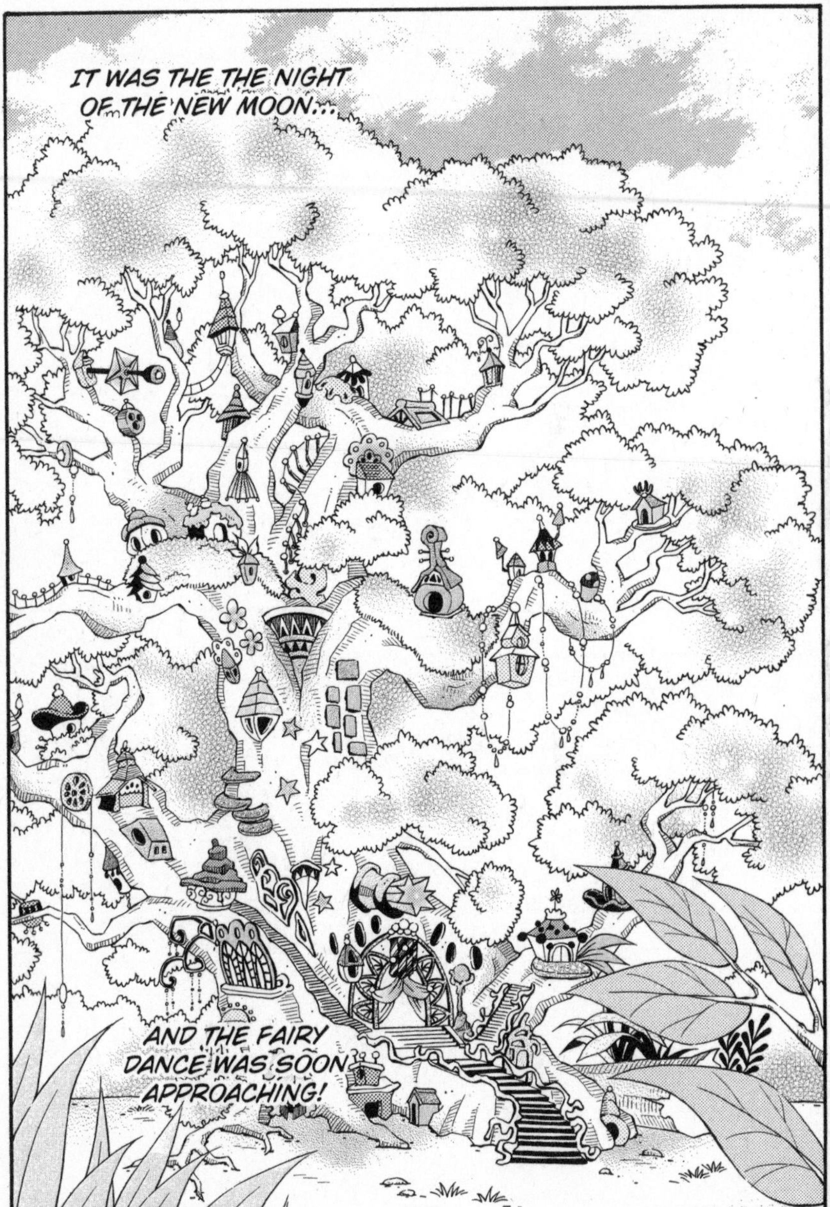
IT WAS THE THE NIGHT OF THE NEW MOON...
AND THE FAIRY DANCE WAS SOON APPROACHING!

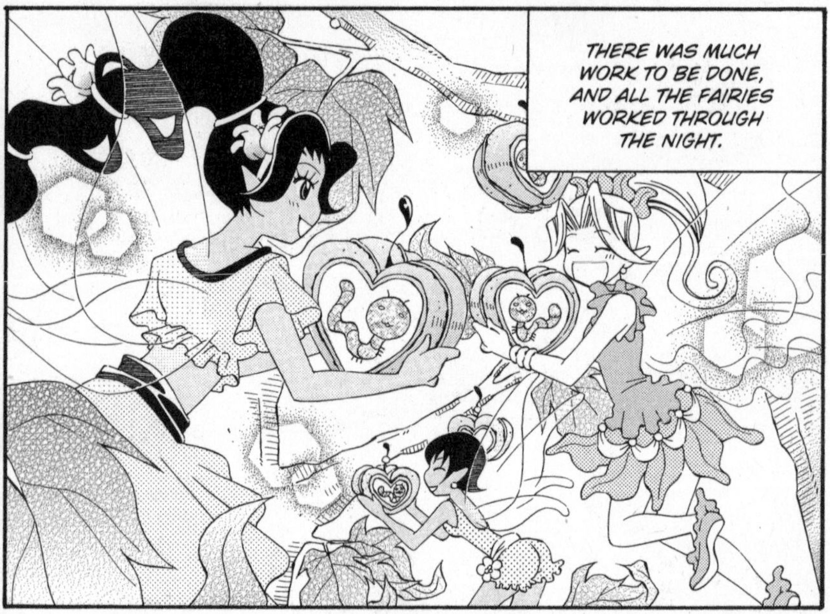
THERE WAS MUCH WORK TO BE DONE, AND ALL THE FAIRIES WORKED THROUGH THE NIGHT.
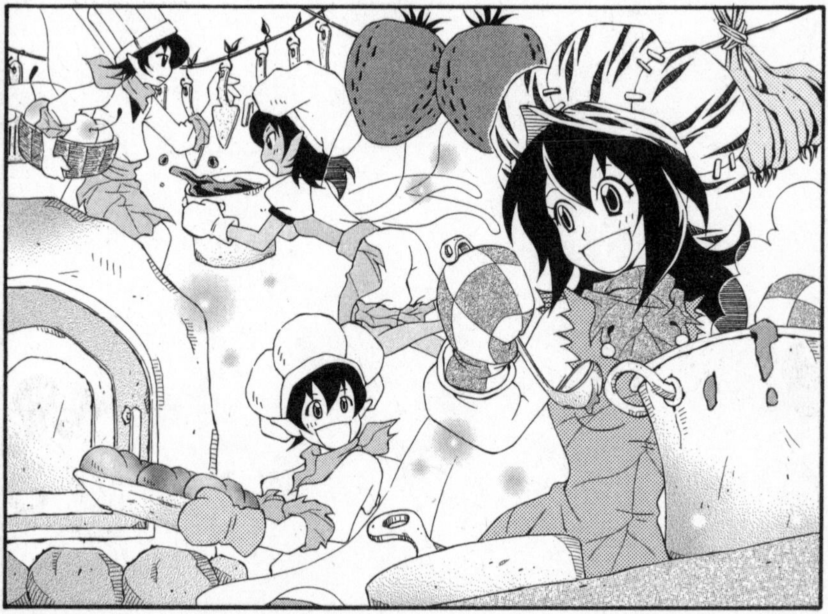

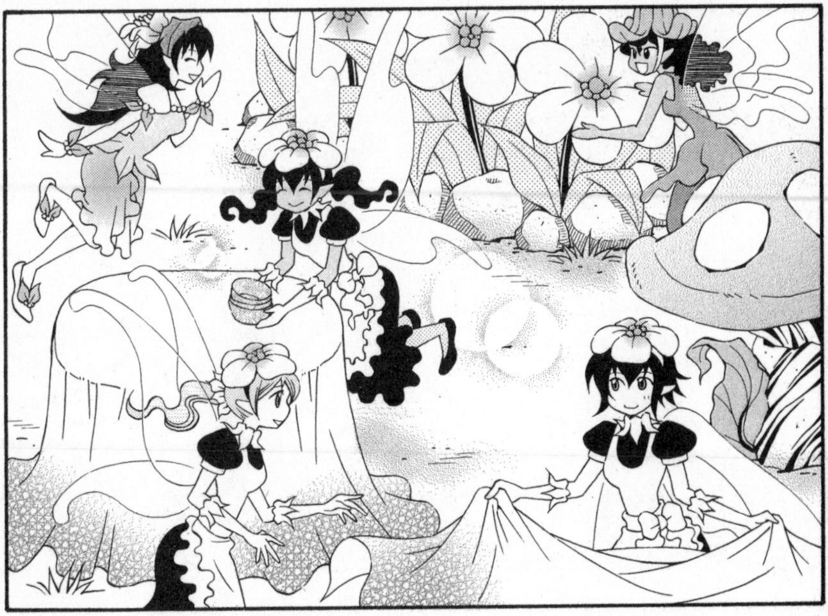

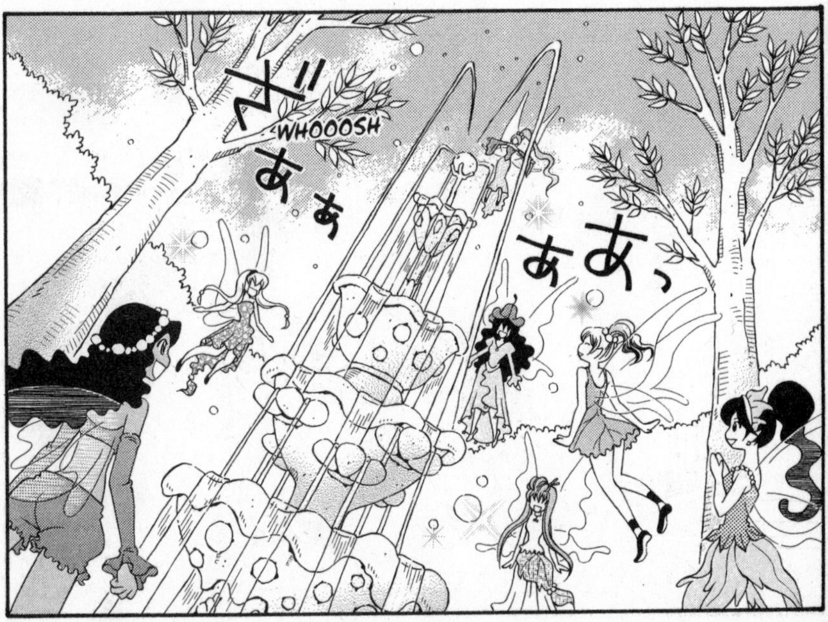
ああっ
ズ
WHOOOSH
あぁ

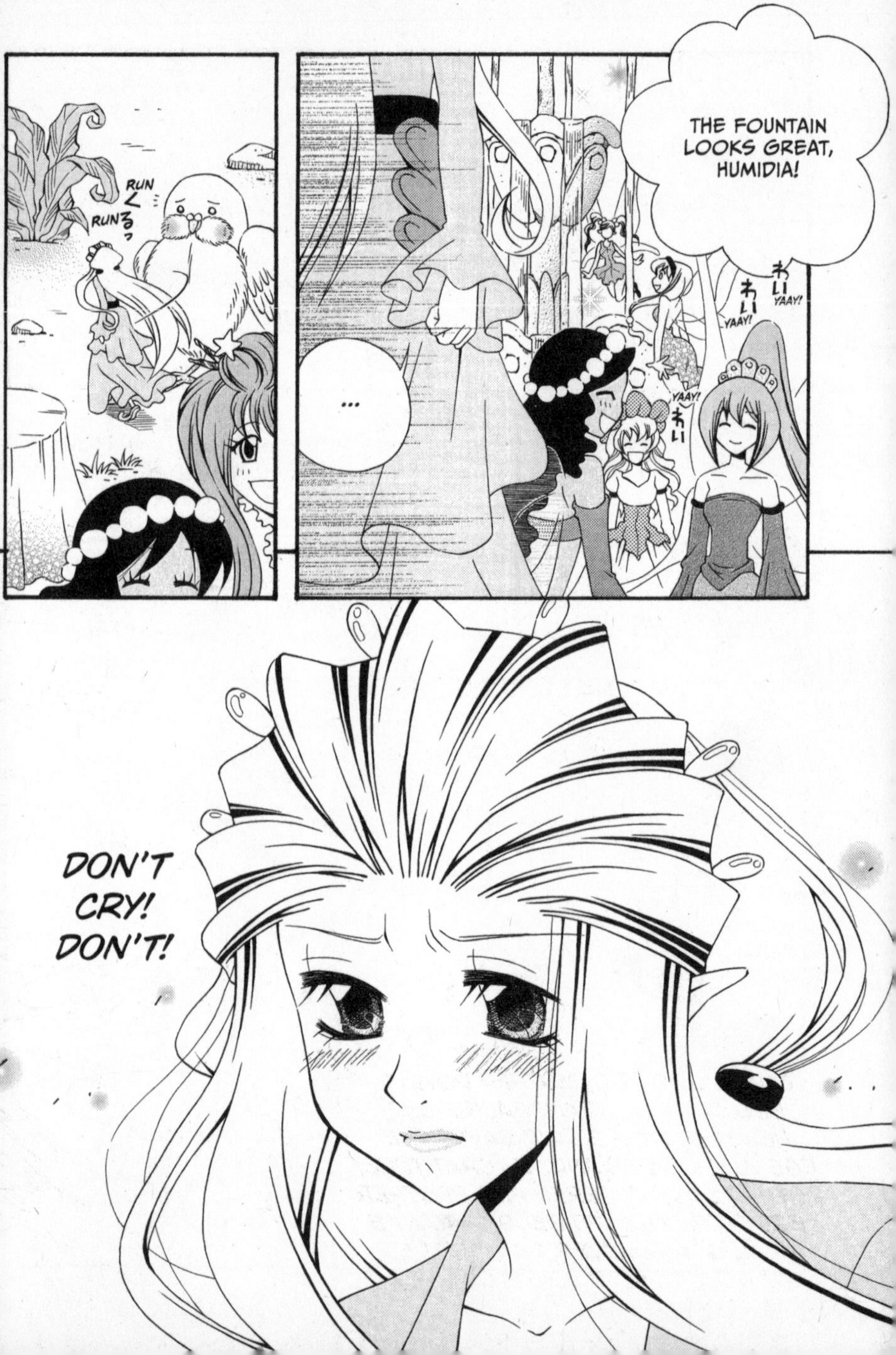
THE FOUNTAIN LOOKS GREAT, HUMIDIA!
わい YAAY!
わい YAAY!
YAAY! わい
...
RUN く
RUN る
DON'T CRY! DON'T!

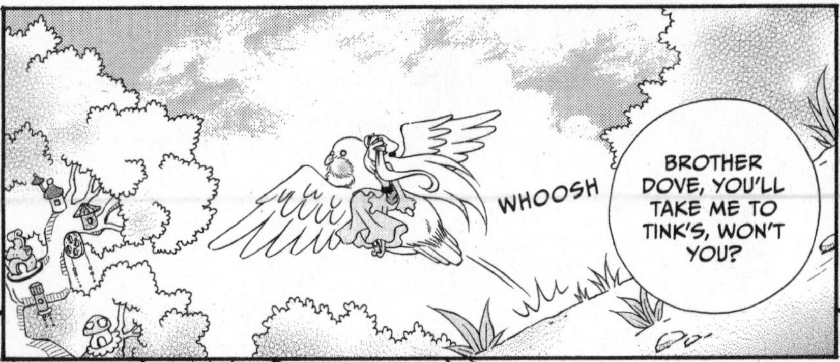
BROTHER DOVE, YOU'LL TAKE ME TO TINK'S, WON'T YOU?
WHOOSH

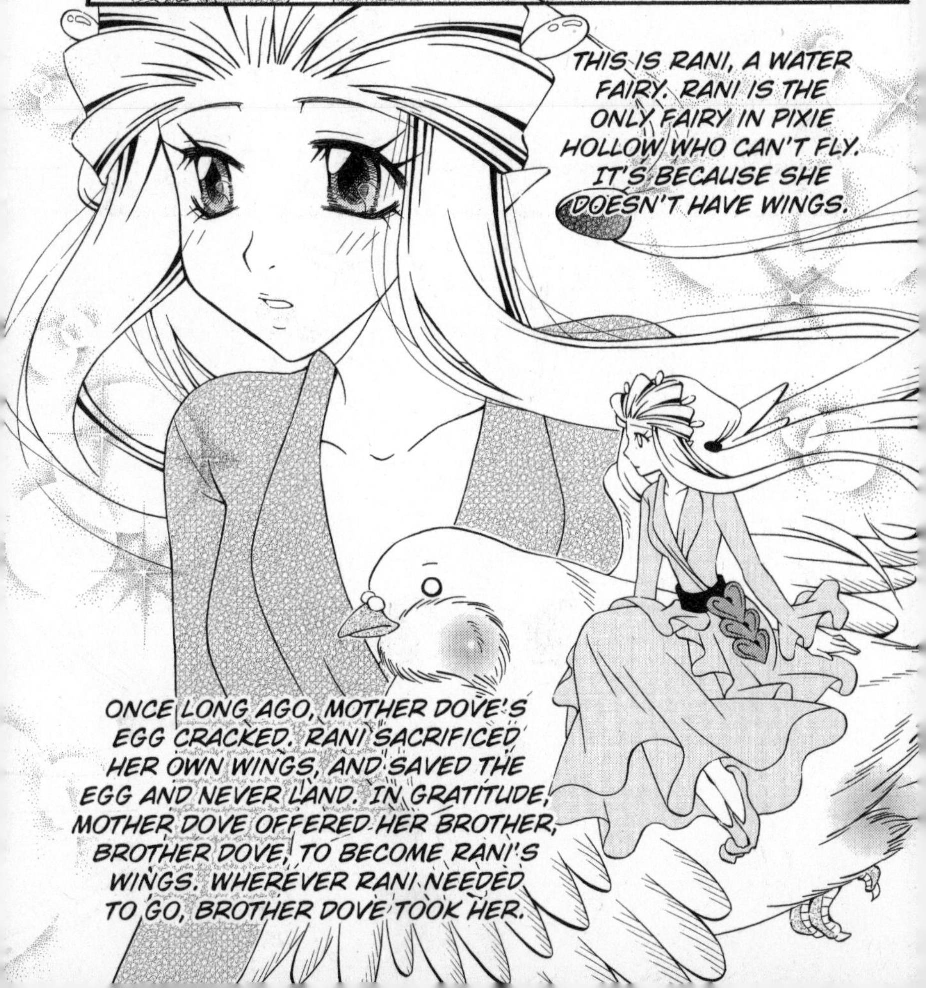
THIS IS RANI, A WATER FAIRY. RANI IS THE ONLY FAIRY IN PIXIE HOLLOW WHO CAN'T FLY. IT'S BECAUSE SHE DOESN'T HAVE WINGS.
ONCE LONG AGO, MOTHER DOVE'S EGG CRACKED. RANI SACRIFICED HER OWN WINGS, AND SAVED THE EGG AND NEVER LAND. IN GRATITUDE, MOTHER DOVE OFFERED HER BROTHER, BROTHER DOVE, TO BECOME RANI'S WINGS. WHEREVER RANI NEEDED TO GO, BROTHER DOVE TOOK HER.

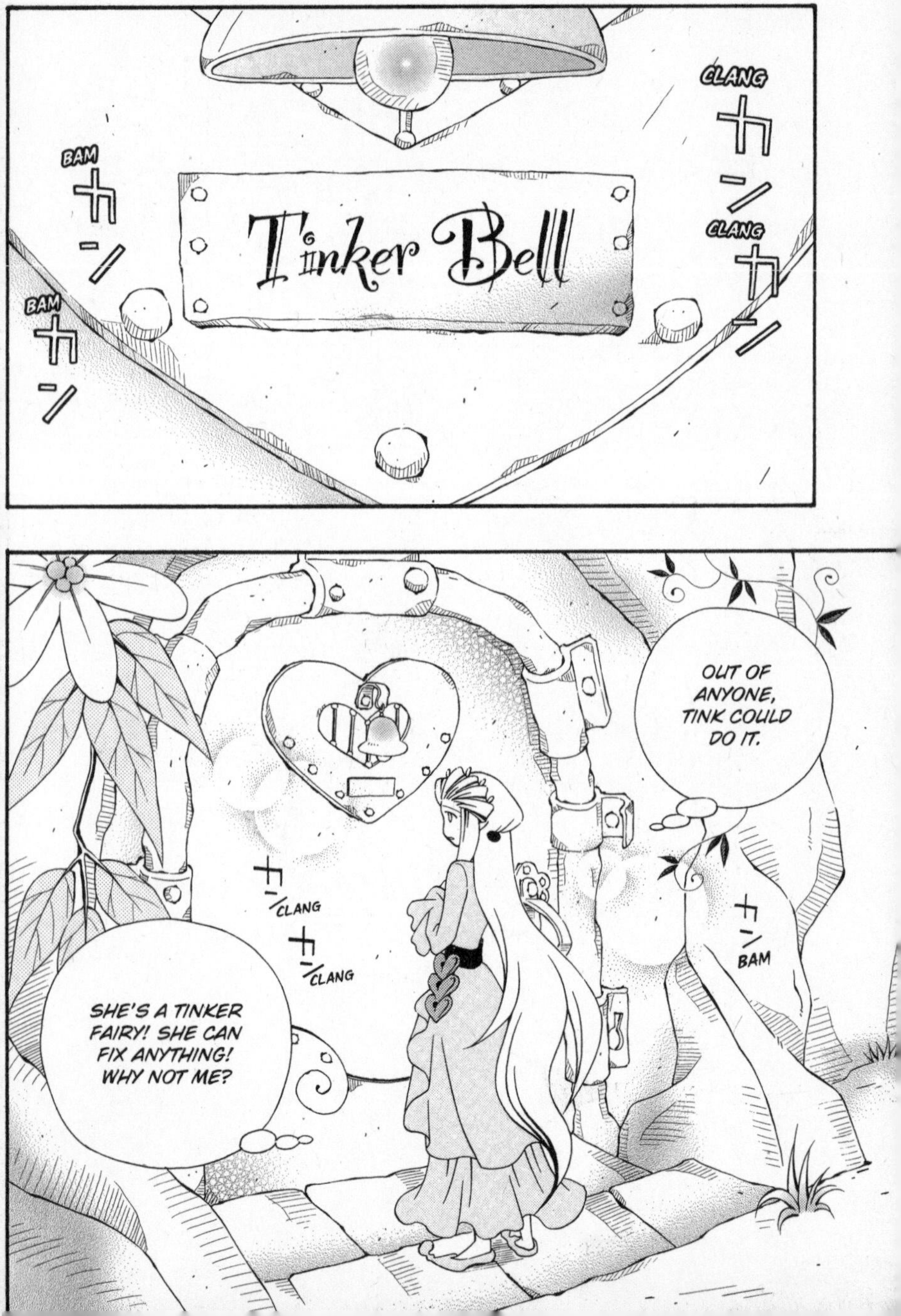
CLANG
CLANG
Tinker Bell
BAM
BAM
OUT OF ANYONE, TINK COULD DO IT.
BAM
CLANG
CLANG
SHE'S A TINKER FAIRY! SHE CAN FIX ANYTHING! WHY NOT ME?

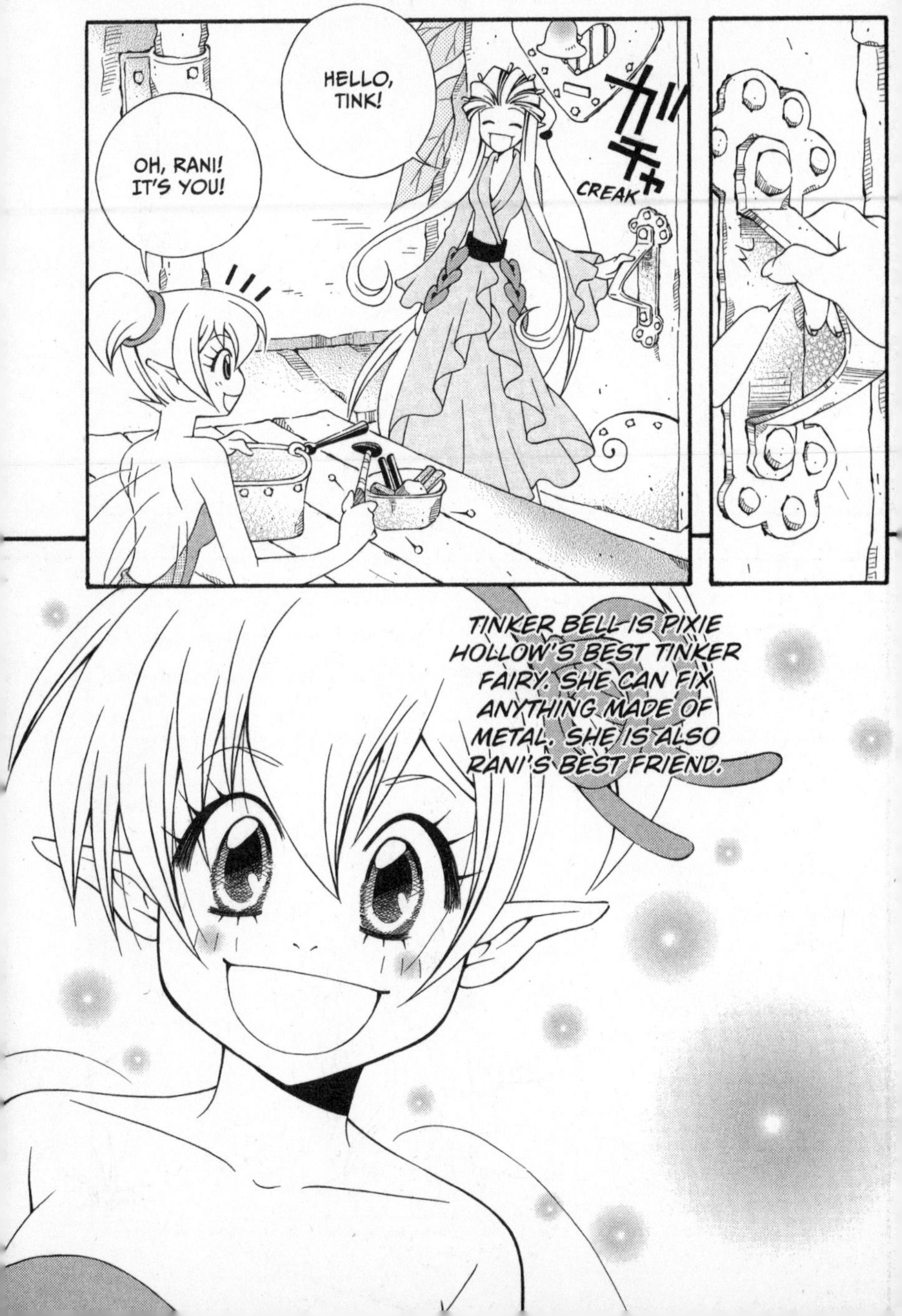
HELLO, TINK!
カチャ
CREAK
OH, RANI! IT'S YOU!
TINKER BELL IS PIXIE HOLLOW'S BEST TINKER FAIRY. SHE CAN FIX ANYTHING MADE OF METAL. SHE IS ALSO RANI'S BEST FRIEND.

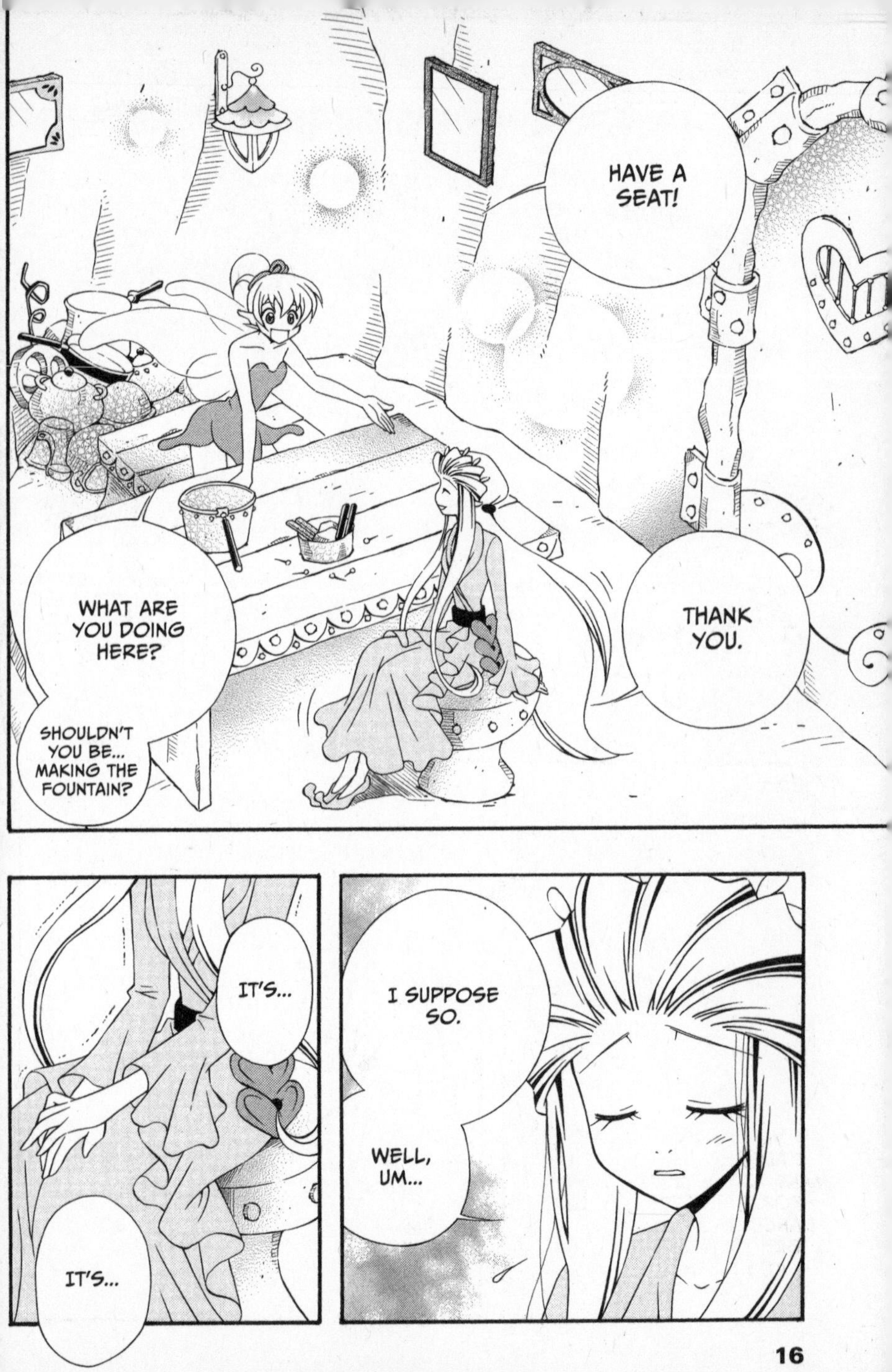
HAVE A SEAT!
THANK YOU.
WHAT ARE YOU DOING HERE?
SHOULDN'T YOU BE... MAKING THE FOUNTAIN?
I SUPPOSE SO.
WELL, UM...
IT'S...
IT'S...

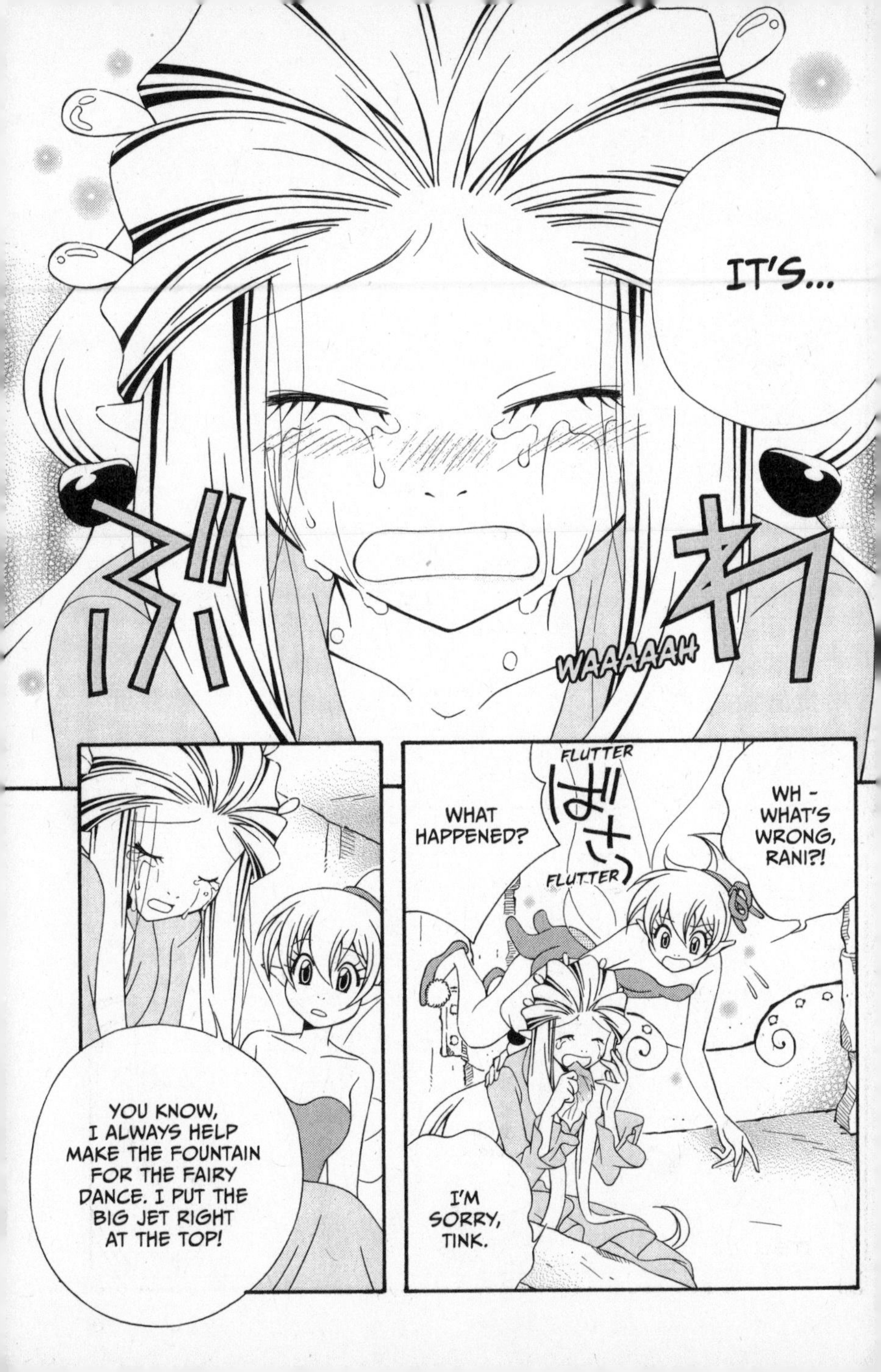
IT'S...
WAAAAAH
WH - WHAT'S WRONG, RANI?!
FLUTTER
FLUTTER
WHAT HAPPENED?
I'M SORRY, TINK.
YOU KNOW, I ALWAYS HELP MAKE THE FOUNTAIN FOR THE FAIRY DANCE. I PUT THE BIG JET RIGHT AT THE TOP!

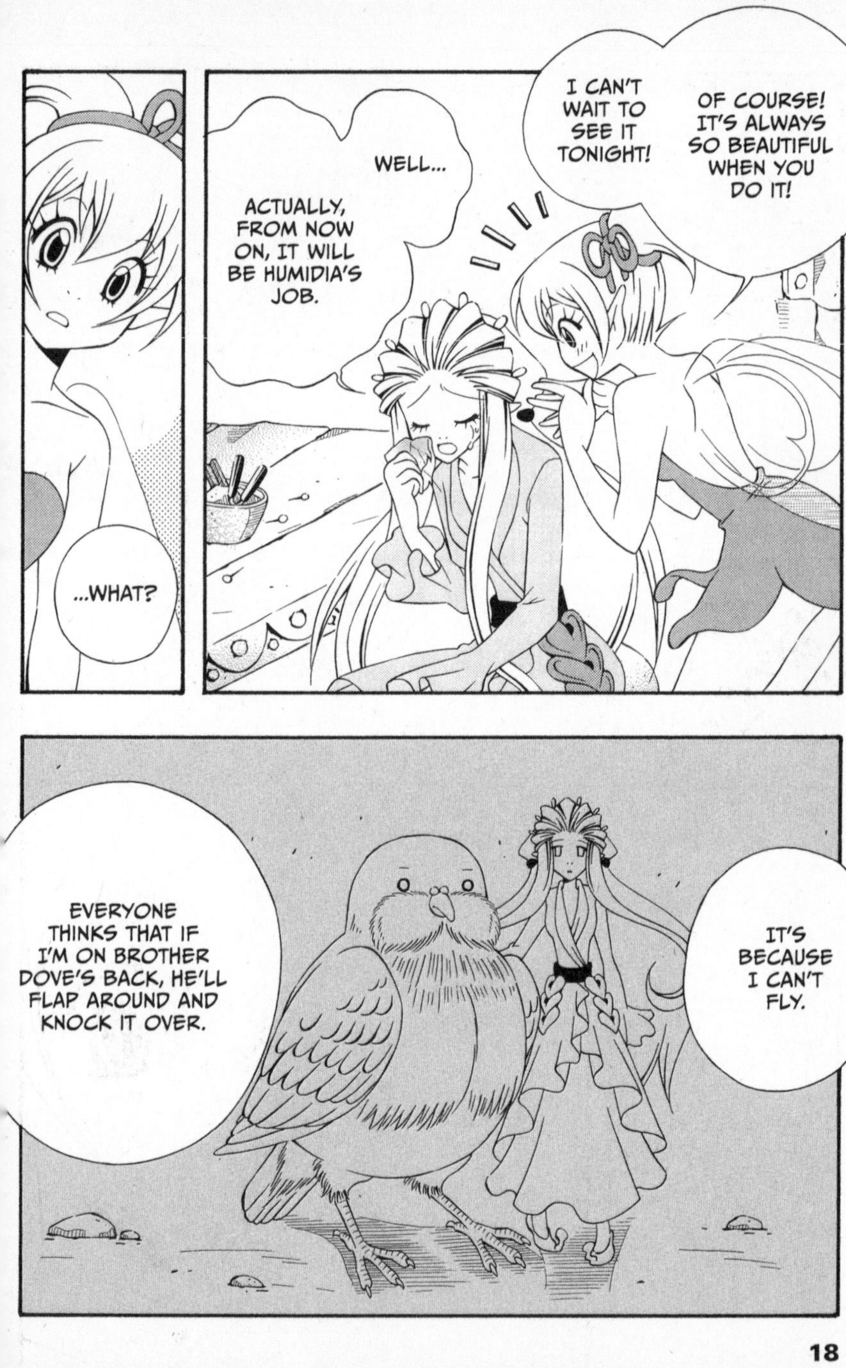
OF COURSE! IT'S ALWAYS SO BEAUTIFUL WHEN YOU DO IT!
I CAN'T WAIT TO SEE IT TONIGHT!
WELL...
ACTUALLY, FROM NOW ON, IT WILL BE HUMIDIA'S JOB.
...WHAT?
IT'S BECAUSE I CAN'T FLY.
EVERYONE THINKS THAT IF I'M ON BROTHER DOVE'S BACK, HE'LL FLAP AROUND AND KNOCK IT OVER.

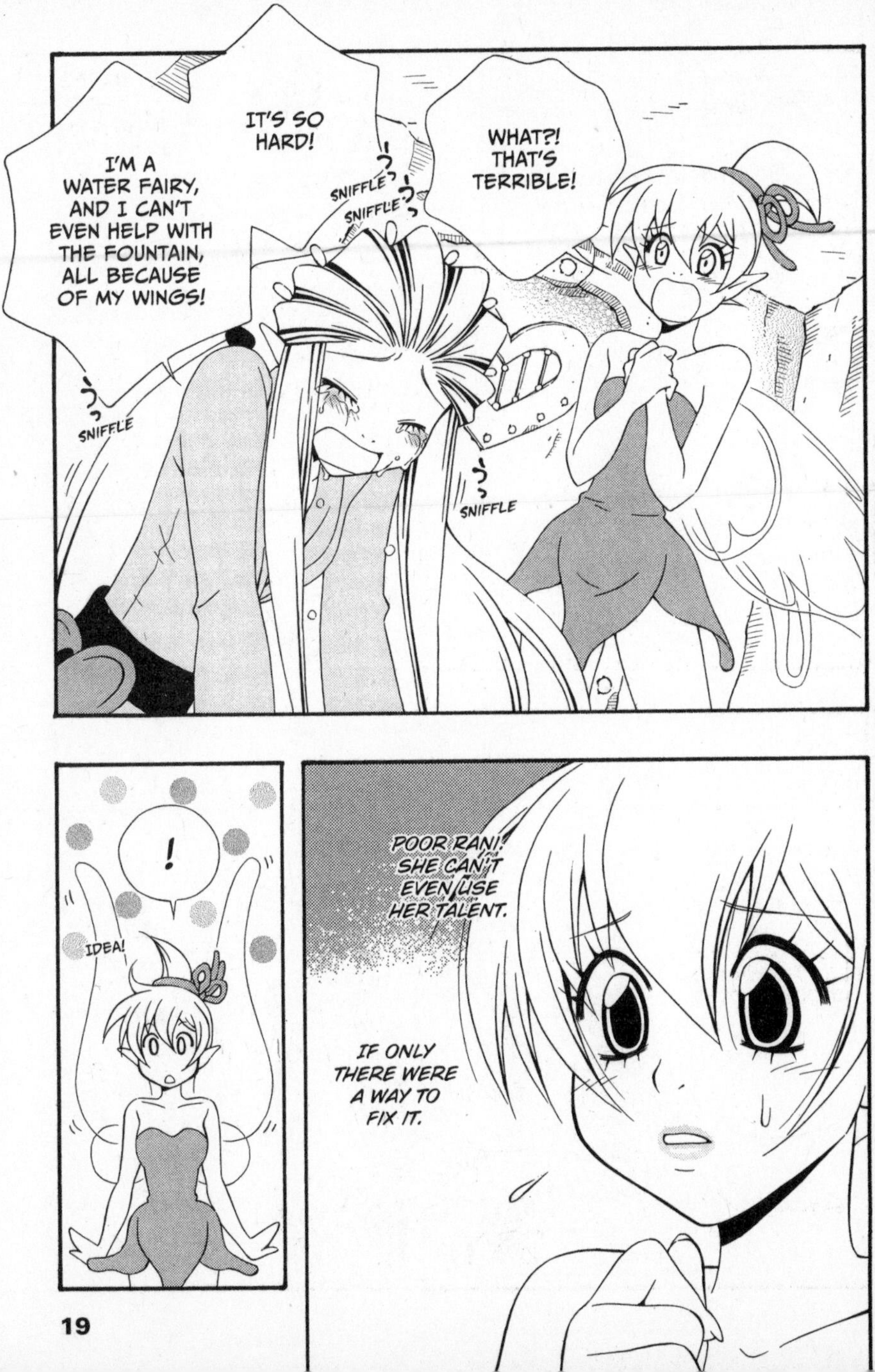
I'M A WATER FAIRY, AND I CAN'T EVEN HELP WITH THE FOUNTAIN, ALL BECAUSE OF MY WINGS!
IT'S SO HARD!
SNIFFLE
SNIFFLE
SNIFFLE
SNIFFLE
WHAT?! THAT'S TERRIBLE!
POOR RANI! SHE CAN'T EVEN USE HER TALENT.
IF ONLY THERE WERE A WAY TO FIX IT.
!
IDEA!

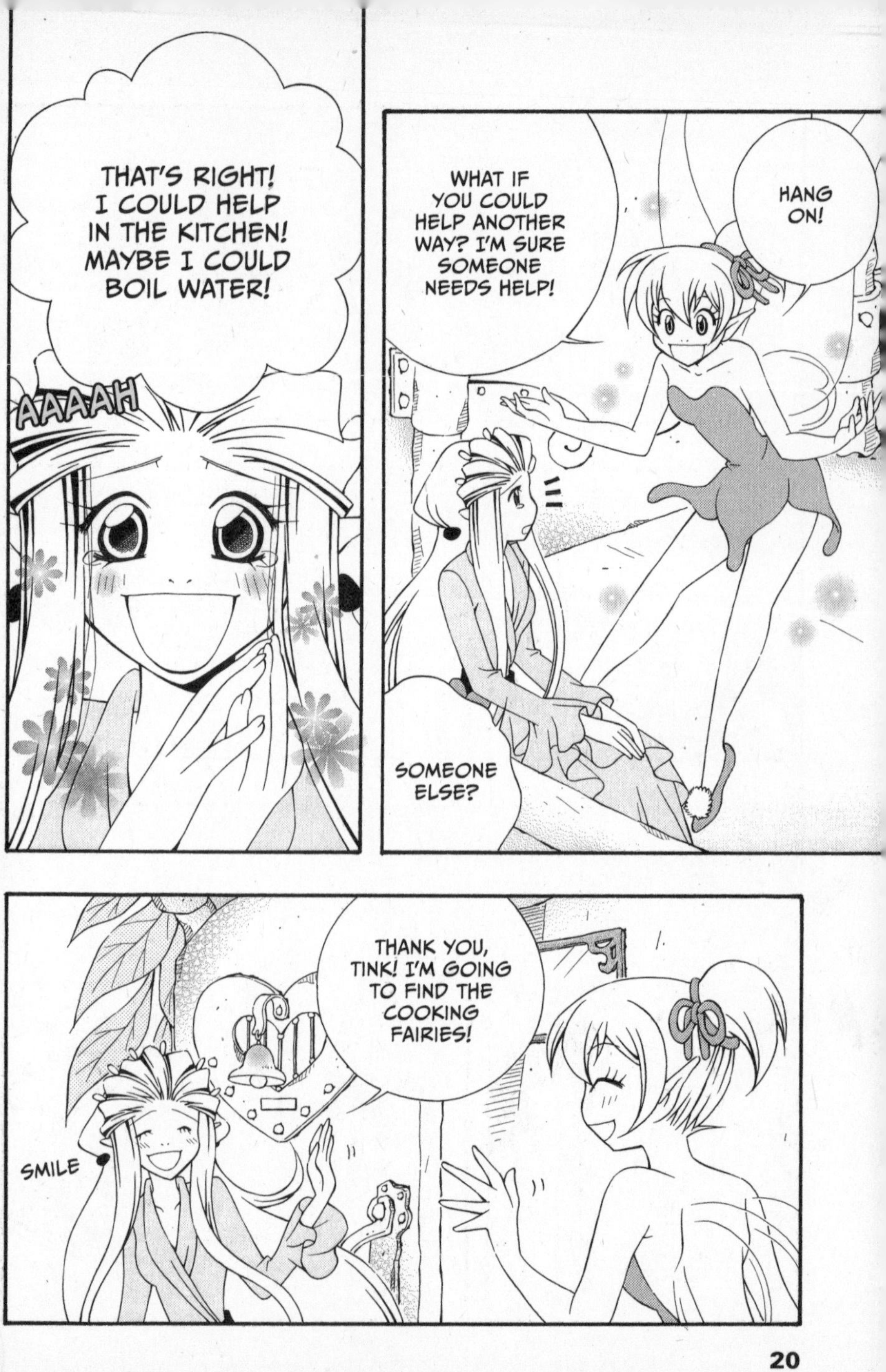
HANG ON!
WHAT IF YOU COULD HELP ANOTHER WAY? I'M SURE SOMEONE NEEDS HELP!
SOMEONE ELSE?
THAT'S RIGHT! I COULD HELP IN THE KITCHEN! MAYBE I COULD BOIL WATER!
AAAAH
THANK YOU, TINK! I'M GOING TO FIND THE COOKING FAIRIES!
SMILE

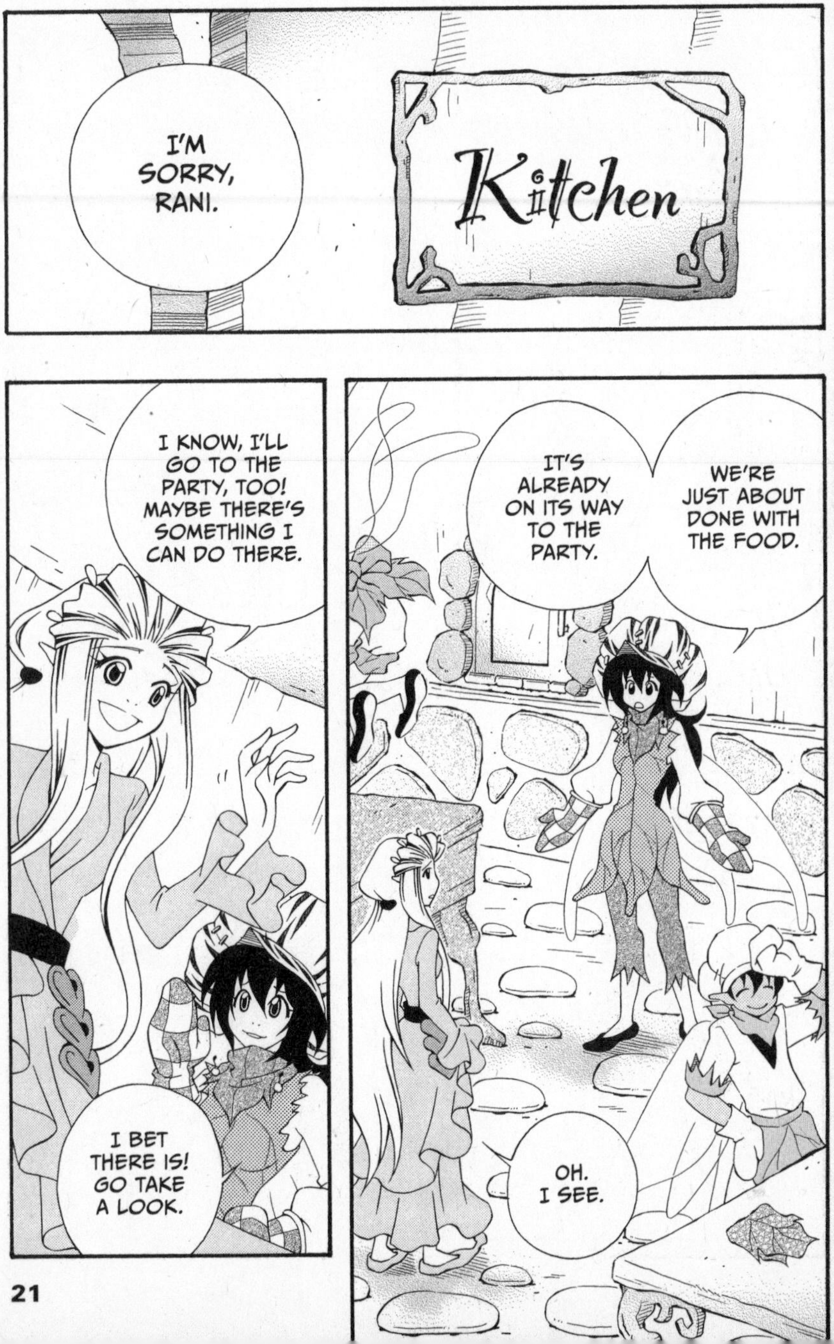
Kitchen
I'M SORRY, RANI.
WE'RE JUST ABOUT DONE WITH THE FOOD.
IT'S ALREADY ON ITS WAY TO THE PARTY.
OH. I SEE.
I KNOW, I'LL GO TO THE PARTY, TOO! MAYBE THERE'S SOMETHING I CAN DO THERE.
I BET THERE IS! GO TAKE A LOOK.

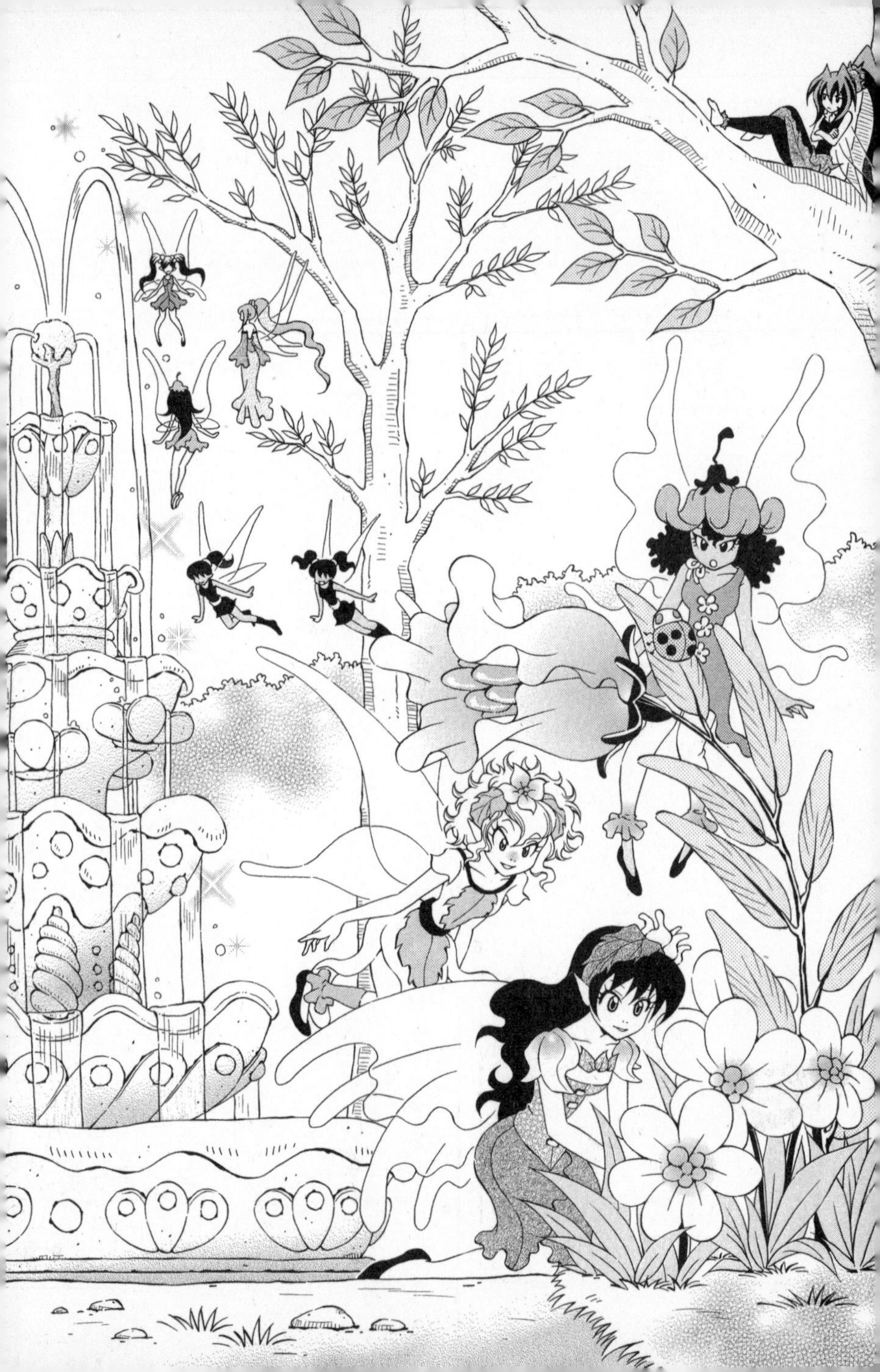

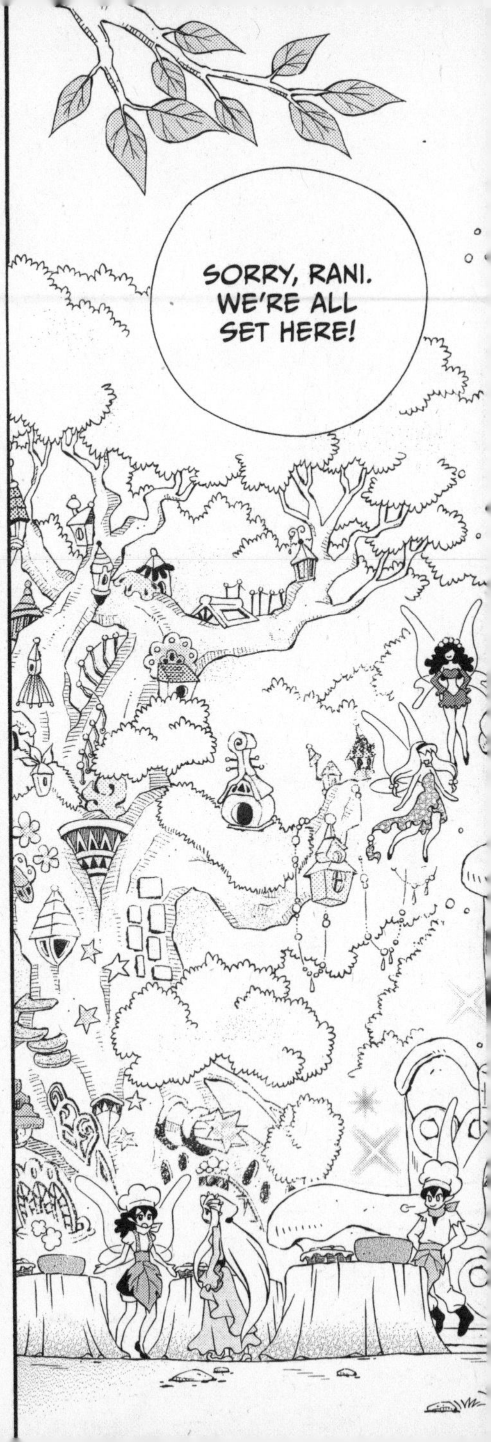
SORRY, RANI. WE'RE ALL SET HERE!

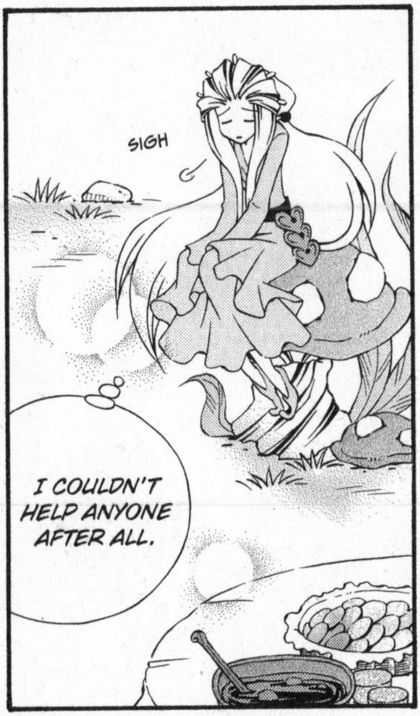
SIGH
I COULDN'T HELP ANYONE AFTER ALL.

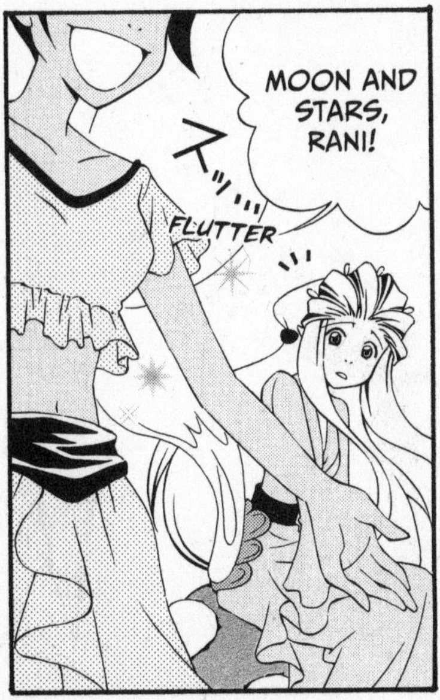
MOON AND STARS, RANI!
FLUTTER

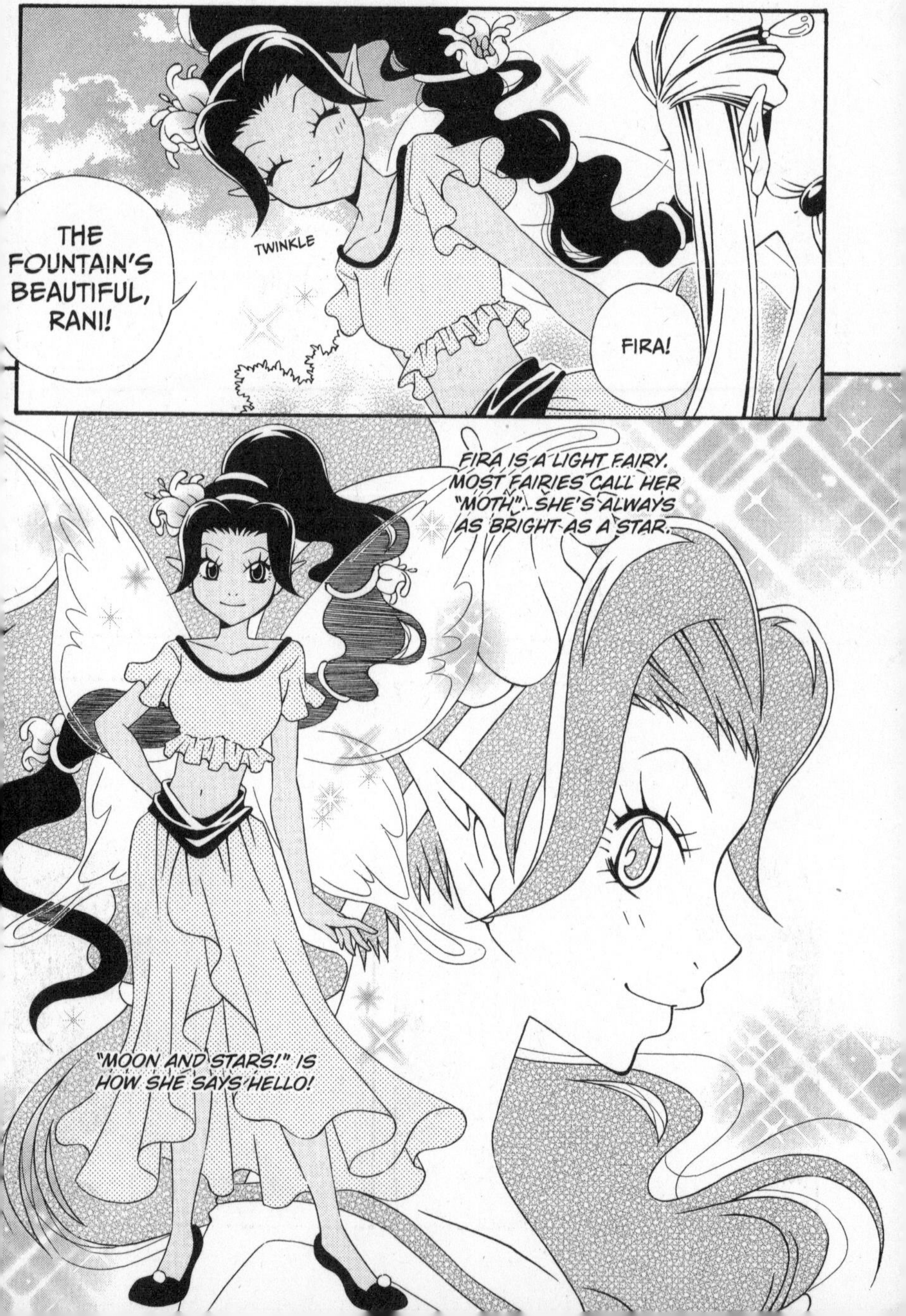
FIRA!
THE FOUNTAIN'S BEAUTIFUL, RANI!
TWINKLE
FIRA IS A LIGHT FAIRY. MOST FAIRIES CALL HER "MOTH". SHE'S ALWAYS AS BRIGHT AS A STAR.
"MOON AND STARS!" IS HOW SHE SAYS HELLO!

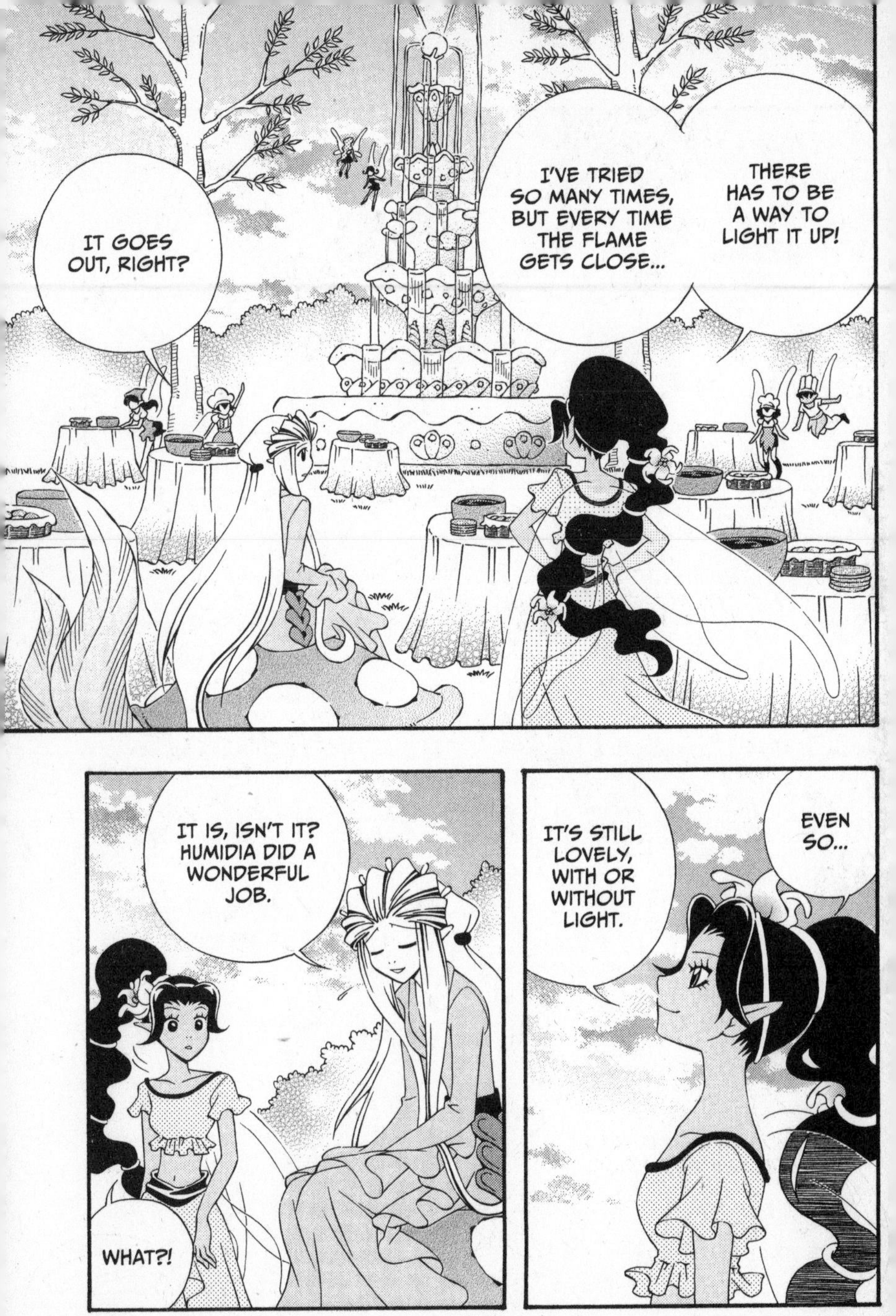
THERE HAS TO BE A WAY TO LIGHT IT UP!
I'VE TRIED SO MANY TIMES, BUT EVERY TIME THE FLAME GETS CLOSE...
IT GOES OUT, RIGHT?
EVEN SO...
IT'S STILL LOVELY, WITH OR WITHOUT LIGHT.
IT IS, ISN'T IT? HUMIDIA DID A WONDERFUL JOB.
WHAT?!

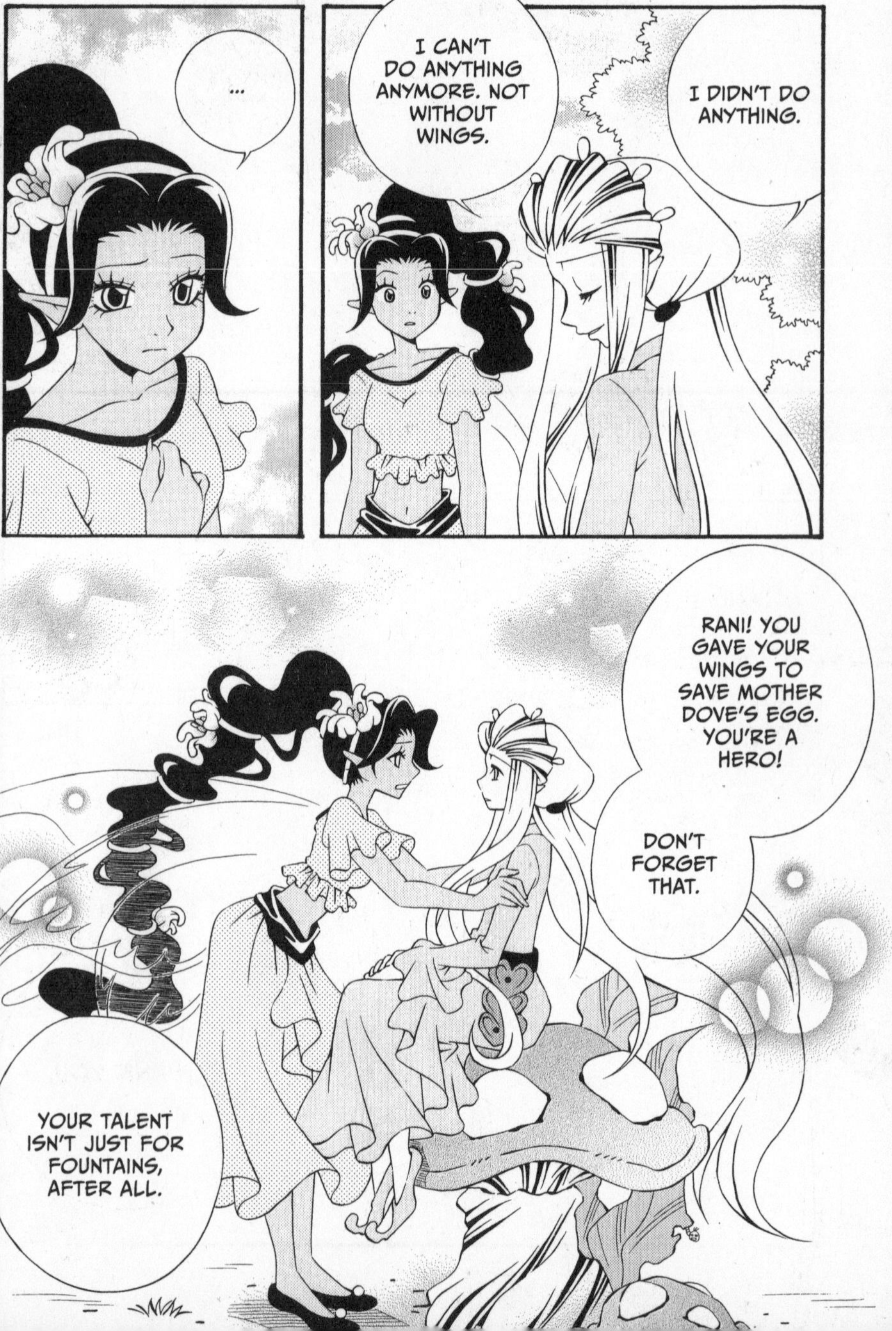
I DIDN'T DO ANYTHING.
I CAN'T DO ANYTHING ANYMORE. NOT WITHOUT WINGS.
...
RANI! YOU GAVE YOUR WINGS TO SAVE MOTHER DOVE'S EGG. YOU'RE A HERO!
DON'T FORGET THAT.
YOUR TALENT ISN'T JUST FOR FOUNTAINS, AFTER ALL.

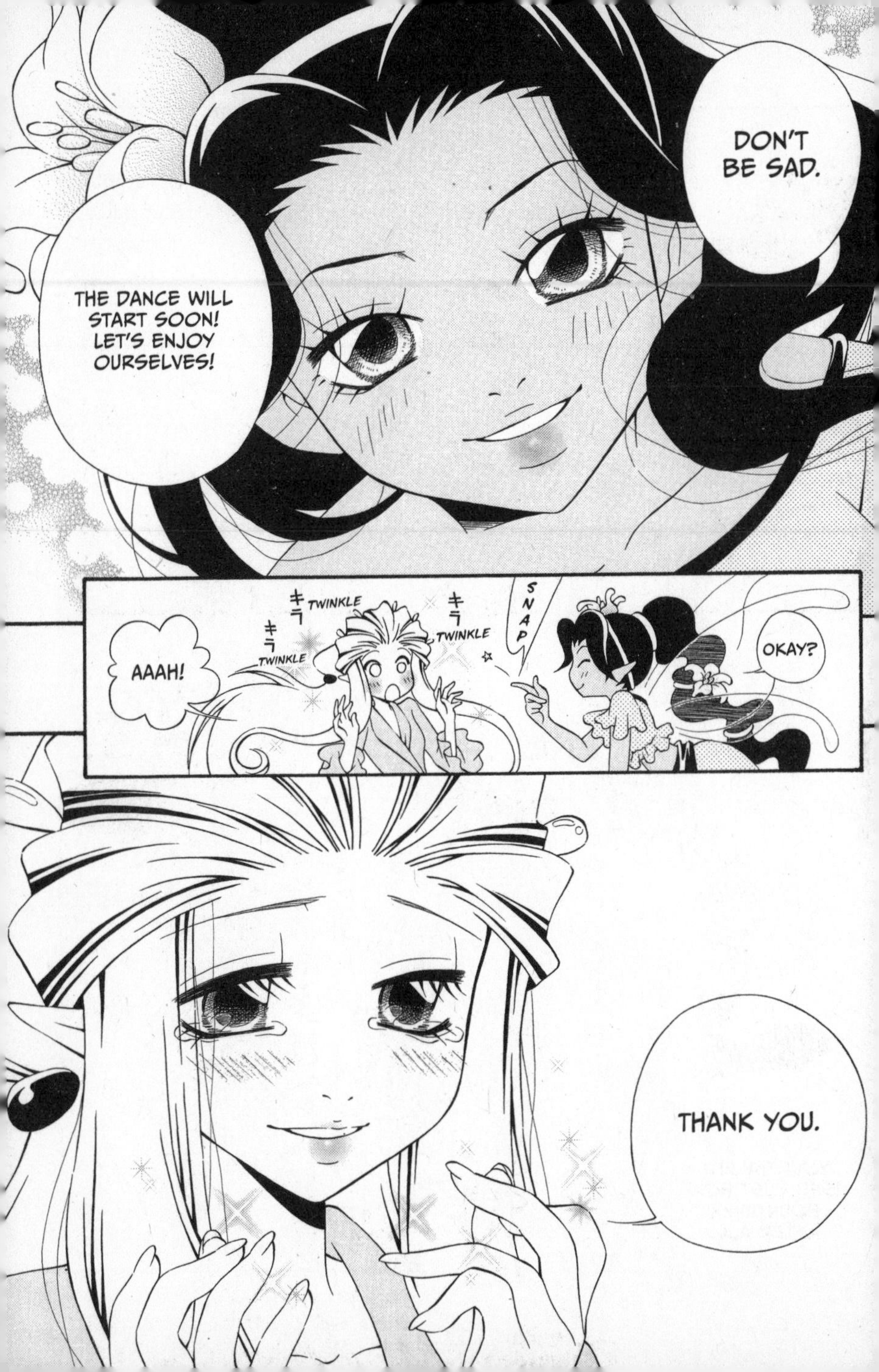
DON'T BE SAD.
THE DANCE WILL START SOON! LET'S ENJOY OURSELVES!
OKAY?
SNAP
キラ TWINKLE
キラ TWINKLE
キラ TWINKLE
AAAH!
THANK YOU.

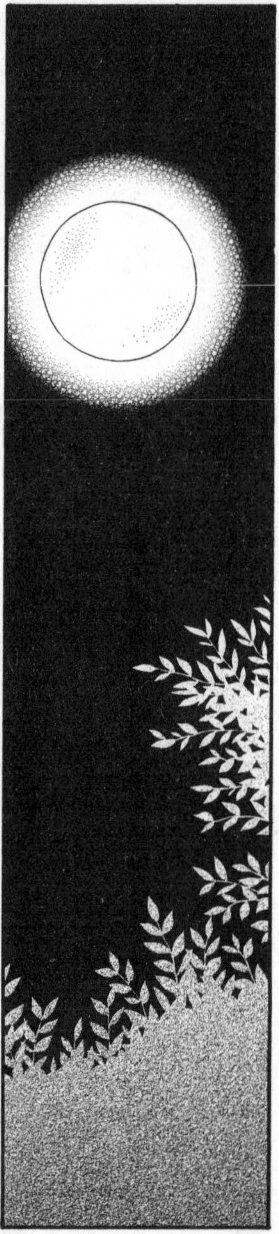

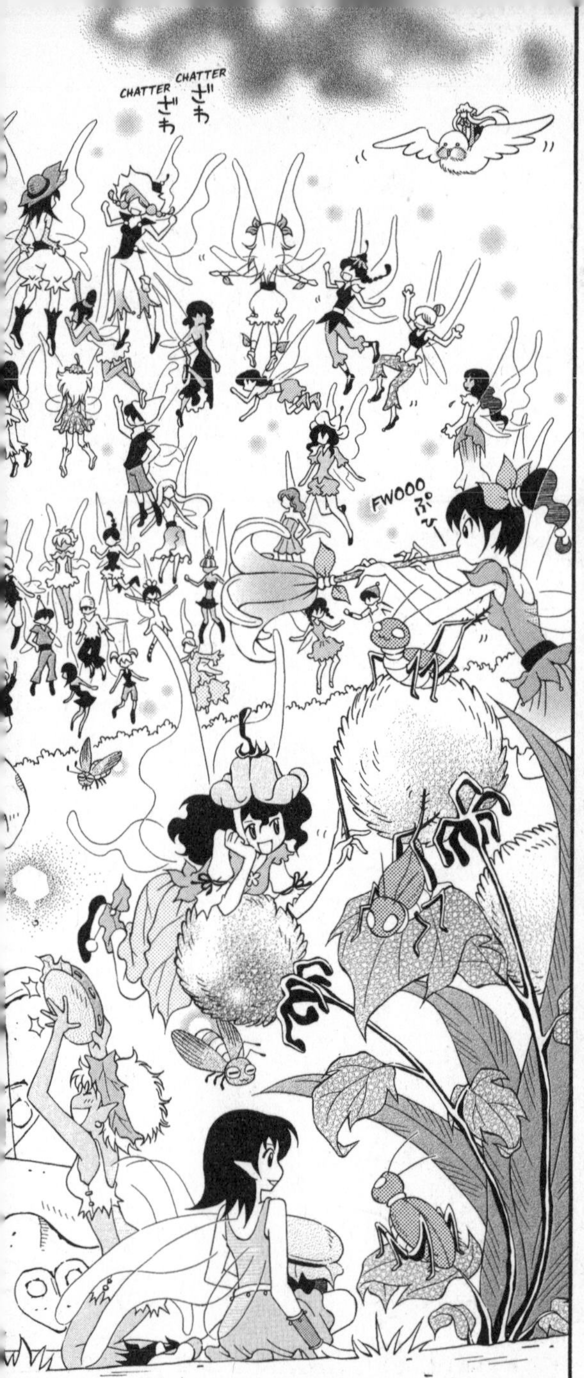
CHATTER CHATTER
ざわ ざわ
FWOOO
ぷひー

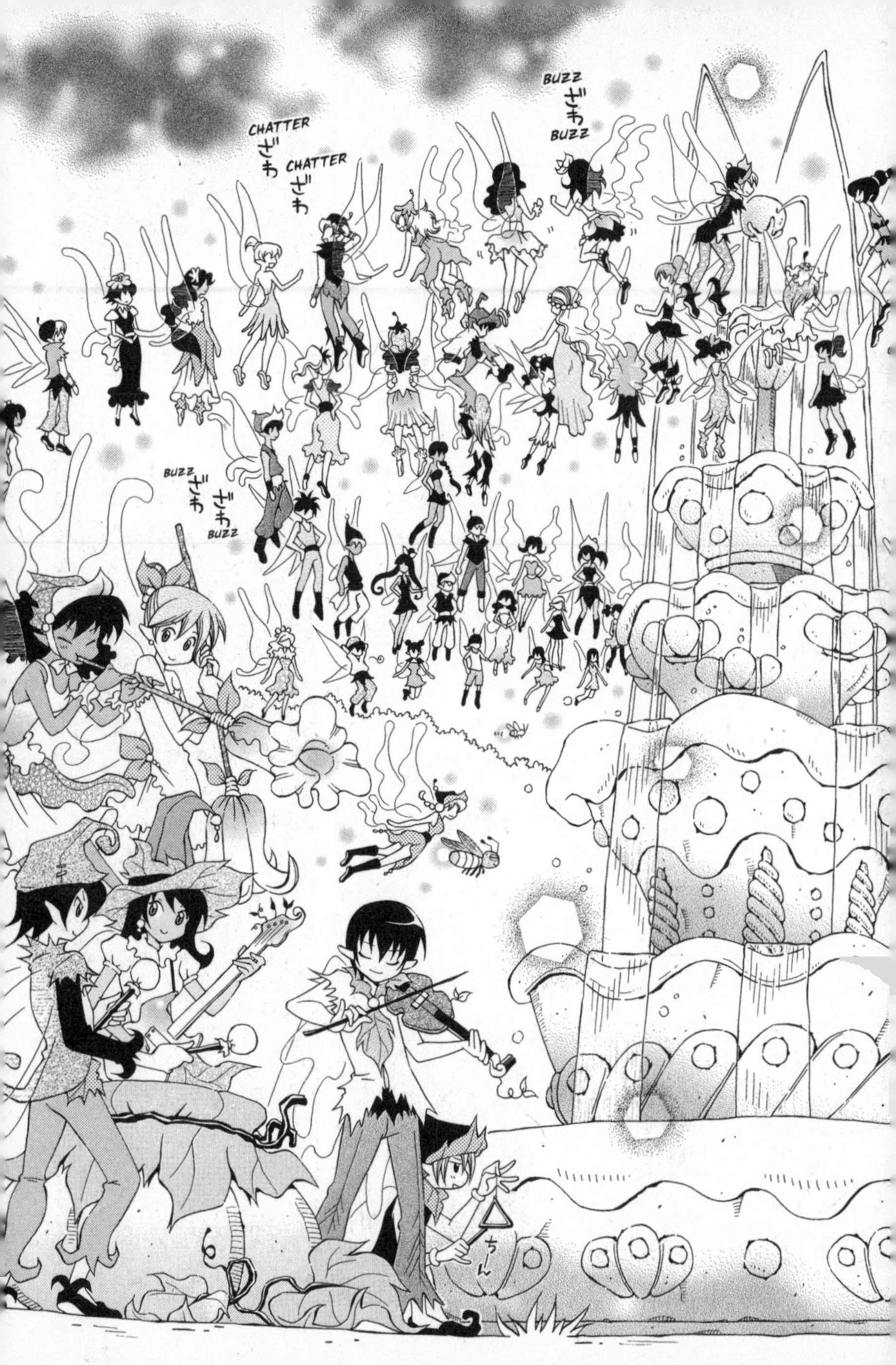
BUZZ ざわ BUZZ
CHATTER ざわ CHATTER ざわ
BUZZ ざわ ざわ BUZZ
ちん

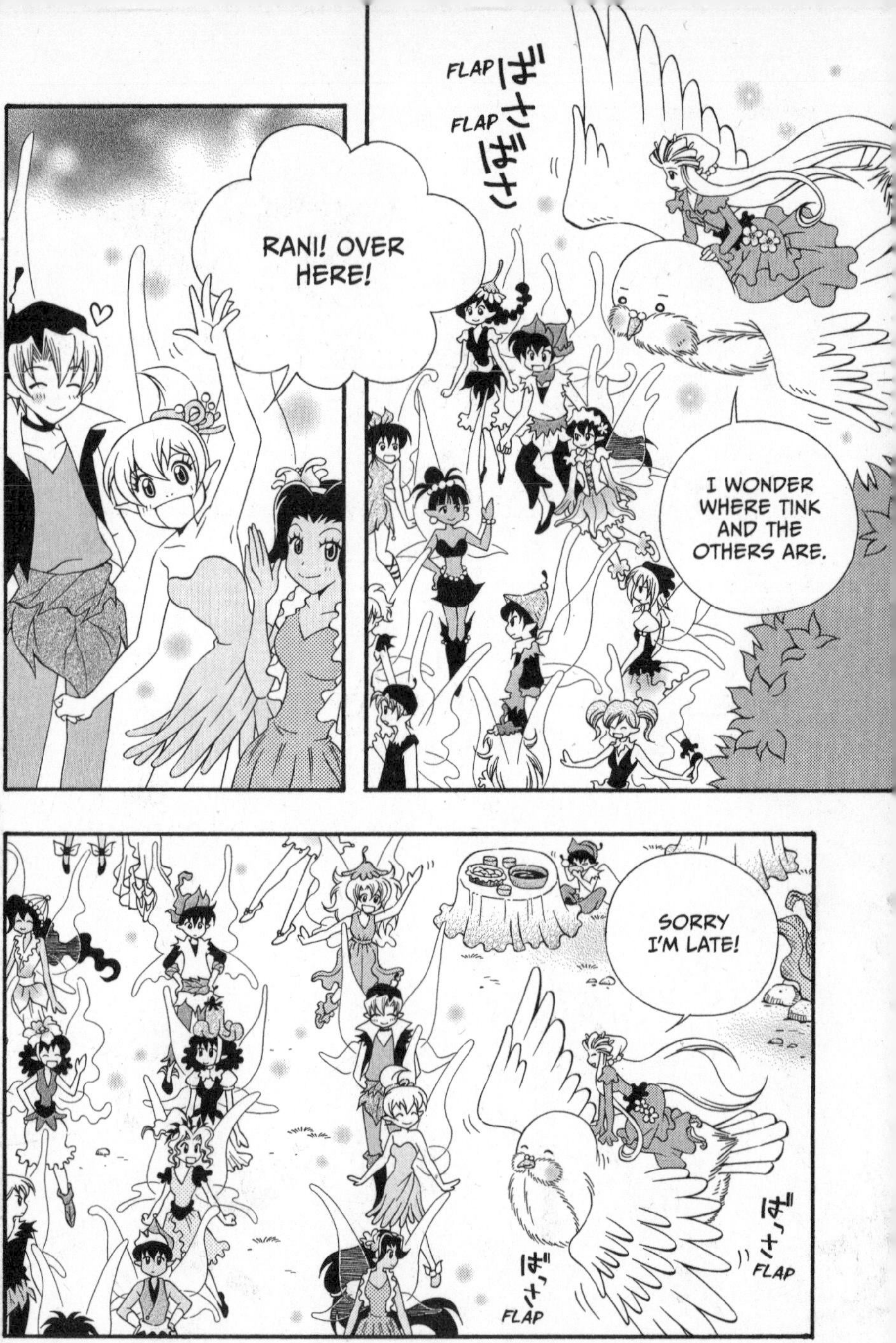
FLAP ばさ
FLAP ばさ
I WONDER WHERE TINK AND THE OTHERS ARE.
RANI! OVER HERE!
SORRY I'M LATE!
ばっさ FLAP
ばっさ FLAP

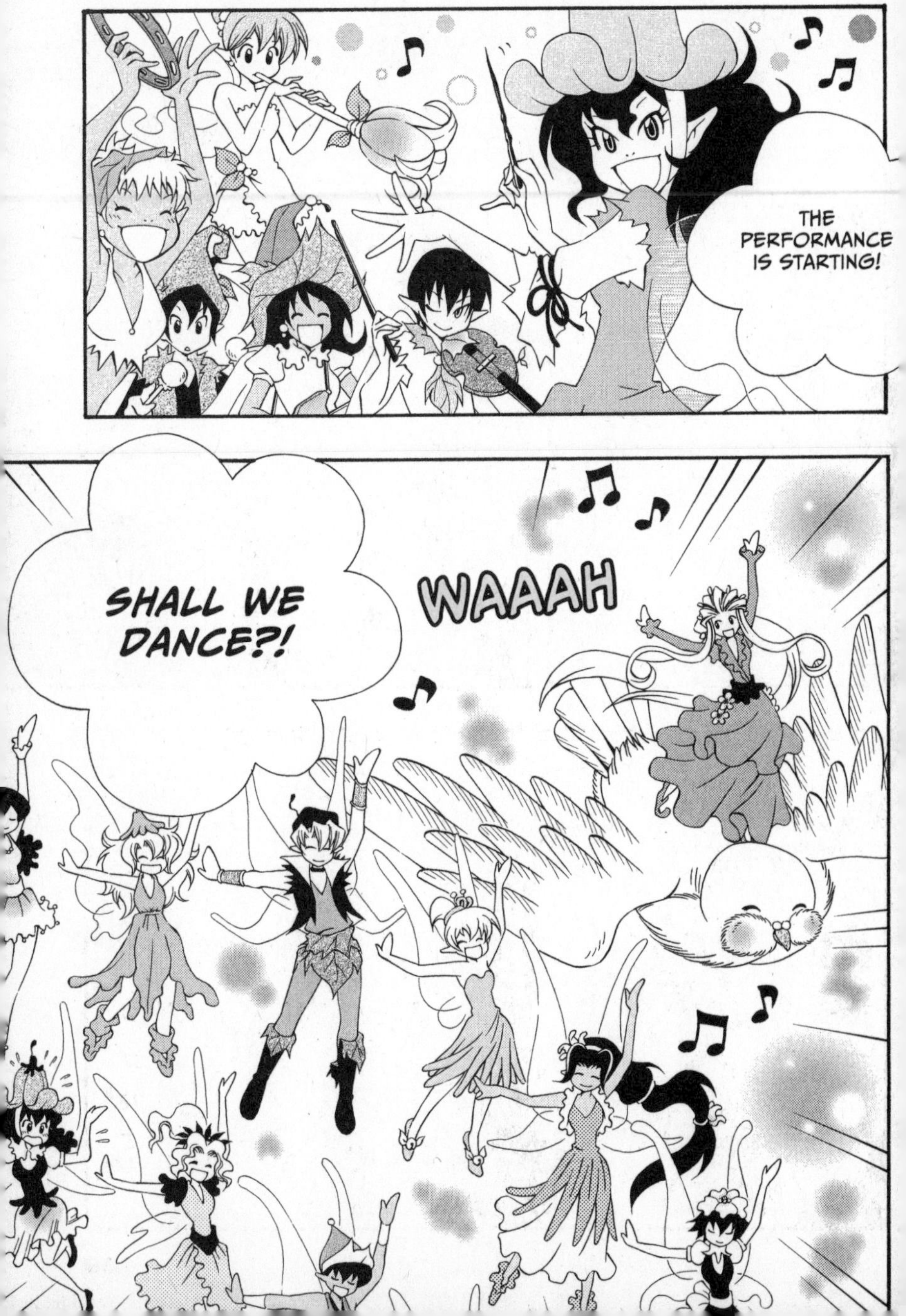
THE PERFORMANCE IS STARTING!
WAAAH
SHALL WE DANCE?!

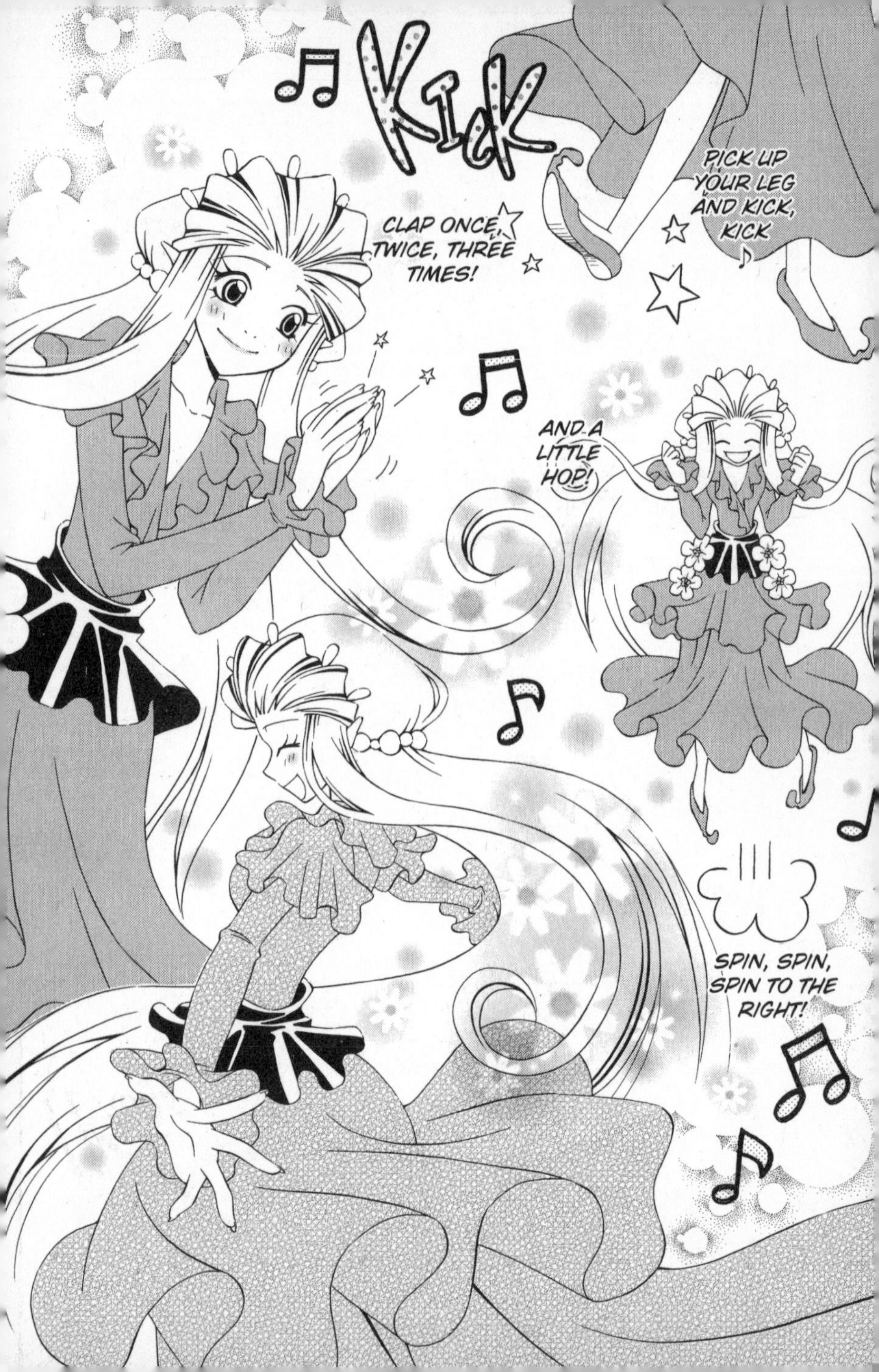
PICK UP YOUR LEG AND KICK, KICK ♪
KICK
CLAP ONCE, TWICE, THREE TIMES!
AND A LITTLE HOP!
SPIN, SPIN, SPIN TO THE RIGHT!

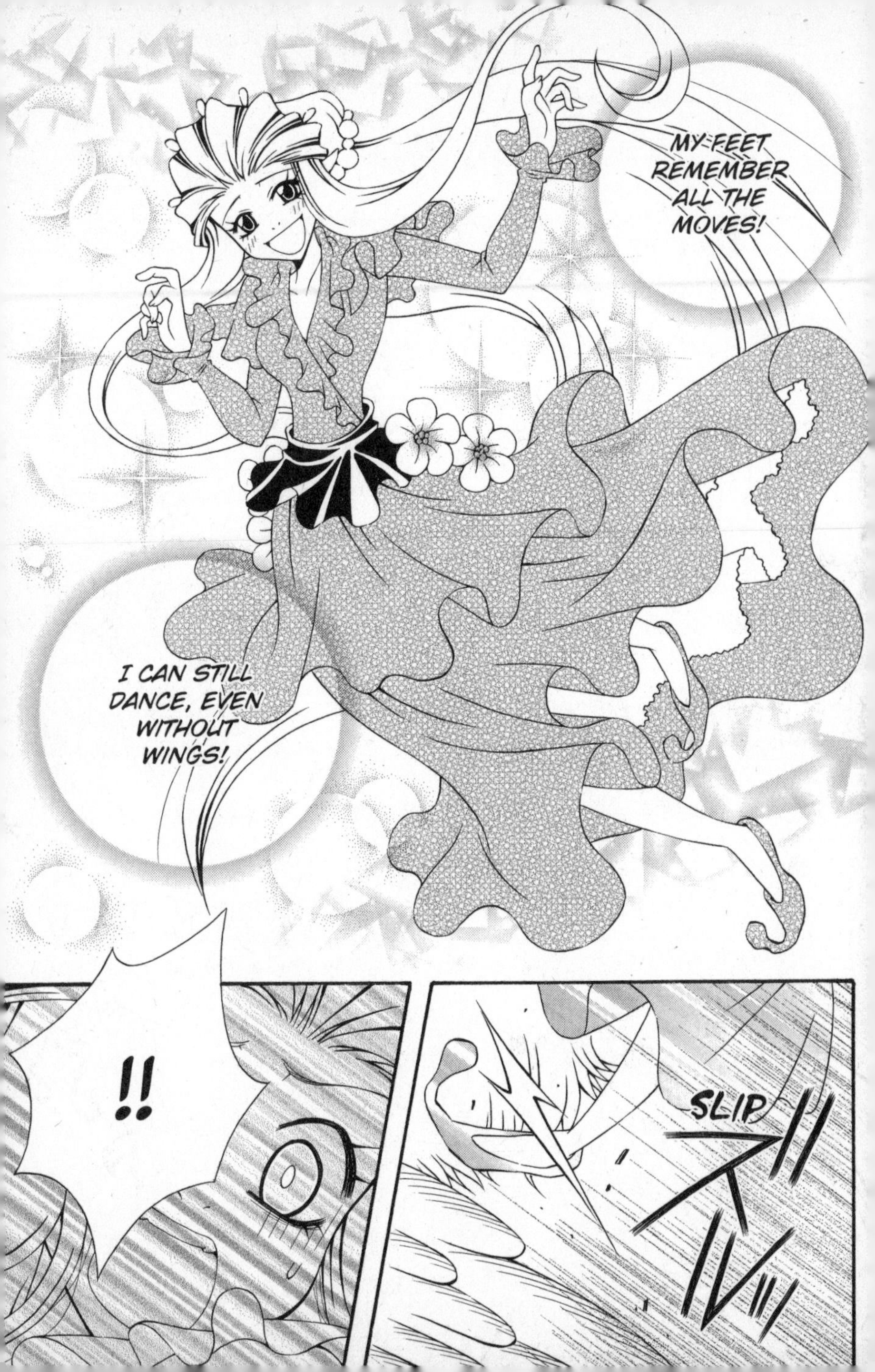
MY FEET REMEMBER ALL THE MOVES!
I CAN STILL DANCE, EVEN WITHOUT WINGS!
SLIP
!!

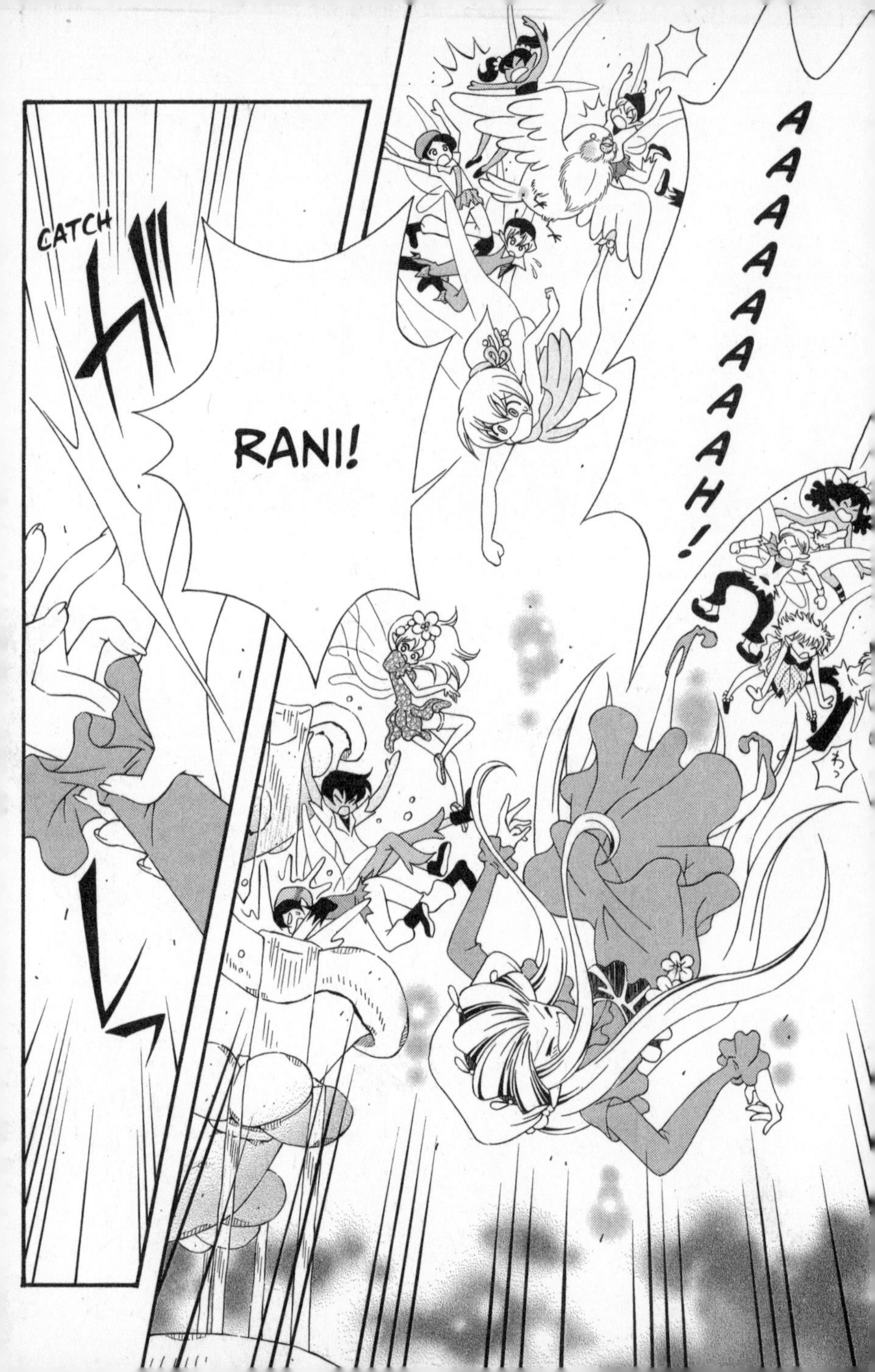
AAAAAAAAH!
RANI!
わっ
CATCH

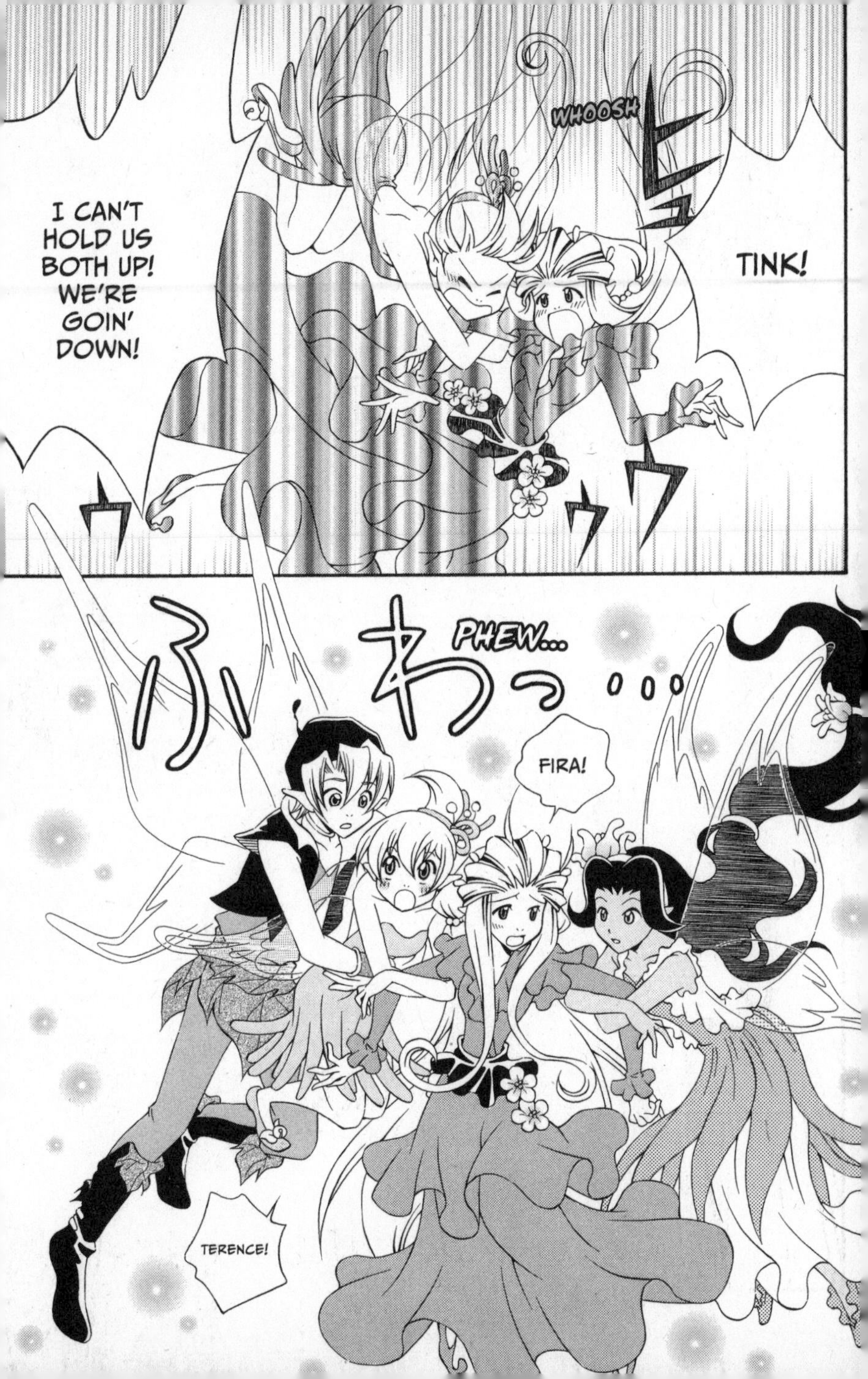
WHOOSH
TINK!
I CAN'T HOLD US BOTH UP! WE'RE GOIN' DOWN!
PHEW...
ふわっ...
FIRA!
TERENCE!

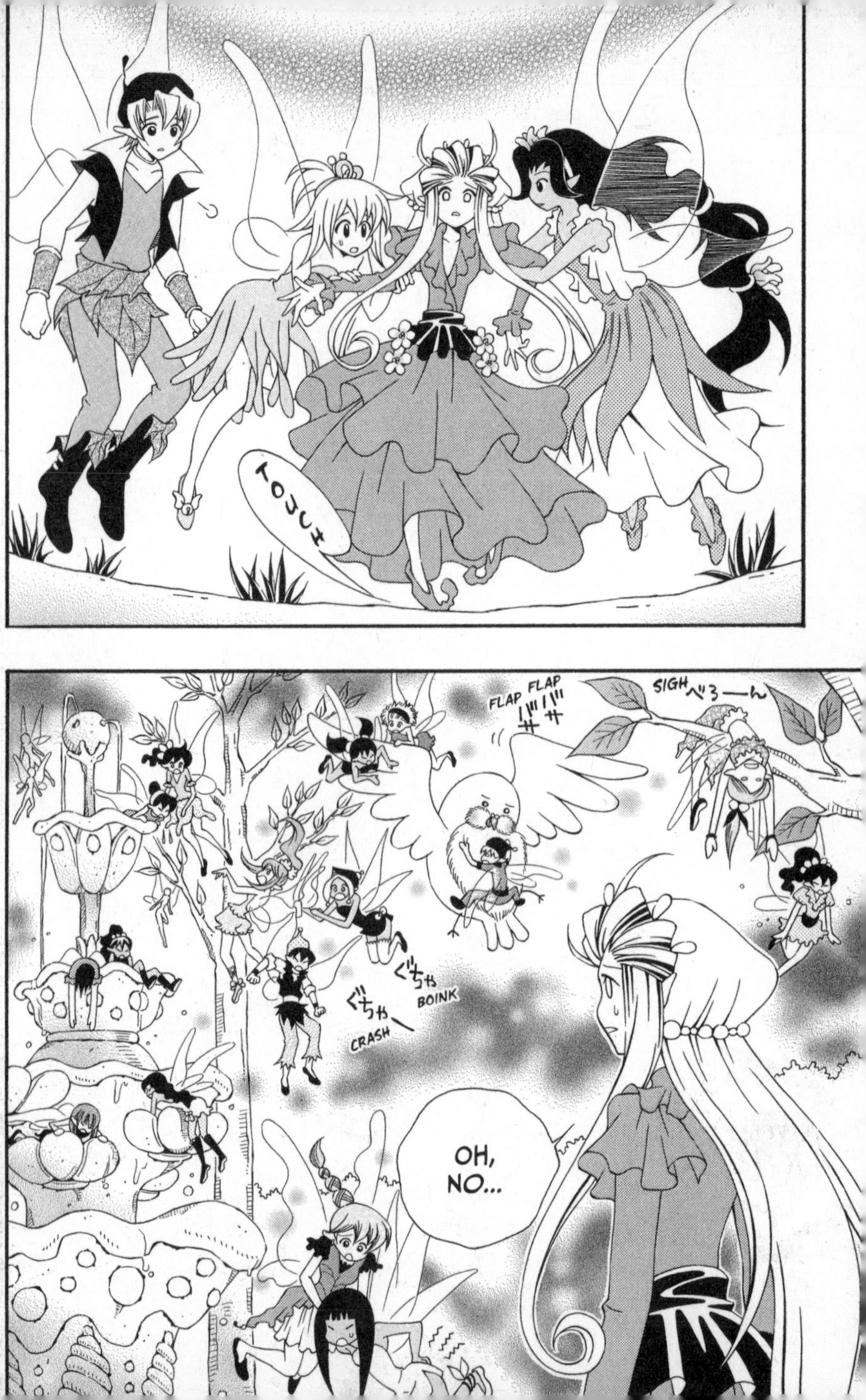
TOUCH
SIGH べろーん
FLAP FLAP バサバサ
ぐちゃ BOINK
ぐちゃ CRASH
OH, NO...

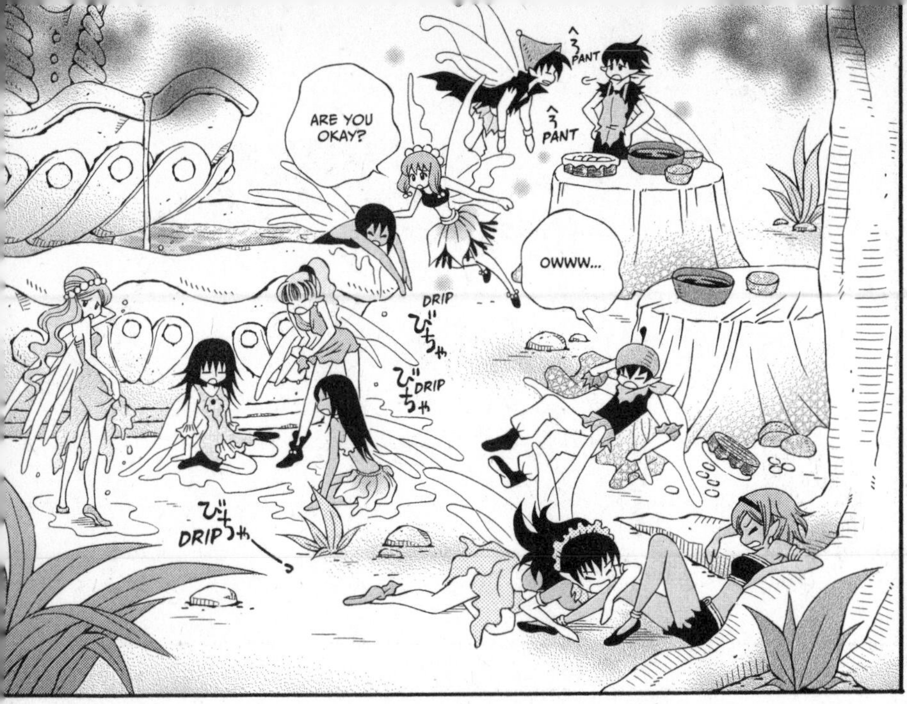
PANT へろ
PANT へろ
ARE YOU OKAY?
OWWW...
DRIP びちゃ
DRIP びちゃ
DRIP びちゃ
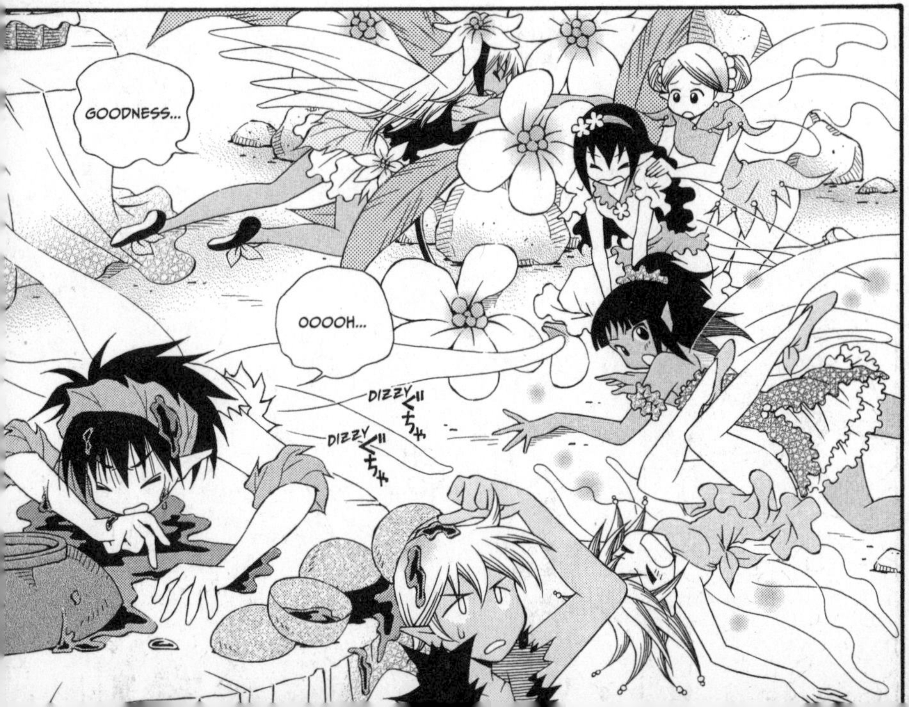
GOODNESS...
OOOOH...
DIZZY ぐちゃ
DIZZY ぐちゃ

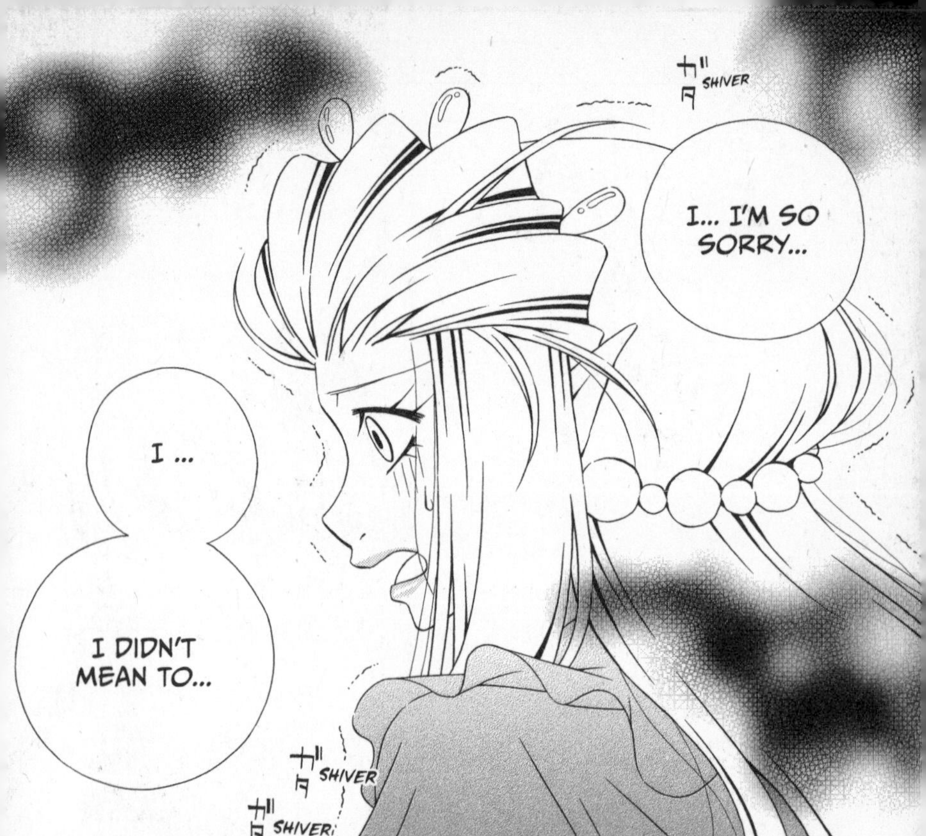
ガタ SHIVER
I... I'M SO SORRY...
I ...
I DIDN'T MEAN TO...
ガタ SHIVER
ガタ SHIVER
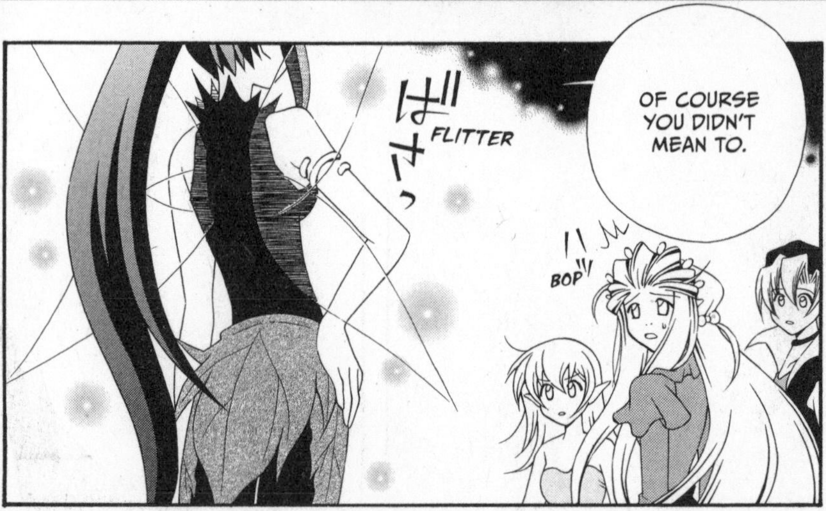
OF COURSE YOU DIDN'T MEAN TO.
ばさっ FLITTER
BOP

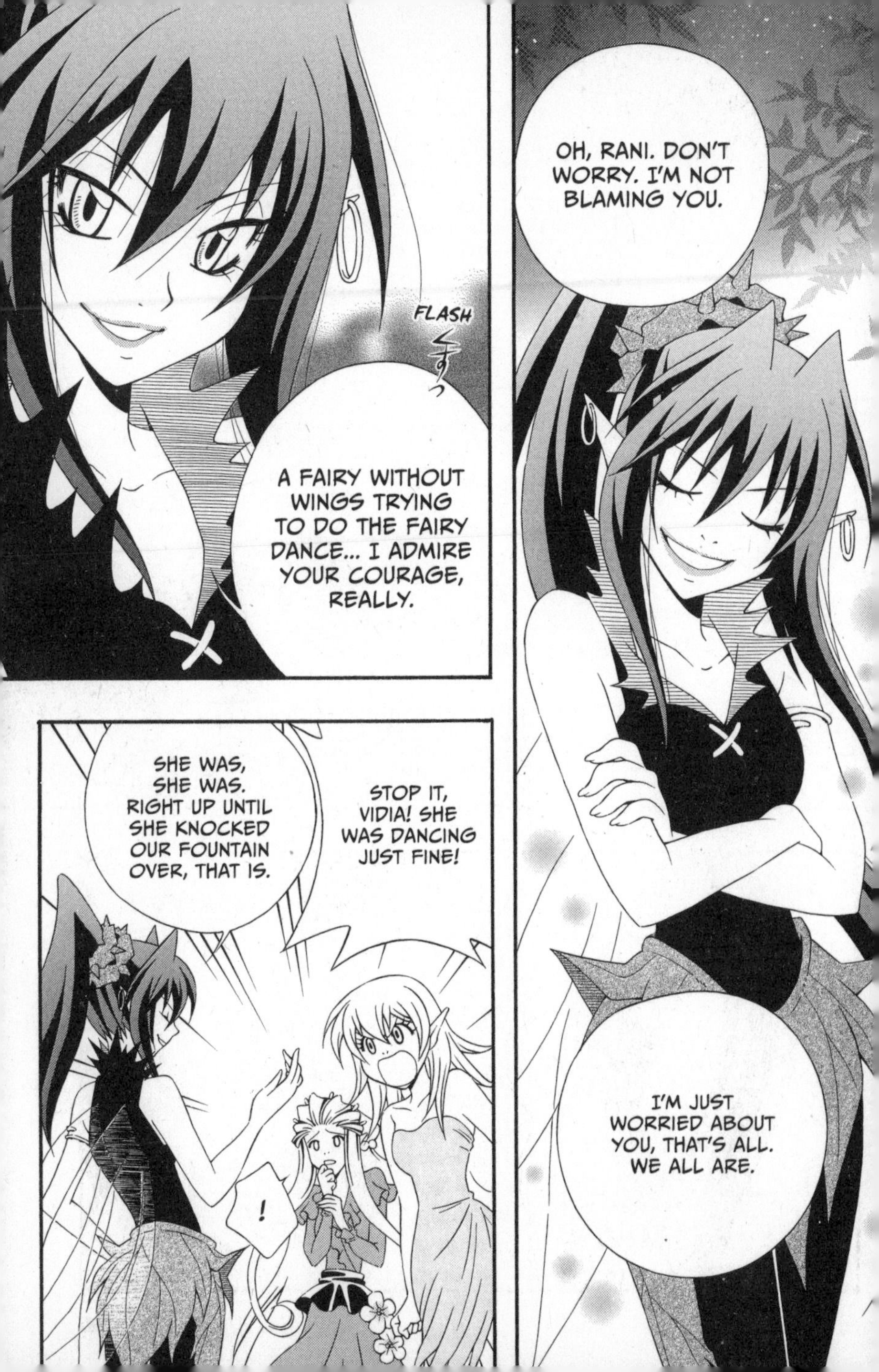
OH, RANI. DON'T WORRY. I'M NOT BLAMING YOU.
I'M JUST WORRIED ABOUT YOU, THAT'S ALL. WE ALL ARE.
FLASH
A FAIRY WITHOUT WINGS TRYING TO DO THE FAIRY DANCE... I ADMIRE YOUR COURAGE, REALLY.
STOP IT, VIDIA! SHE WAS DANCING JUST FINE!
SHE WAS, SHE WAS. RIGHT UP UNTIL SHE KNOCKED OUR FOUNTAIN OVER, THAT IS.
!

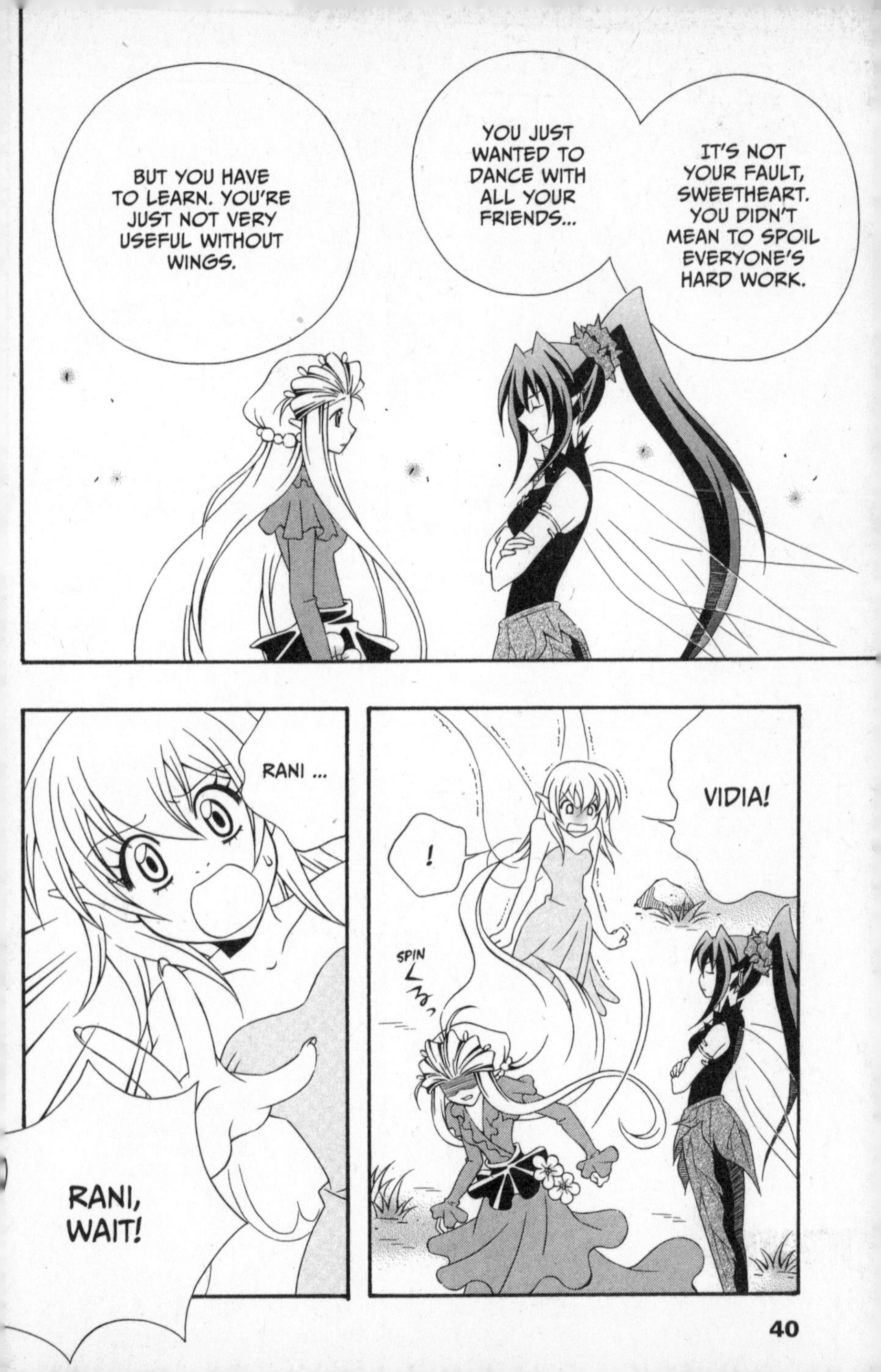
IT'S NOT YOUR FAULT, SWEETHEART. YOU DIDN'T MEAN TO SPOIL EVERYONE'S HARD WORK.
YOU JUST WANTED TO DANCE WITH ALL YOUR FRIENDS...
BUT YOU HAVE TO LEARN. YOU'RE JUST NOT VERY USEFUL WITHOUT WINGS.
VIDIA!
!
SPIN
RANI ...
RANI, WAIT!

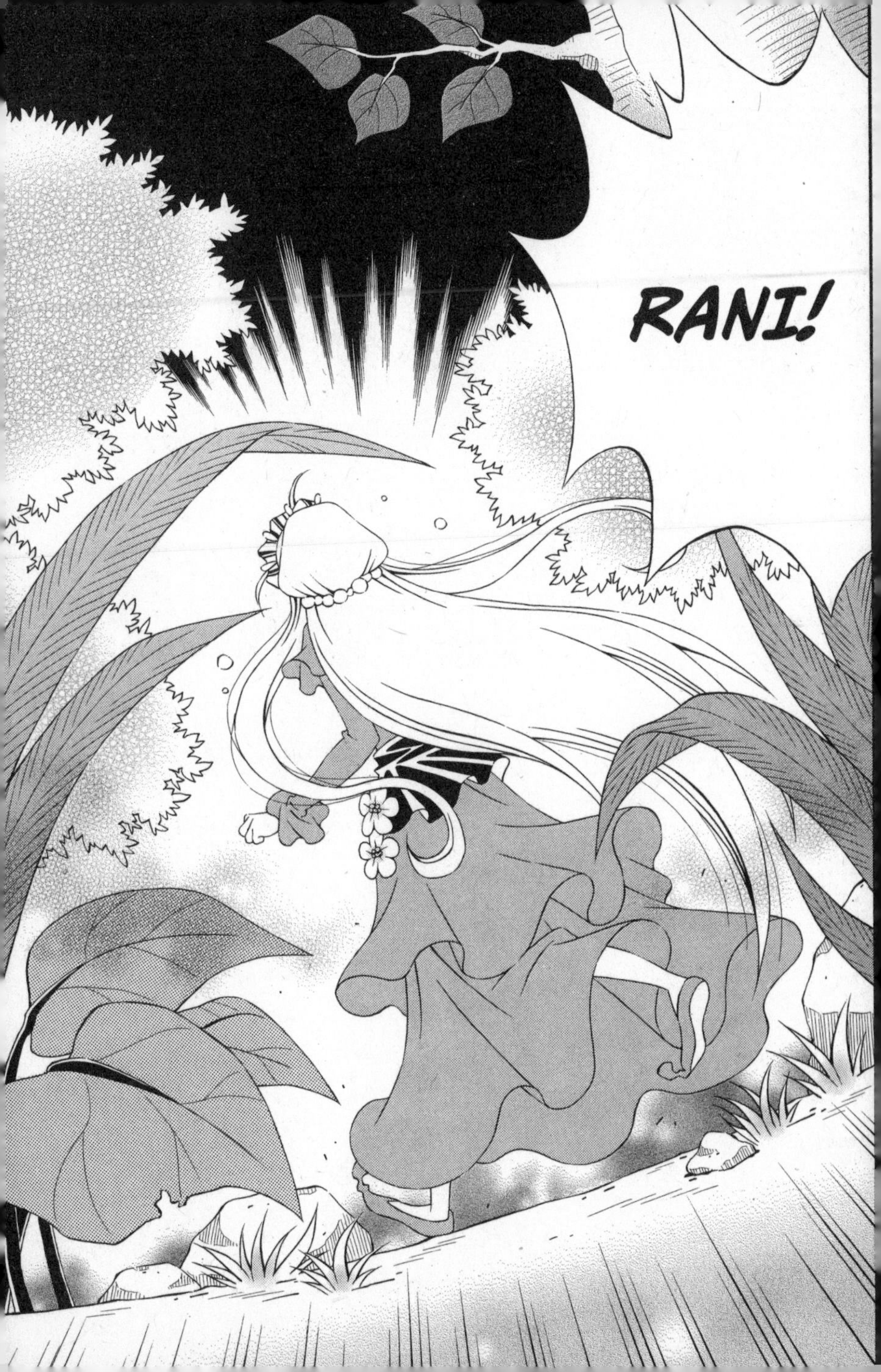
RANI!

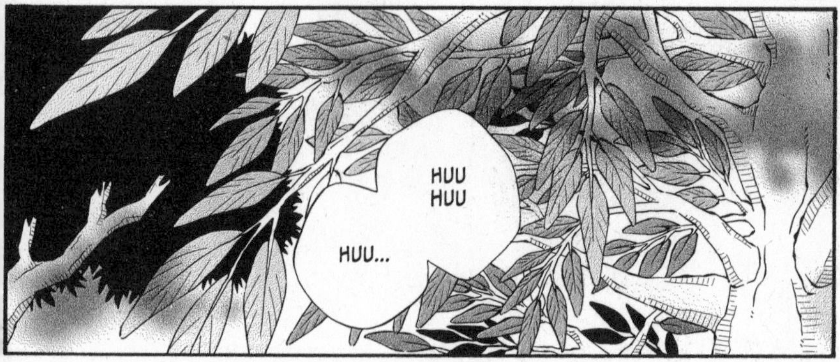
HUU
HUU
HUU...
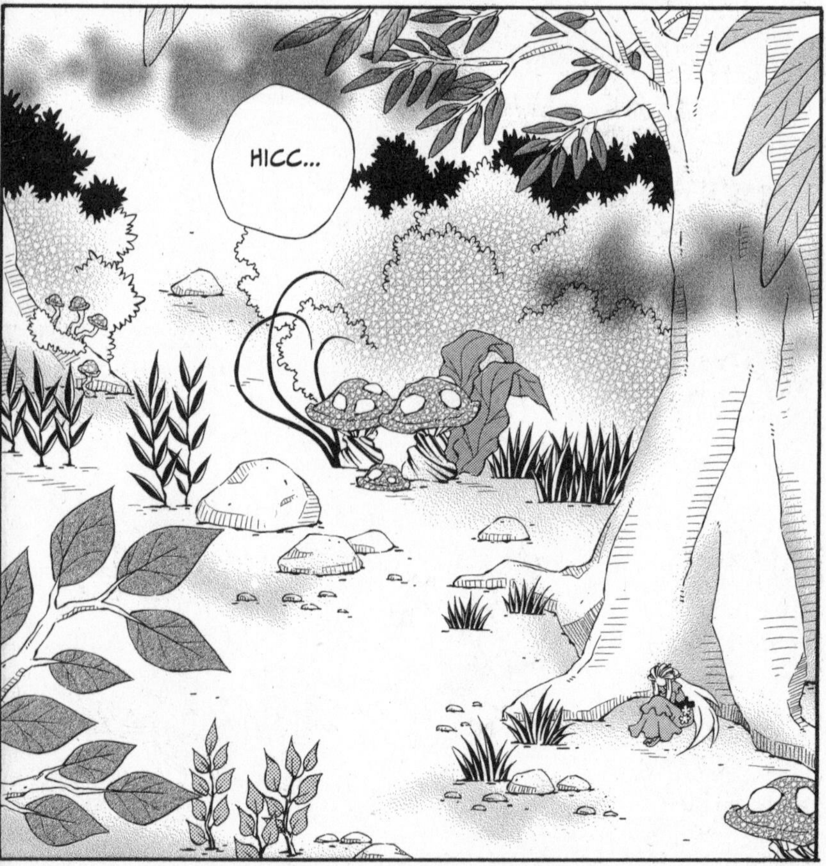
HICC...

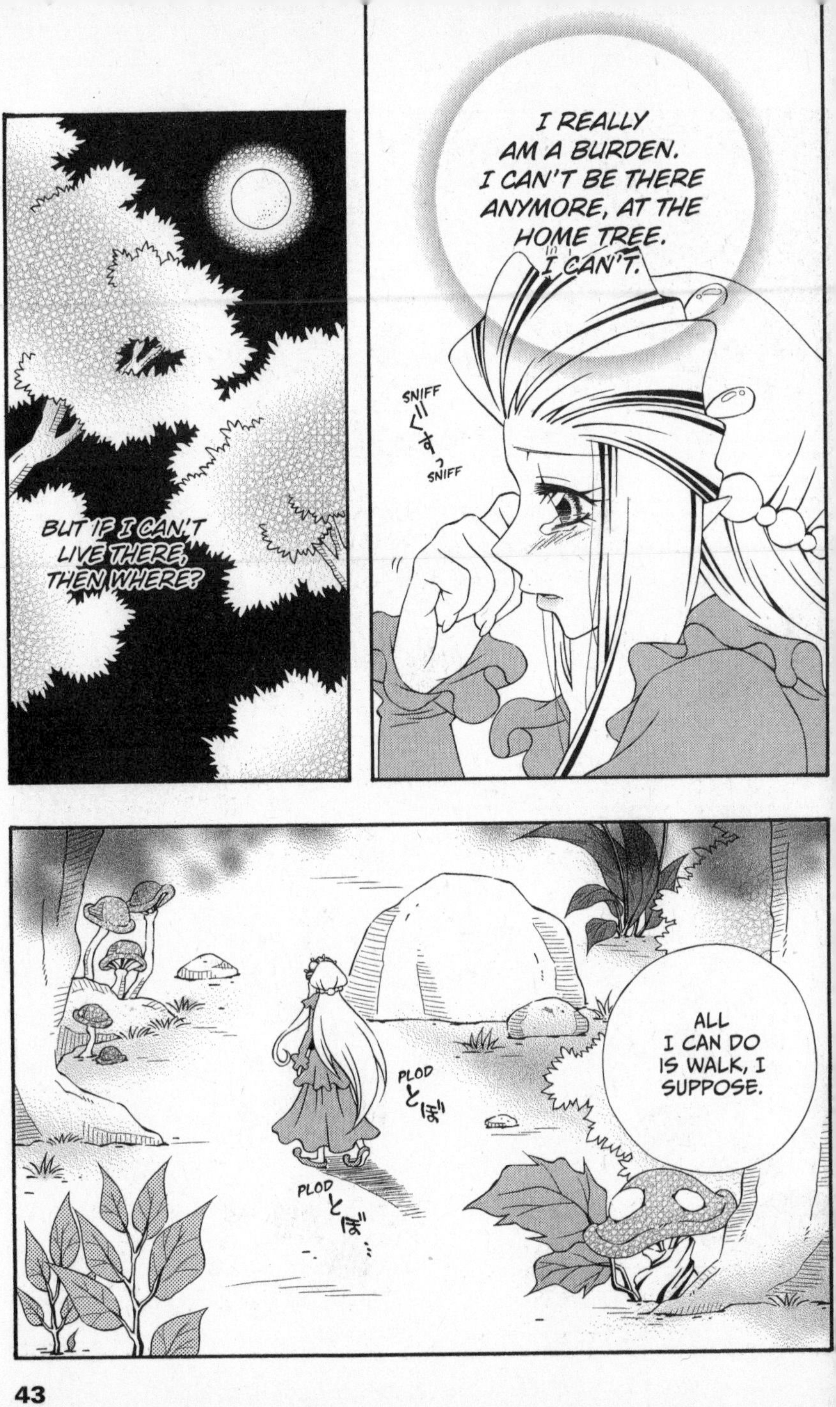
I REALLY AM A BURDEN. I CAN'T BE THERE ANYMORE, AT THE HOME TREE. I CAN'T.
SNIFF
ぐすっ
SNIFF
BUT IF I CAN'T LIVE THERE, THEN WHERE?
ALL I CAN DO IS WALK, I SUPPOSE.
PLOD
とぼ
PLOD
とぼ

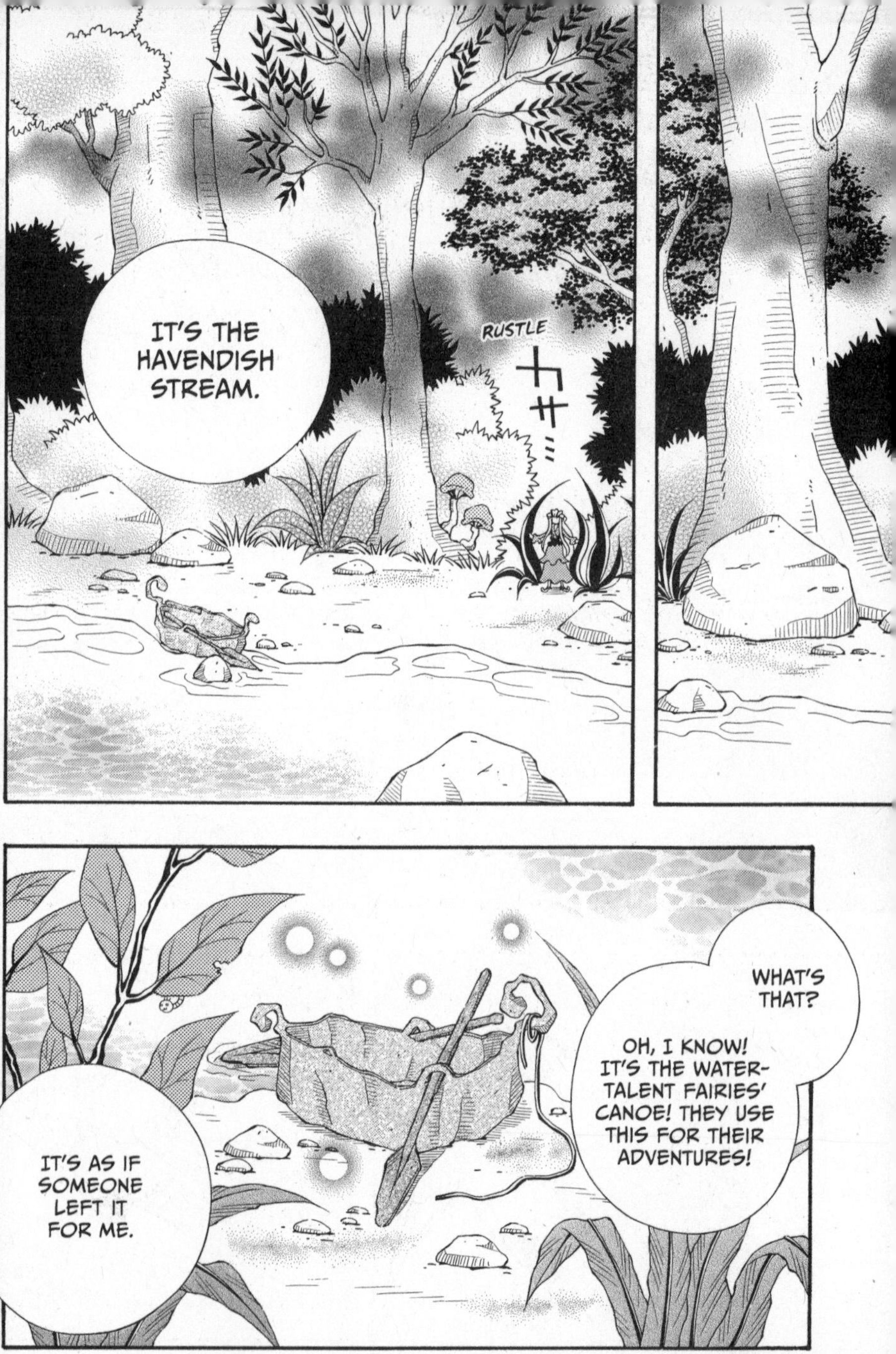
RUSTLE
IT'S THE HAVENDISH STREAM.
WHAT'S THAT?
OH, I KNOW! IT'S THE WATER-TALENT FAIRIES' CANOE! THEY USE THIS FOR THEIR ADVENTURES!
IT'S AS IF SOMEONE LEFT IT FOR ME.

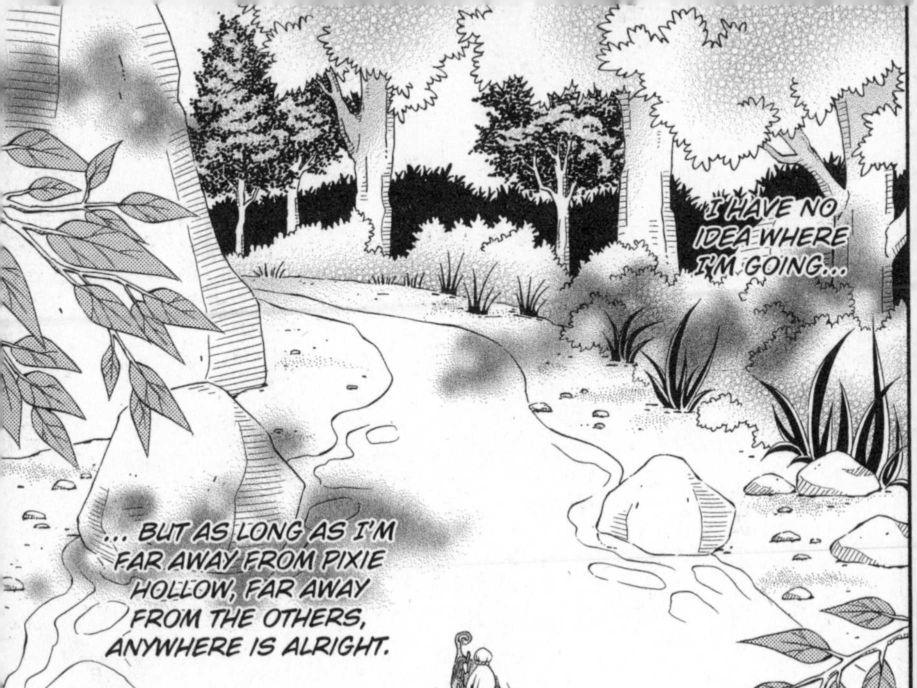
I HAVE NO IDEA WHERE I'M GOING...
... BUT AS LONG AS I'M FAR AWAY FROM PIXIE HOLLOW, FAR AWAY FROM THE OTHERS, ANYWHERE IS ALRIGHT.

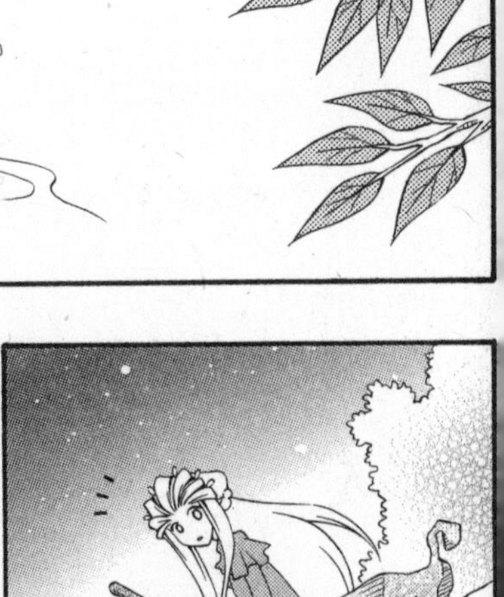

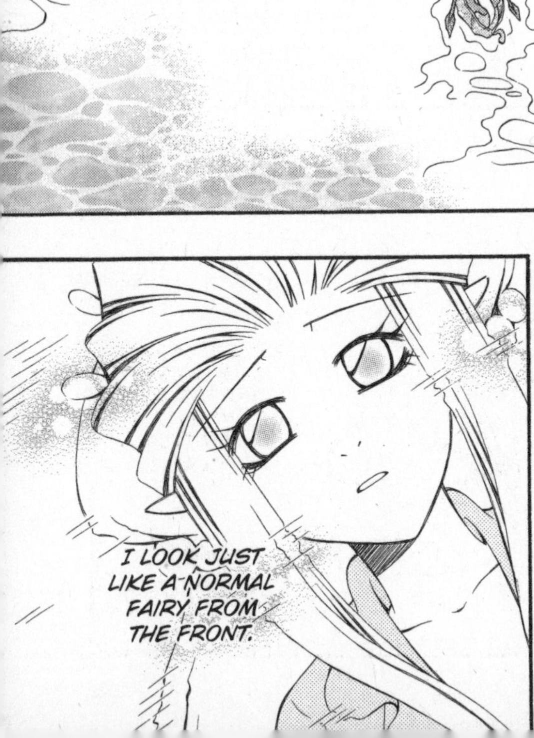
I LOOK JUST LIKE A NORMAL FAIRY FROM THE FRONT.

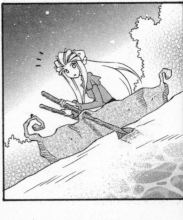

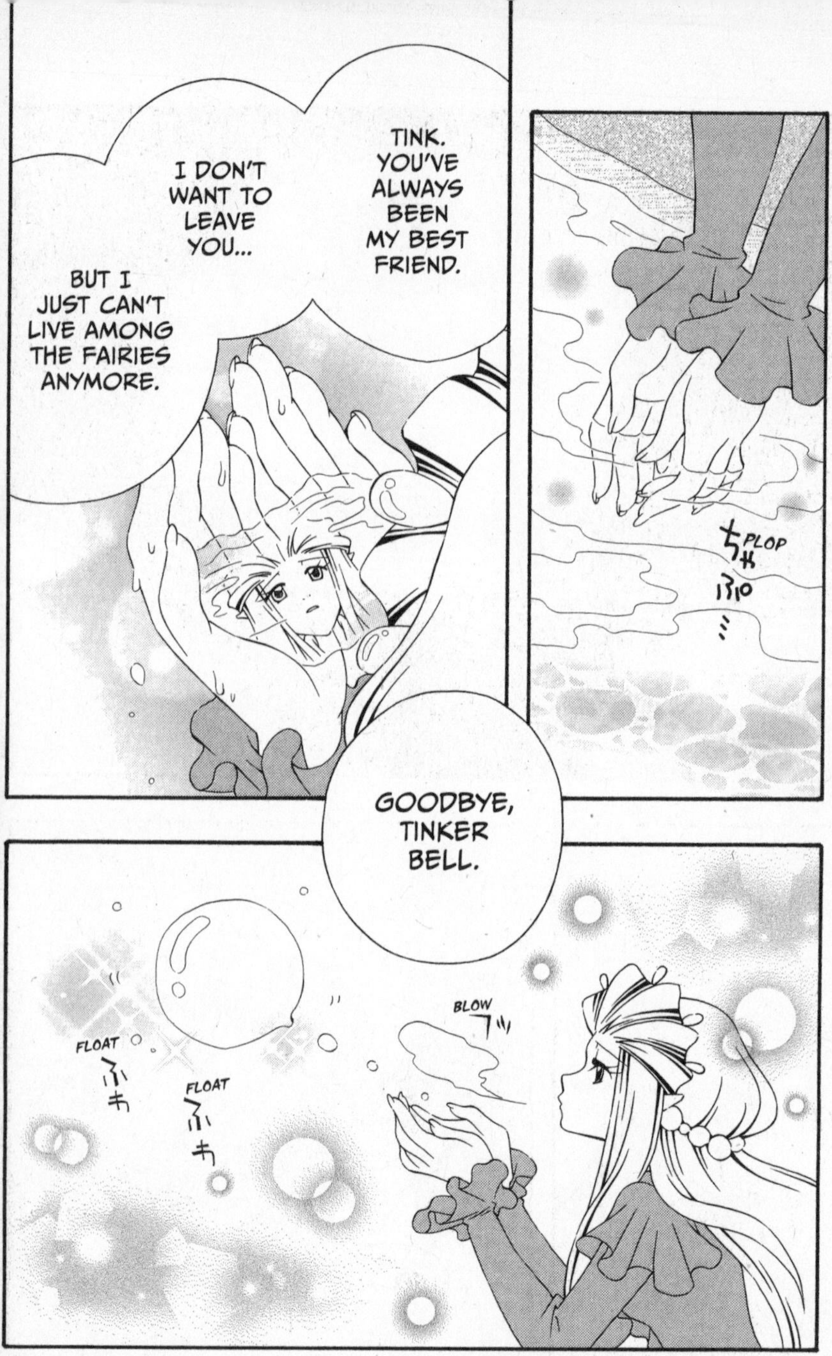
PLOP
TINK. YOU'VE ALWAYS BEEN MY BEST FRIEND.
I DON'T WANT TO LEAVE YOU...
BUT I JUST CAN'T LIVE AMONG THE FAIRIES ANYMORE.
GOODBYE, TINKER BELL.
BLOW
FLOAT
FLOAT

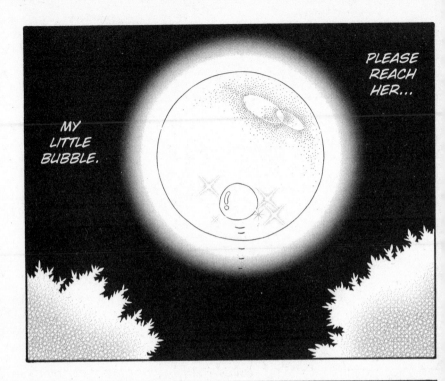

PLEASE REACH HER...

MY LITTLE BUBBLE.

WHAT'S THAT?

HMM?

SLITHER

SPLASH

SPLASH

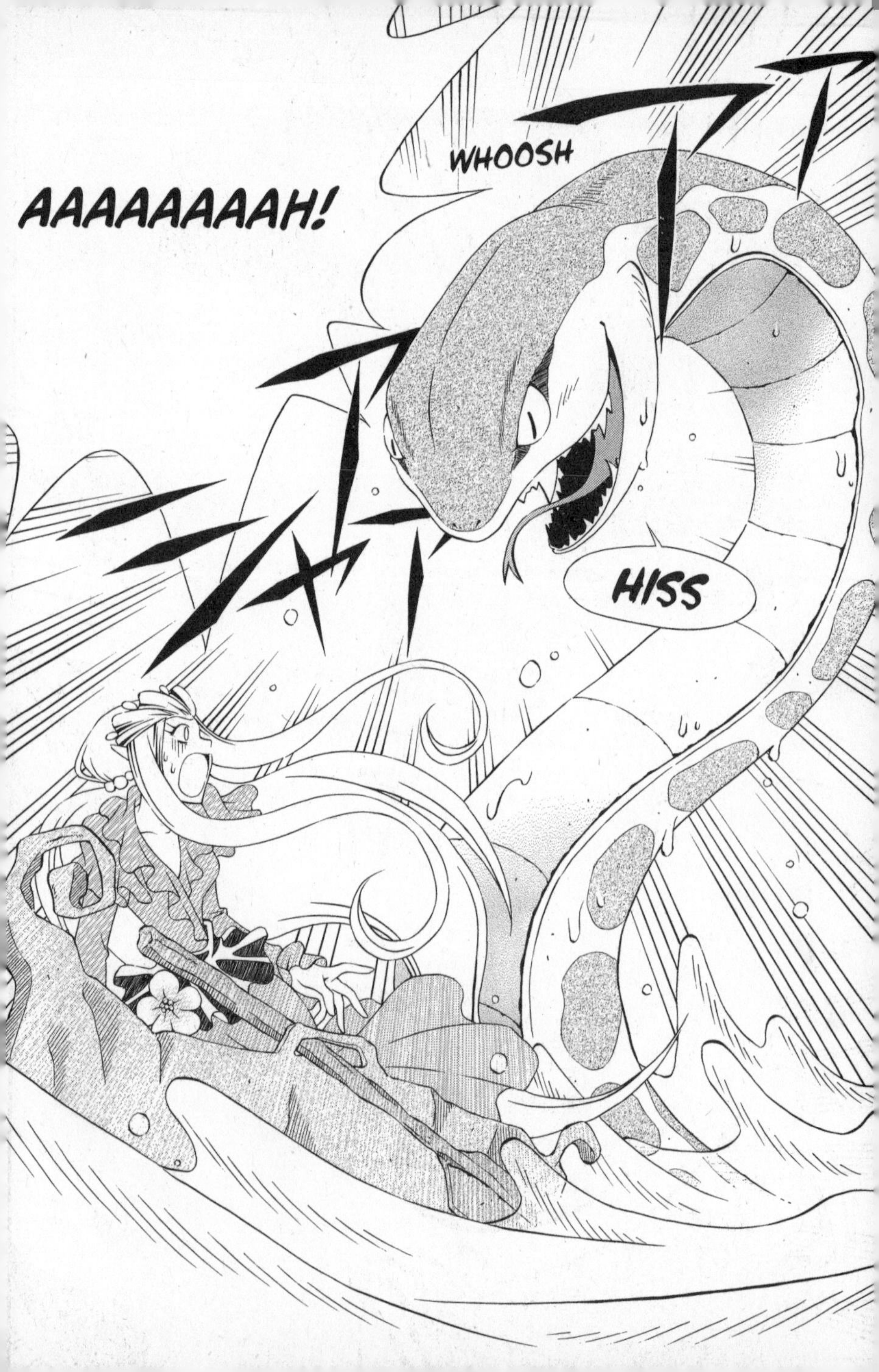
WHOOSH
AAAAAAAAH!
HISS

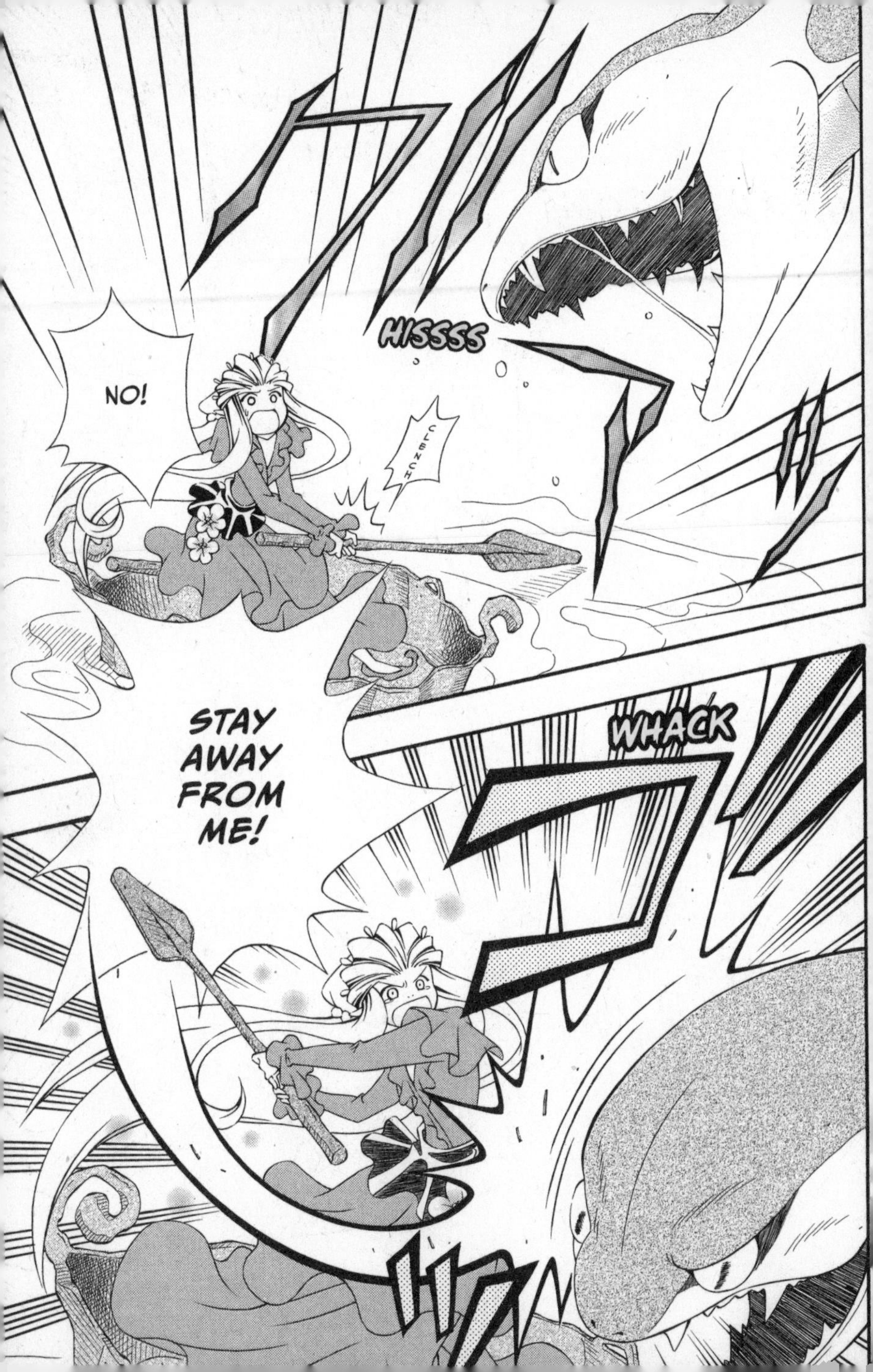
HISSSS
CLENCH
NO!
WHACK
STAY AWAY FROM ME!

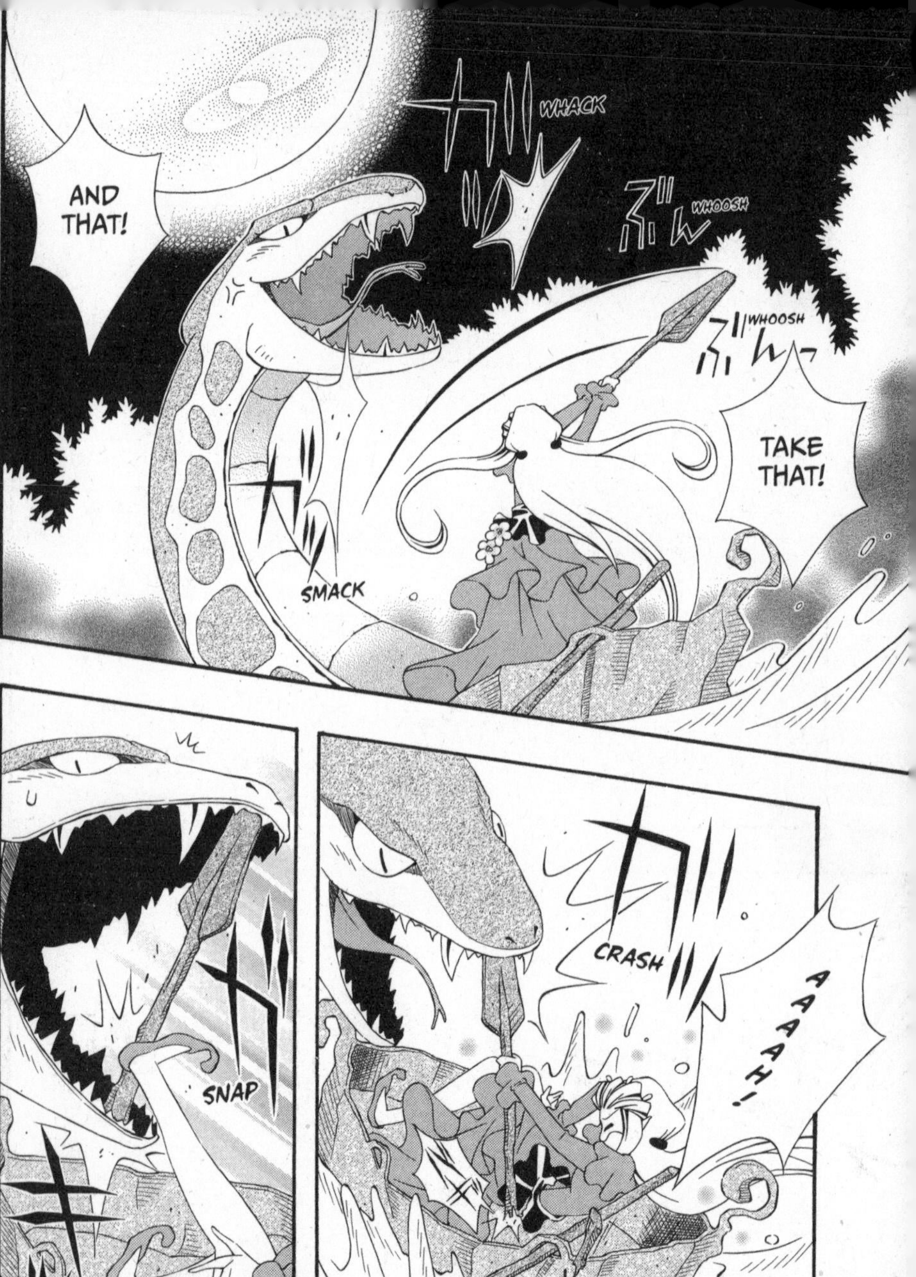
WHACK
WHOOSH
WHOOSH
TAKE THAT!
AND THAT!
SMACK
CRASH
AAAAAH!
SNAP

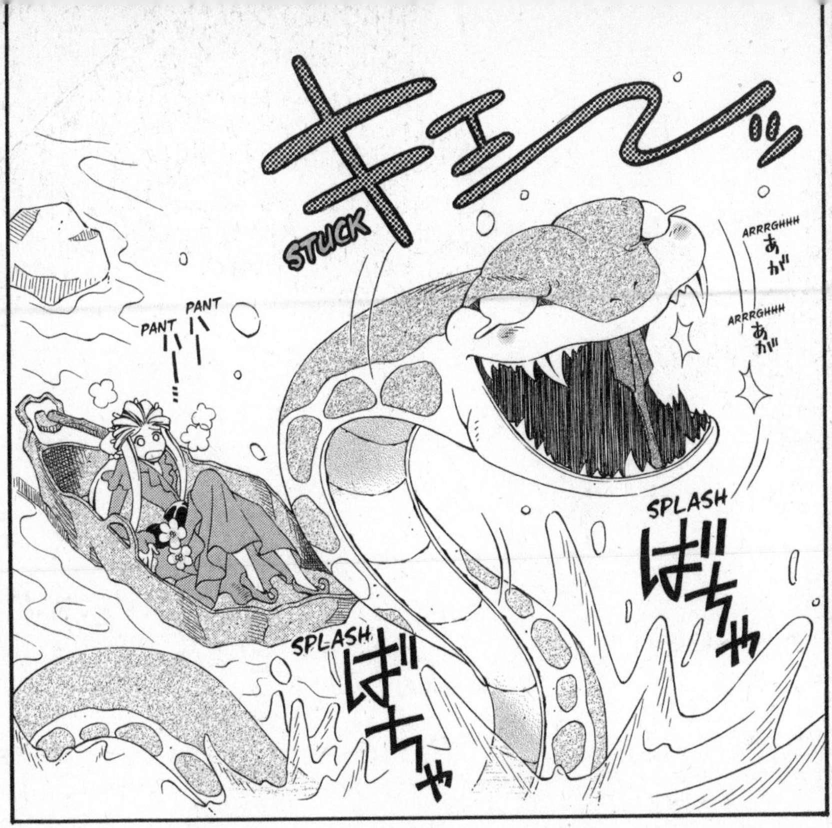

キェ〜ッ
STUCK
ARRRGHHH
あが
ARRRGHHH
あが
SPLASH
ばちゃ
PANT
ハー!!
PANT
ハ
SPLASH
ばちゃ

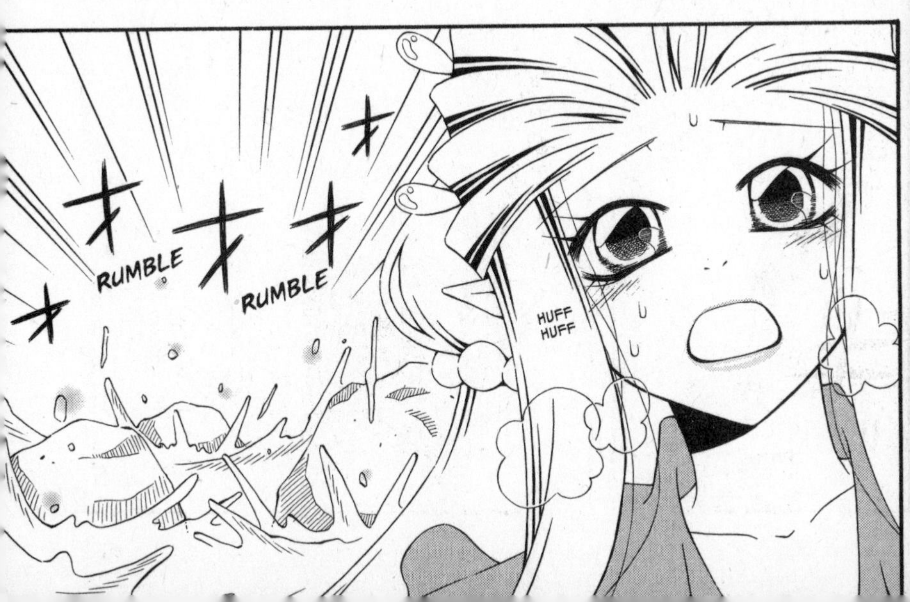

HUFF HUFF
RUMBLE
RUMBLE

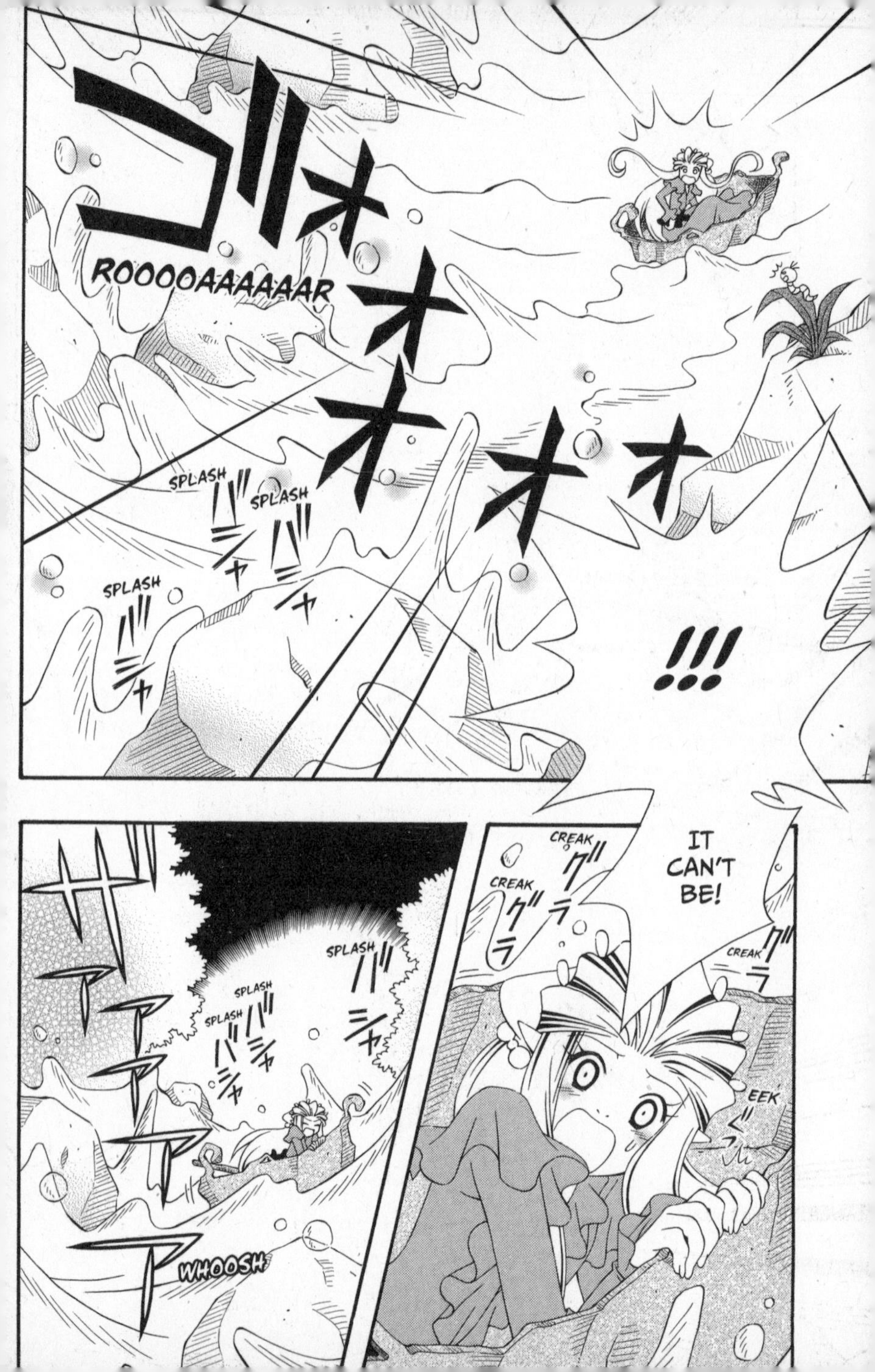

ゴォオオオオ
ROOOOAAAAAAR
SPLASH
バシャ
SPLASH
バシャ
SPLASH
バシャ
!!!
CREAK
グラ
CREAK
グラ
IT CAN'T BE!
CREAK
グラ
EEK
SPLASH
バシャ
SPLASH
バシャ
SPLASH
バシャ
ザァァァァ
WHOOSH

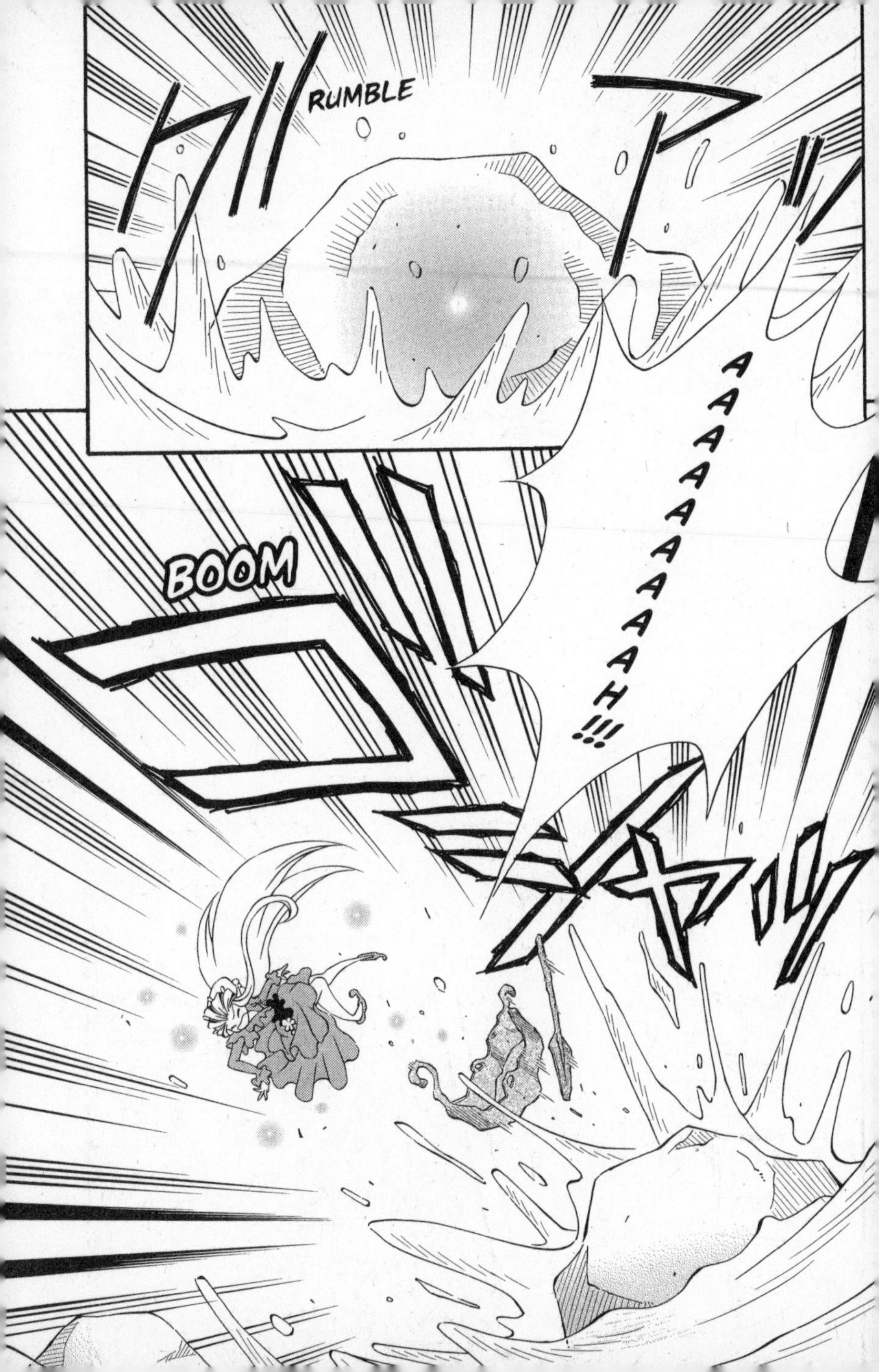
RUMBLE
AAAAAAAAAH!!!
BOOM

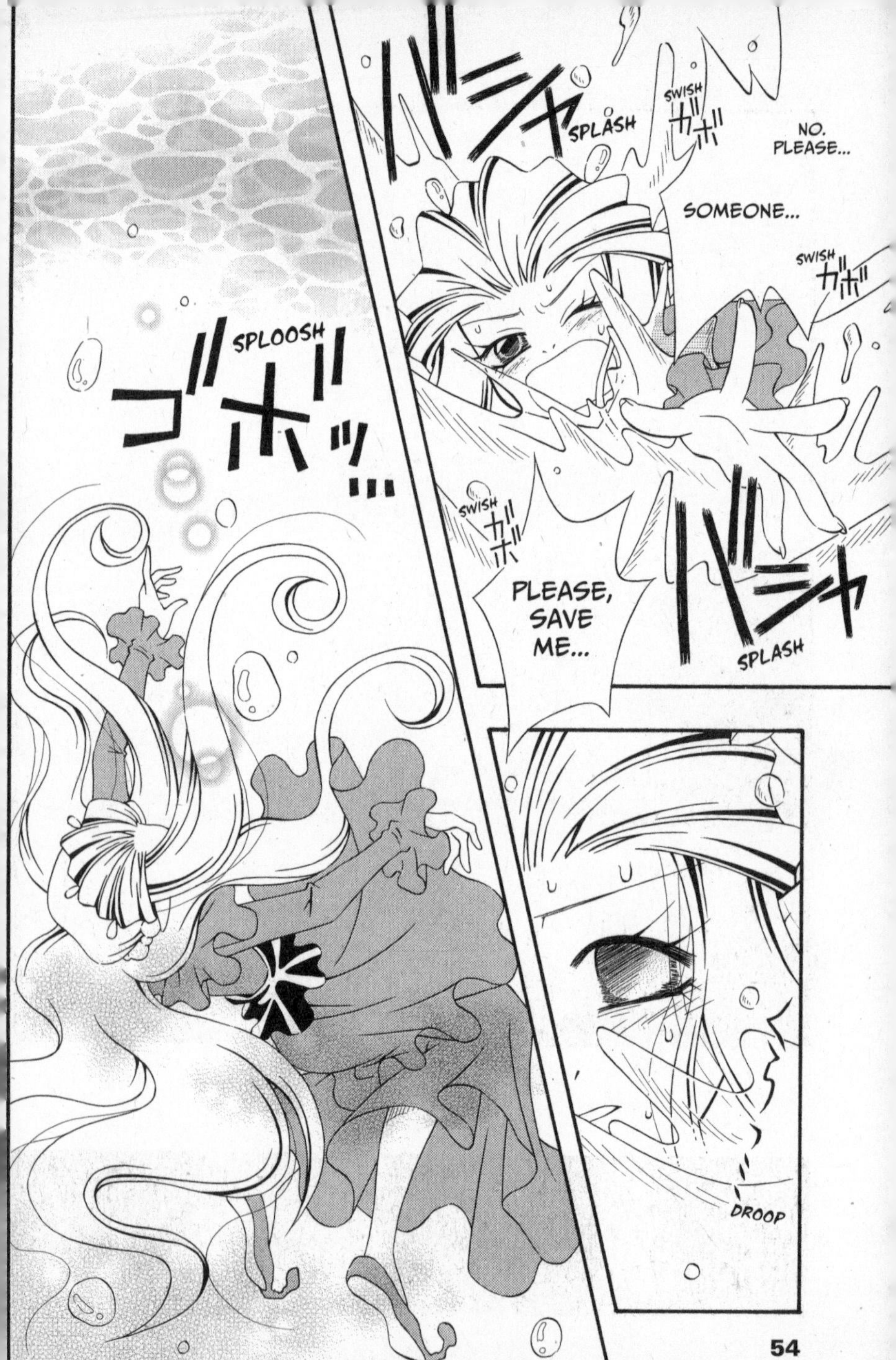
NO. PLEASE...
SWISH
ガボ
バシャ
SPLASH
SOMEONE...
SWISH
ガボ
バシャ
SPLASH
PLEASE, SAVE ME...
SWISH
ガボ
DROOP
SPLOOSH
ゴボッ...

WHOOSH
ゴボ・・・

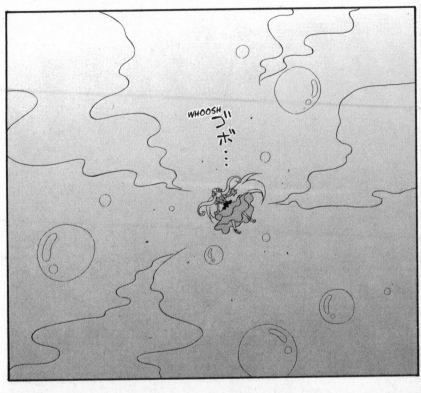

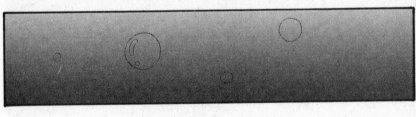

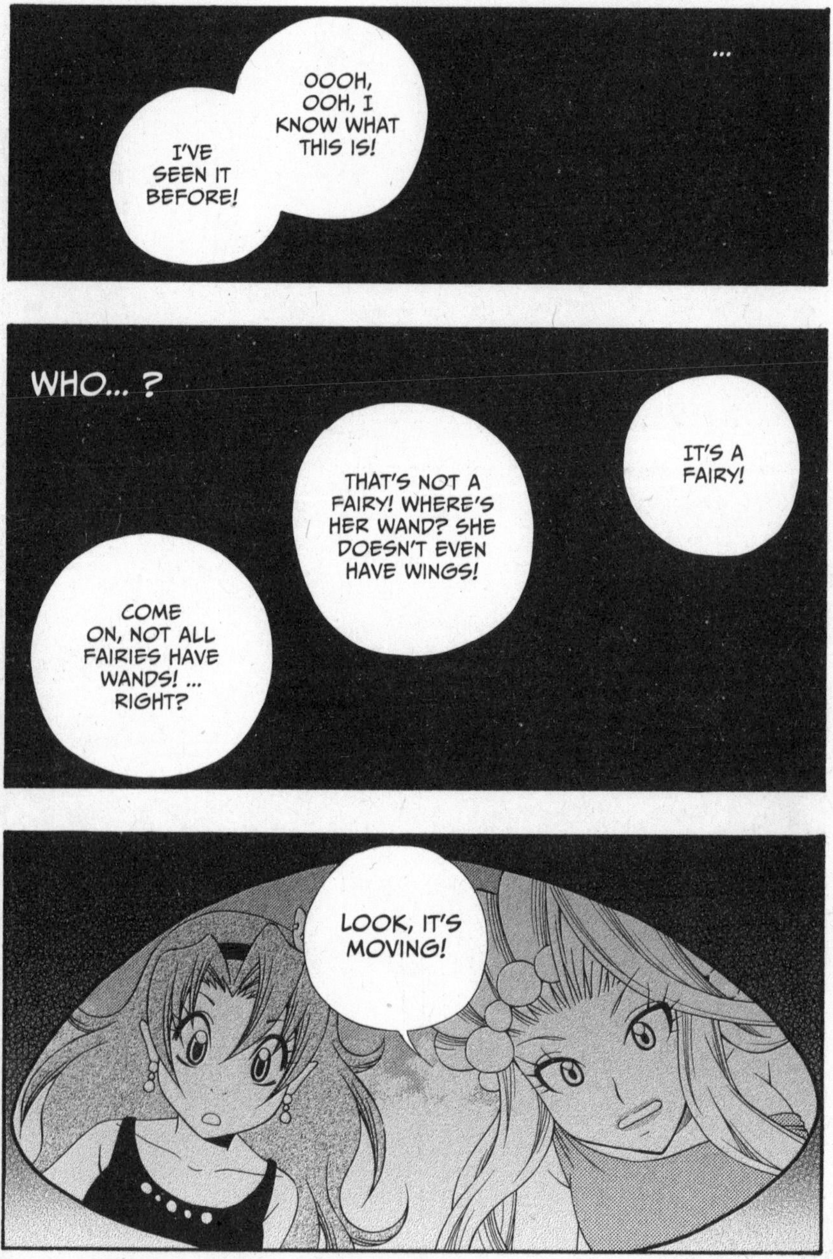
...
OOOH, OOH, I KNOW WHAT THIS IS!
I'VE SEEN IT BEFORE!
WHO... ?
IT'S A FAIRY!
THAT'S NOT A FAIRY! WHERE'S HER WAND? SHE DOESN'T EVEN HAVE WINGS!
COME ON, NOT ALL FAIRIES HAVE WANDS! ... RIGHT?
LOOK, IT'S MOVING!

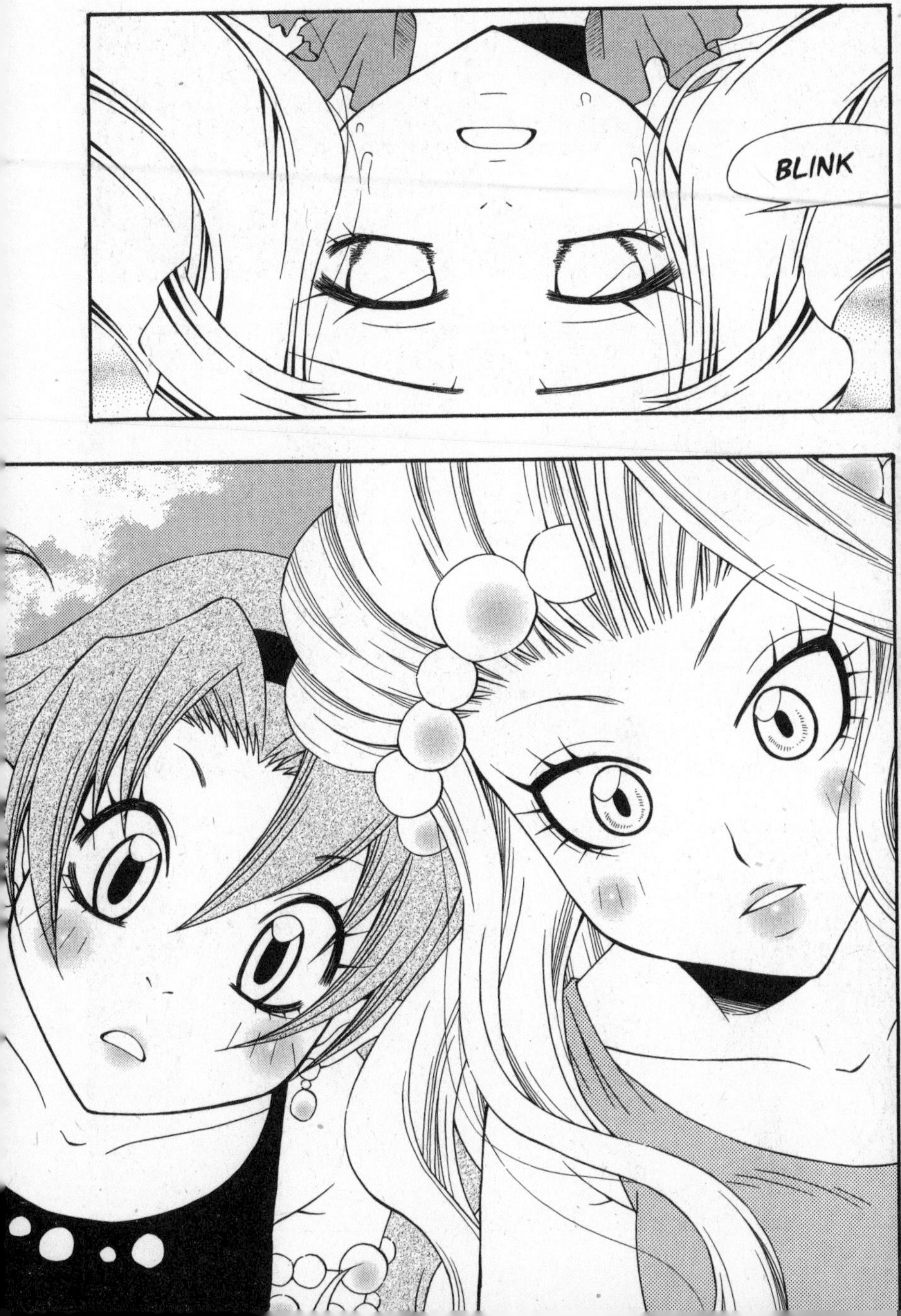
BLINK

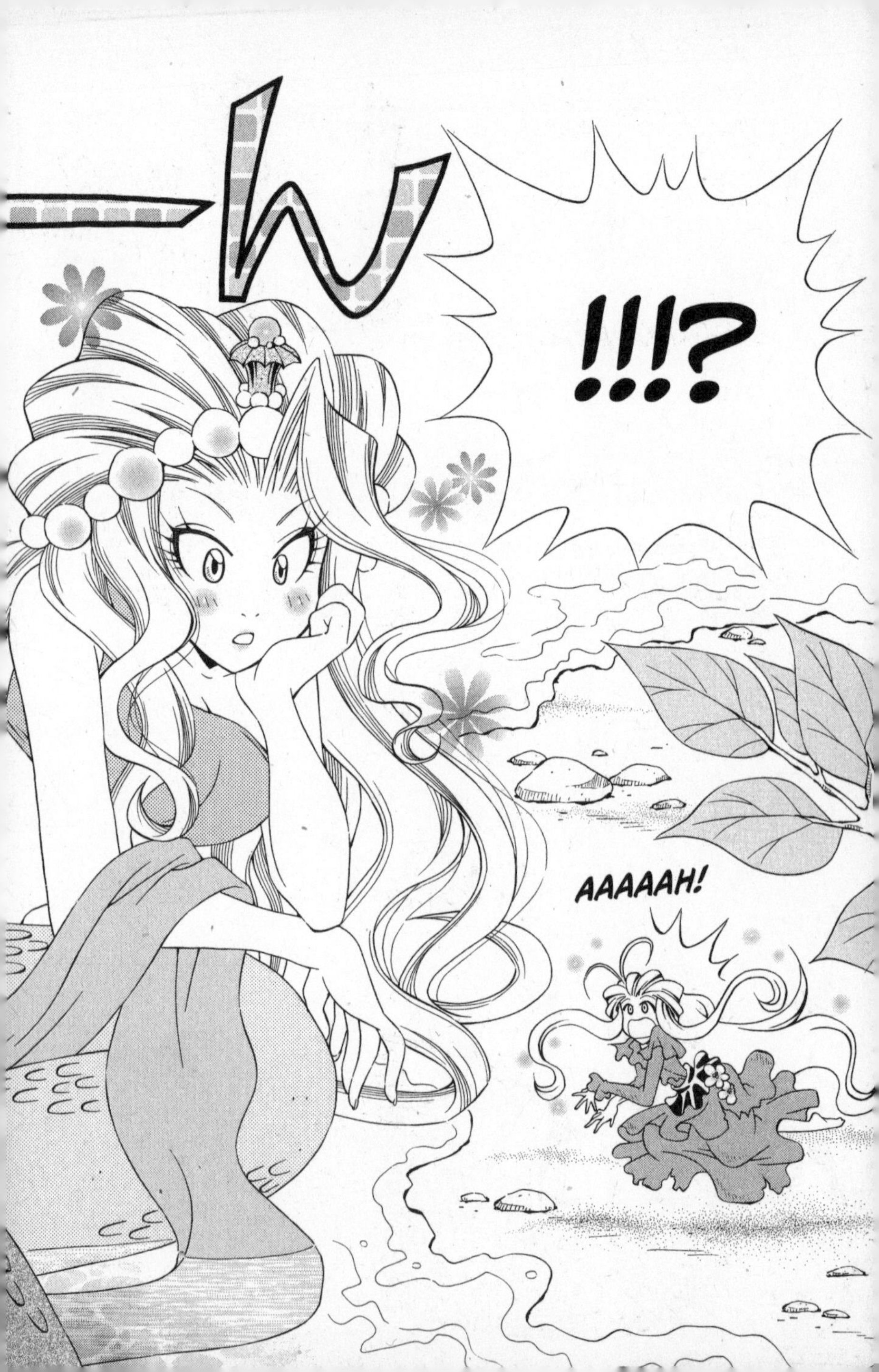
—N
!!!?
AAAAAH!

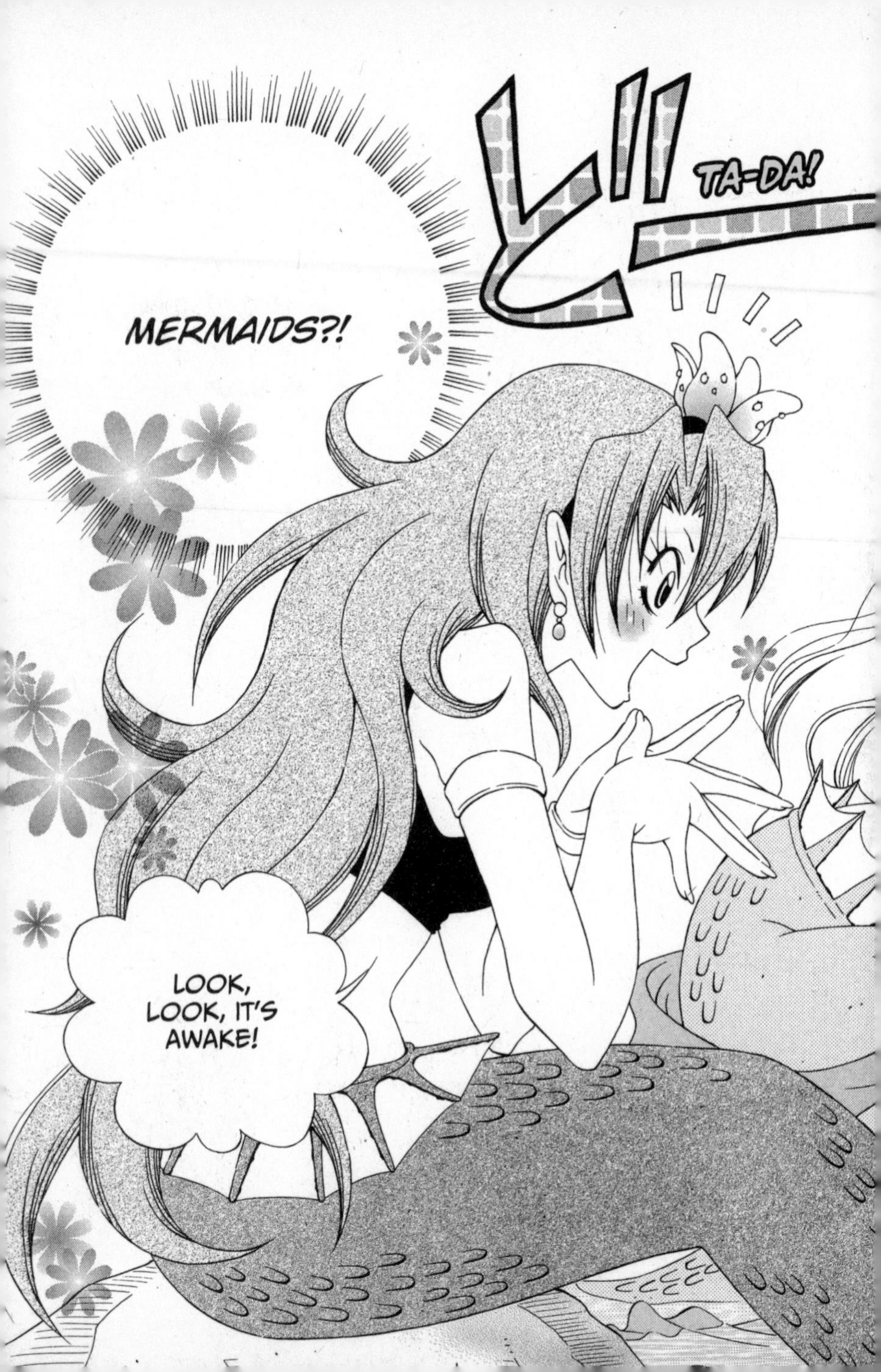
TA-DA!
MERMAIDS?!
LOOK, LOOK, IT'S AWAKE!

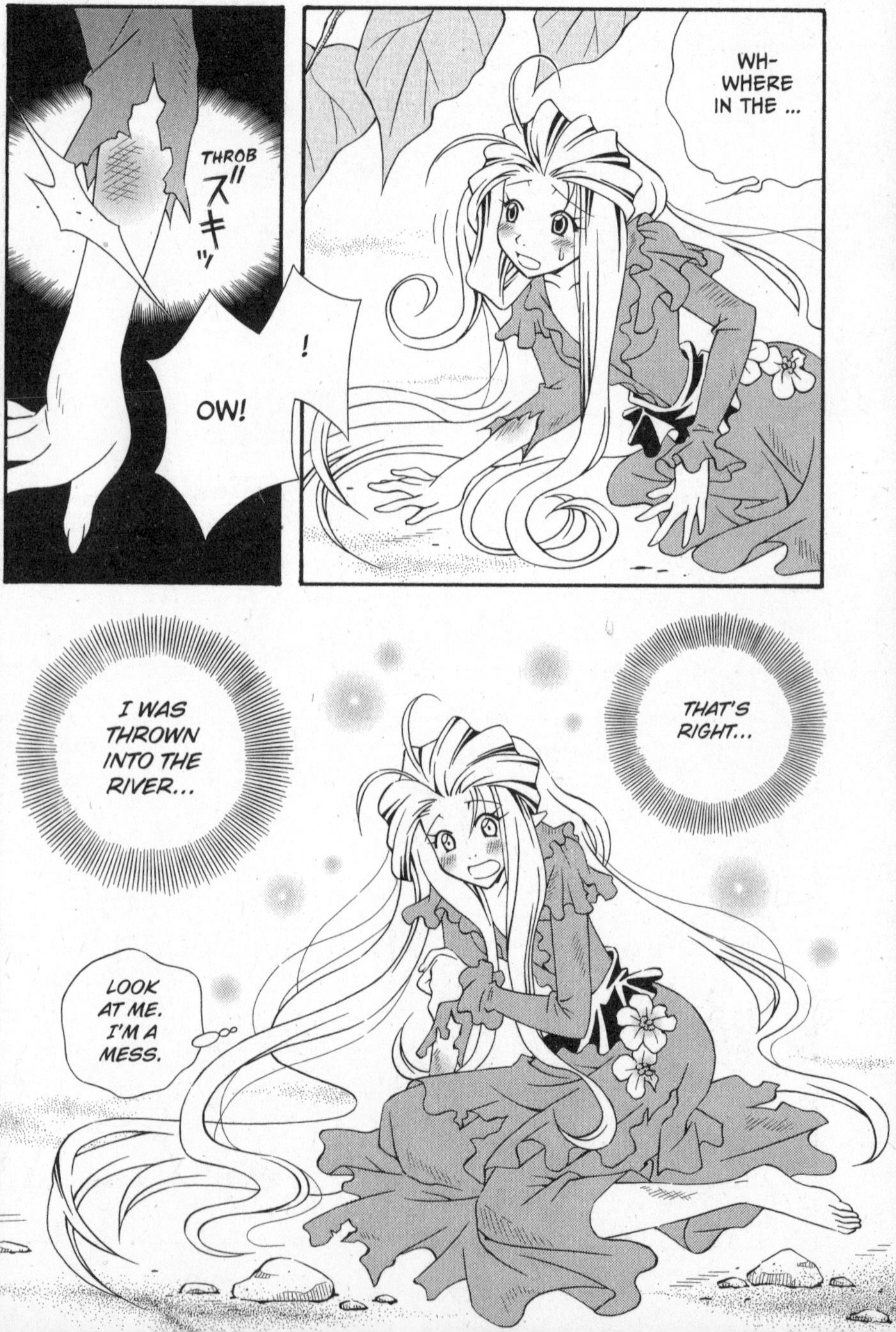
WH- WHERE IN THE ...
THROB
ズキッ
!
OW!
THAT'S RIGHT...
I WAS THROWN INTO THE RIVER...
LOOK AT ME. I'M A MESS.

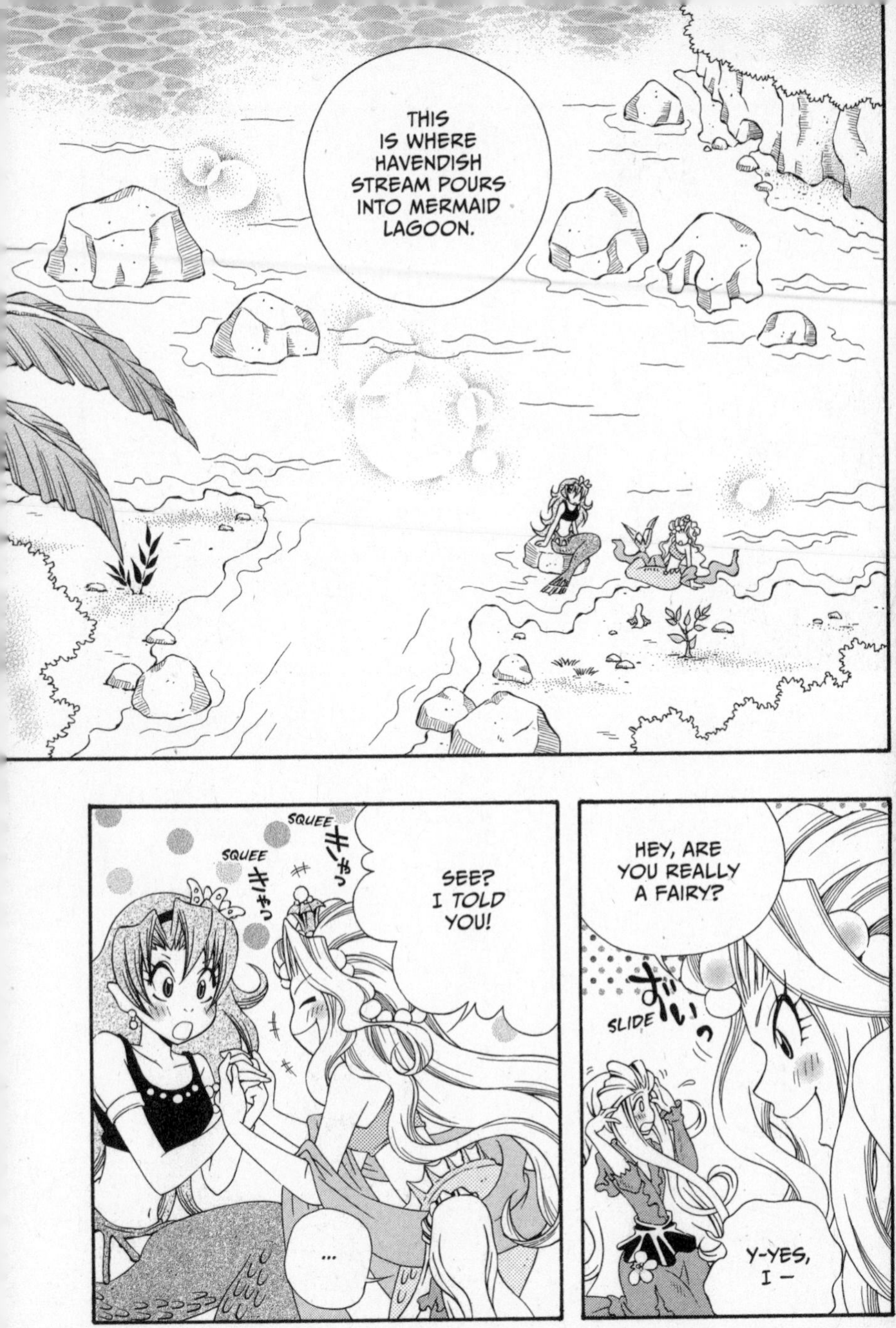
THIS IS WHERE HAVENDISH STREAM POURS INTO MERMAID LAGOON.
HEY, ARE YOU REALLY A FAIRY?
SLIDE
Y-YES, I —
SQUEE
SQUEE
SEE? I TOLD YOU!
...

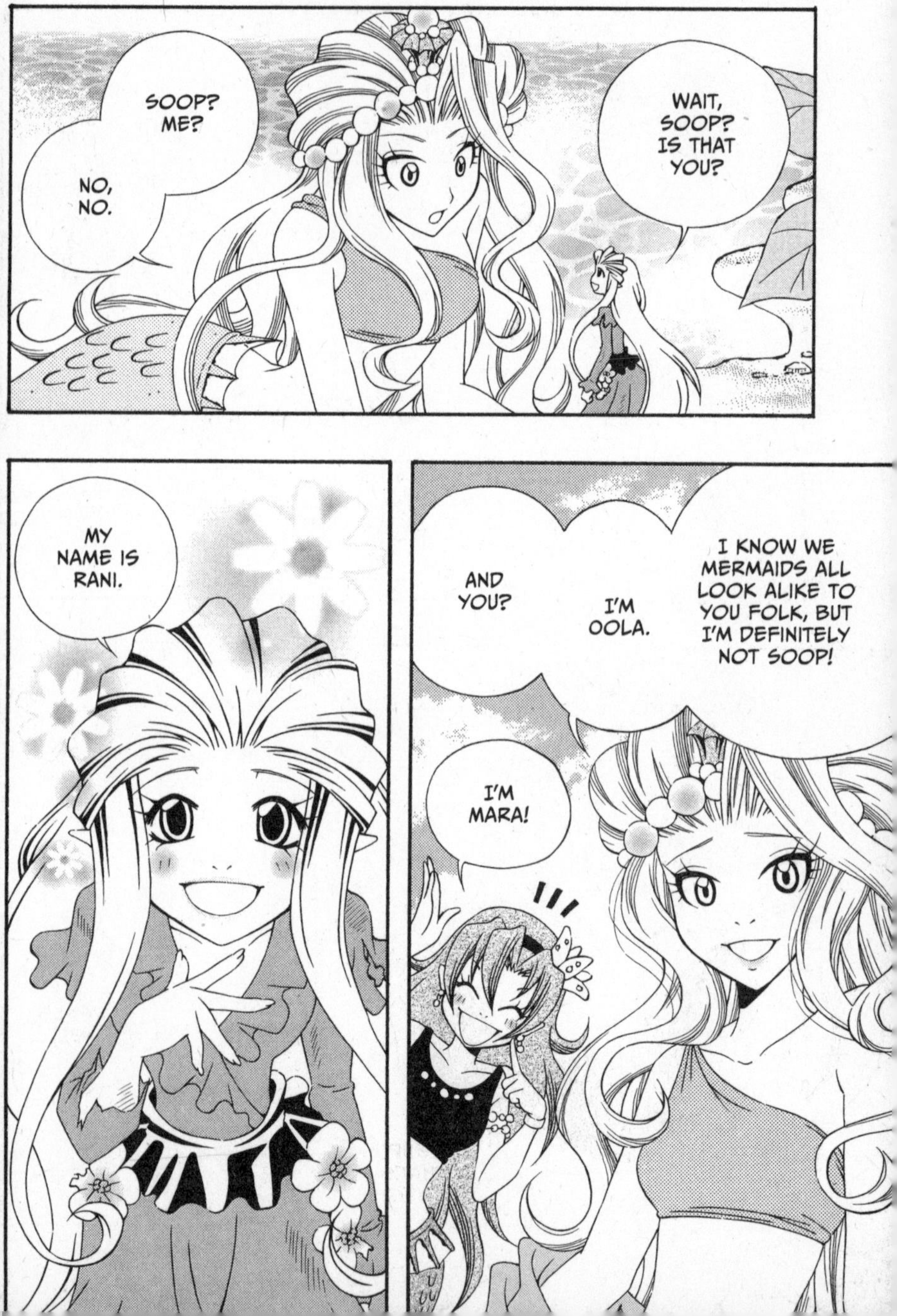
WAIT, SOOP? IS THAT YOU?
SOOP? ME?
NO, NO.
I KNOW WE MERMAIDS ALL LOOK ALIKE TO YOU FOLK, BUT I'M DEFINITELY NOT SOOP!
I'M OOLA.
AND YOU?
I'M MARA!
MY NAME IS RANI.

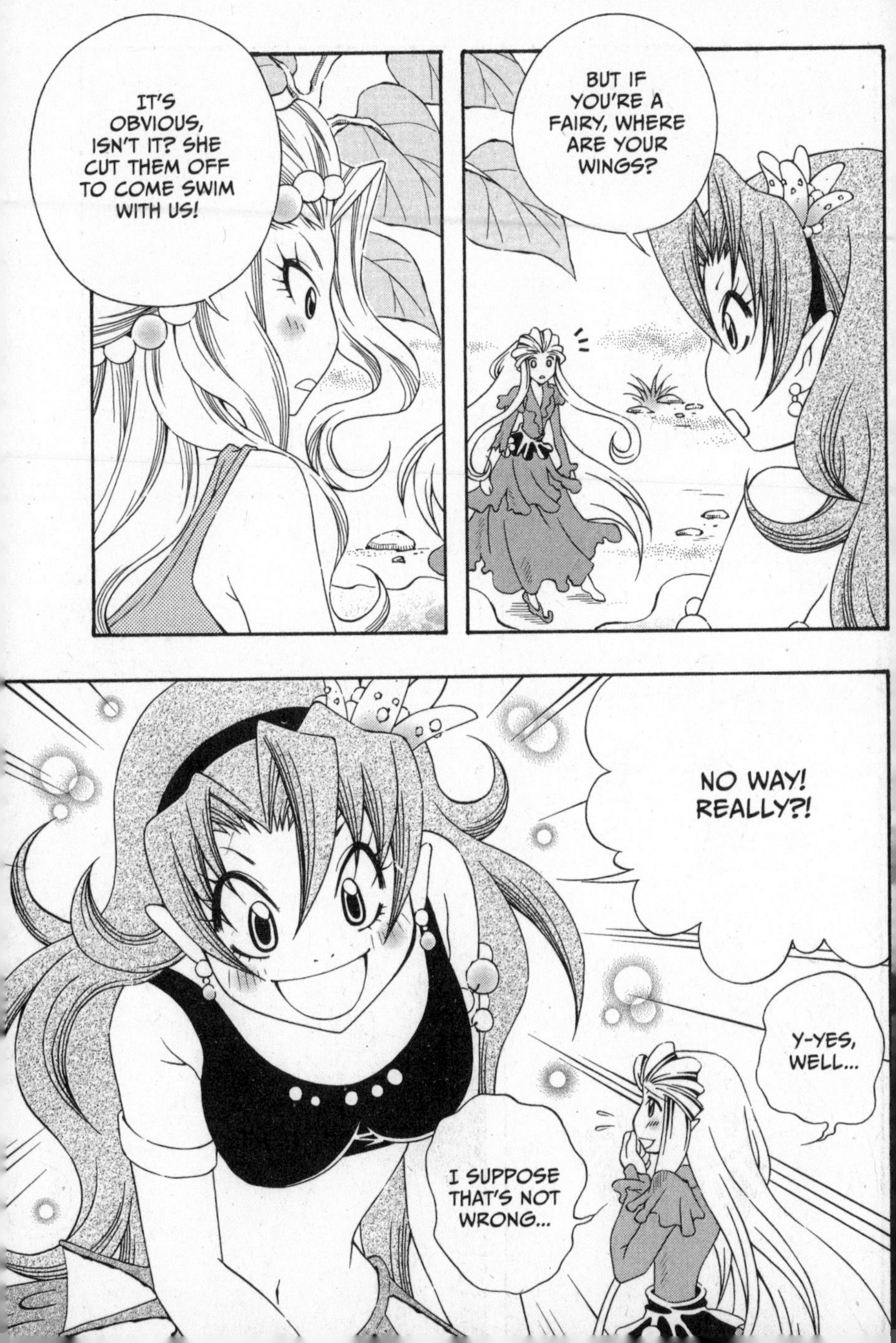
BUT IF YOU'RE A FAIRY, WHERE ARE YOUR WINGS?
IT'S OBVIOUS, ISN'T IT? SHE CUT THEM OFF TO COME SWIM WITH US!
NO WAY! REALLY?!
Y-YES, WELL...
I SUPPOSE THAT'S NOT WRONG...

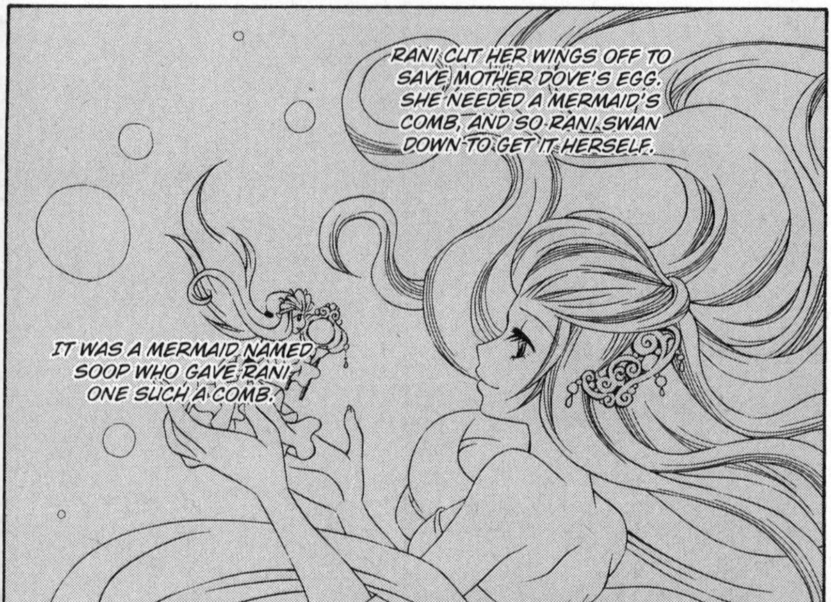
RANI CUT HER WINGS OFF TO SAVE MOTHER DOVE'S EGG. SHE NEEDED A MERMAID'S COMB, AND SO RANI SWAN DOWN TO GET IT HERSELF.
IT WAS A MERMAID NAMED SOOP WHO GAVE RANI ONE SUCH A COMB.
SO, IT WAS QUITE REASONABLE TO SAY SHE HAD CUT OFF HER WINGS TO SWIM WITH THE MERMAIDS.
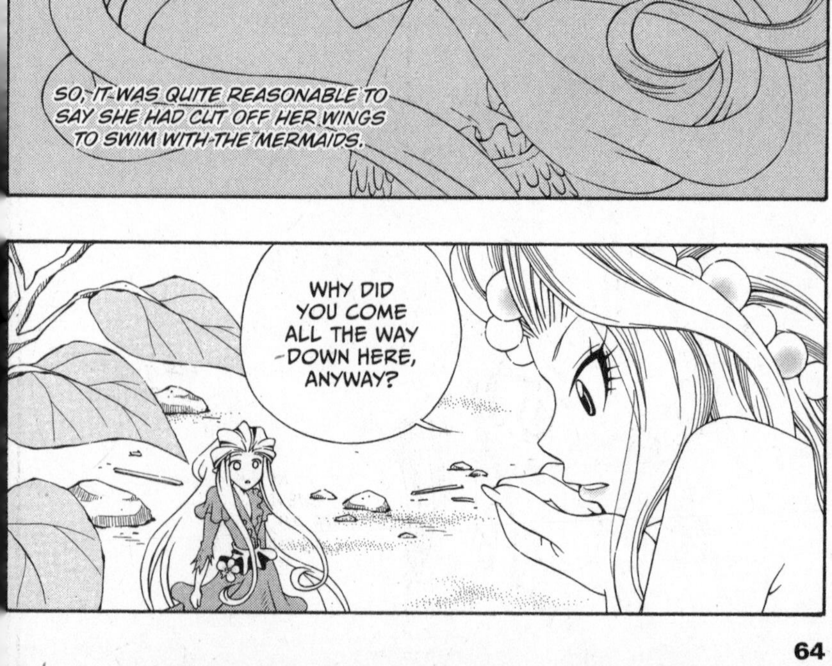
WHY DID YOU COME ALL THE WAY DOWN HERE, ANYWAY?

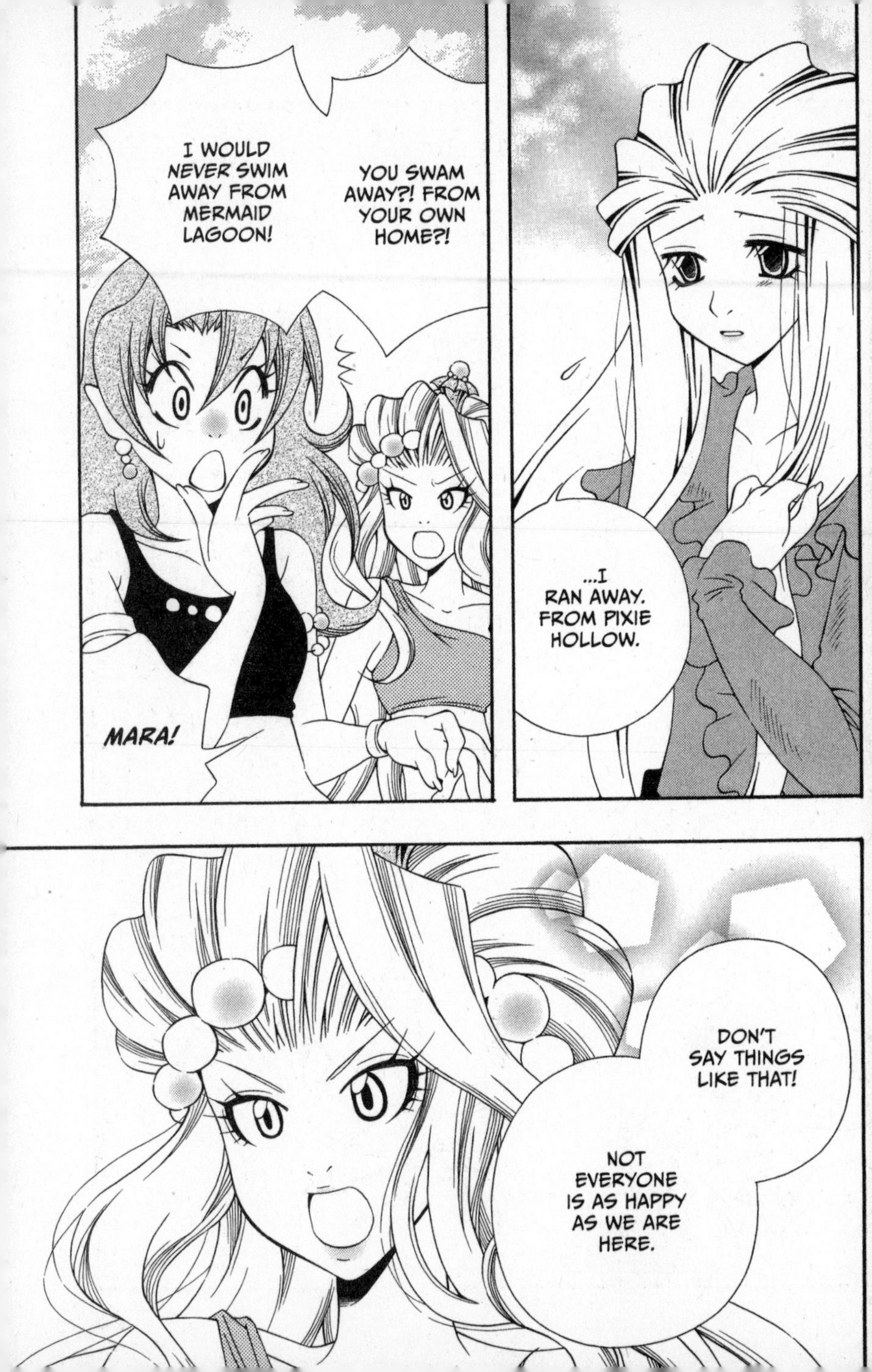
...I RAN AWAY. FROM PIXIE HOLLOW.
YOU SWAM AWAY?! FROM YOUR OWN HOME?!
I WOULD NEVER SWIM AWAY FROM MERMAID LAGOON!
MARA!
DON'T SAY THINGS LIKE THAT!
NOT EVERYONE IS AS HAPPY AS WE ARE HERE.

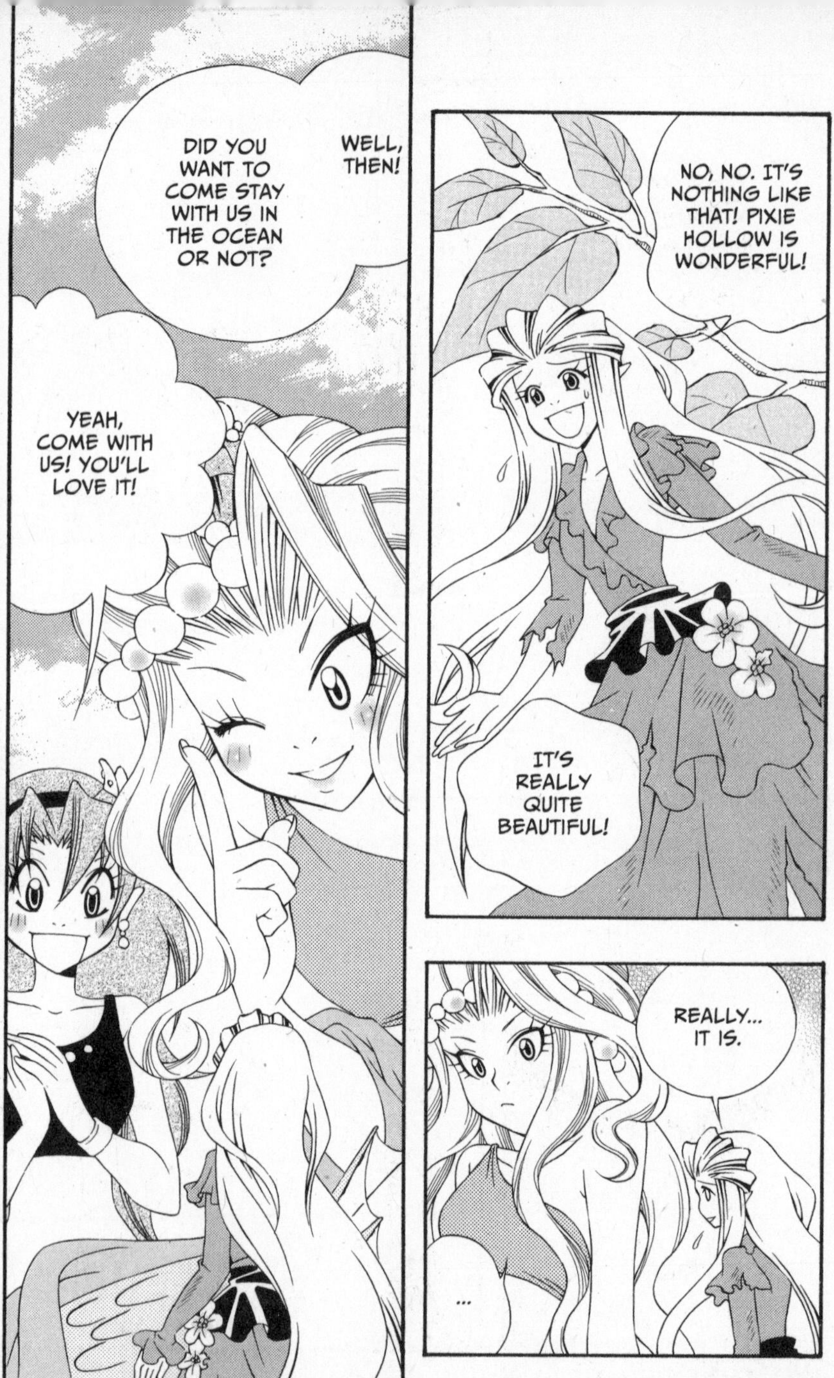
NO, NO. IT'S NOTHING LIKE THAT! PIXIE HOLLOW IS WONDERFUL!
IT'S REALLY QUITE BEAUTIFUL!
REALLY... IT IS.
...
WELL, THEN!
DID YOU WANT TO COME STAY WITH US IN THE OCEAN OR NOT?
YEAH, COME WITH US! YOU'LL LOVE IT!

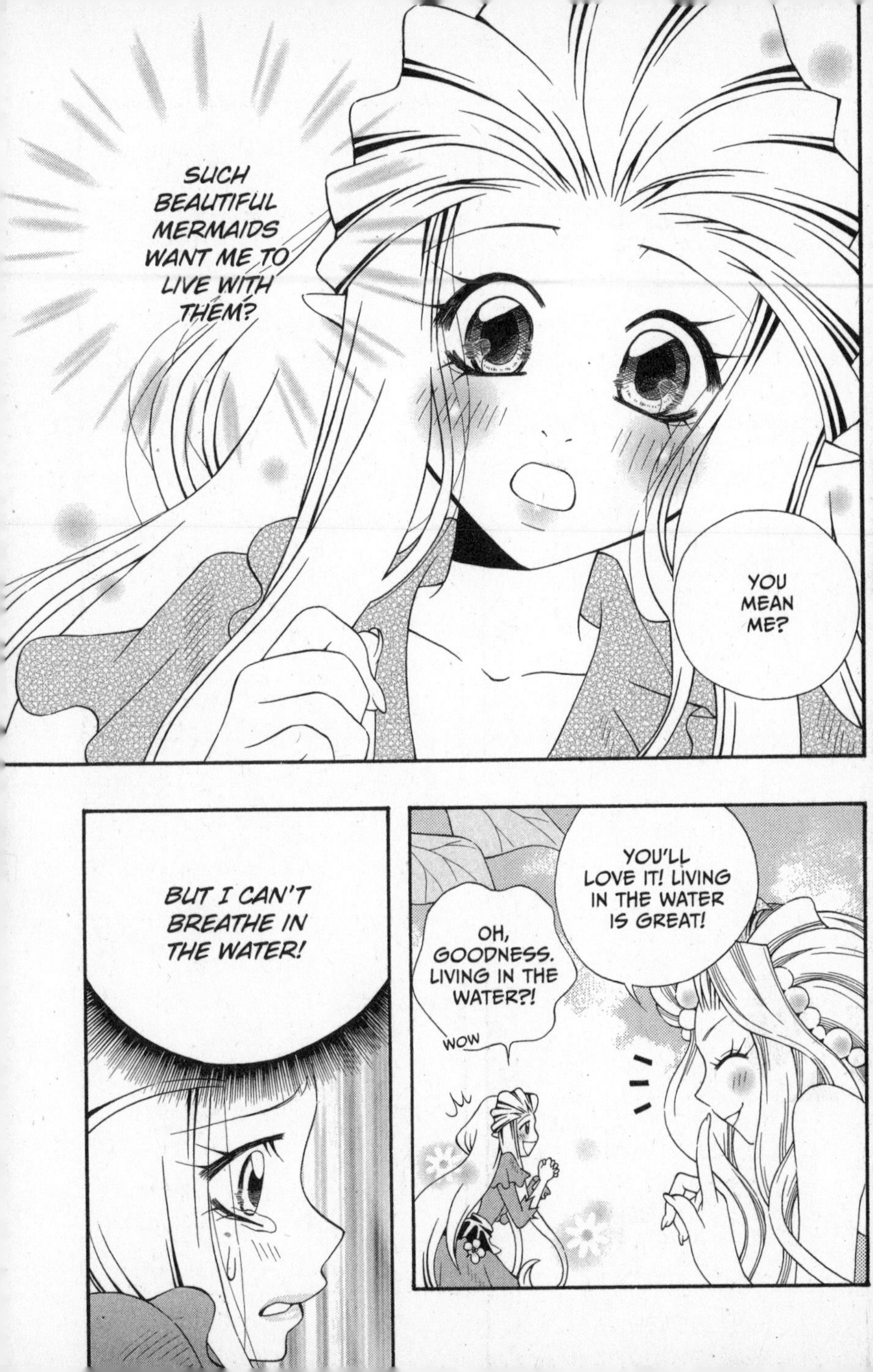
SUCH BEAUTIFUL MERMAIDS WANT ME TO LIVE WITH THEM?
YOU MEAN ME?
YOU'LL LOVE IT! LIVING IN THE WATER IS GREAT!
OH, GOODNESS. LIVING IN THE WATER?!
WOW
BUT I CAN'T BREATHE IN THE WATER!

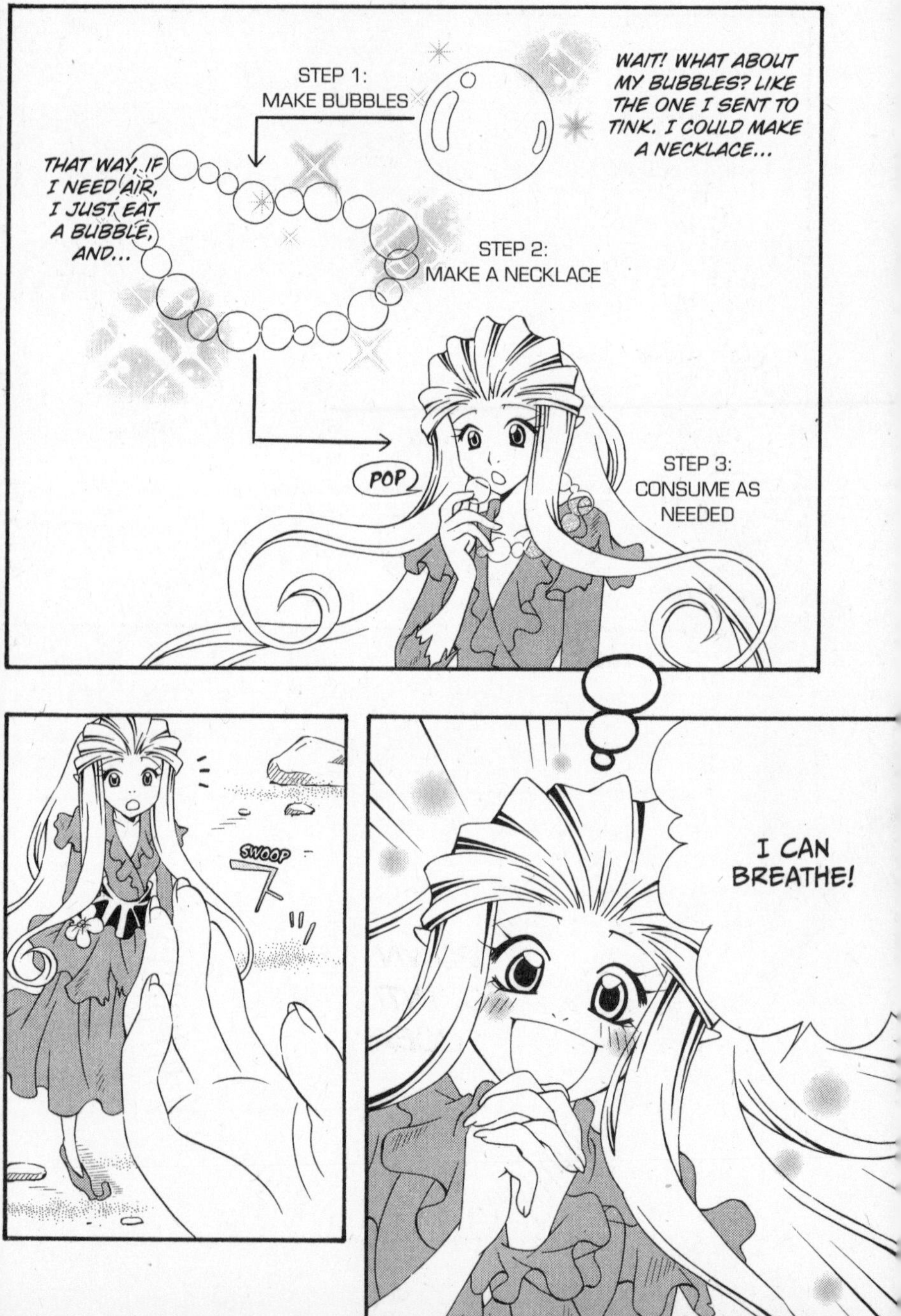
WAIT! WHAT ABOUT MY BUBBLES? LIKE THE ONE I SENT TO TINK. I COULD MAKE A NECKLACE...
STEP 1: MAKE BUBBLES
THAT WAY, IF I NEED AIR, I JUST EAT A BUBBLE, AND...
STEP 2: MAKE A NECKLACE
STEP 3: CONSUME AS NEEDED
POP
I CAN BREATHE!
SWOOP

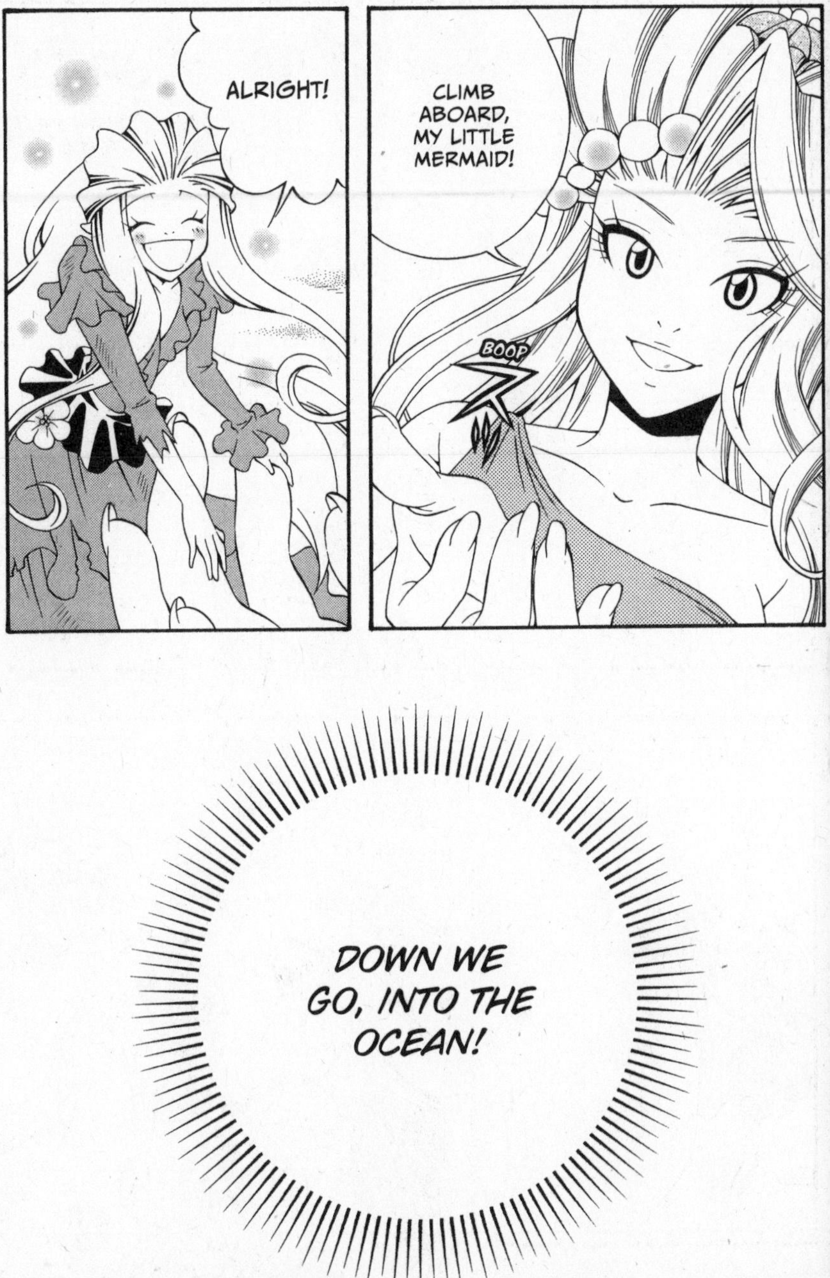
CLIMB ABOARD, MY LITTLE MERMAID!
BOOP
ALRIGHT!
DOWN WE GO, INTO THE OCEAN!

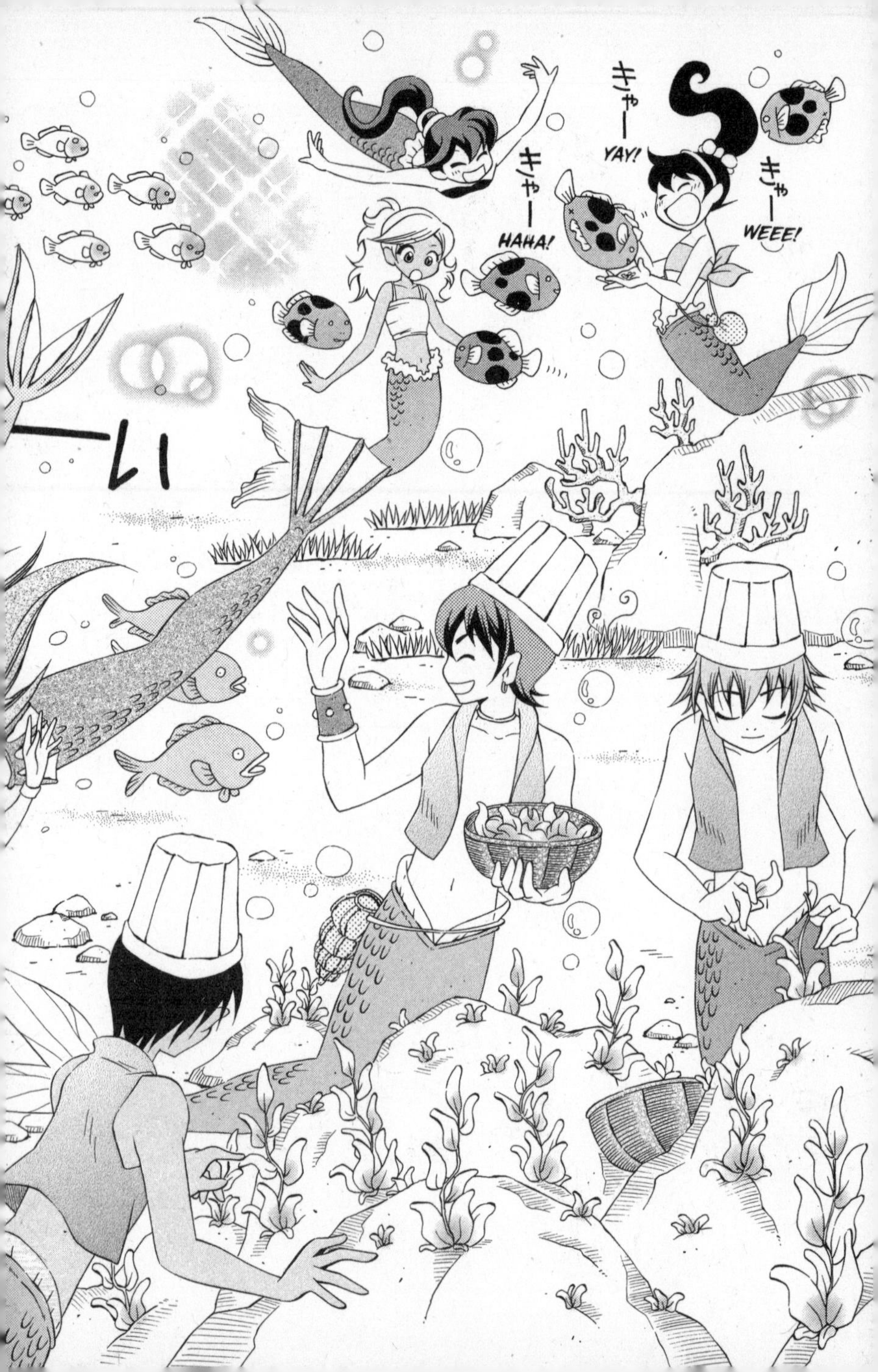

きゃー
WEEE!
キャー
YAY!
キャー
HAHA!

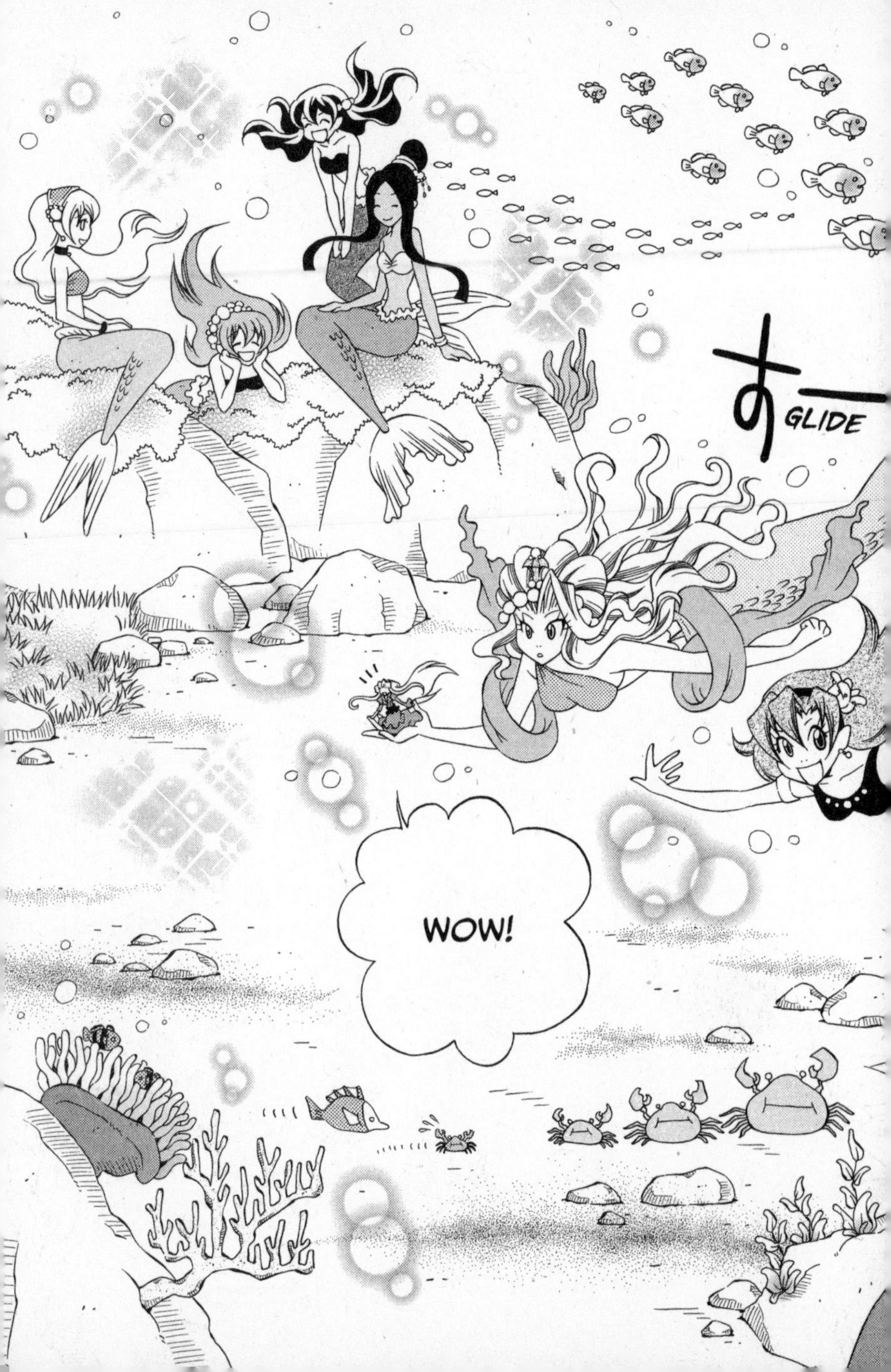
すー GLIDE
WOW!

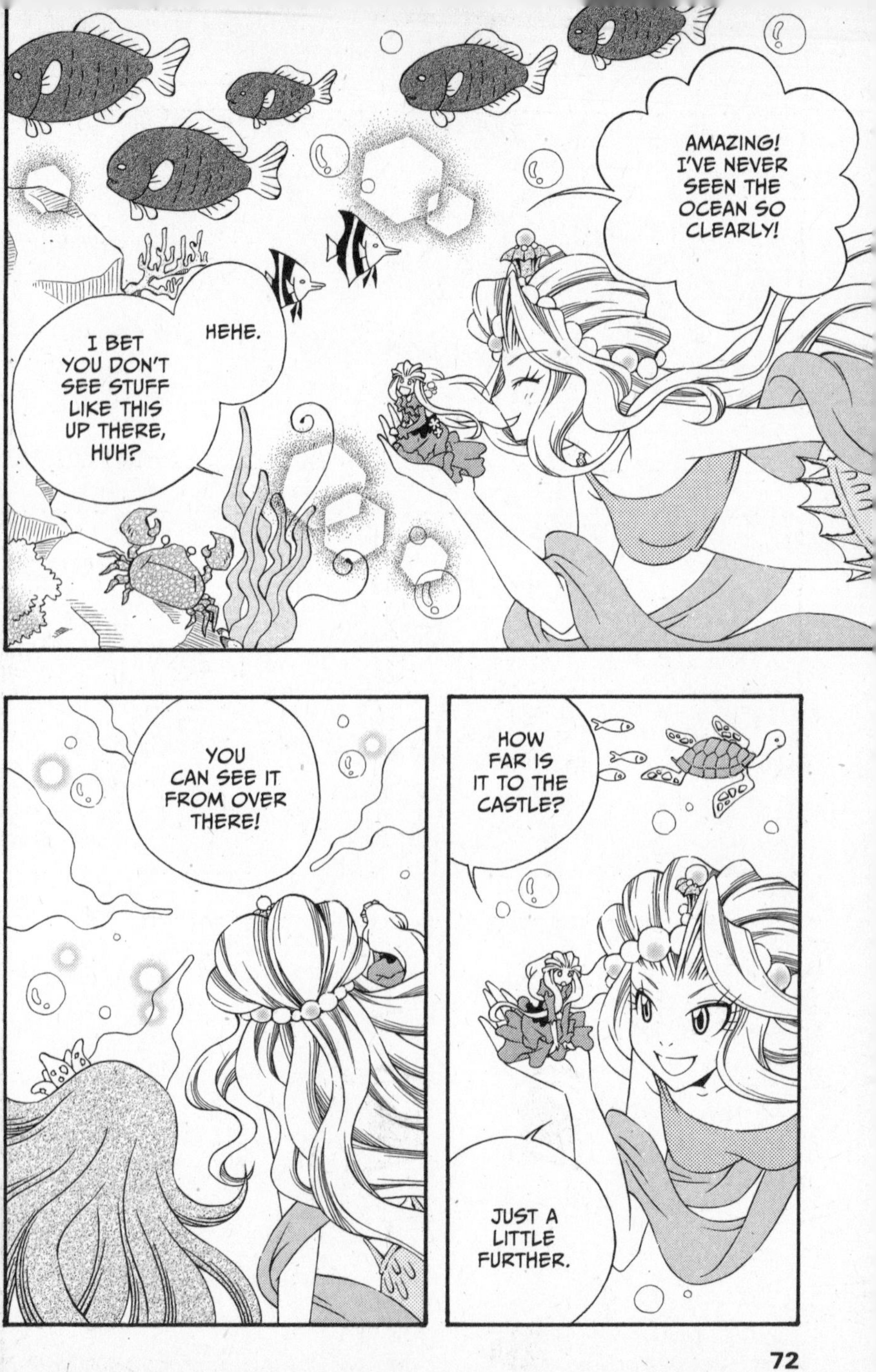
AMAZING! I'VE NEVER SEEN THE OCEAN SO CLEARLY!
HEHE.
I BET YOU DON'T SEE STUFF LIKE THIS UP THERE, HUH?
HOW FAR IS IT TO THE CASTLE?
JUST A LITTLE FURTHER.
YOU CAN SEE IT FROM OVER THERE!

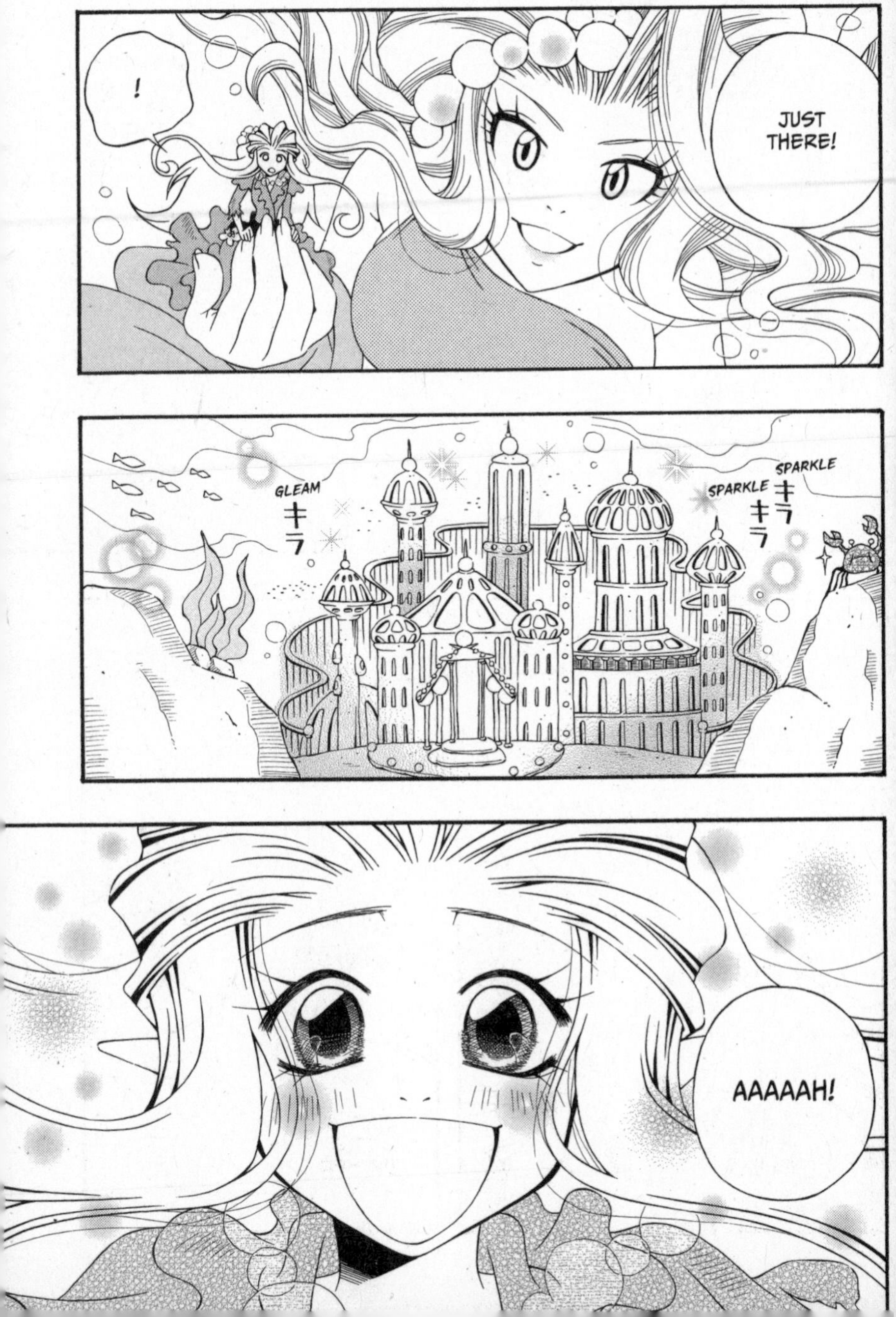
JUST THERE!
!
SPARKLE キラ
SPARKLE キラ
GLEAM キラ
AAAAH!

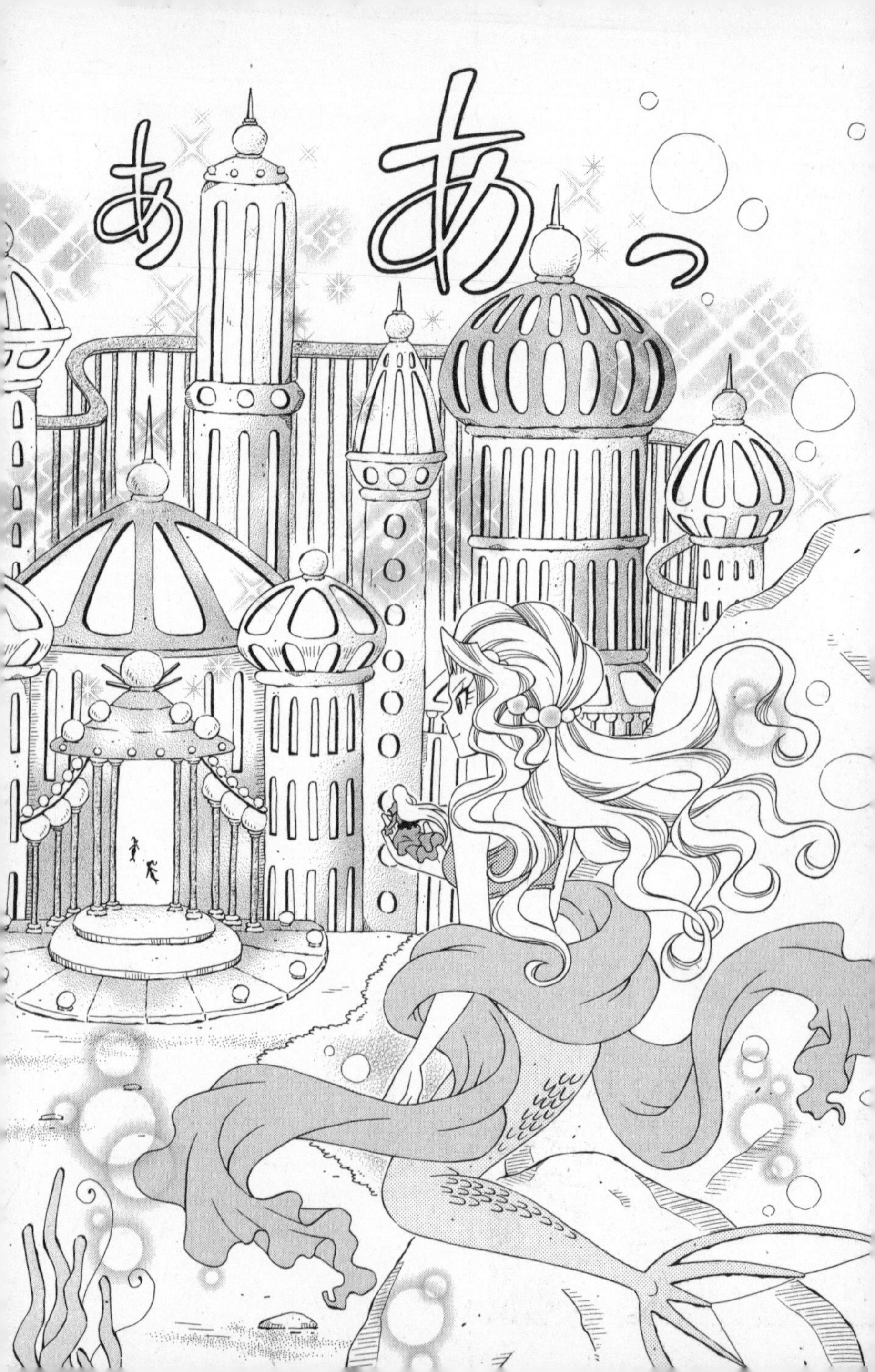
あ あっ

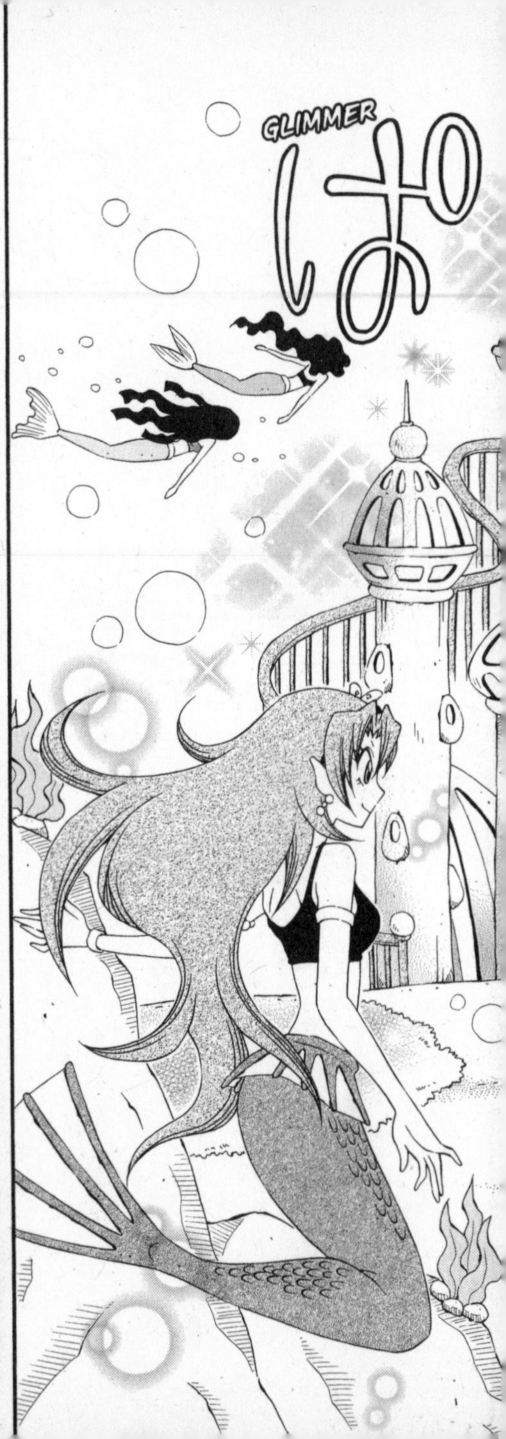
GLIMMER

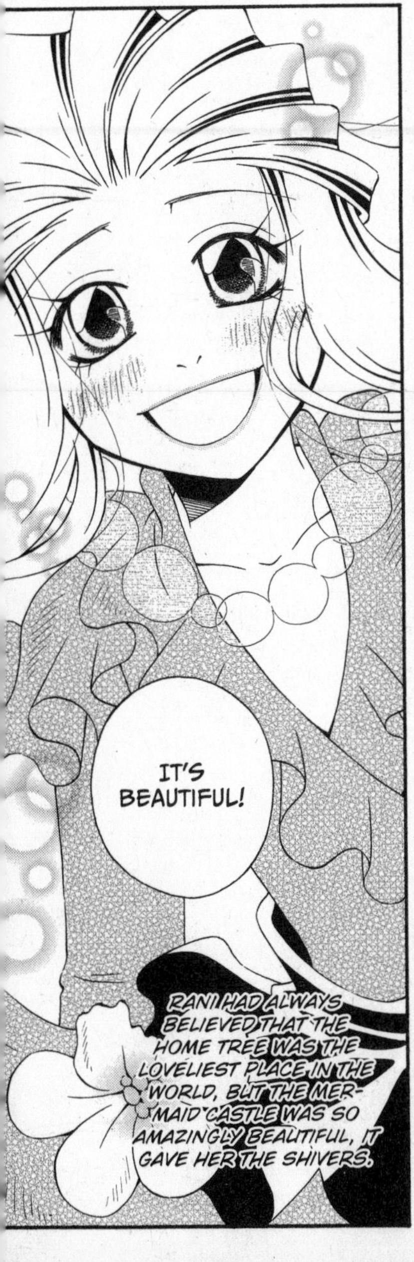
IT'S BEAUTIFUL!
RANI HAD ALWAYS BELIEVED THAT THE HOME TREE WAS THE LOVELIEST PLACE IN THE WORLD, BUT THE MER-MAID CASTLE WAS SO AMAZINGLY BEAUTIFUL, IT GAVE HER THE SHIVERS.

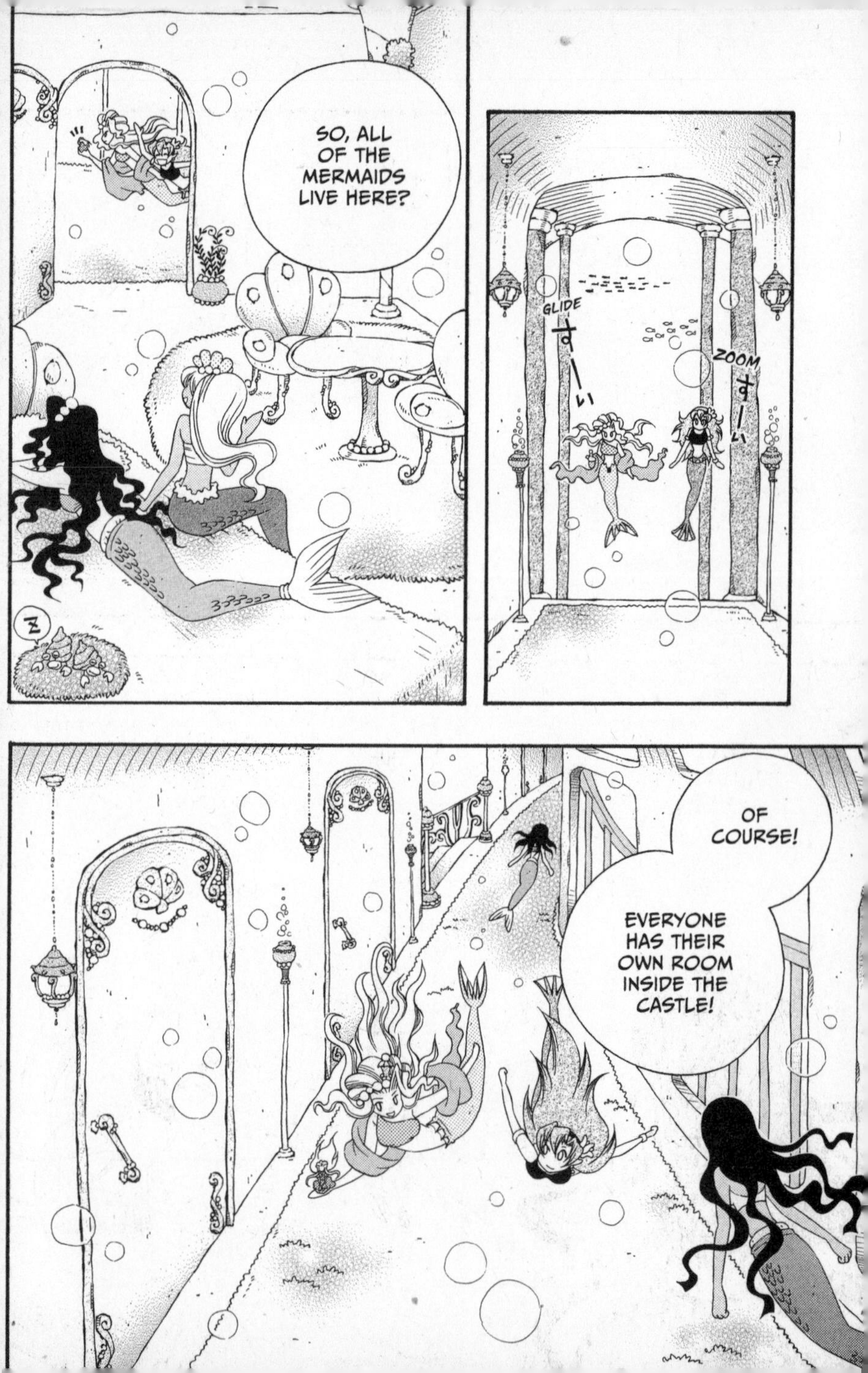
GLIDE
すーい
ZOOM
すーい
SO, ALL OF THE MERMAIDS LIVE HERE?
OF COURSE!
EVERYONE HAS THEIR OWN ROOM INSIDE THE CASTLE!

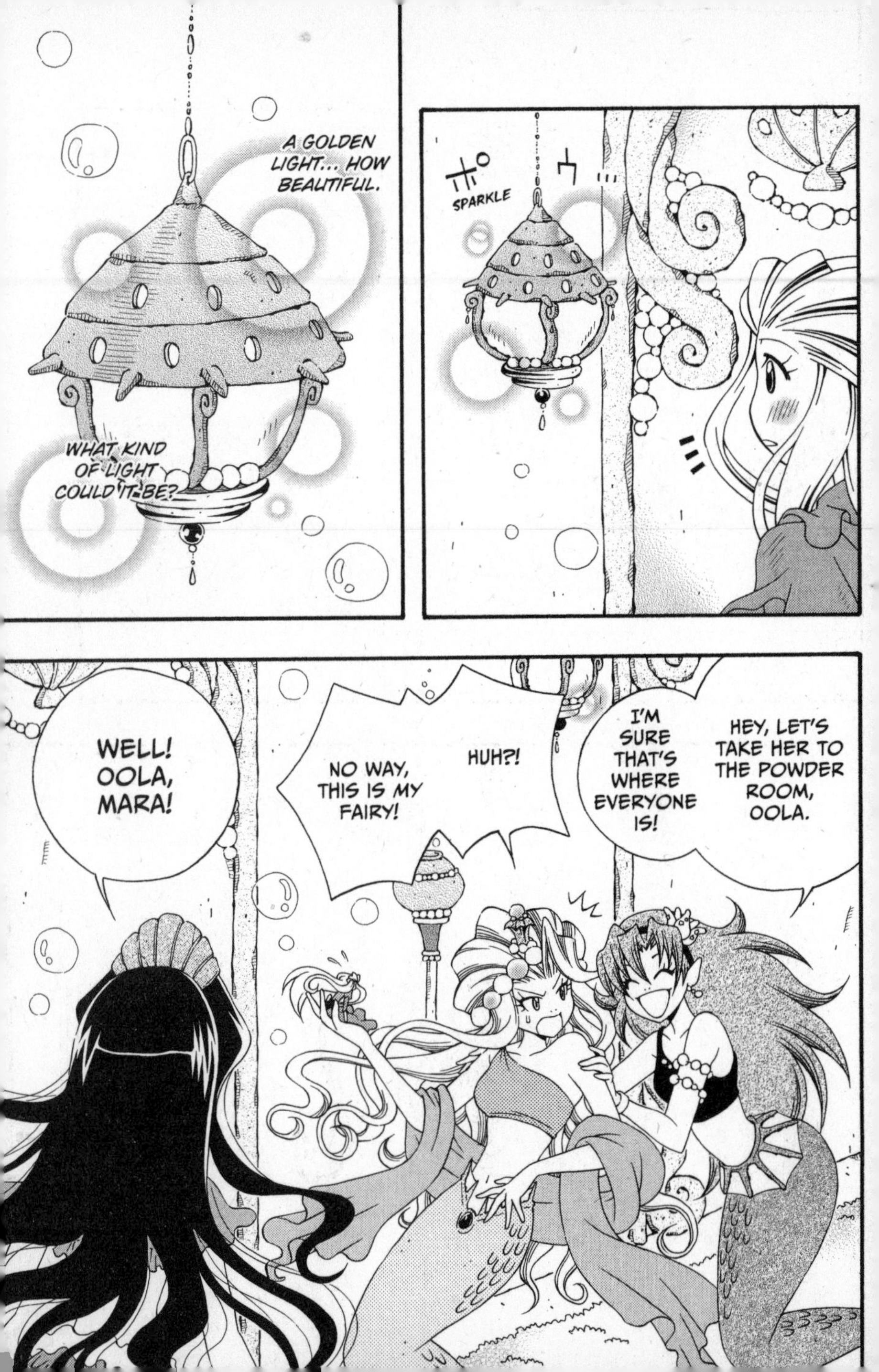
SPARKLE
A GOLDEN LIGHT... HOW BEAUTIFUL.
WHAT KIND OF LIGHT COULD IT BE?
HEY, LET'S TAKE HER TO THE POWDER ROOM, OOLA.
I'M SURE THAT'S WHERE EVERYONE IS!
HUH?!
NO WAY, THIS IS MY FAIRY!
WELL! OOLA, MARA!

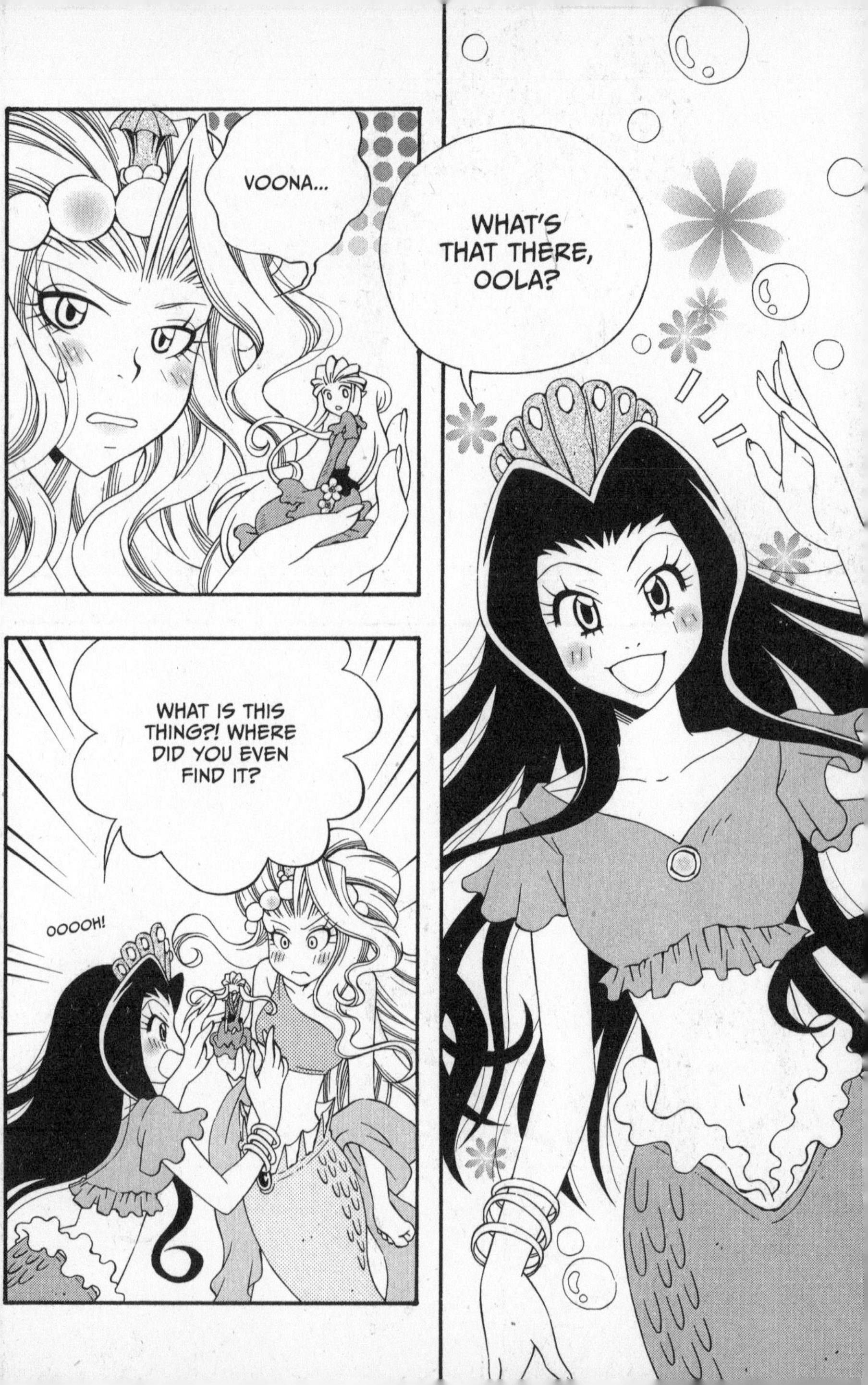
WHAT'S THAT THERE, OOLA?
VOONA...
WHAT IS THIS THING?! WHERE DID YOU EVEN FIND IT?
OOOOH!

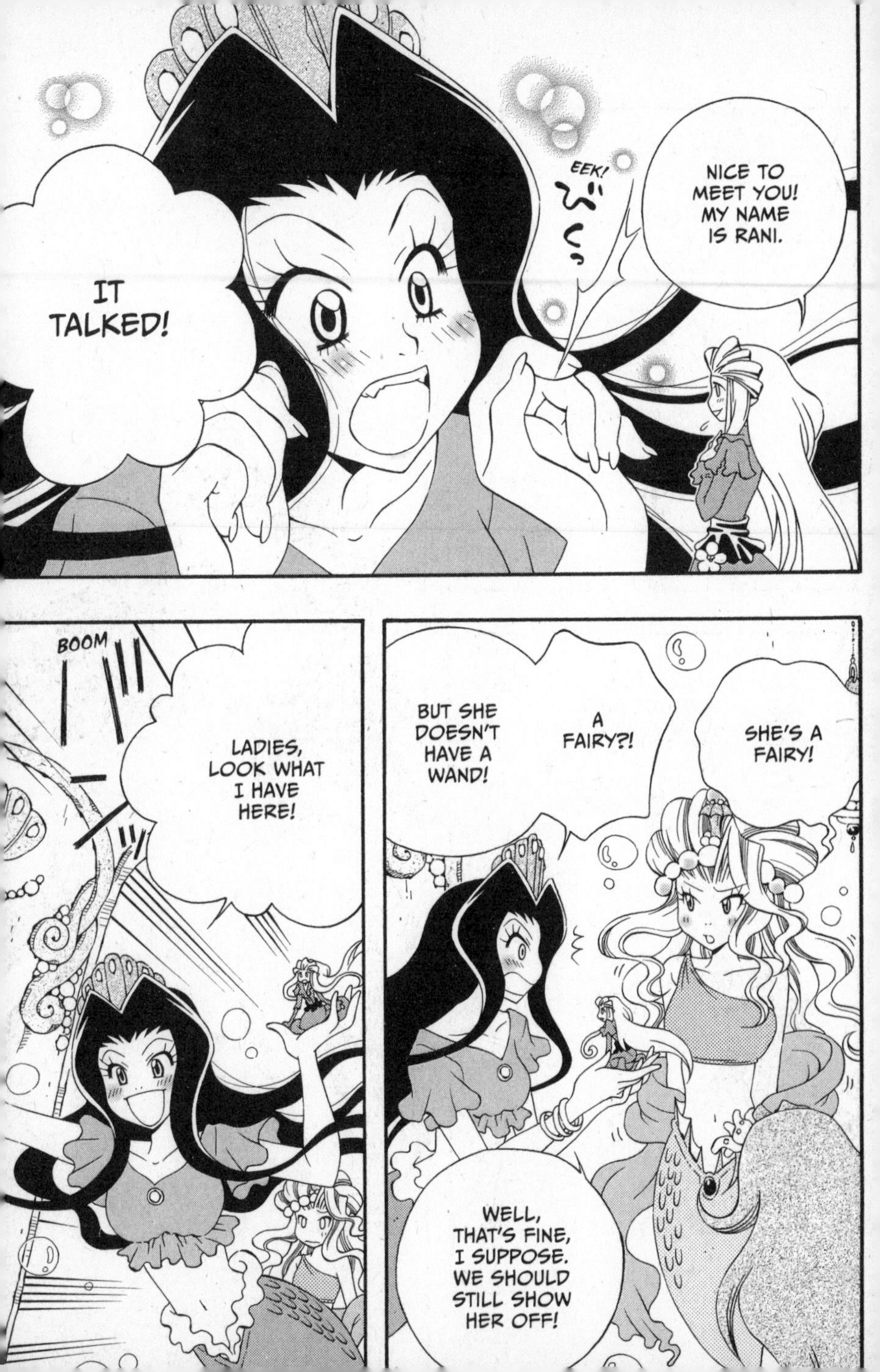
NICE TO MEET YOU! MY NAME IS RANI.
EEK!
びくっ
IT TALKED!
SHE'S A FAIRY!
A FAIRY?!
BUT SHE DOESN'T HAVE A WAND!
WELL, THAT'S FINE, I SUPPOSE. WE SHOULD STILL SHOW HER OFF!
BOOM
LADIES, LOOK WHAT I HAVE HERE!

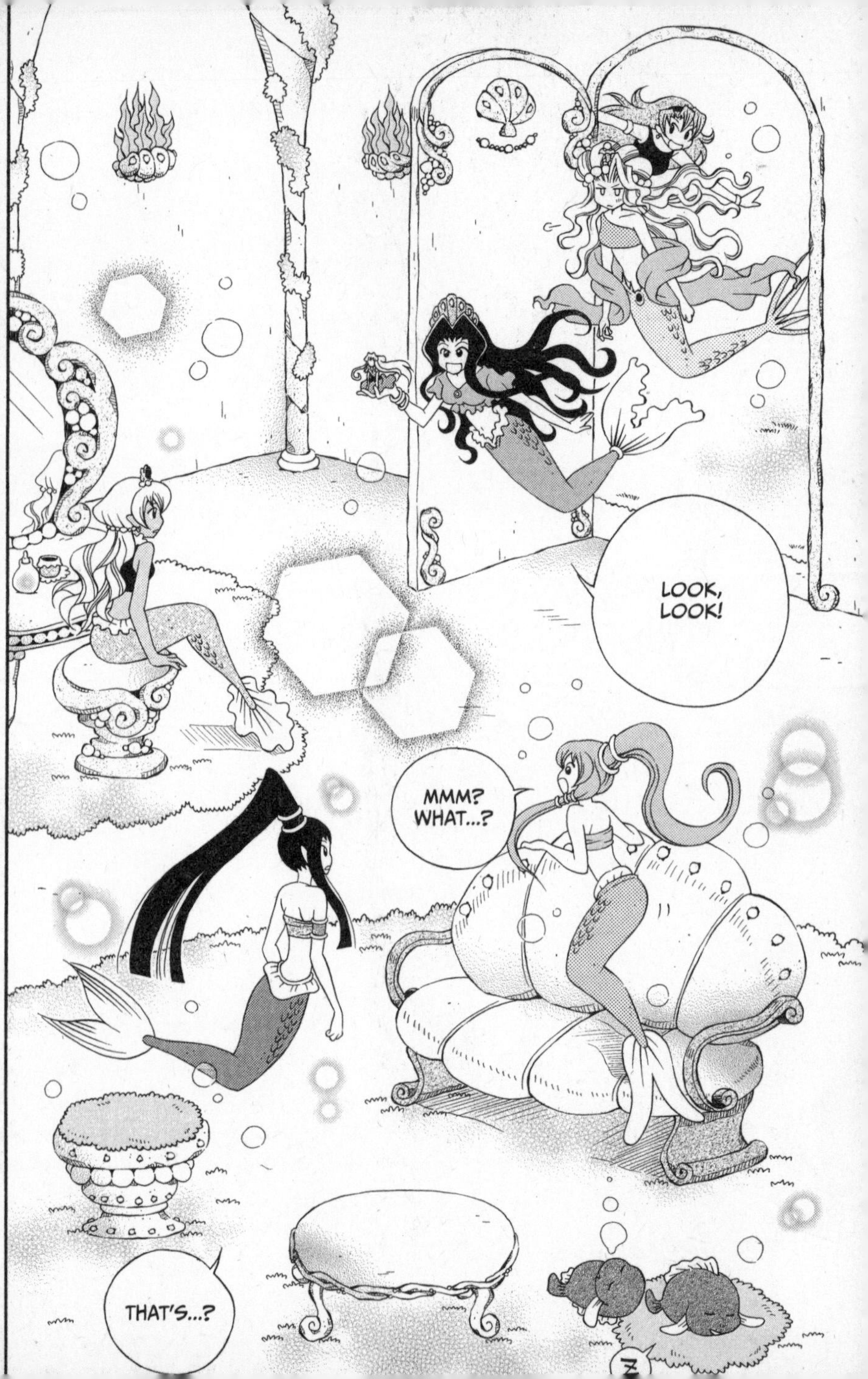
LOOK, LOOK!
MMM? WHAT...?
THAT'S...?

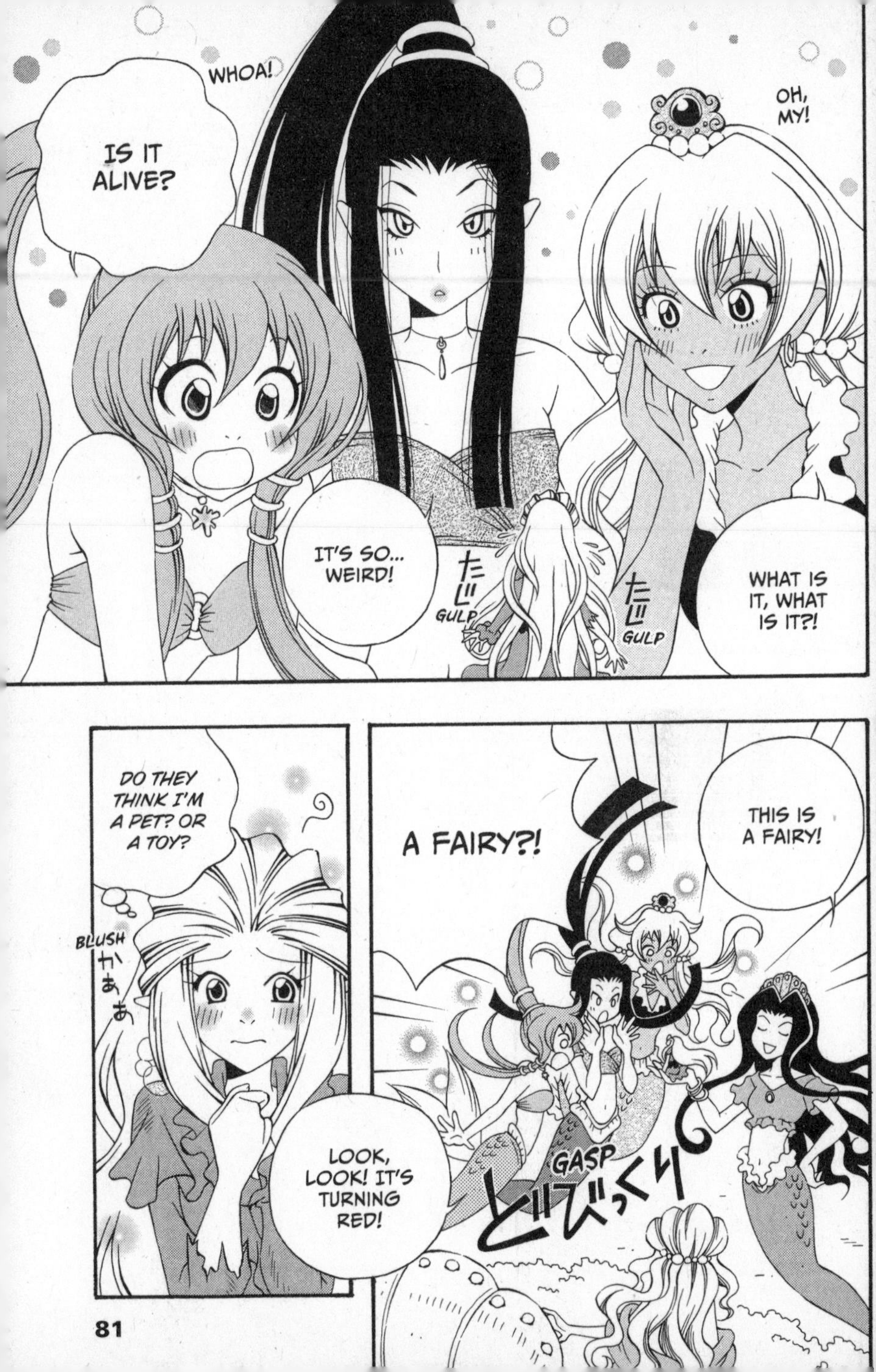

OH, MY!
WHOA!
IS IT ALIVE?
WHAT IS IT, WHAT IS IT?!
たじ
GULP
IT'S SO... WEIRD!
たじ
GULP
THIS IS A FAIRY!
A FAIRY?!
GASP
どびっくり
DO THEY THINK I'M A PET? OR A TOY?
BLUSH
かぁぁ
LOOK, LOOK! IT'S TURNING RED!

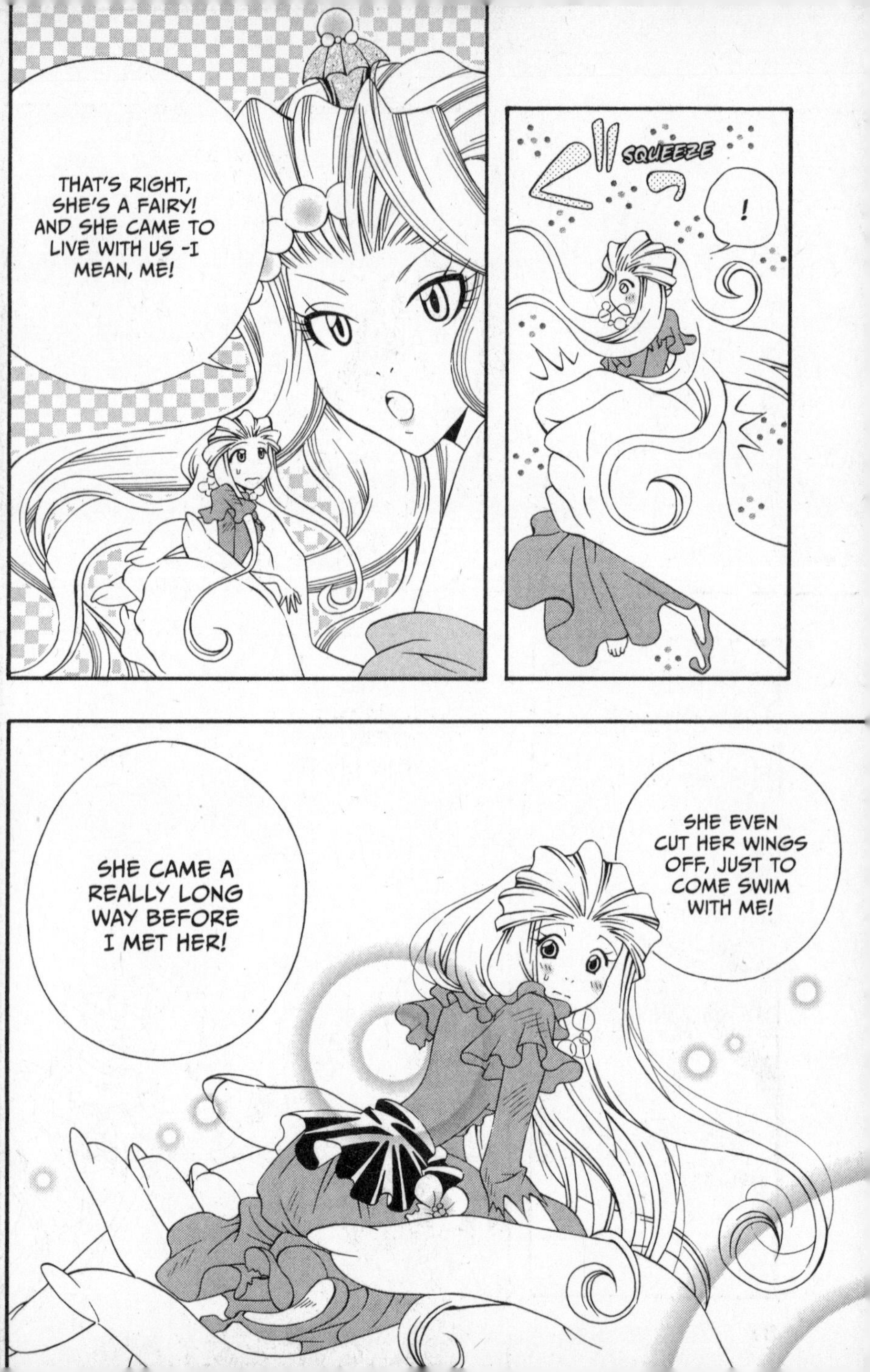
SQUEEZE
!
THAT'S RIGHT, SHE'S A FAIRY! AND SHE CAME TO LIVE WITH US -I MEAN, ME!
SHE EVEN CUT HER WINGS OFF, JUST TO COME SWIM WITH ME!
SHE CAME A REALLY LONG WAY BEFORE I MET HER!

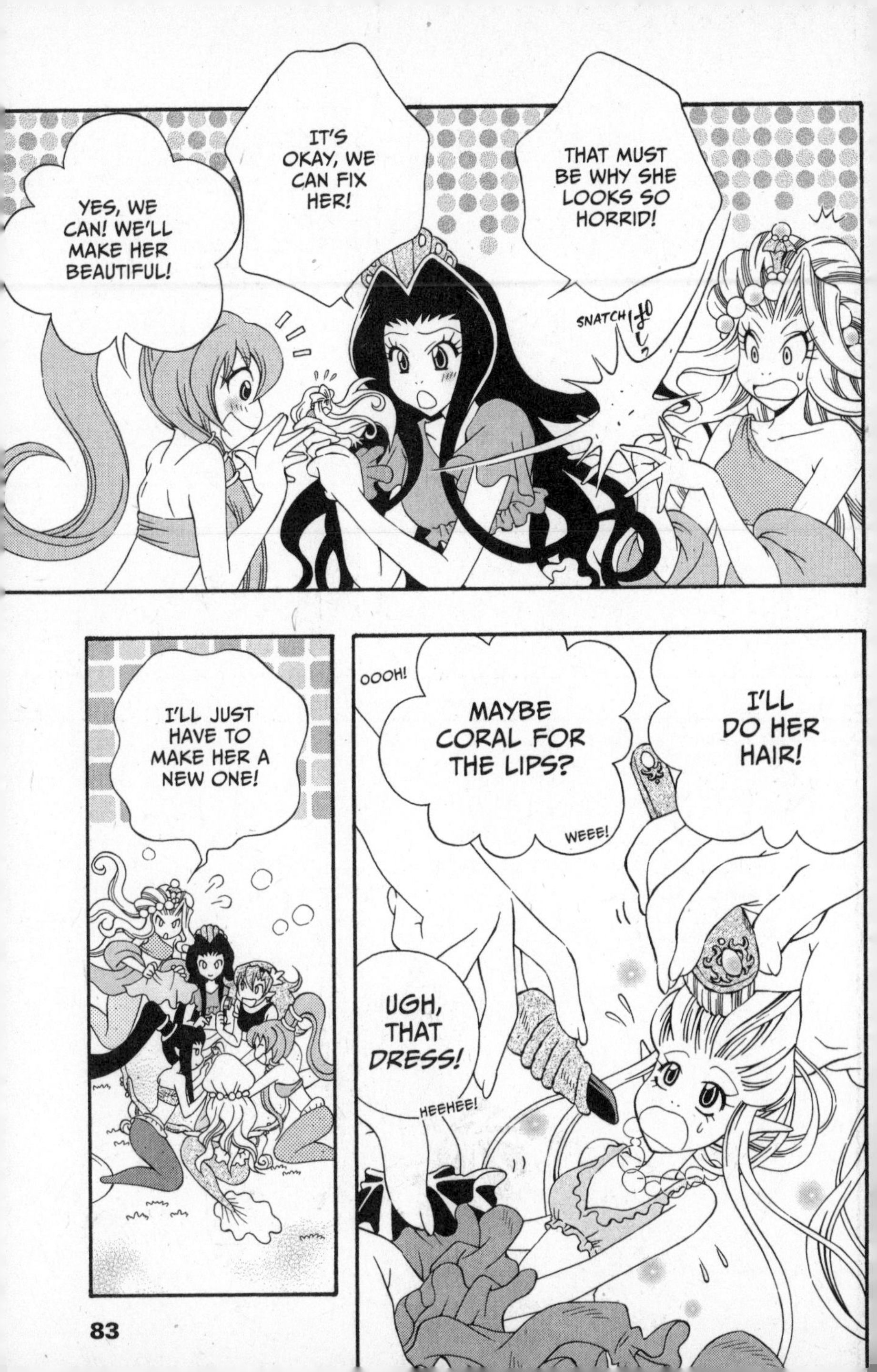
THAT MUST BE WHY SHE LOOKS SO HORRID!
SNATCH
IT'S OKAY, WE CAN FIX HER!
YES, WE CAN! WE'LL MAKE HER BEAUTIFUL!
I'LL DO HER HAIR!
MAYBE CORAL FOR THE LIPS?
OOOH!
WEEE!
UGH, THAT DRESS!
HEEHEE!
I'LL JUST HAVE TO MAKE HER A NEW ONE!

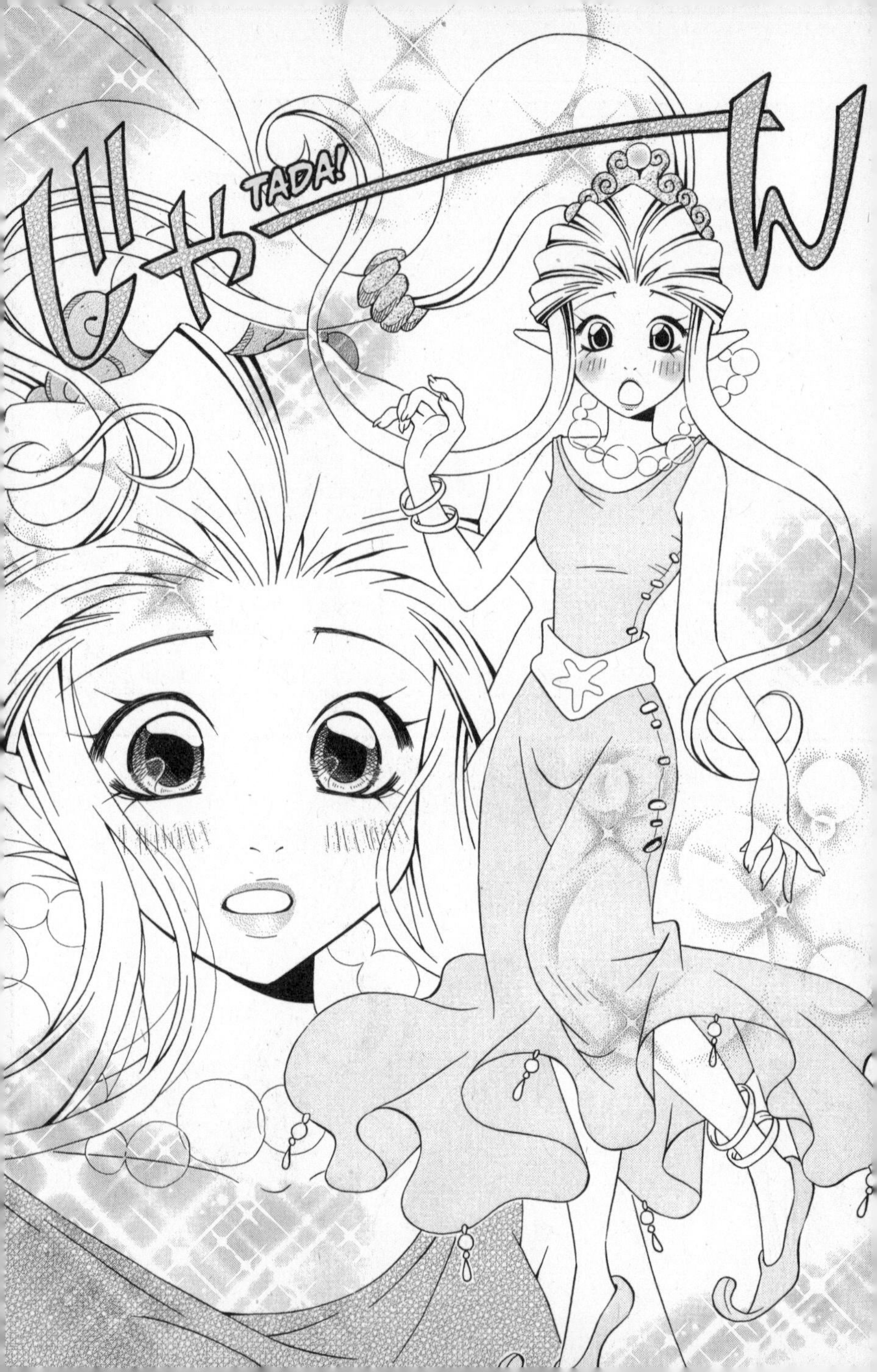
じゃーん
TADA!

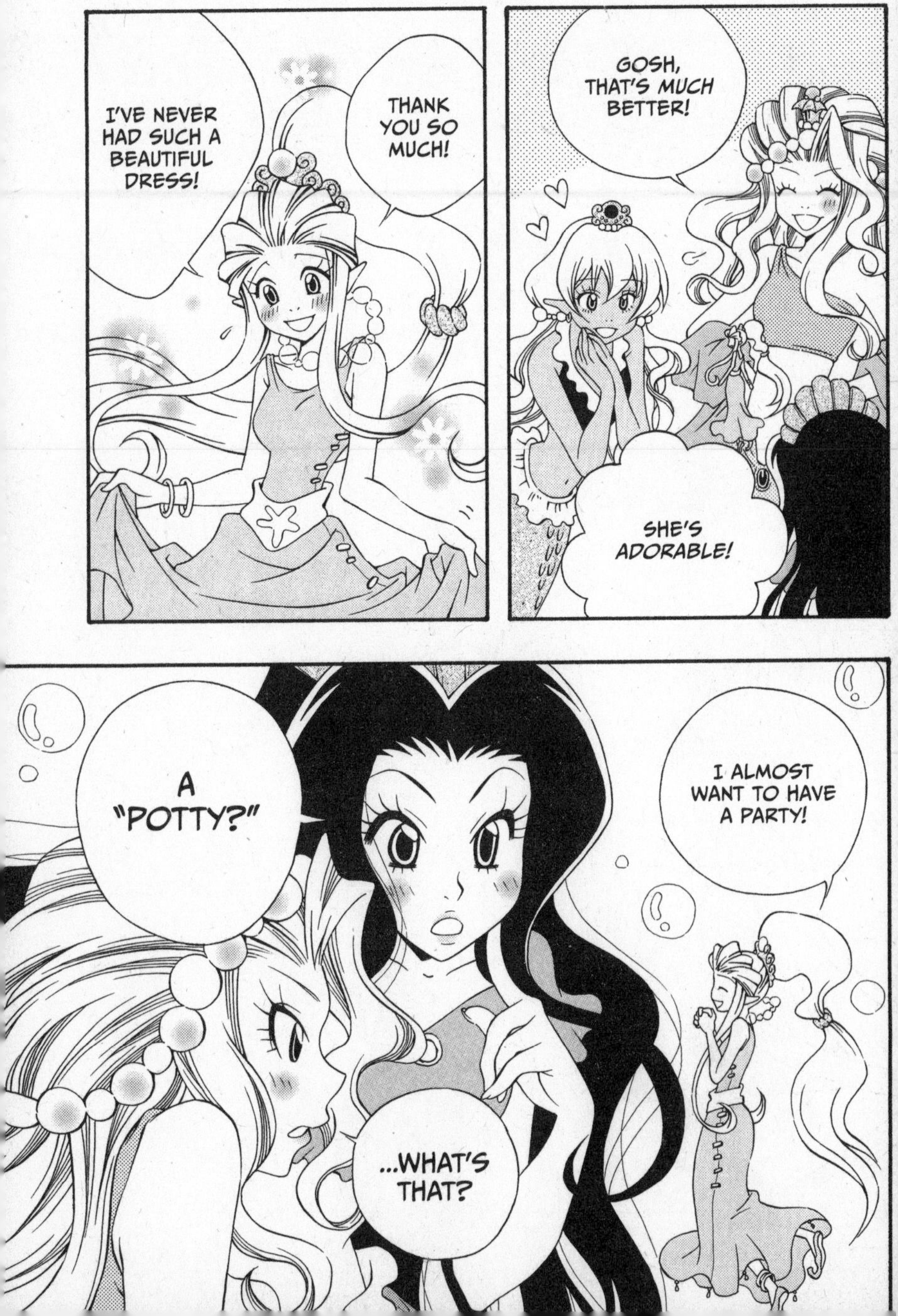
GOSH, THAT'S MUCH BETTER!
SHE'S ADORABLE!
THANK YOU SO MUCH!
I'VE NEVER HAD SUCH A BEAUTIFUL DRESS!
I ALMOST WANT TO HAVE A PARTY!
A "POTTY?"
...WHAT'S THAT?

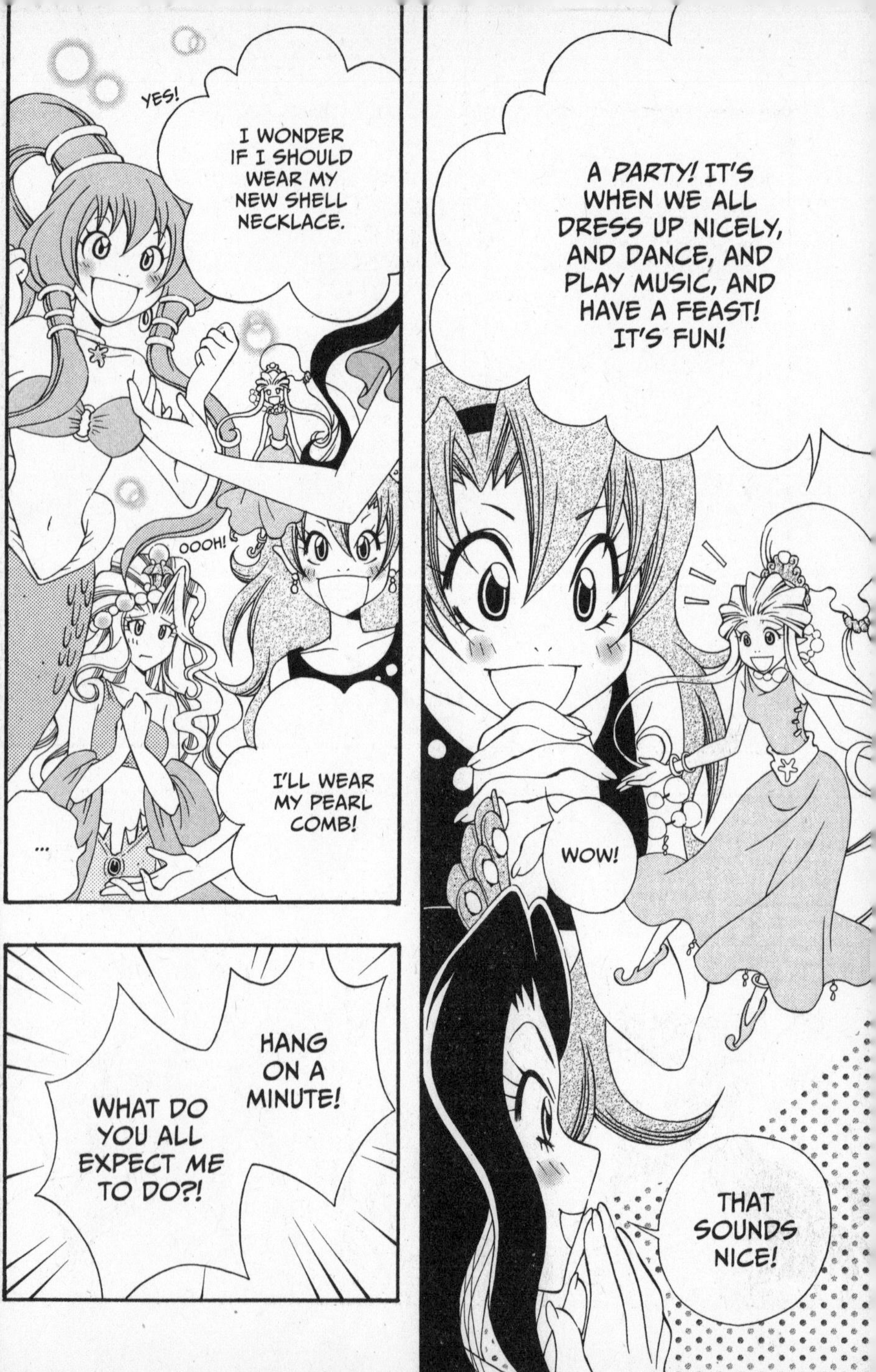
A *PARTY!* IT'S WHEN WE ALL DRESS UP NICELY, AND DANCE, AND PLAY MUSIC, AND HAVE A FEAST! IT'S FUN!
WOW!
THAT SOUNDS NICE!
I WONDER IF I SHOULD WEAR MY NEW SHELL NECKLACE.
YES!
OOOH!
I'LL WEAR MY PEARL COMB!
...
HANG ON A MINUTE!
WHAT DO YOU ALL EXPECT ME TO DO?!

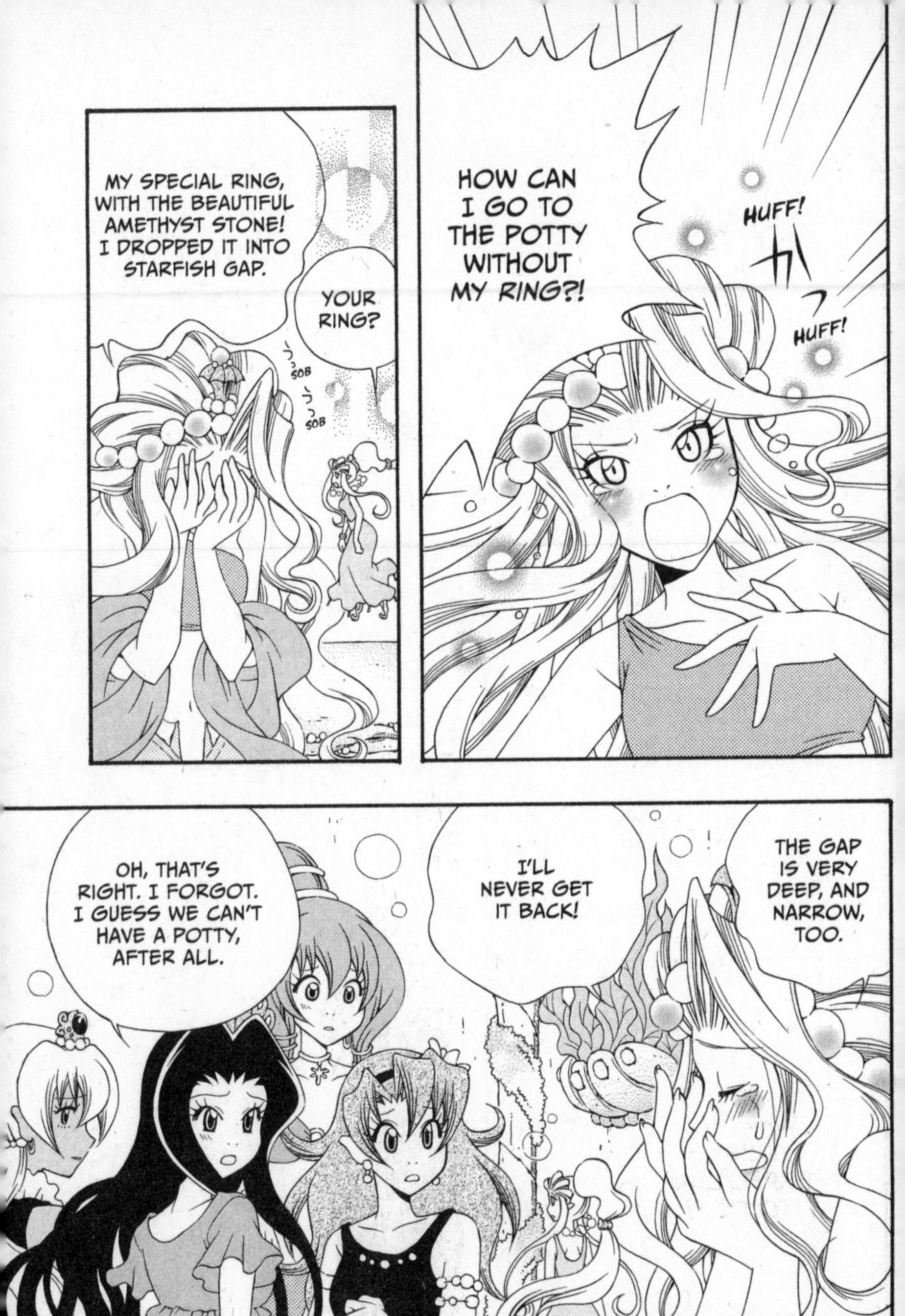
HOW CAN I GO TO THE POTTY WITHOUT MY RING?!
HUFF!
カッ
HUFF!
YOUR RING?
SOB
SOB
MY SPECIAL RING, WITH THE BEAUTIFUL AMETHYST STONE! I DROPPED IT INTO STARFISH GAP.
THE GAP IS VERY DEEP, AND NARROW, TOO.
I'LL NEVER GET IT BACK!
OH, THAT'S RIGHT. I FORGOT. I GUESS WE CAN'T HAVE A POTTY, AFTER ALL.

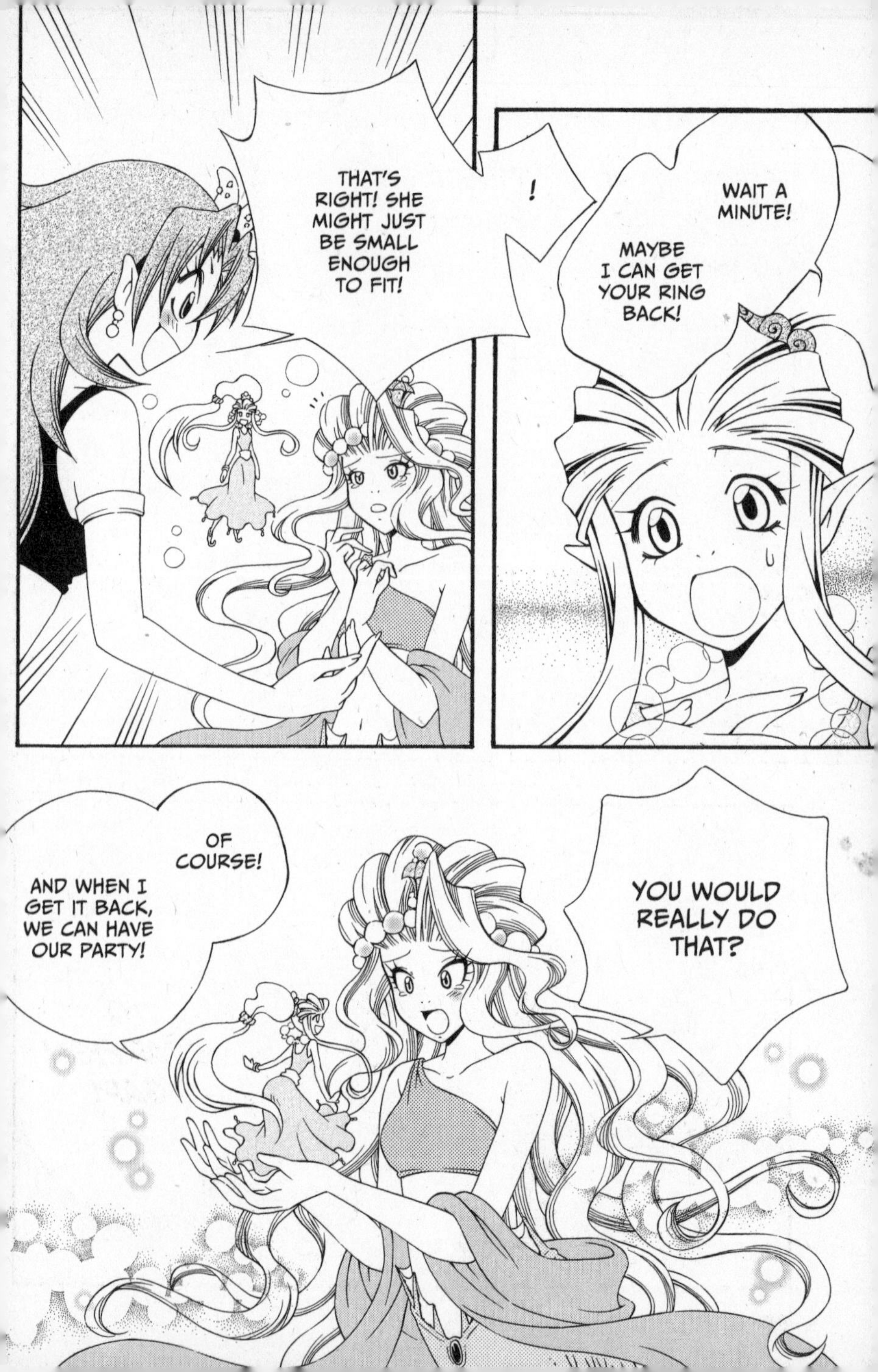
WAIT A MINUTE!
MAYBE I CAN GET YOUR RING BACK!
!
THAT'S RIGHT! SHE MIGHT JUST BE SMALL ENOUGH TO FIT!
YOU WOULD REALLY DO THAT?
OF COURSE!
AND WHEN I GET IT BACK, WE CAN HAVE OUR PARTY!

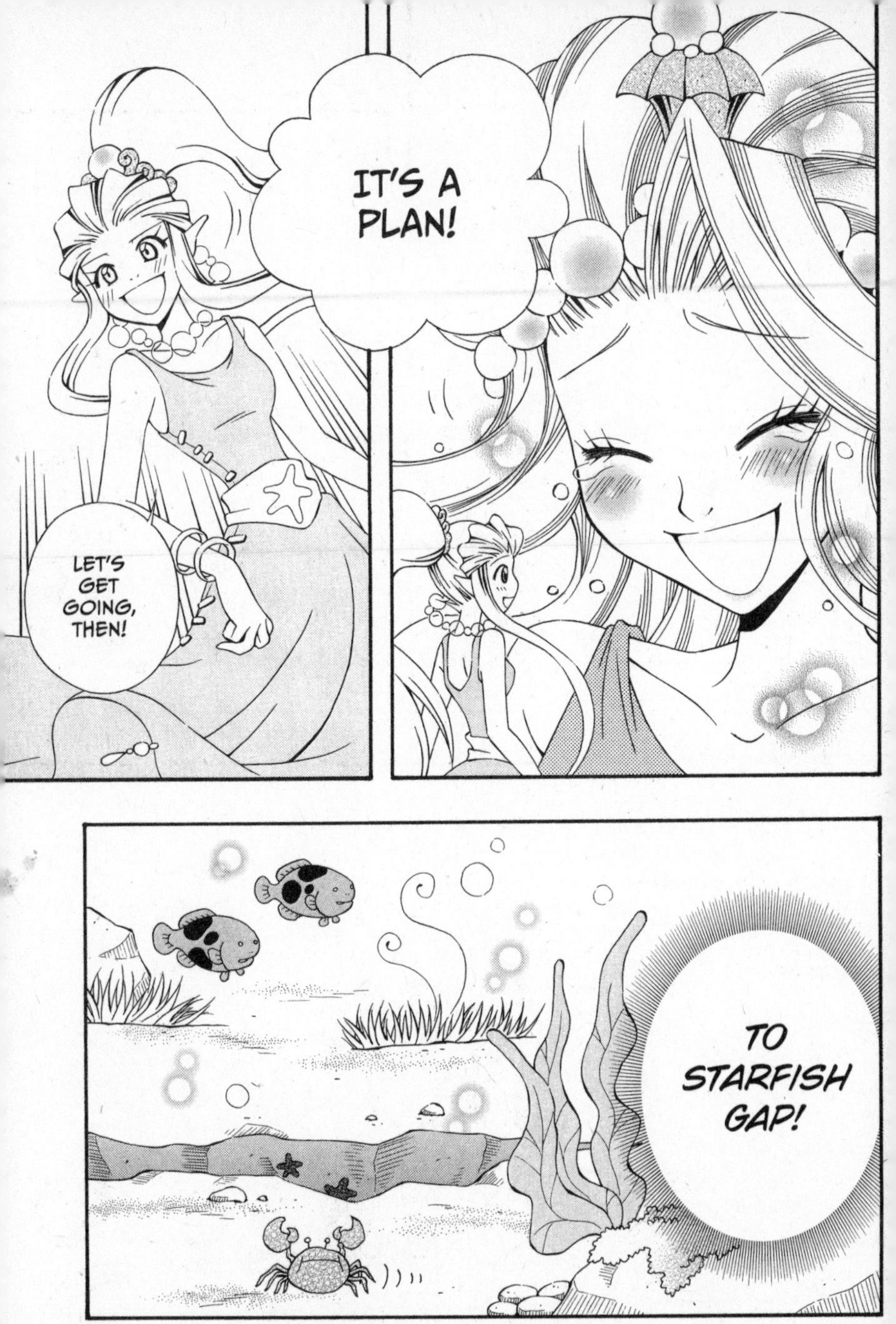
IT'S A PLAN!
LET'S GET GOING, THEN!
TO STARFISH GAP!

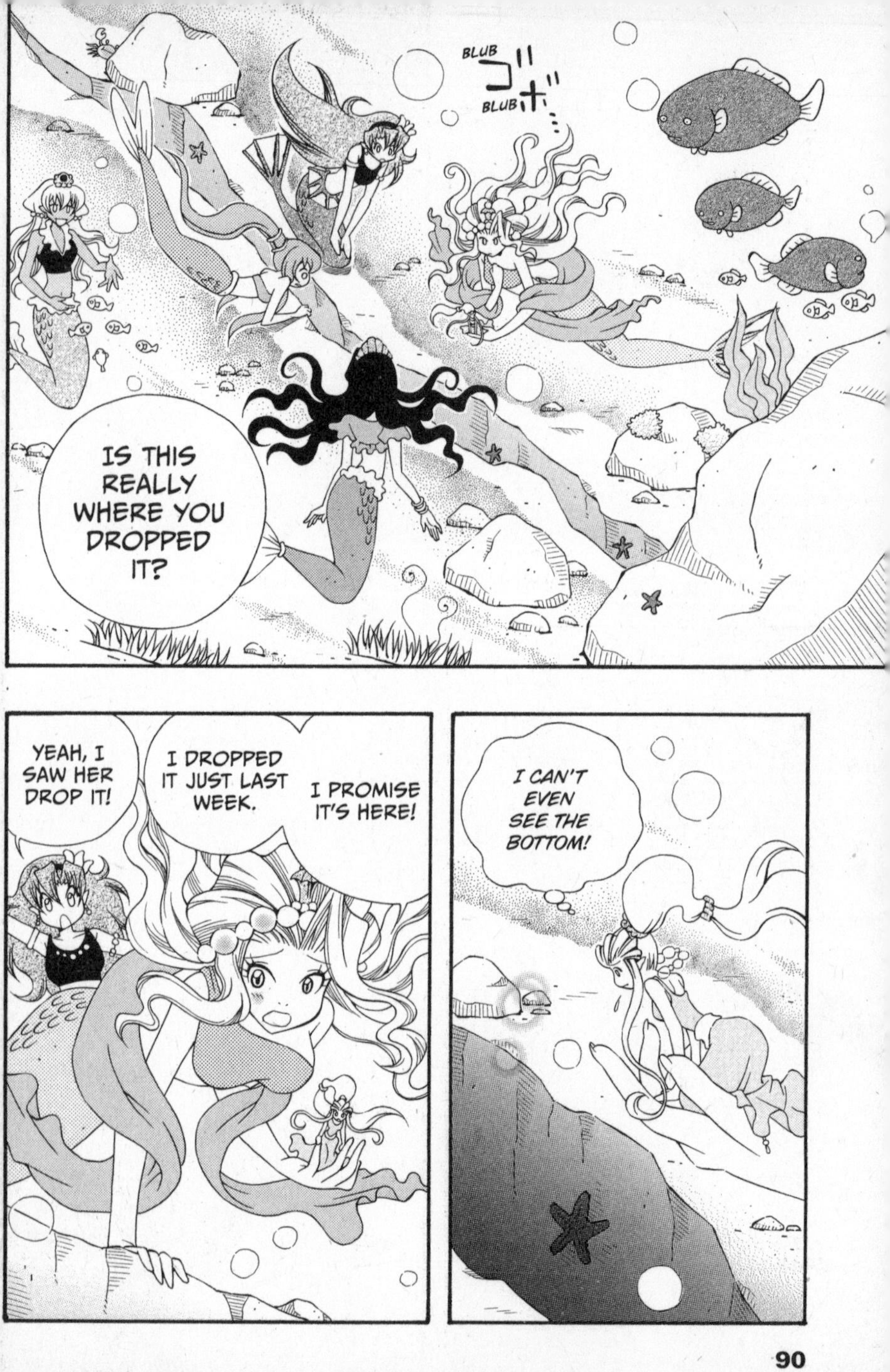
BLUB
BLUB
ゴボ
IS THIS REALLY WHERE YOU DROPPED IT?
I CAN'T EVEN SEE THE BOTTOM!
I PROMISE IT'S HERE!
I DROPPED IT JUST LAST WEEK.
YEAH, I SAW HER DROP IT!

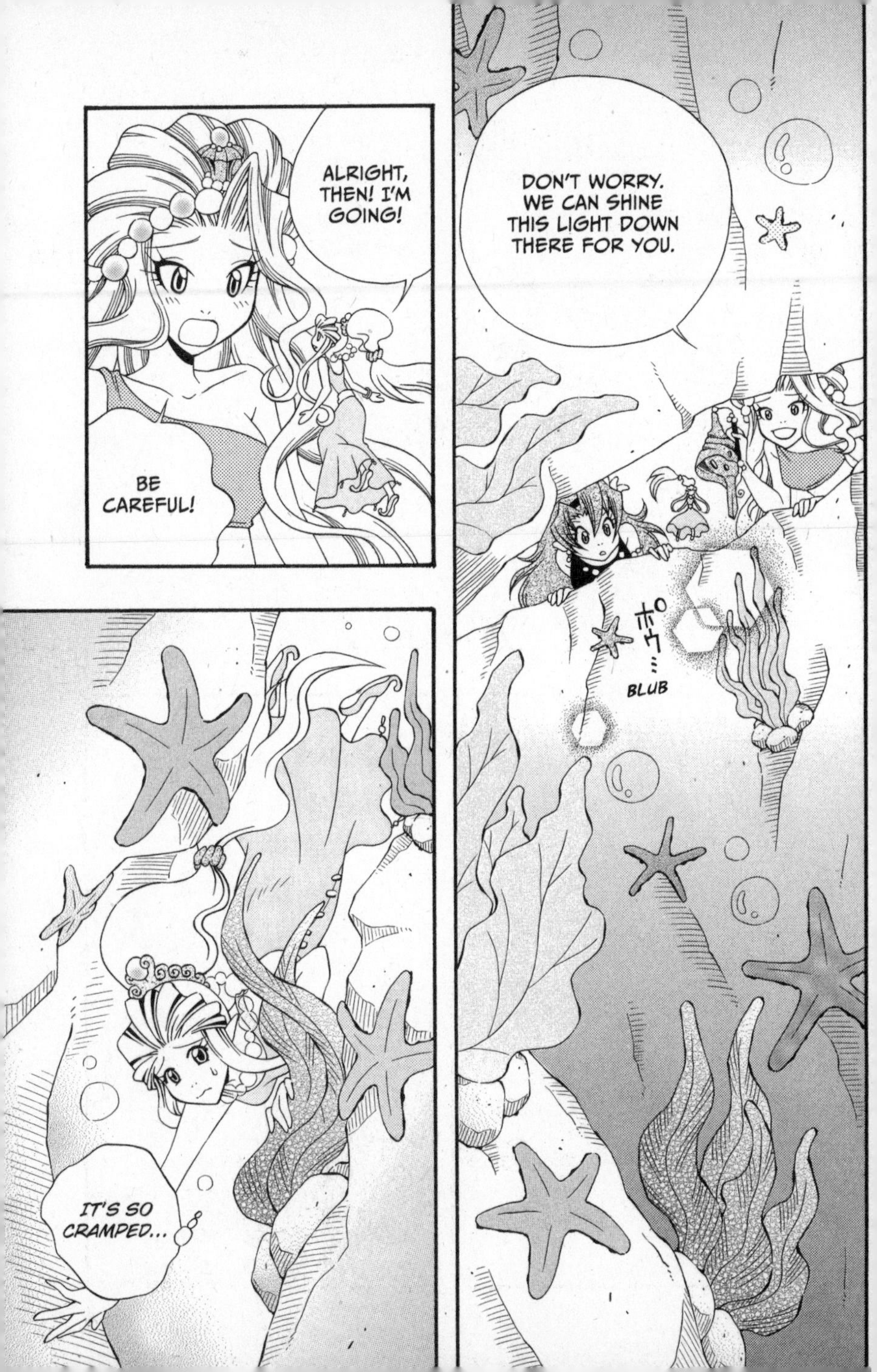
DON'T WORRY. WE CAN SHINE THIS LIGHT DOWN THERE FOR YOU.
ポウ…
BLUB
ALRIGHT, THEN! I'M GOING!
BE CAREFUL!
IT'S SO CRAMPED...

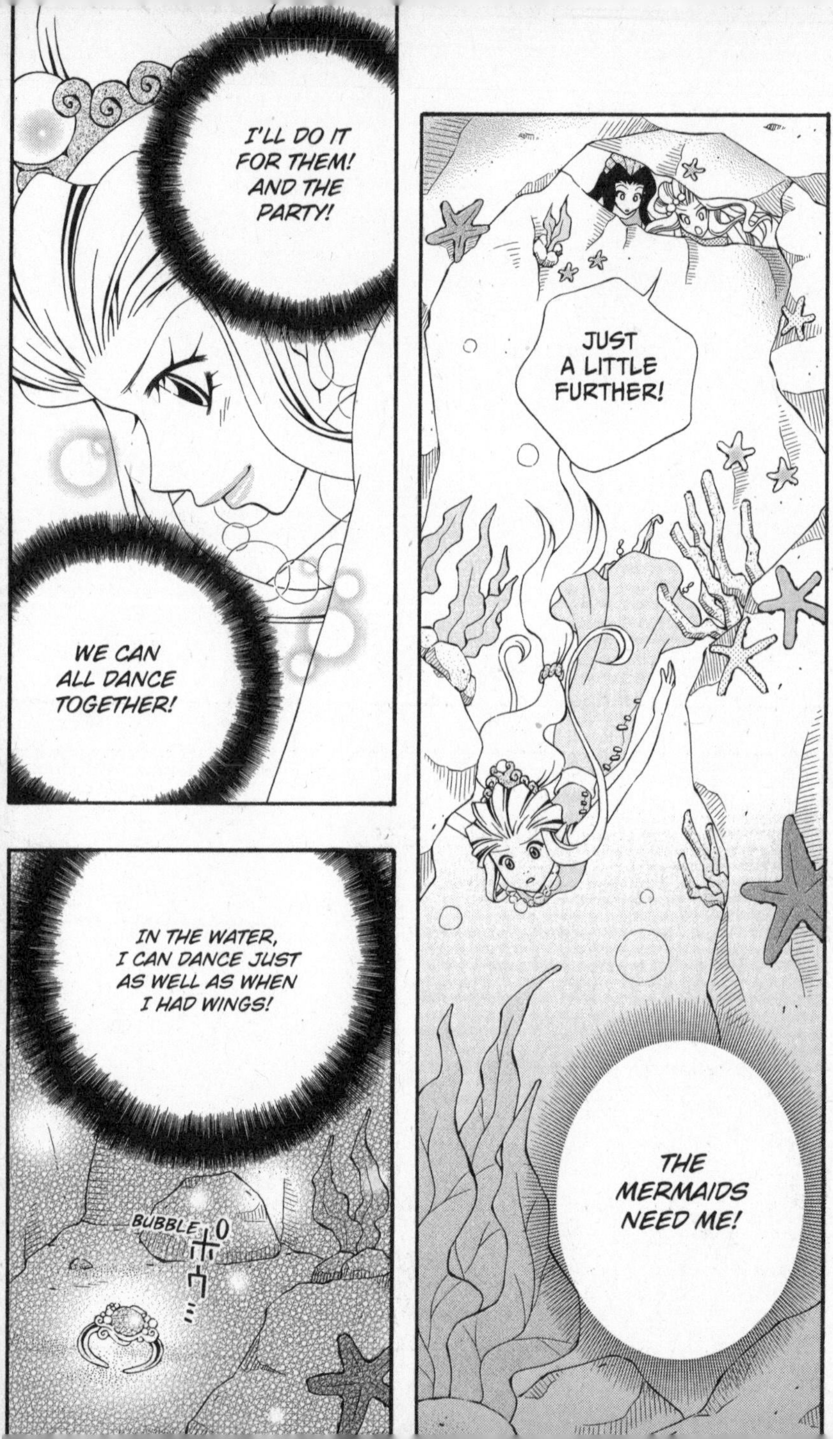
JUST A LITTLE FURTHER!
THE MERMAIDS NEED ME!
I'LL DO IT FOR THEM! AND THE PARTY!
WE CAN ALL DANCE TOGETHER!
IN THE WATER, I CAN DANCE JUST AS WELL AS WHEN I HAD WINGS!
BUBBLE
ホウ

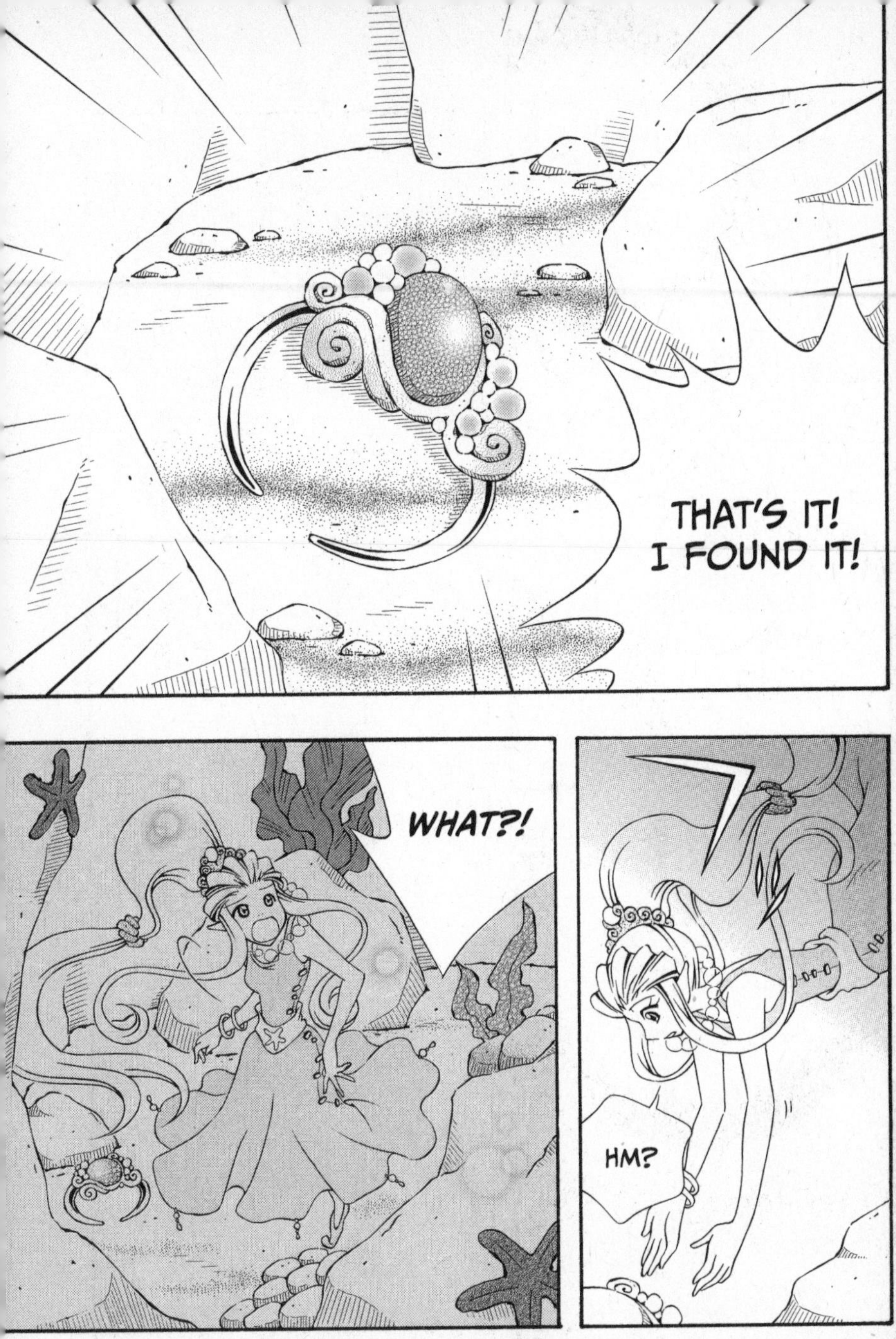
THAT'S IT! I FOUND IT!
HM?
WHAT?!

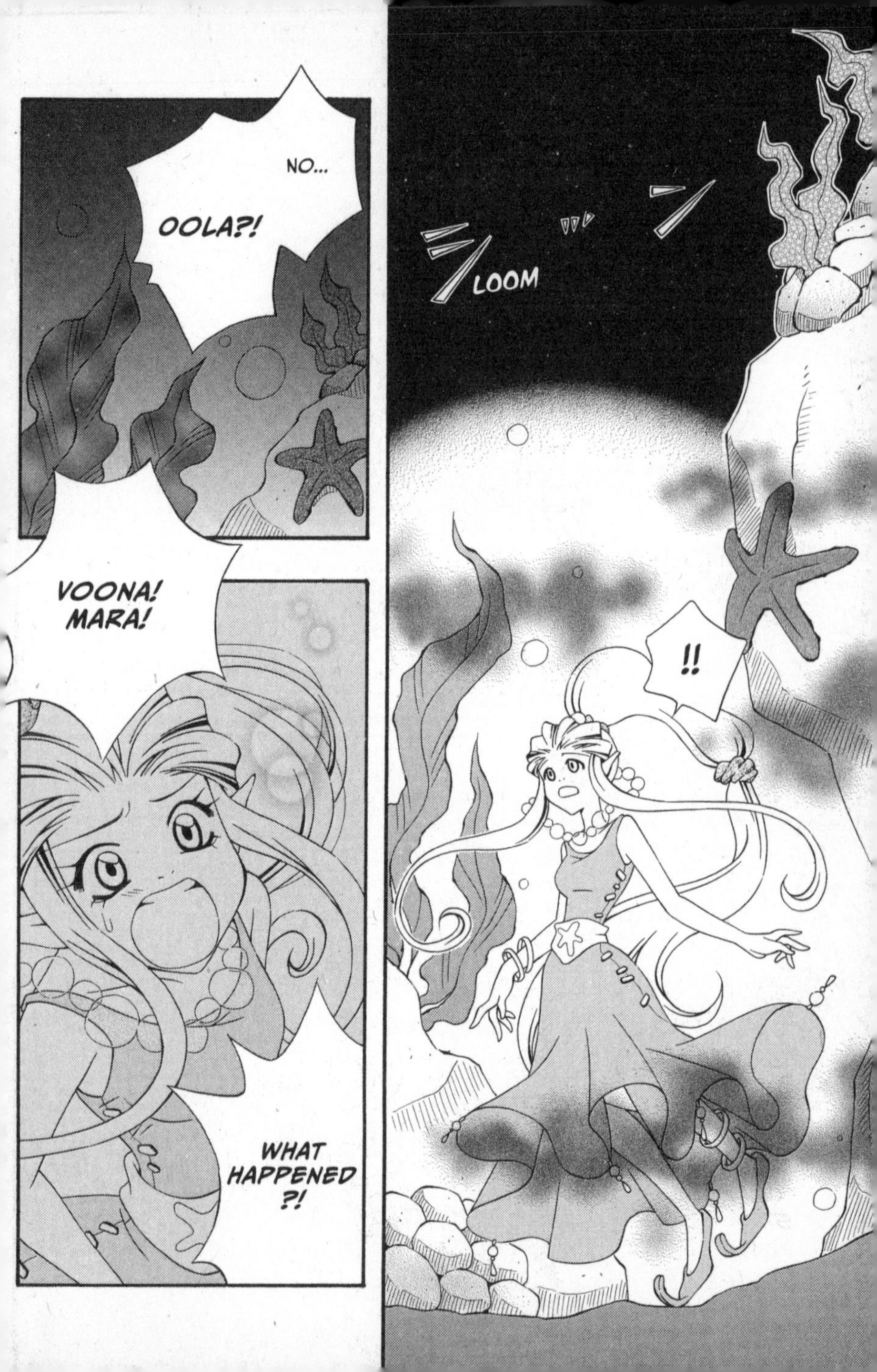
LOOM
!!
NO...
OOLA?!
VOONA! MARA!
WHAT HAPPENED ?!

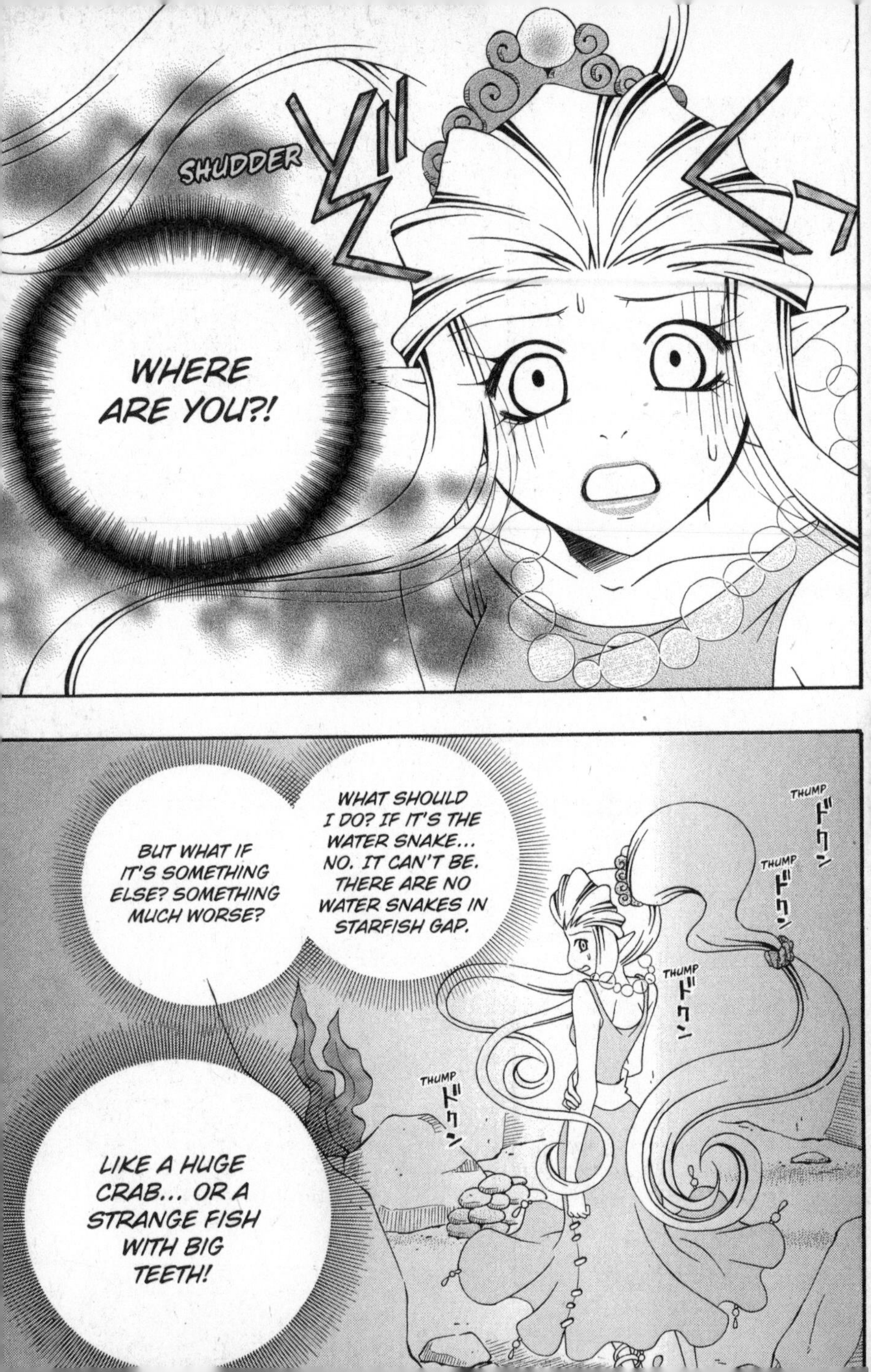
SHUDDER
WHERE ARE YOU?!
THUMP ドクン
THUMP ドクン
WHAT SHOULD I DO? IF IT'S THE WATER SNAKE... NO. IT CAN'T BE. THERE ARE NO WATER SNAKES IN STARFISH GAP.
BUT WHAT IF IT'S SOMETHING ELSE? SOMETHING MUCH WORSE?
THUMP ドクン
THUMP ドクン
LIKE A HUGE CRAB... OR A STRANGE FISH WITH BIG TEETH!

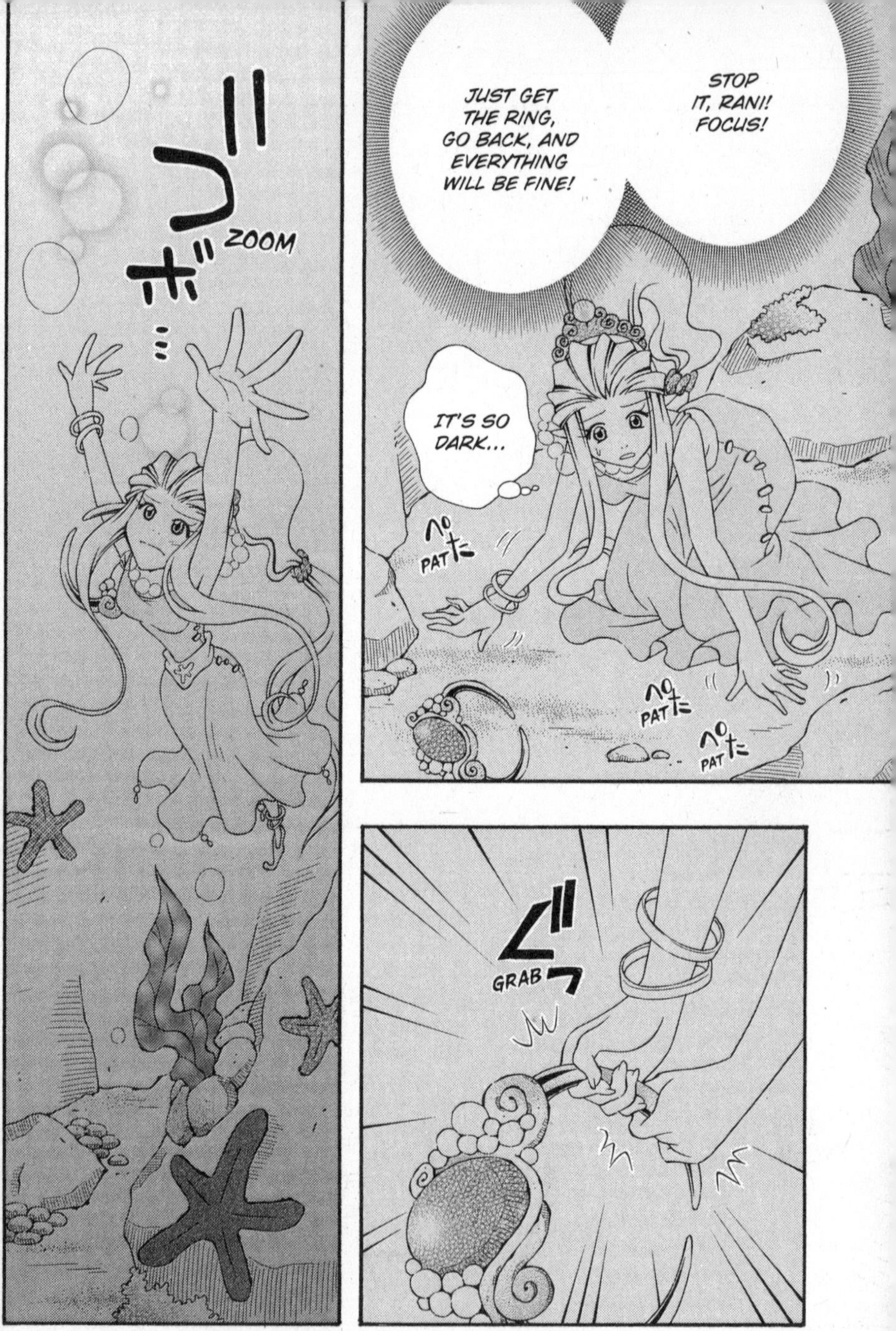
STOP IT, RANI! FOCUS!
JUST GET THE RING, GO BACK, AND EVERYTHING WILL BE FINE!
IT'S SO DARK...
PAT
PAT
PAT
GRAB
ZOOM

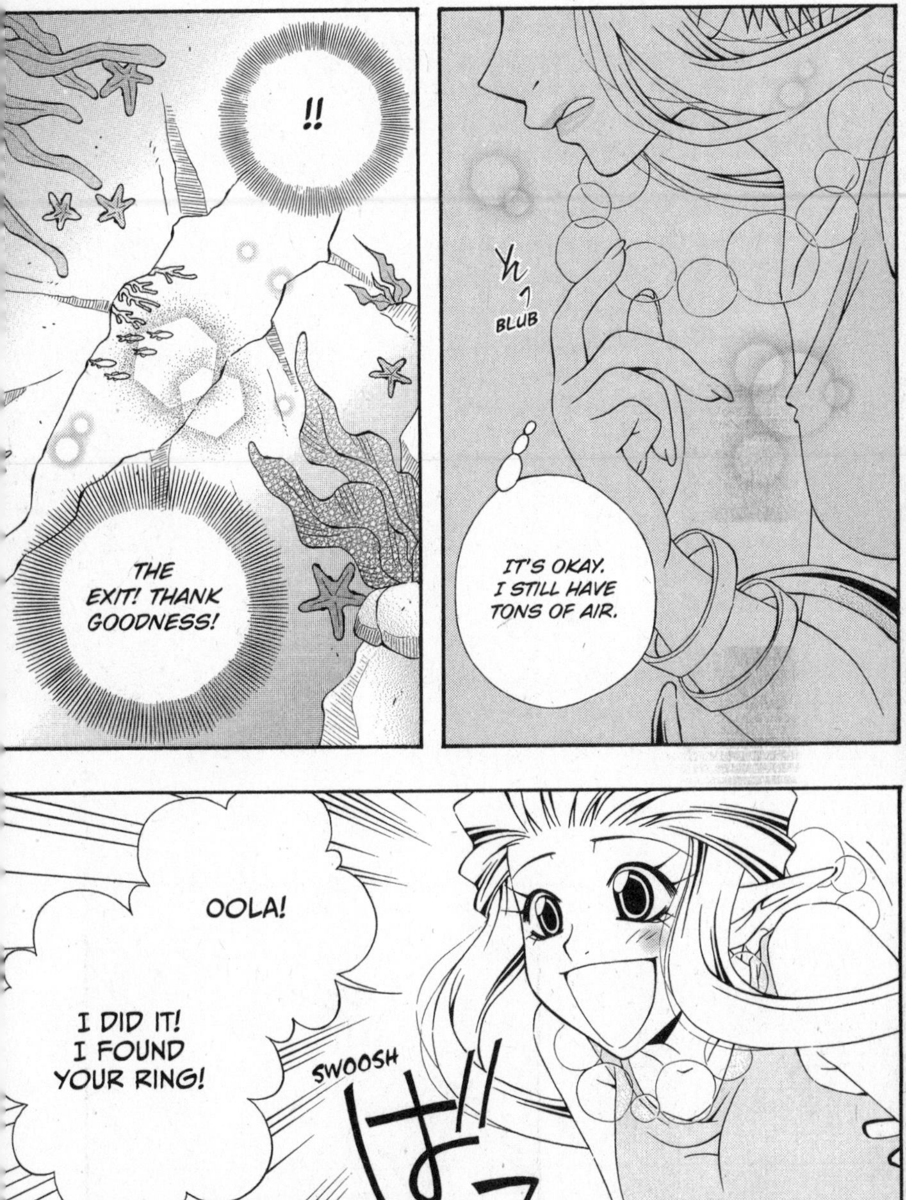
BLUB
IT'S OKAY. I STILL HAVE TONS OF AIR.
!!
THE EXIT! THANK GOODNESS!
OOLA!
I DID IT! I FOUND YOUR RING!
SWOOSH

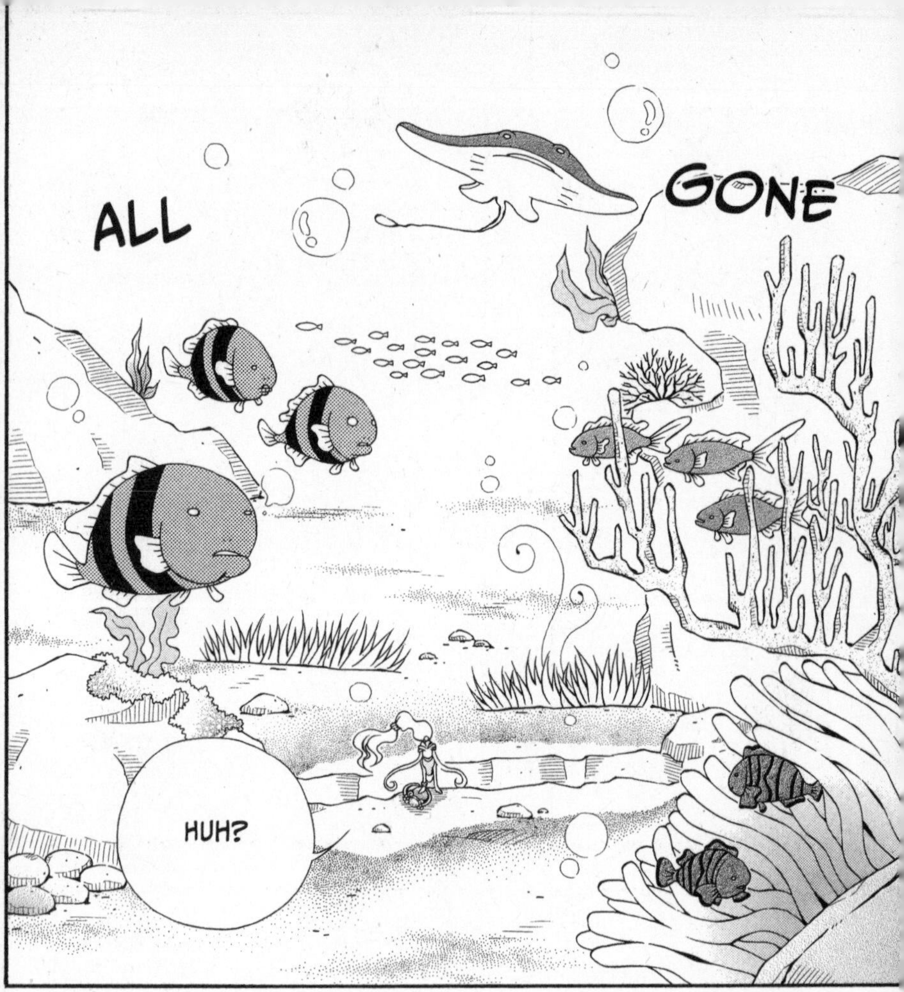
ALL GONE
HUH?
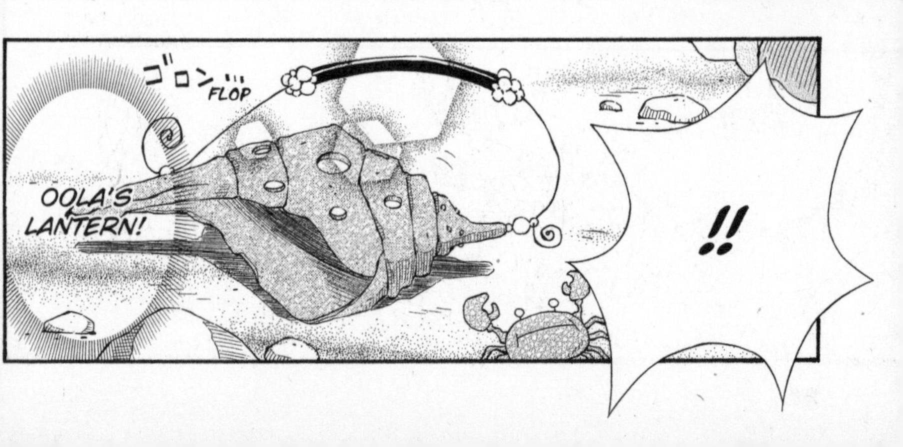
ゴロン FLOP
!!
OOLA'S LANTERN!

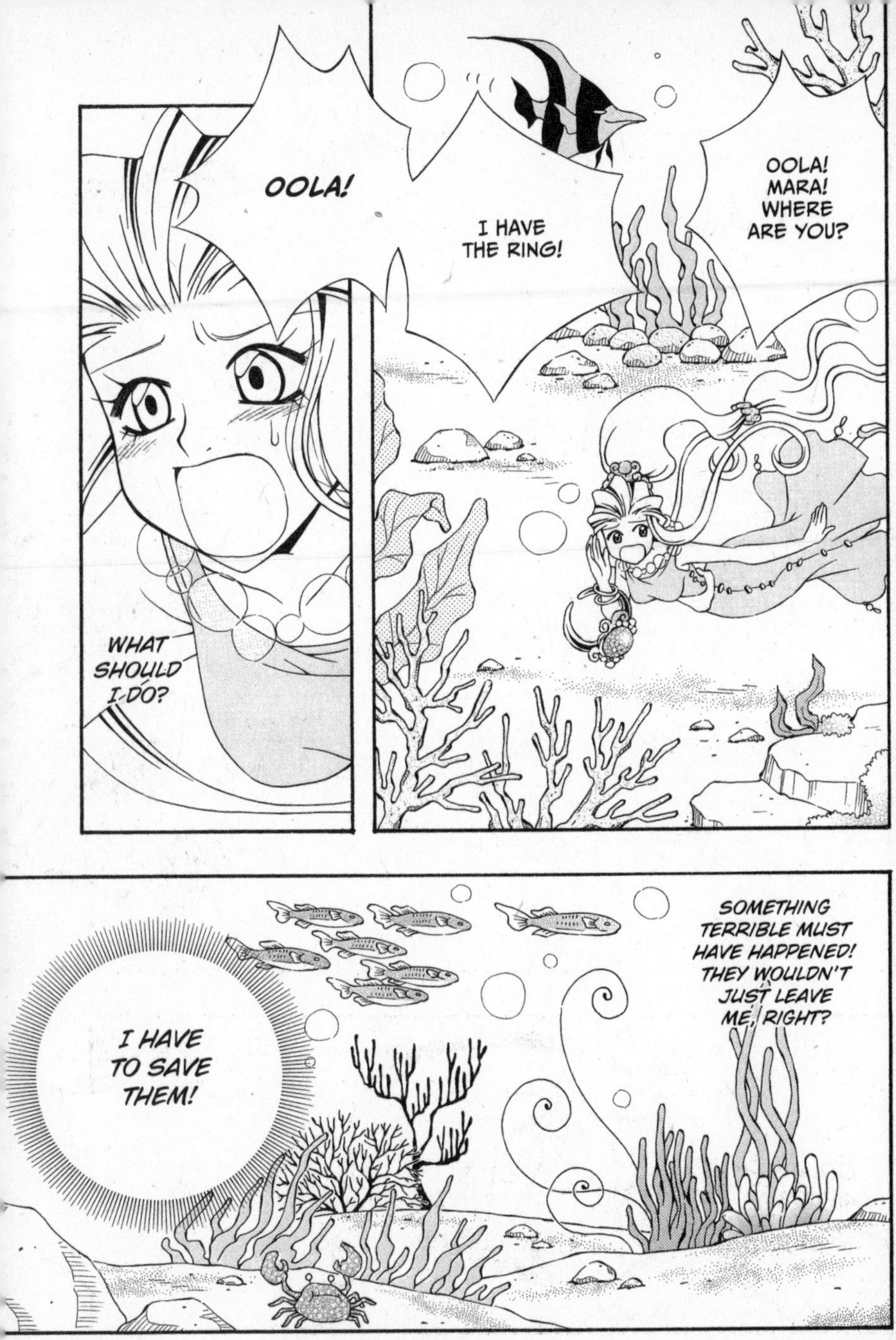
OOLA! MARA! WHERE ARE YOU?
I HAVE THE RING!
OOLA!
WHAT SHOULD I DO?
SOMETHING TERRIBLE MUST HAVE HAPPENED! THEY WOULDN'T JUST LEAVE ME, RIGHT?
I HAVE TO SAVE THEM!

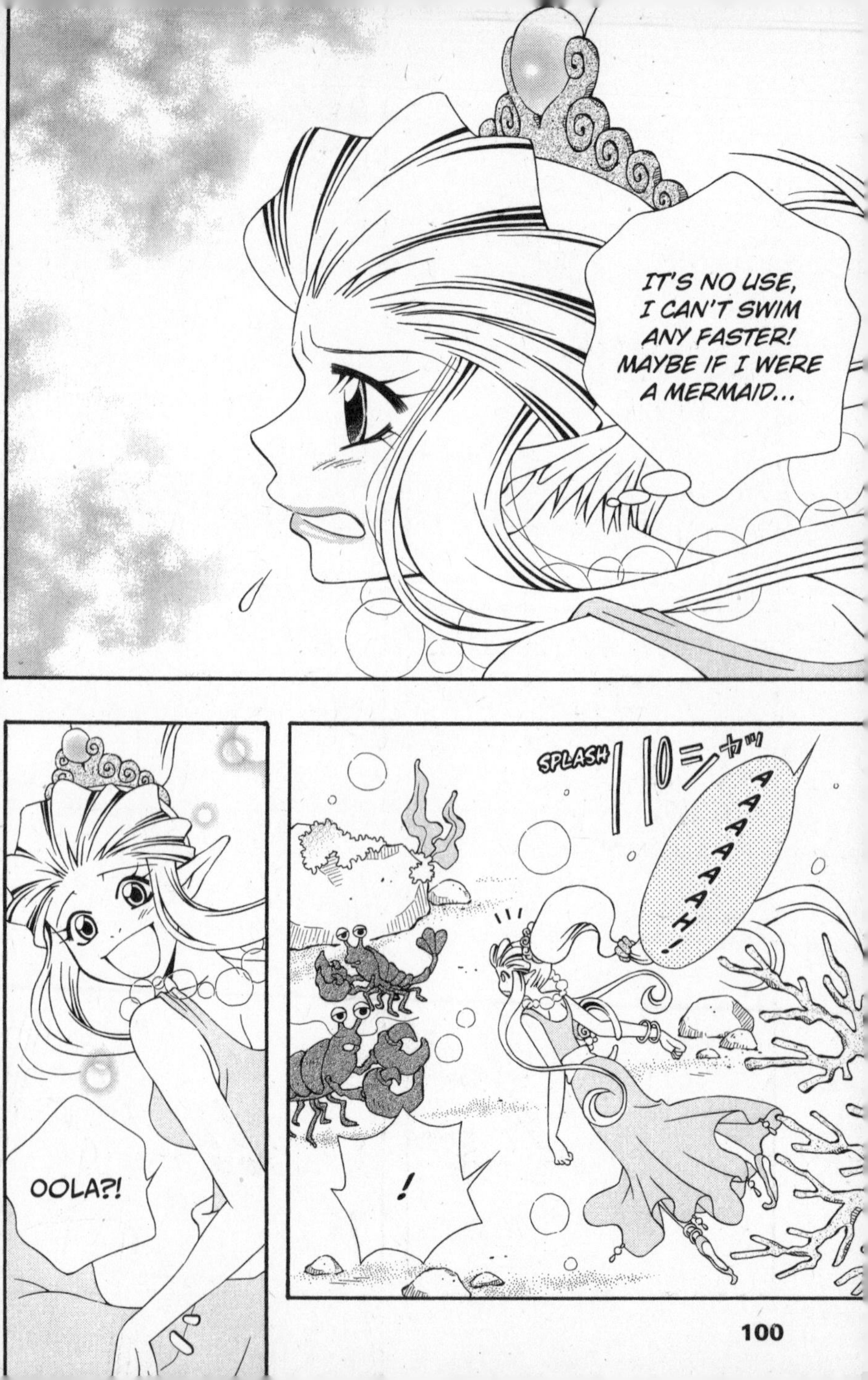
IT'S NO USE, I CAN'T SWIM ANY FASTER! MAYBE IF I WERE A MERMAID...
SPLASH
AAAAAAAH!
!
OOLA?!

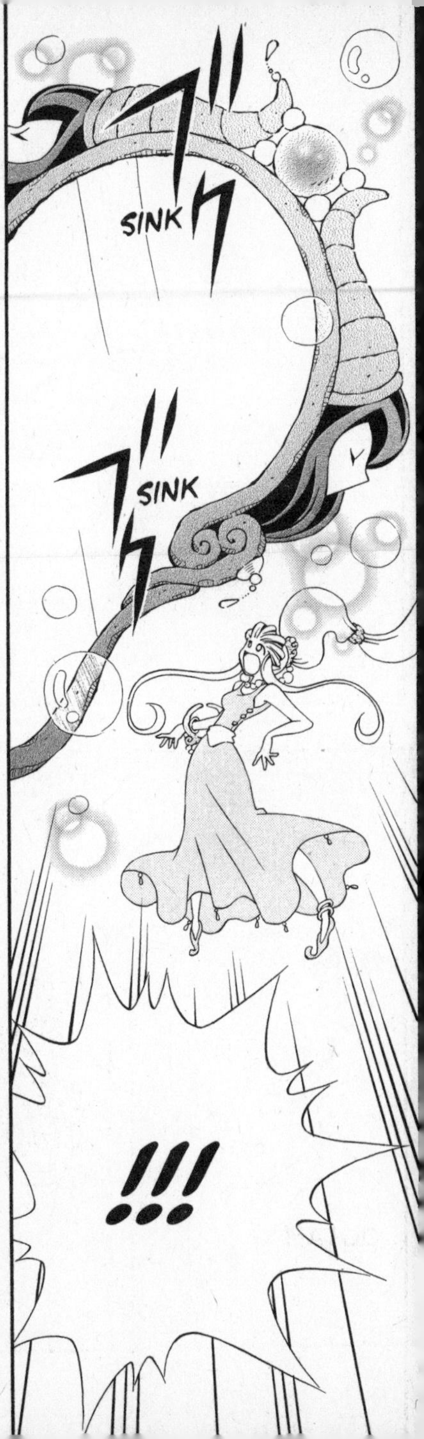
SINK
SINK
!!!
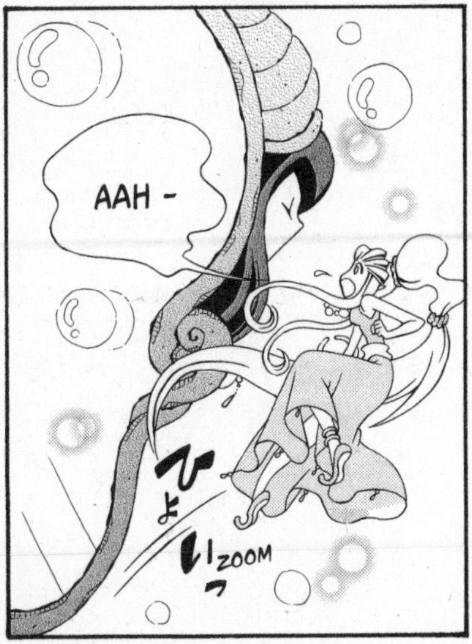
AAH -
ひょい
ZOOM
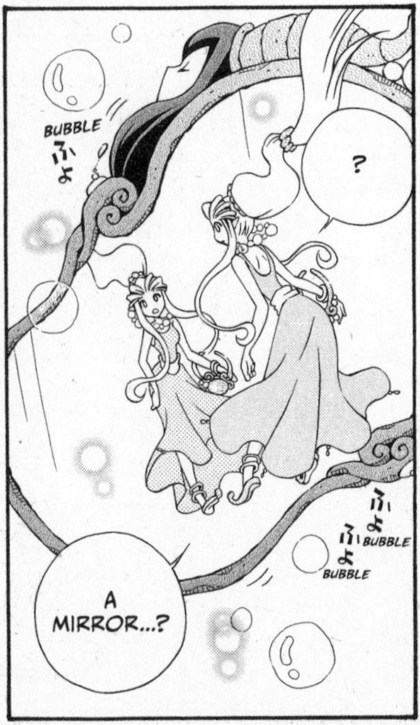
?
ふよ
BUBBLE
ふよ
BUBBLE
ふよ
BUBBLE
A MIRROR...?

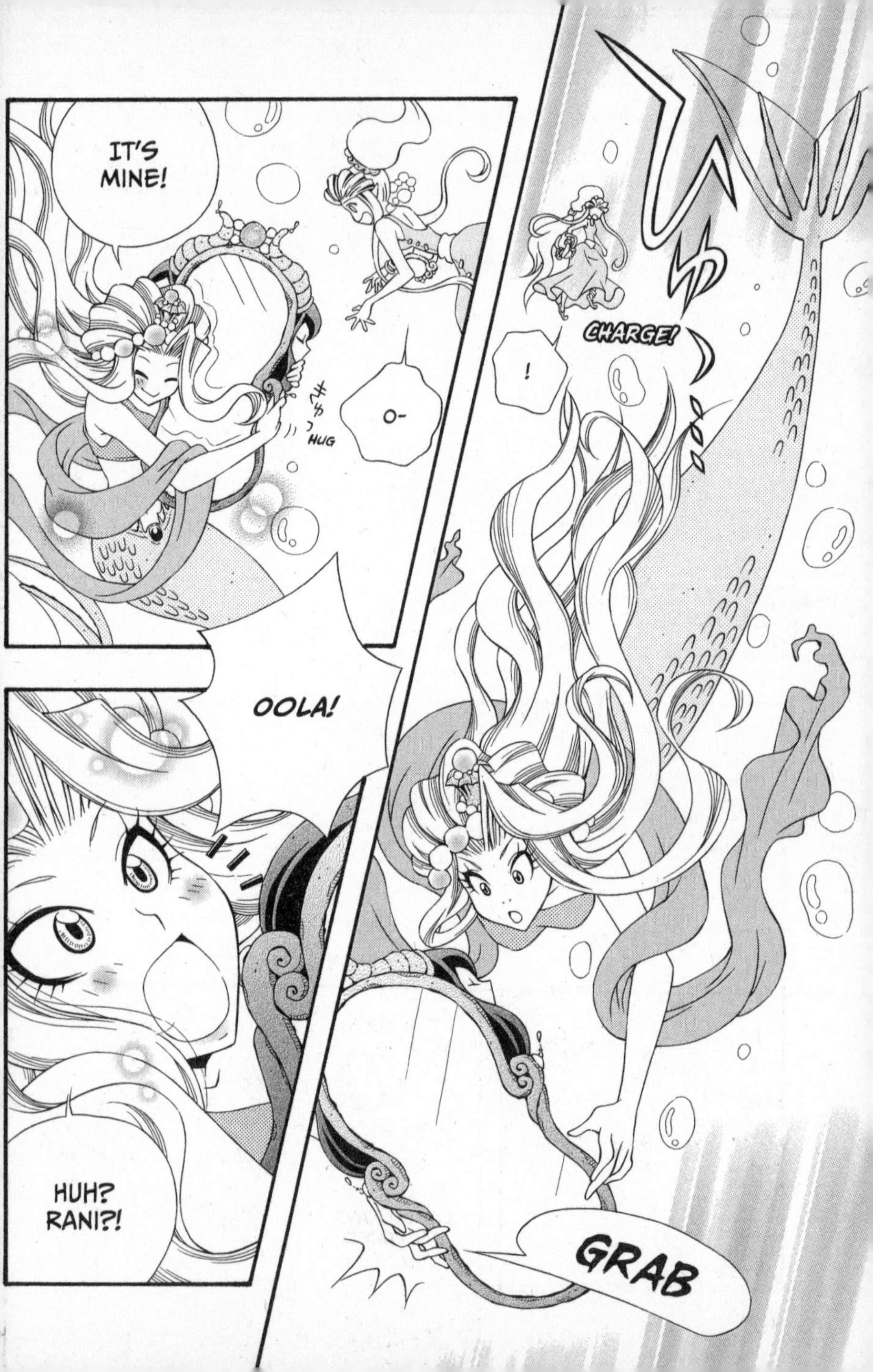
CHARGE!
!
GRAB
IT'S MINE!
きゅっ HUG
O-
OOLA!
HUH? RANI?!

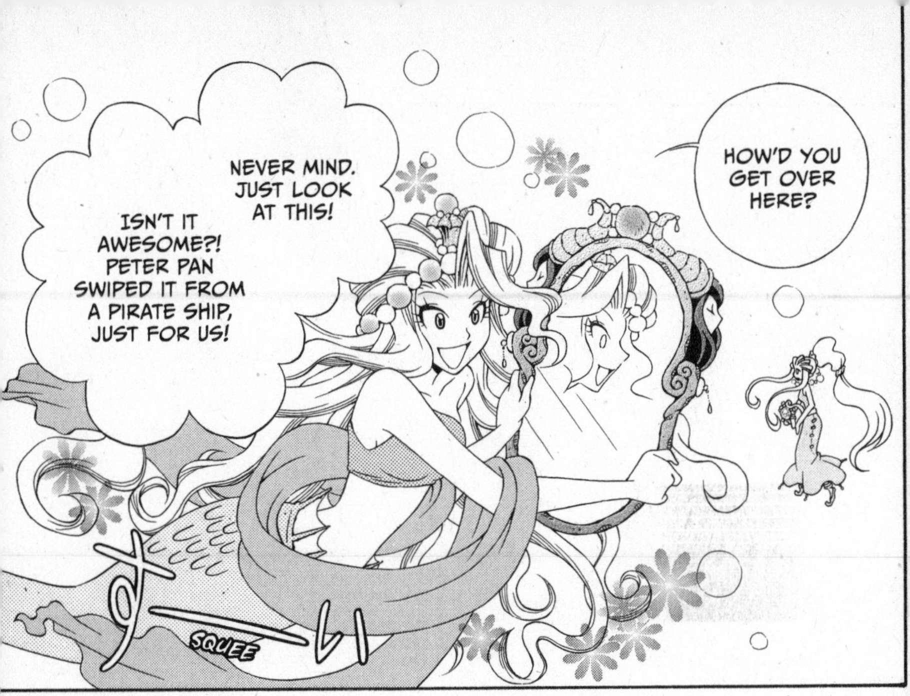
HOW'D YOU GET OVER HERE?
NEVER MIND. JUST LOOK AT THIS!
ISN'T IT AWESOME?! PETER PAN SWIPED IT FROM A PIRATE SHIP, JUST FOR US!
SQUEE

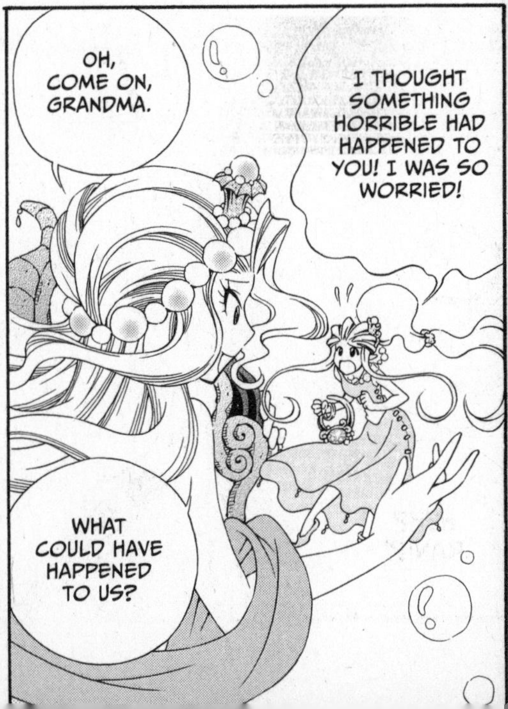
I THOUGHT SOMETHING HORRIBLE HAD HAPPENED TO YOU! I WAS SO WORRIED!
OH, COME ON, GRANDMA.
WHAT COULD HAVE HAPPENED TO US?

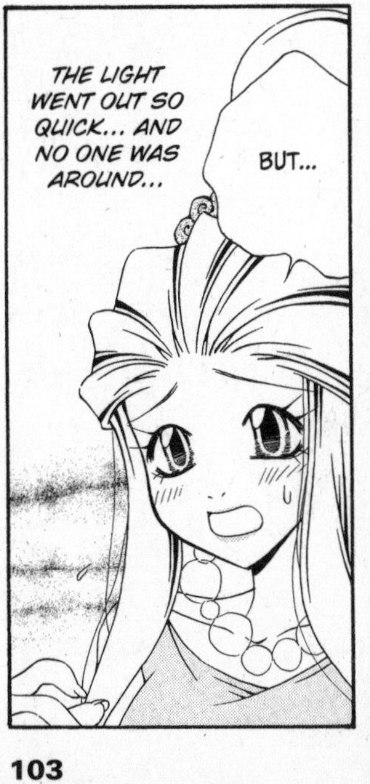
BUT...
THE LIGHT WENT OUT SO QUICK... AND NO ONE WAS AROUND...

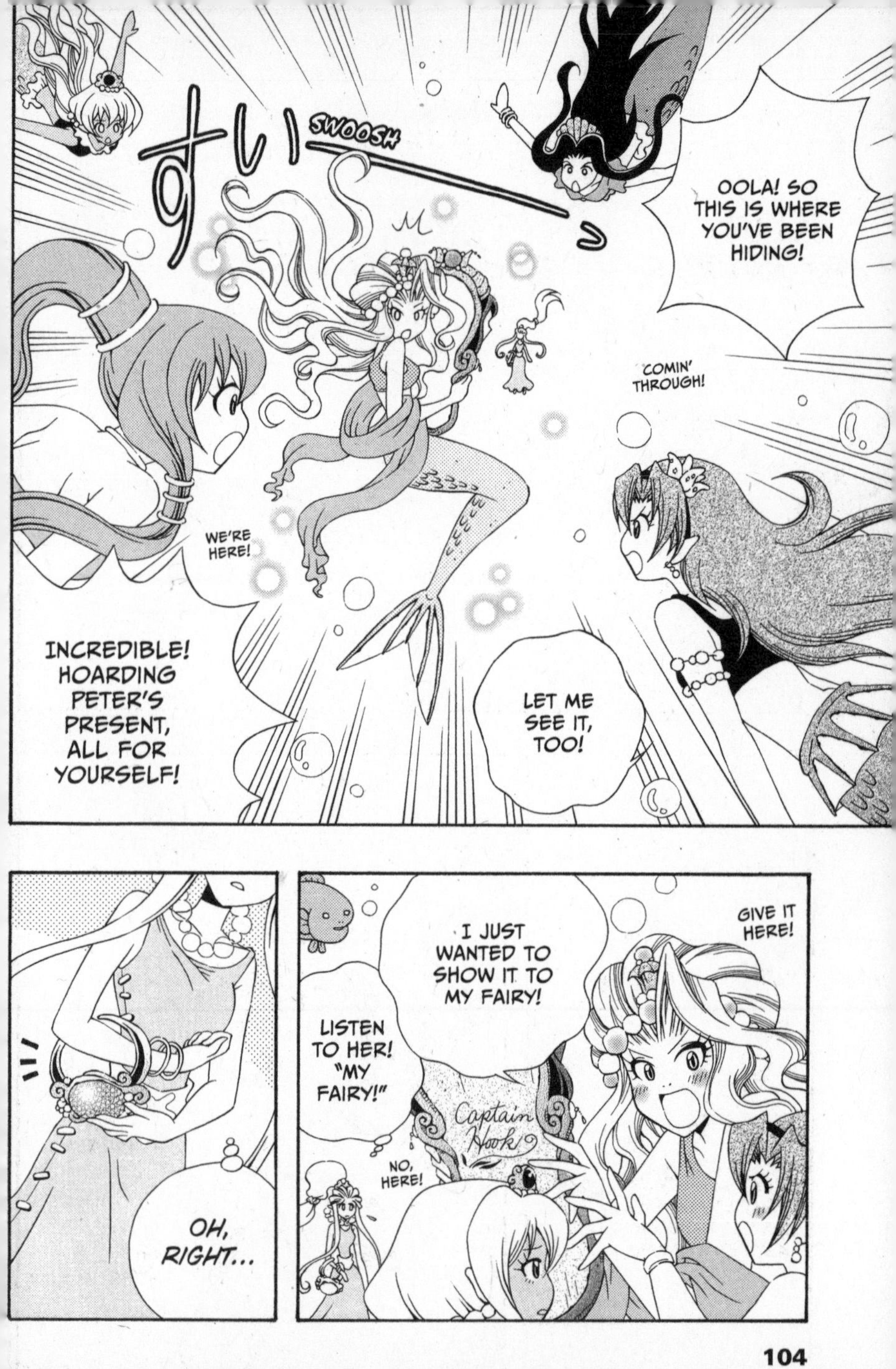
OOLA! SO THIS IS WHERE YOU'VE BEEN HIDING!
すい
SWOOSH
COMIN' THROUGH!
WE'RE HERE!
LET ME SEE IT, TOO!
INCREDIBLE! HOARDING PETER'S PRESENT, ALL FOR YOURSELF!
GIVE IT HERE!
I JUST WANTED TO SHOW IT TO MY FAIRY!
LISTEN TO HER! "MY FAIRY!"
Captain Hook
NO, HERE!
OH, RIGHT...

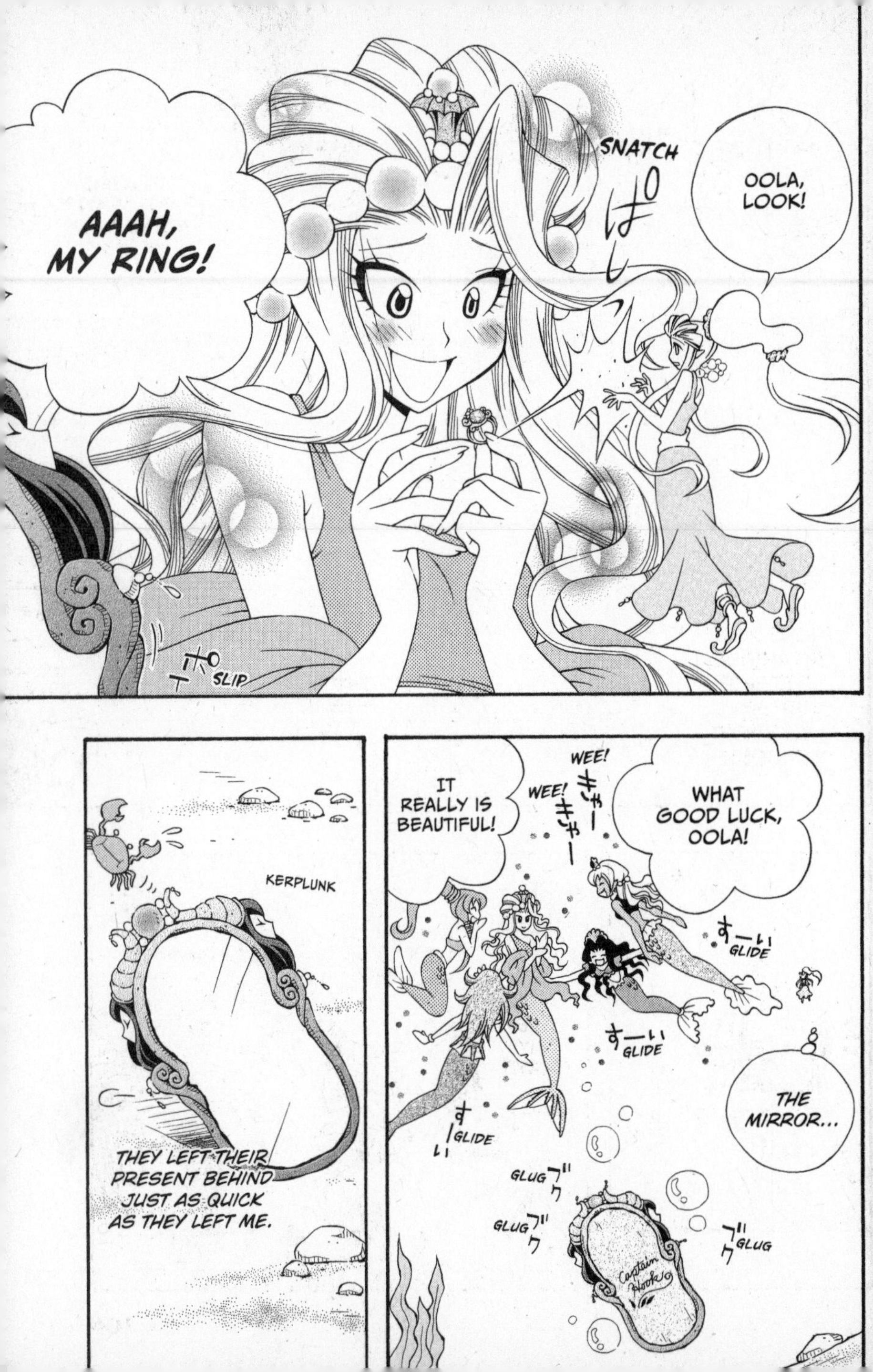
OOLA, LOOK!
SNATCH
AAAH, MY RING!
SLIP
WHAT GOOD LUCK, OOLA!
WEE!
WEE!
IT REALLY IS BEAUTIFUL!
GLIDE
GLIDE
THE MIRROR...
GLIDE
GLUG
GLUG
GLUG
Captain Hook
KERPLUNK
THEY LEFT THEIR PRESENT BEHIND JUST AS QUICK AS THEY LEFT ME.

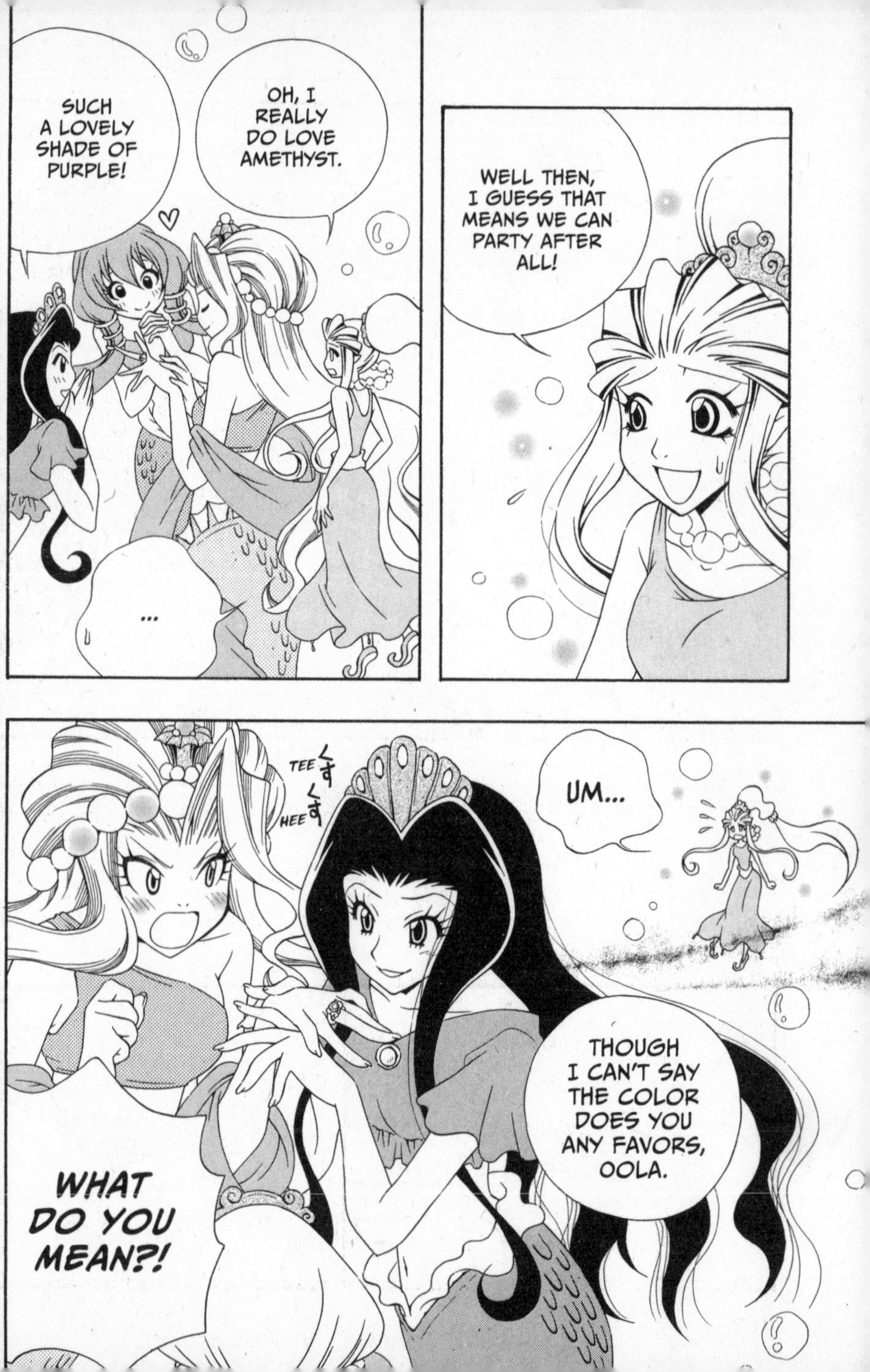
WELL THEN, I GUESS THAT MEANS WE CAN PARTY AFTER ALL!
OH, I REALLY DO LOVE AMETHYST.
SUCH A LOVELY SHADE OF PURPLE!
...
UM...
TEE くす くす HEE
THOUGH I CAN'T SAY THE COLOR DOES YOU ANY FAVORS, OOLA.
WHAT DO YOU MEAN?!

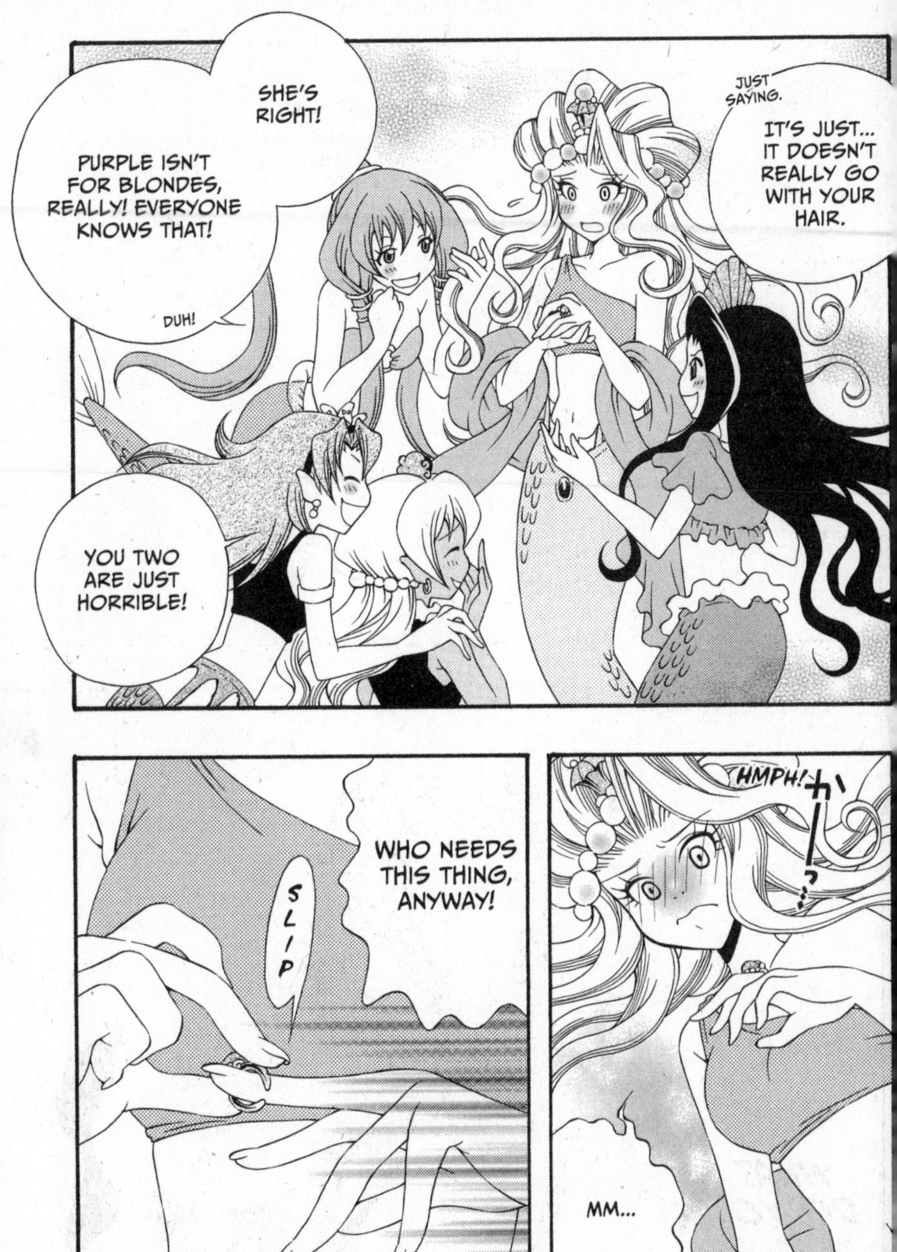
JUST SAYING.
IT'S JUST... IT DOESN'T REALLY GO WITH YOUR HAIR.
SHE'S RIGHT!
PURPLE ISN'T FOR BLONDES, REALLY! EVERYONE KNOWS THAT!
DUH!
YOU TWO ARE JUST HORRIBLE!
HMPH!
MM...
WHO NEEDS THIS THING, ANYWAY!
SLIP

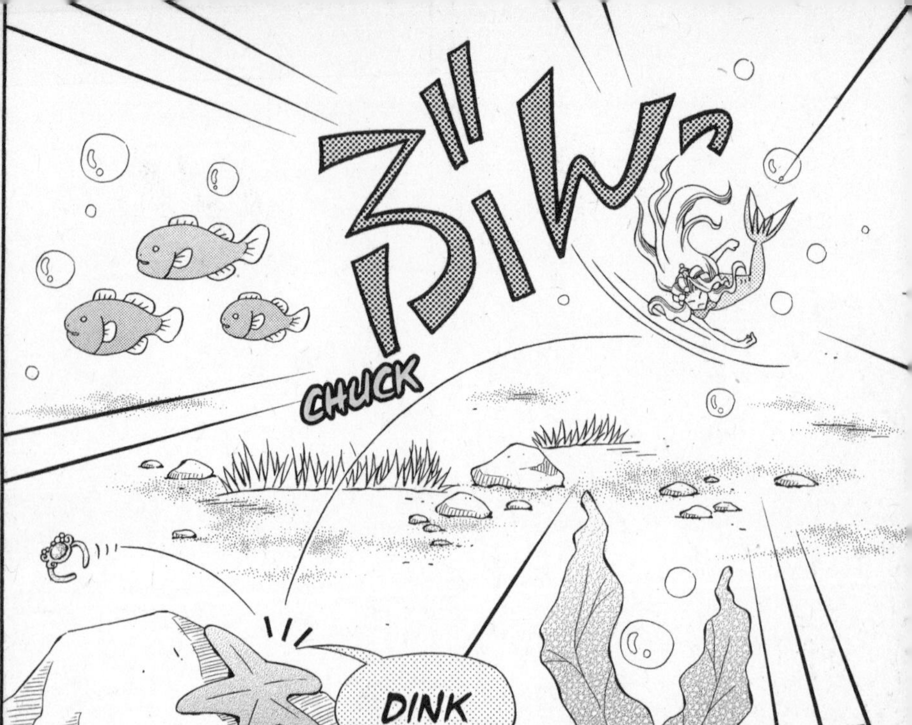
CHUCK
DINK
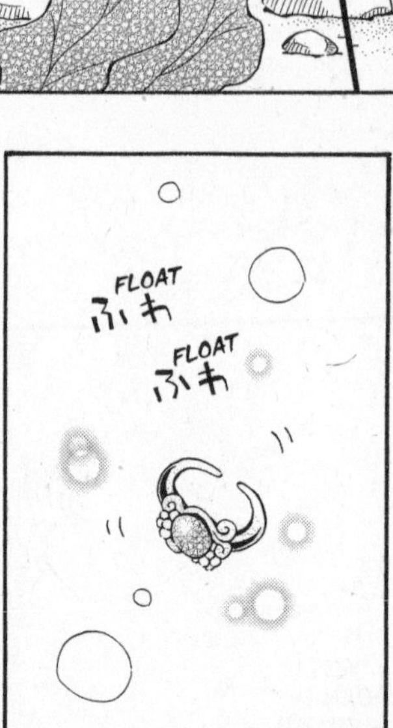
FLOAT
ふわ
FLOAT
ふわ
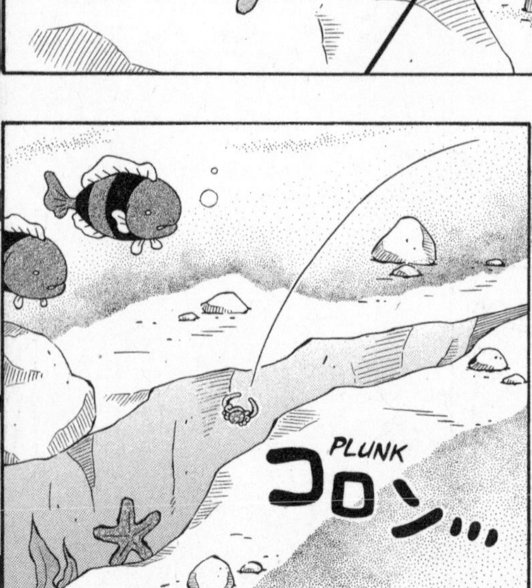
PLUNK
コロン

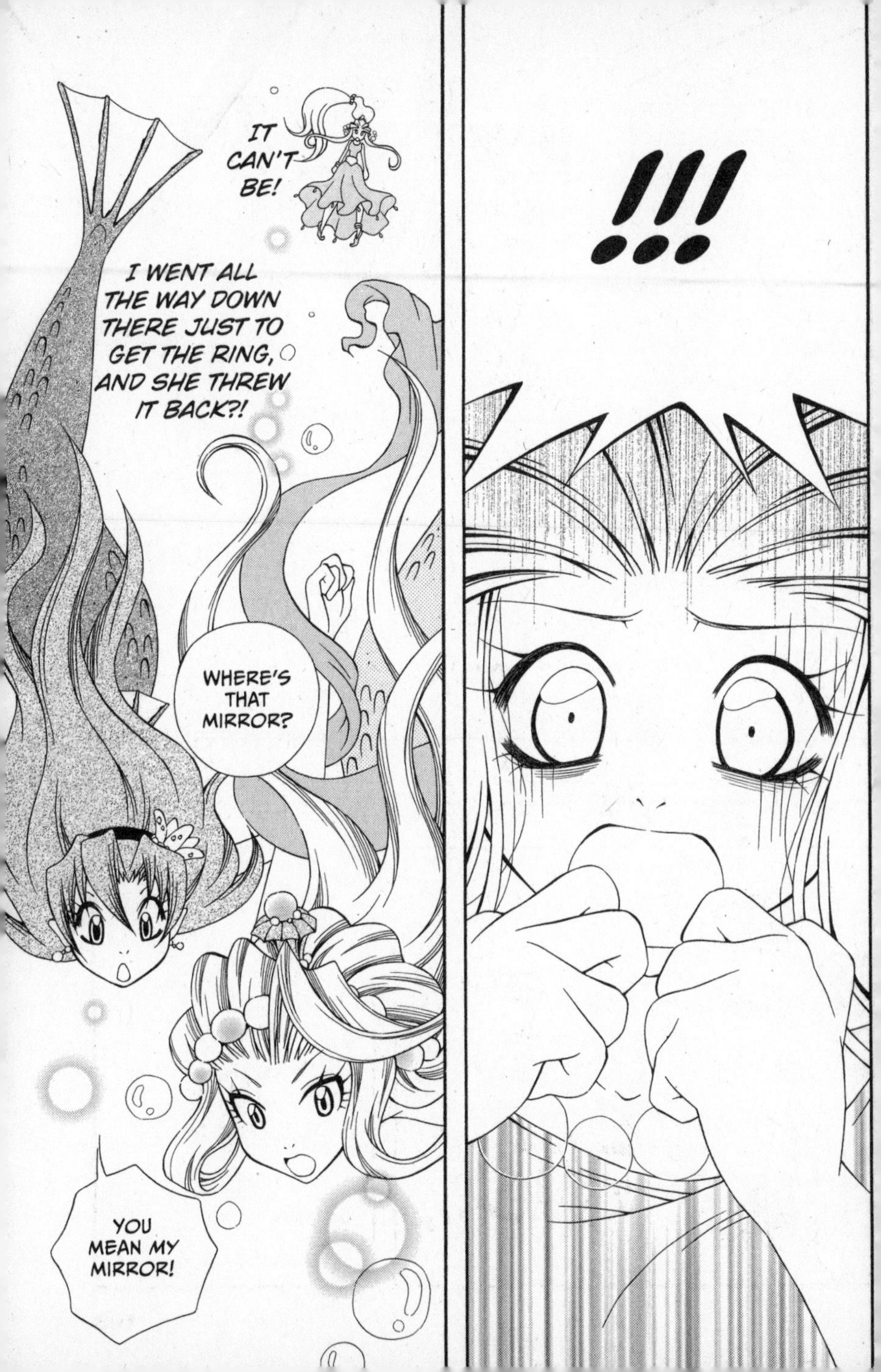
!!!
IT CAN'T BE!
I WENT ALL THE WAY DOWN THERE JUST TO GET THE RING, AND SHE THREW IT BACK?!
WHERE'S THAT MIRROR?
YOU MEAN MY MIRROR!

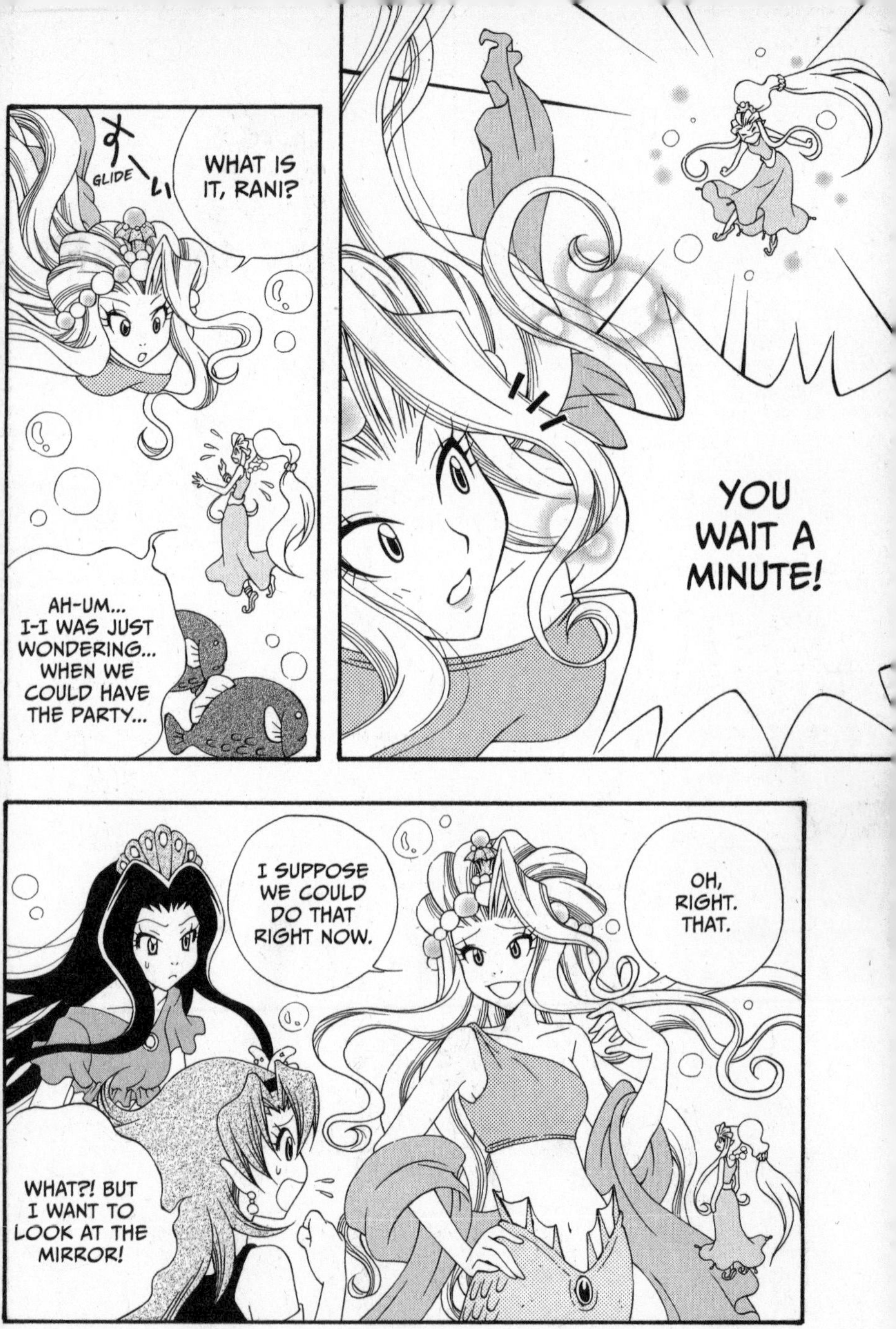
YOU WAIT A MINUTE!
GLIDE
WHAT IS IT, RANI?
AH-UM... I-I WAS JUST WONDERING... WHEN WE COULD HAVE THE PARTY...
OH, RIGHT. THAT.
I SUPPOSE WE COULD DO THAT RIGHT NOW.
WHAT?! BUT I WANT TO LOOK AT THE MIRROR!

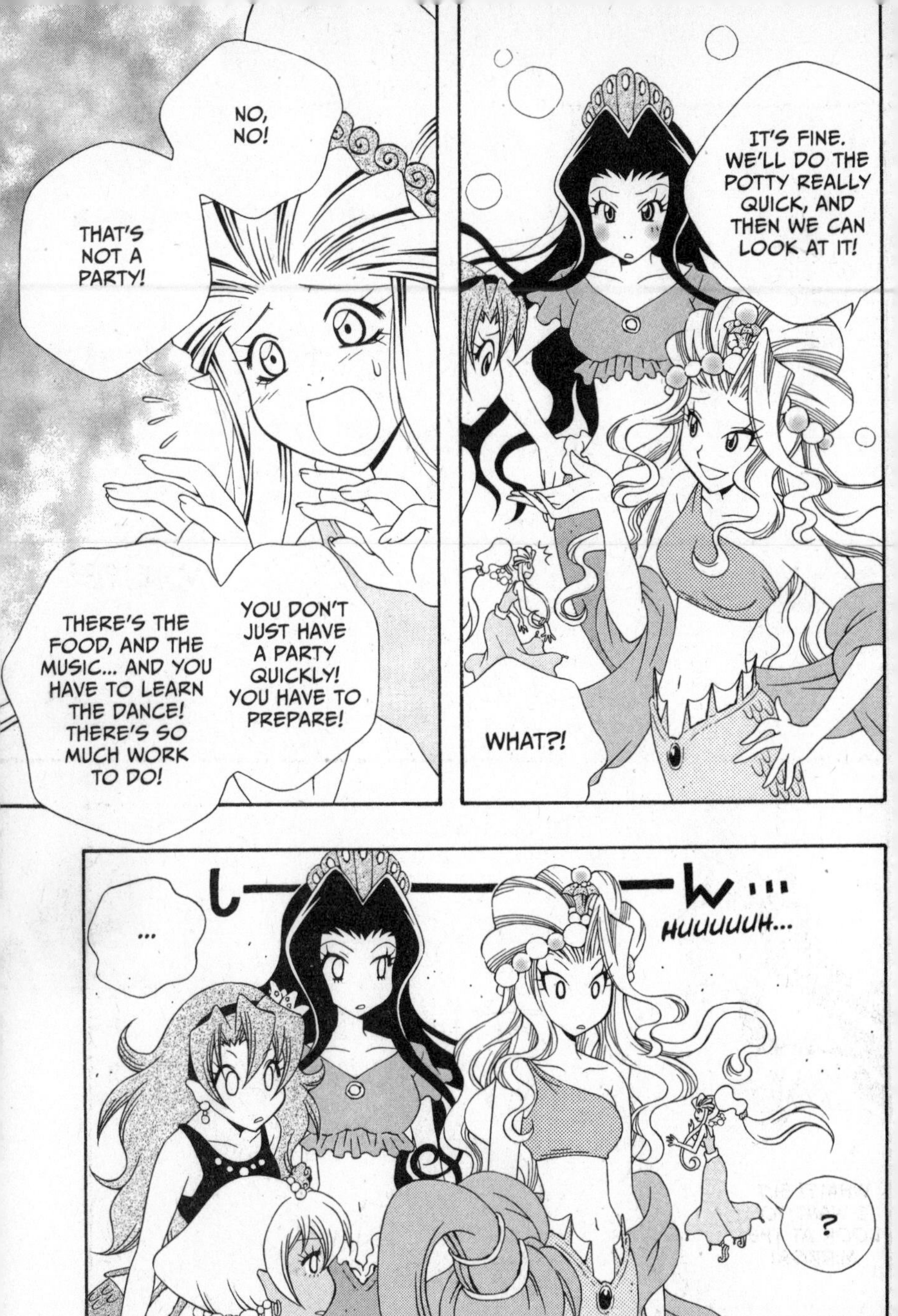
IT'S FINE. WE'LL DO THE POTTY REALLY QUICK, AND THEN WE CAN LOOK AT IT!
WHAT?!
NO, NO!
THAT'S NOT A PARTY!
YOU DON'T JUST HAVE A PARTY QUICKLY! YOU HAVE TO PREPARE!
THERE'S THE FOOD, AND THE MUSIC... AND YOU HAVE TO LEARN THE DANCE! THERE'S SO MUCH WORK TO DO!
L———W...
HUUUUUH...
...
?

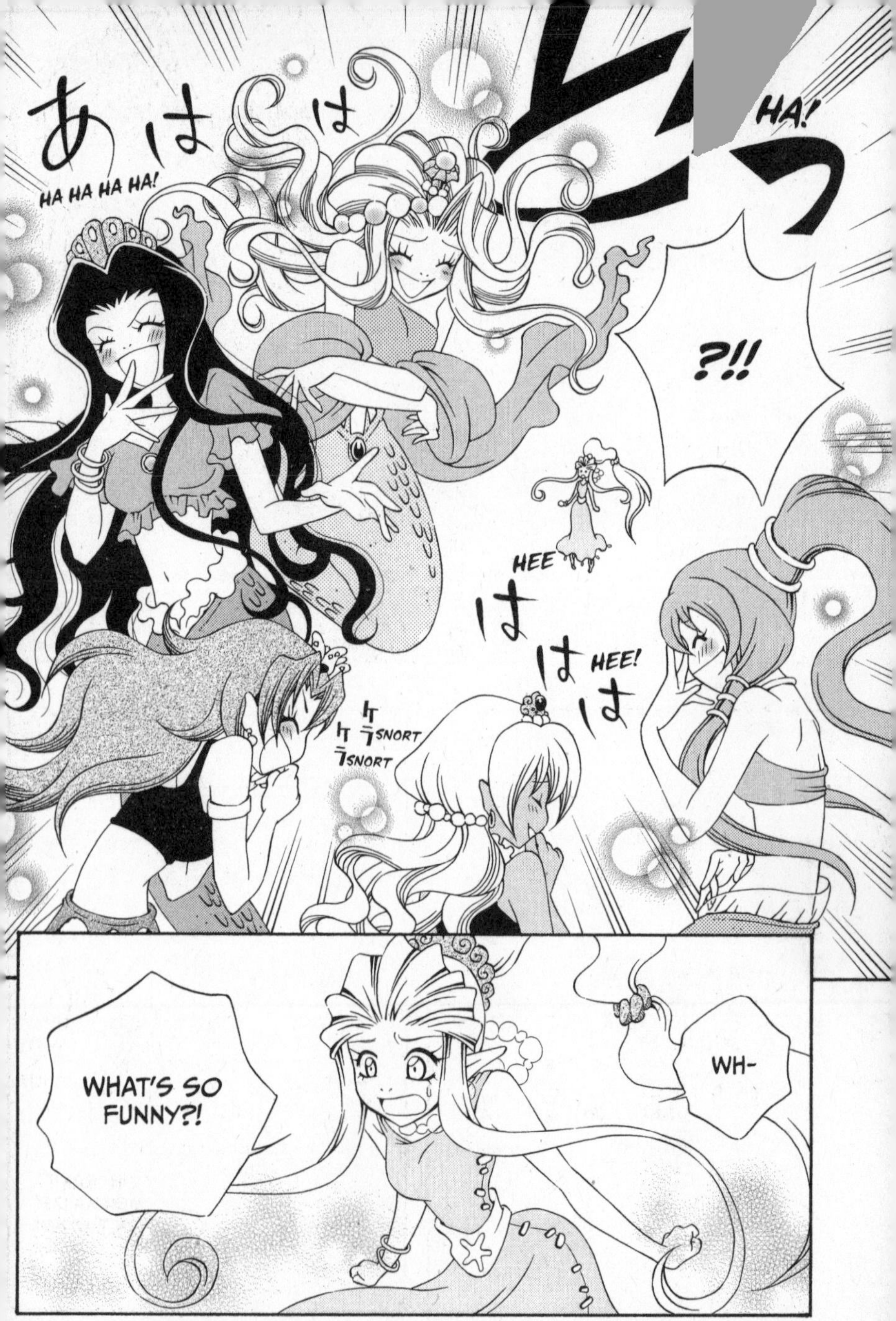

HA!
あはは
HA HA HA HA!
?!!
HEE
ははは
HEE!
SNORT
SNORT
WH-
WHAT'S SO FUNNY?!

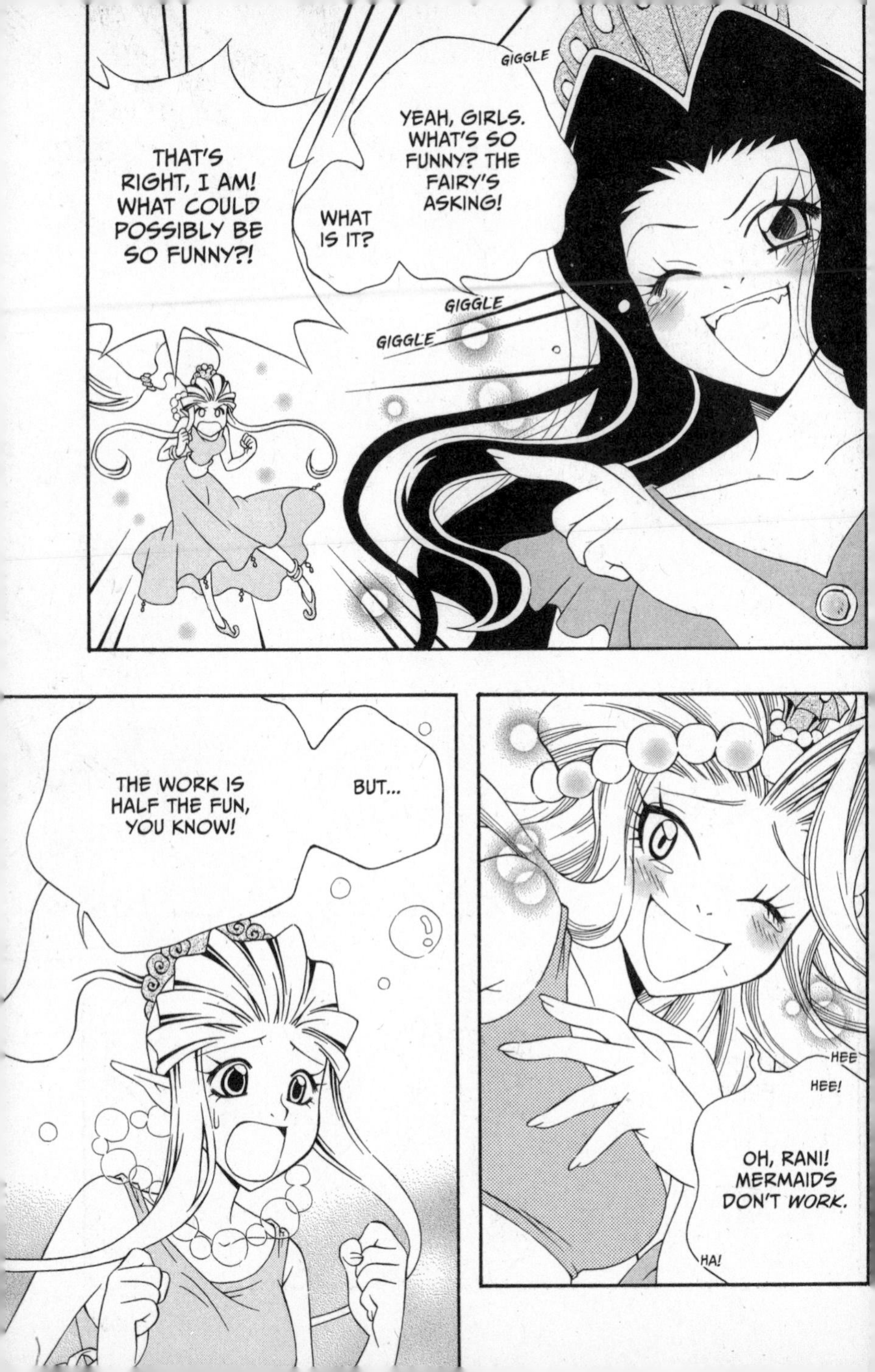
GIGGLE
YEAH, GIRLS. WHAT'S SO FUNNY? THE FAIRY'S ASKING!
WHAT IS IT?
THAT'S RIGHT, I AM! WHAT COULD POSSIBLY BE SO FUNNY?!
GIGGLE
GIGGLE
HEE
HEE!
OH, RANI! MERMAIDS DON'T *WORK*.
HA!
BUT...
THE WORK IS HALF THE FUN, YOU KNOW!

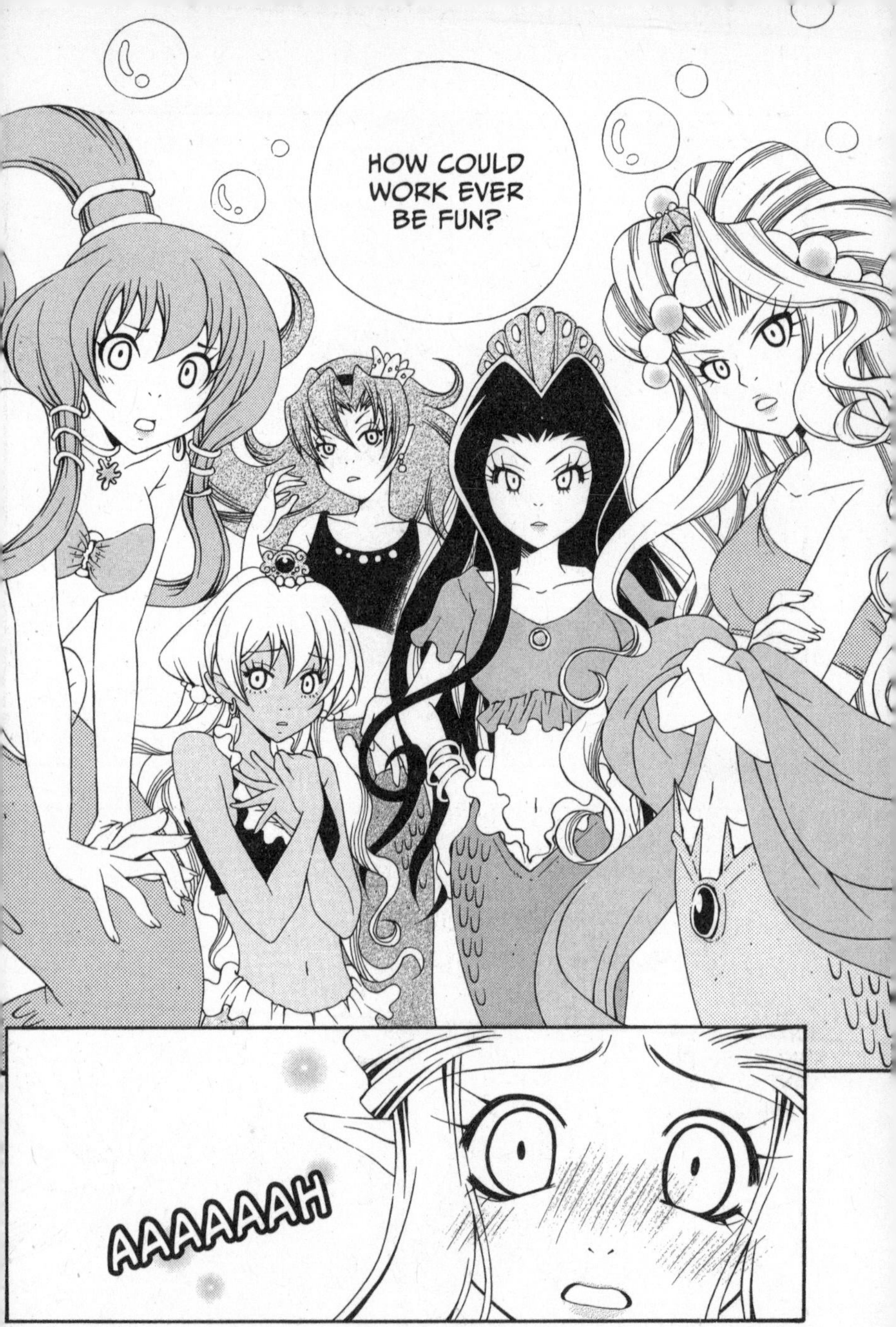
HOW COULD WORK EVER BE FUN?
AAAAAAH

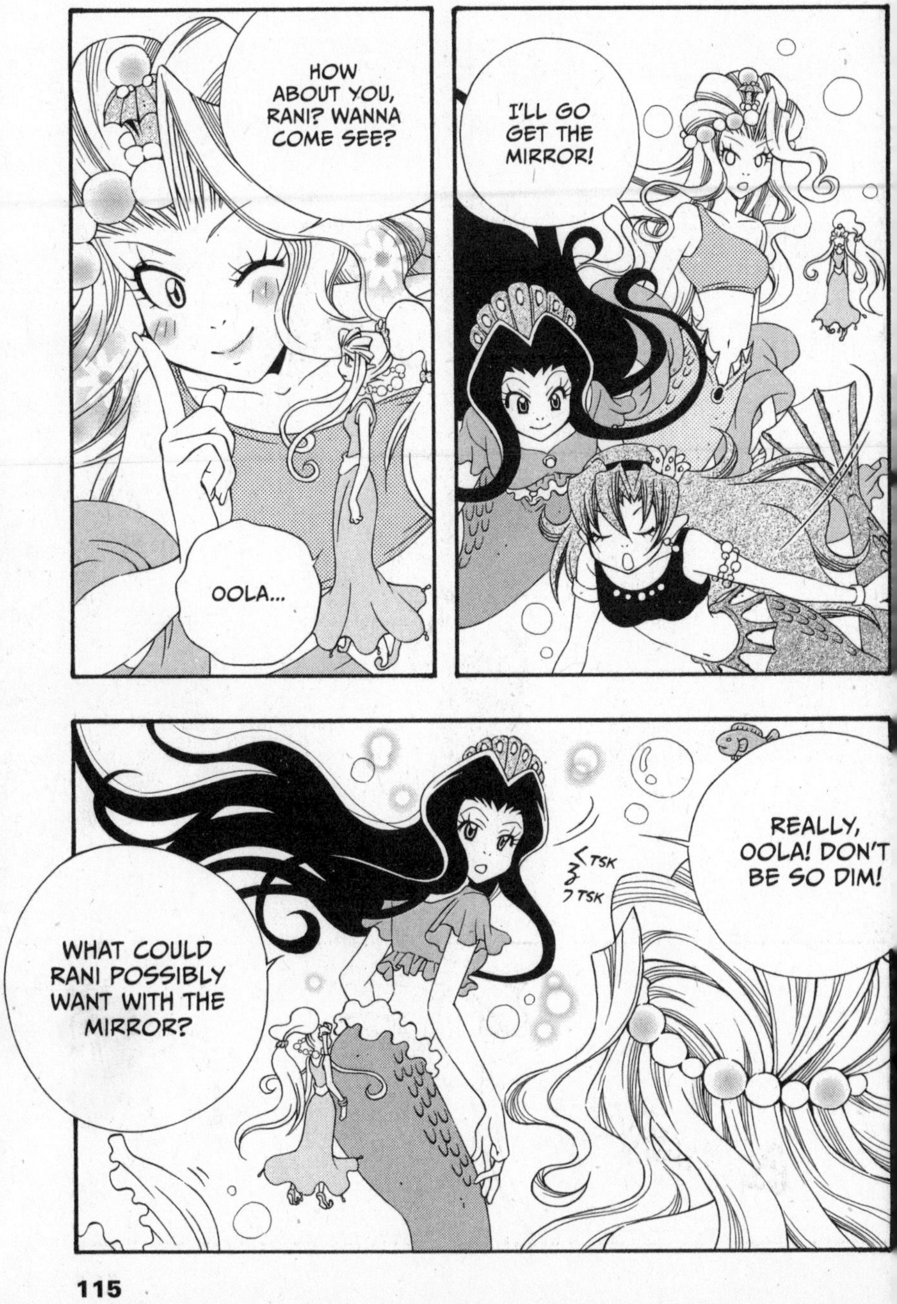
I'LL GO GET THE MIRROR!
HOW ABOUT YOU, RANI? WANNA COME SEE?
OOLA...
REALLY, OOLA! DON'T BE SO DIM!
TSK TSK
WHAT COULD RANI POSSIBLY WANT WITH THE MIRROR?

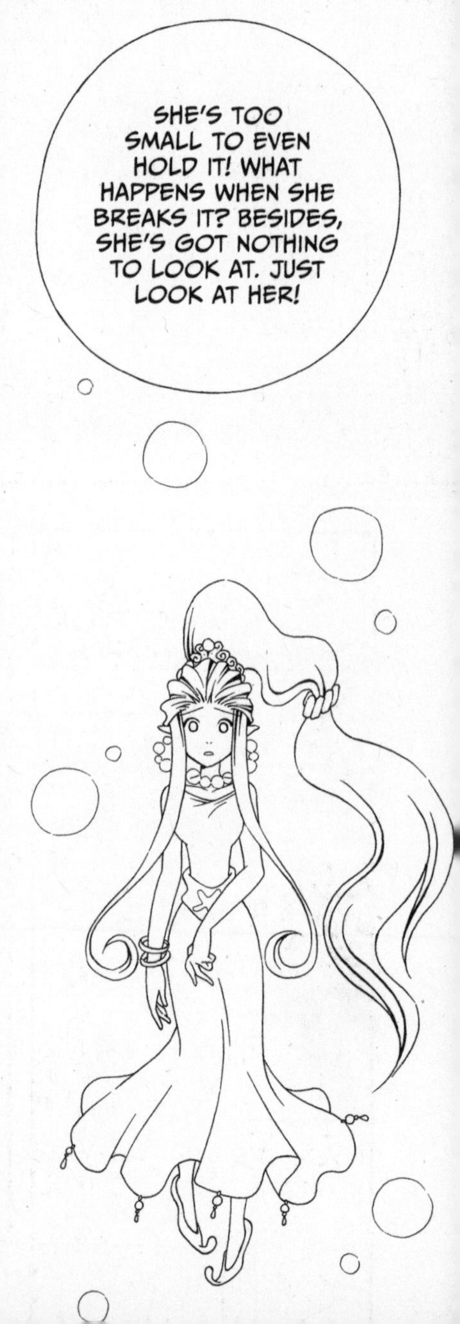
SHE'S TOO SMALL TO EVEN HOLD IT! WHAT HAPPENS WHEN SHE BREAKS IT? BESIDES, SHE'S GOT NOTHING TO LOOK AT. JUST LOOK AT HER!

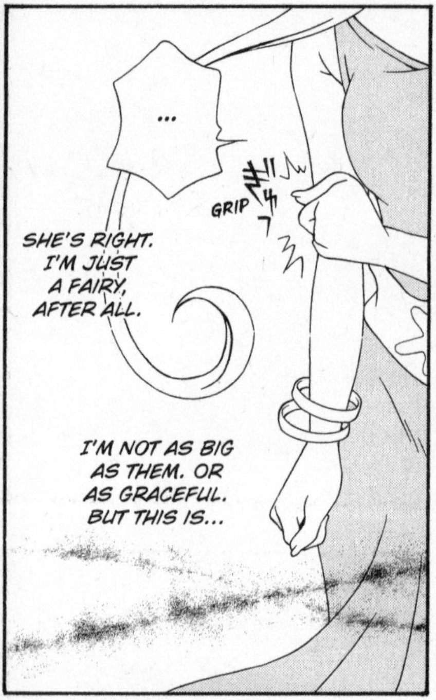
...
GRIP
SHE'S RIGHT. I'M JUST A FAIRY, AFTER ALL.
I'M NOT AS BIG AS THEM. OR AS GRACEFUL. BUT THIS IS...

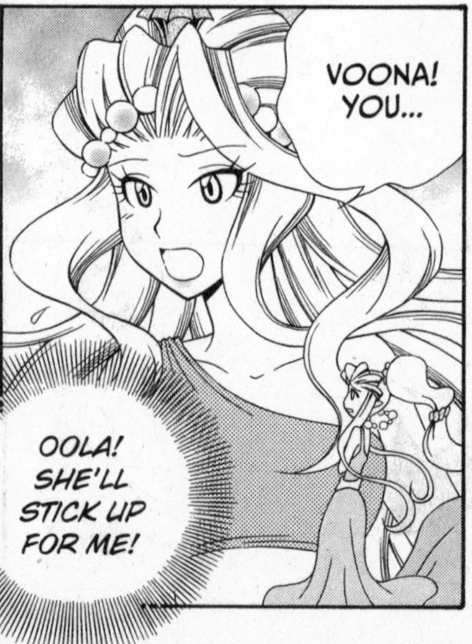
VOONA! YOU...
OOLA! SHE'LL STICK UP FOR ME!

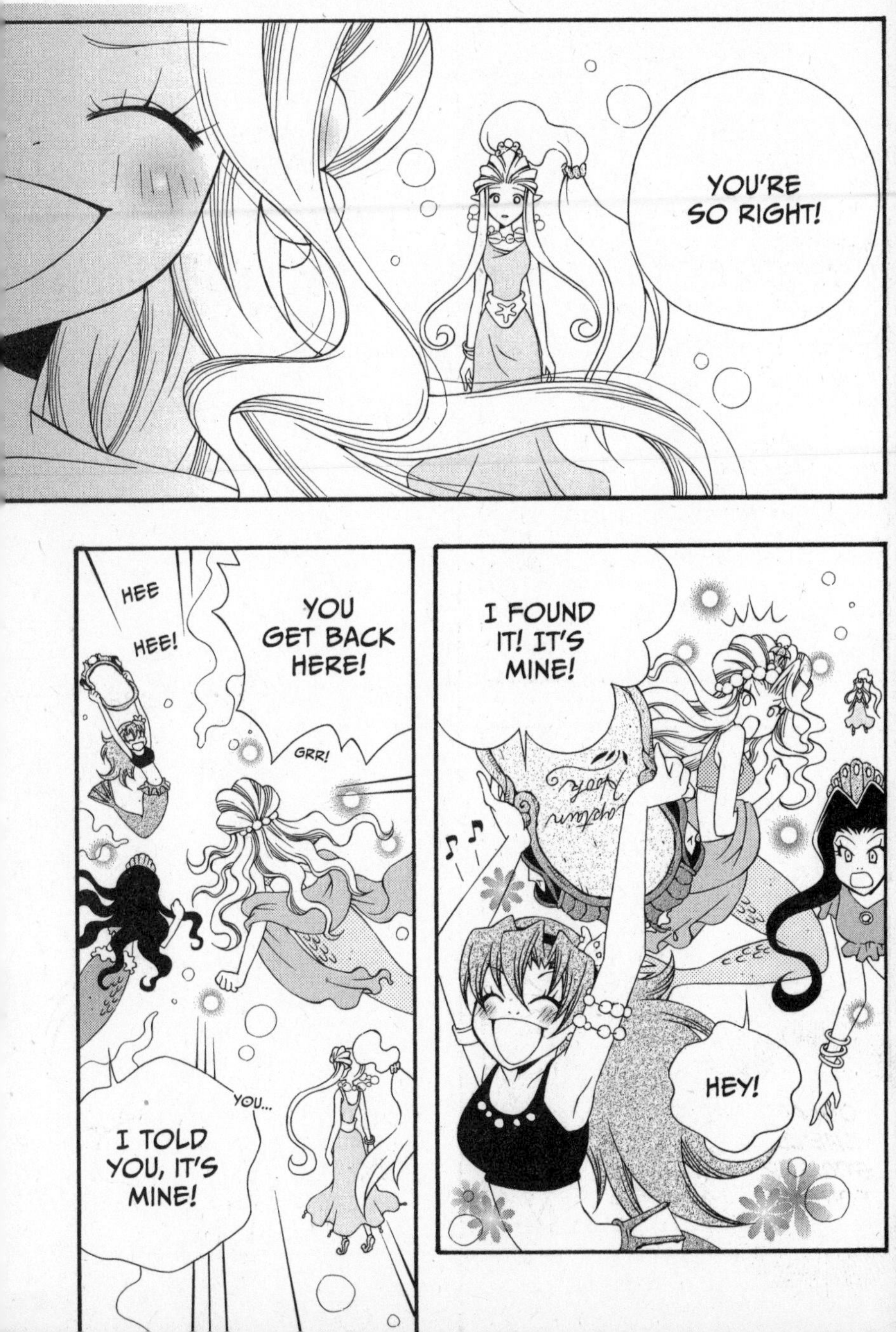
YOU'RE SO RIGHT!
I FOUND IT! IT'S MINE!
HEY!
HEE HEE!
YOU GET BACK HERE!
GRR!
YOU...
I TOLD YOU, IT'S MINE!

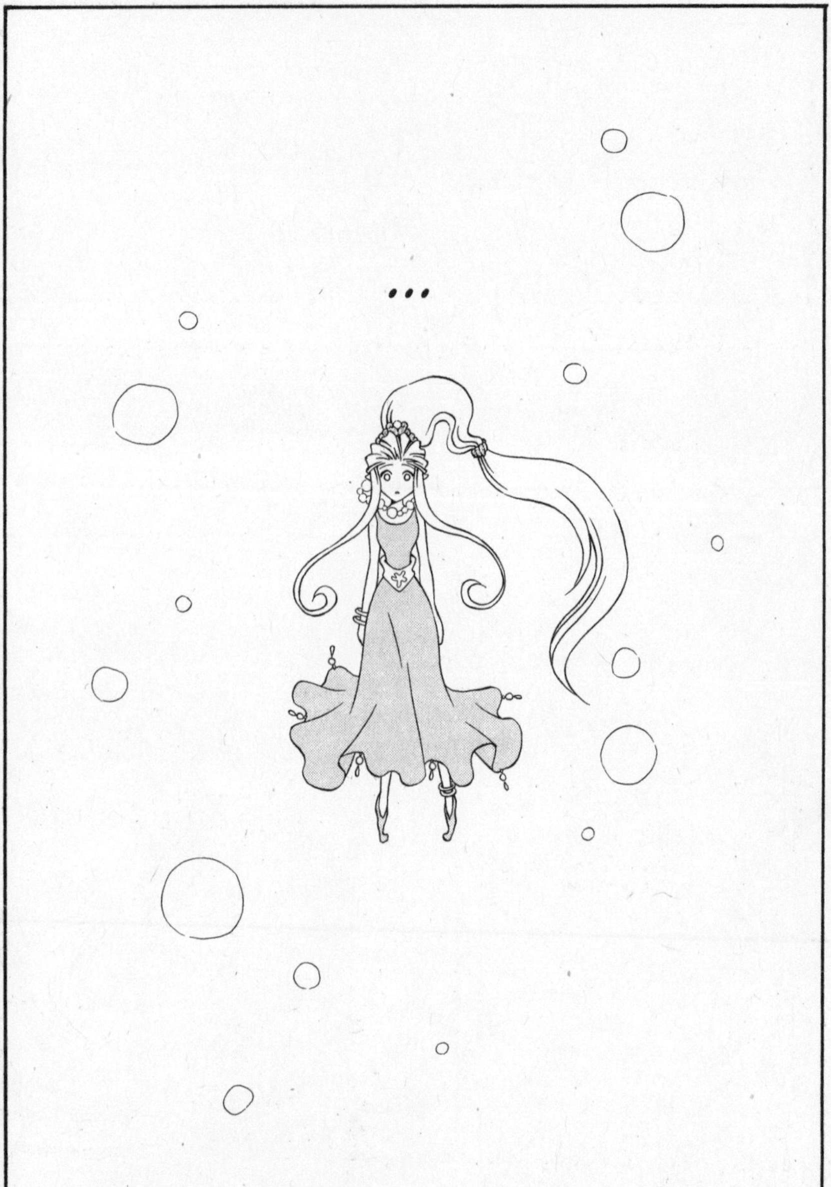
...

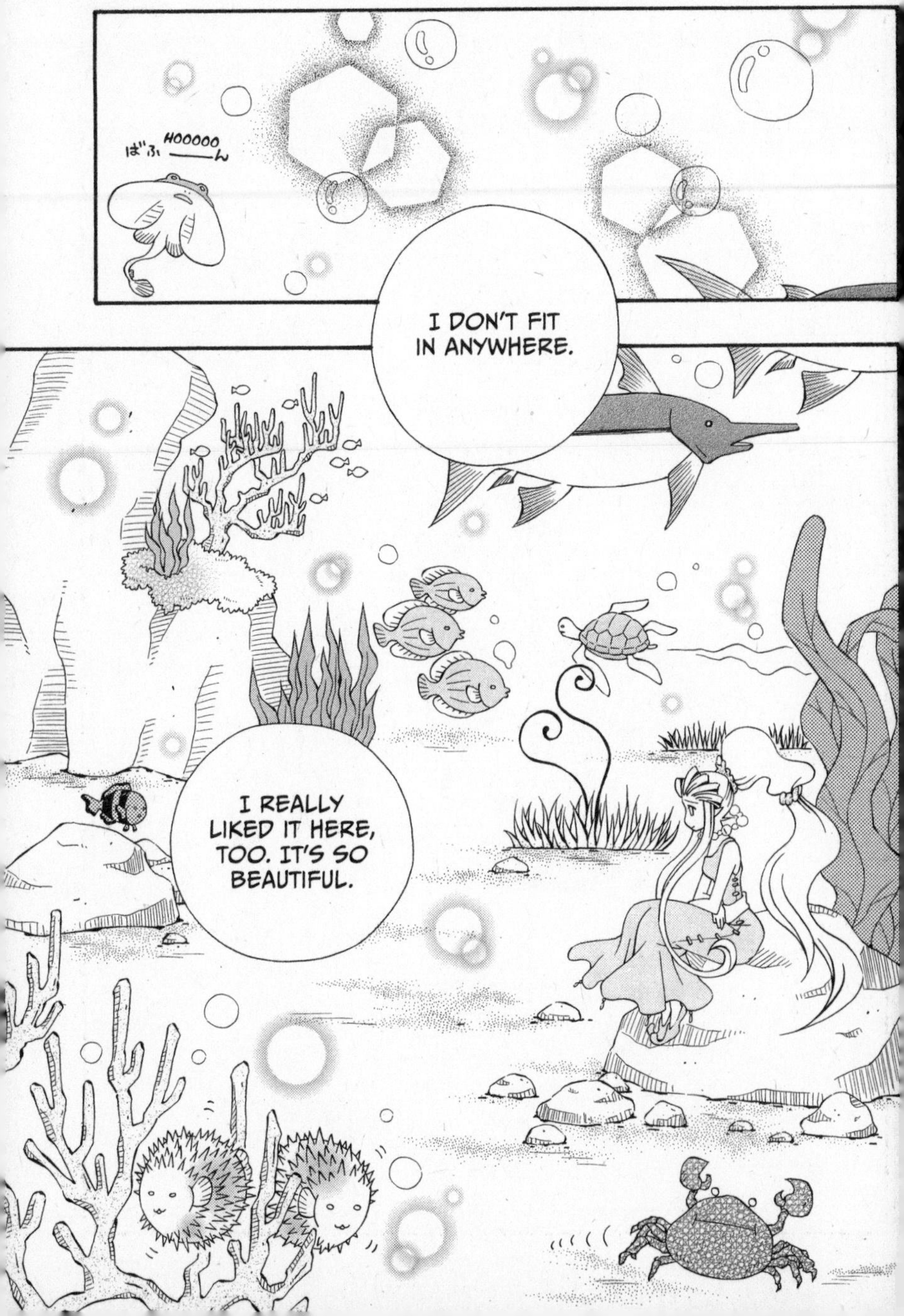
ばふ HOOOOO——ん
I DON'T FIT IN ANYWHERE.
I REALLY LIKED IT HERE, TOO. IT'S SO BEAUTIFUL.

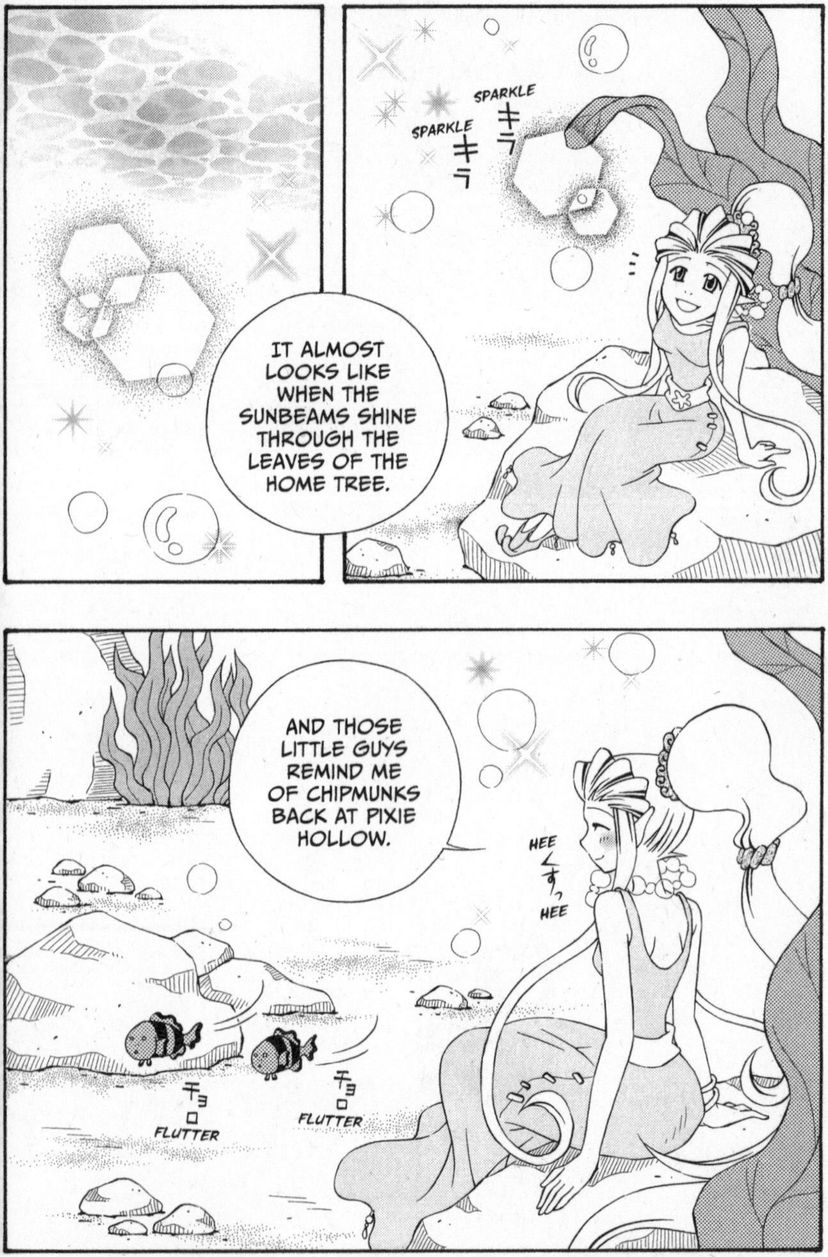
SPARKLE キラ
SPARKLE キラ
IT ALMOST LOOKS LIKE WHEN THE SUNBEAMS SHINE THROUGH THE LEAVES OF THE HOME TREE.
AND THOSE LITTLE GUYS REMIND ME OF CHIPMUNKS BACK AT PIXIE HOLLOW.
HEE くすっ HEE
チョロ FLUTTER
チョロ FLUTTER

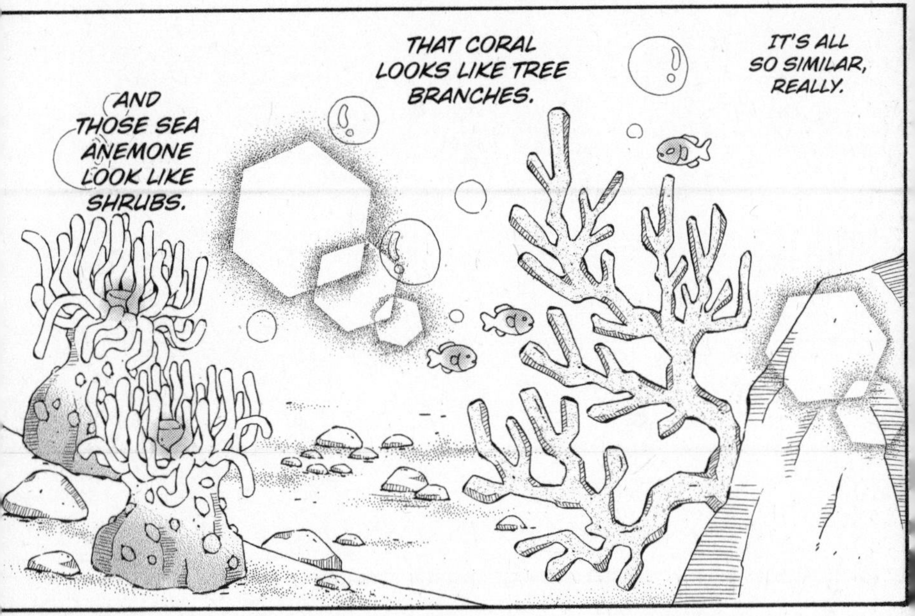
IT'S ALL SO SIMILAR, REALLY.
THAT CORAL LOOKS LIKE TREE BRANCHES.
AND THOSE SEA ANEMONE LOOK LIKE SHRUBS.

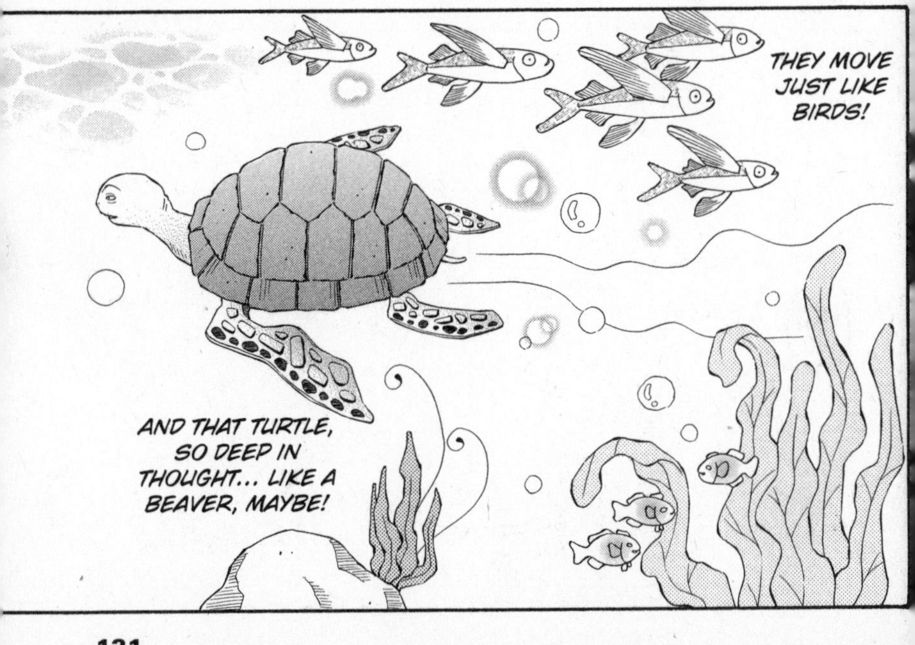
THEY MOVE JUST LIKE BIRDS!
AND THAT TURTLE, SO DEEP IN THOUGHT... LIKE A BEAVER, MAYBE!

I WONDER IF THE CHIPMUNK-FISH WILL-WANT TO PLAY WITH ME.

すい GLIDE

HELLO!

UM...

REACH

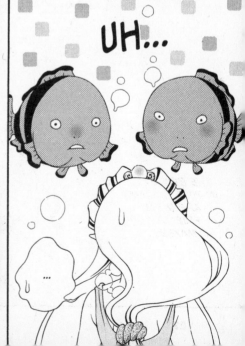

UH...

...

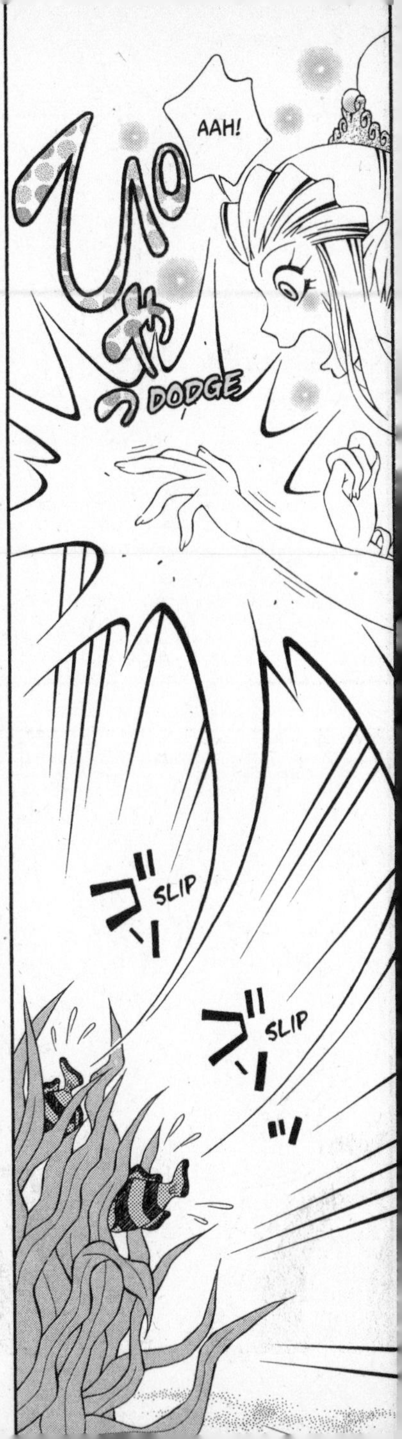
AAH!
ひゅっ DODGE
SLIP
SLIP

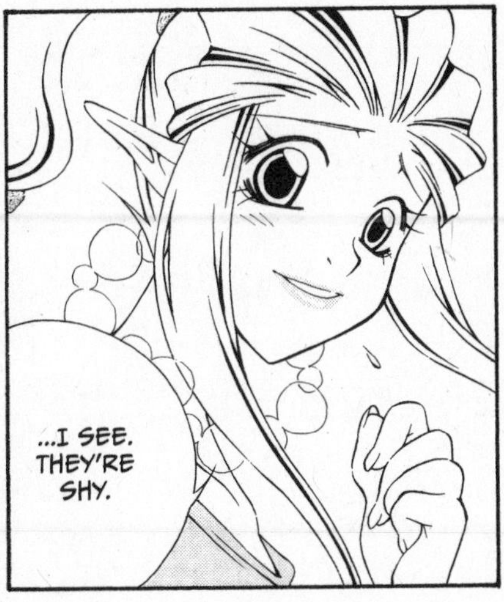
...I SEE. THEY'RE SHY.

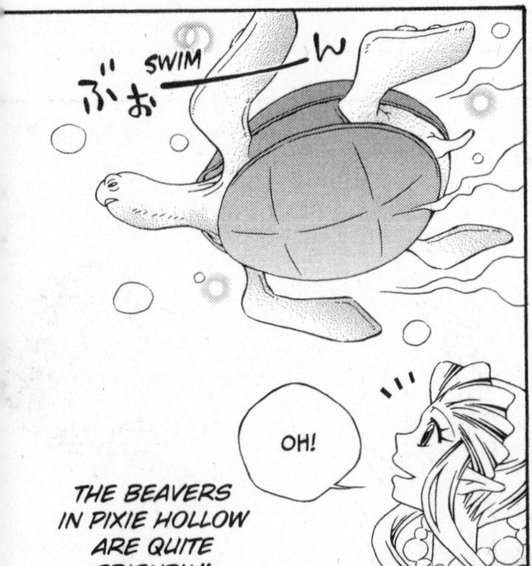
ぶおーん SWIM
OH!
THE BEAVERS IN PIXIE HOLLOW ARE QUITE FRIENDLY! MAYBE...

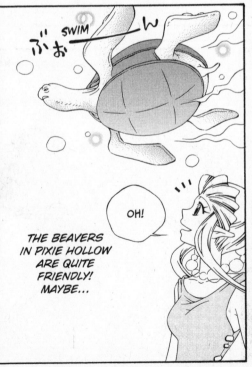

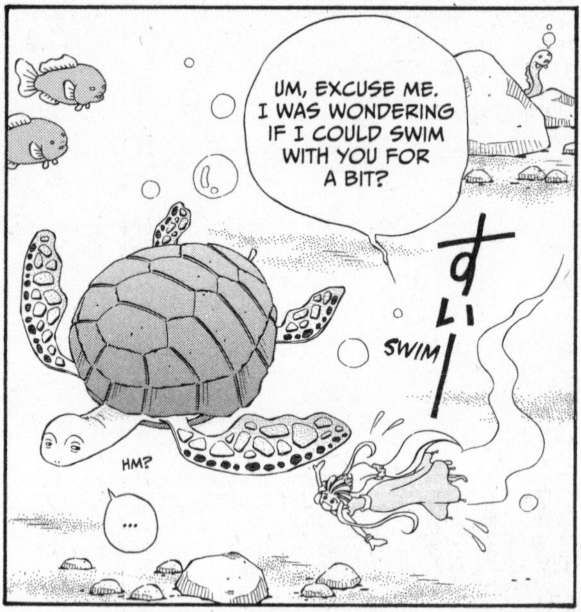
UM, EXCUSE ME. I WAS WONDERING IF I COULD SWIM WITH YOU FOR A BIT?
すいー
SWIM
HM?
...
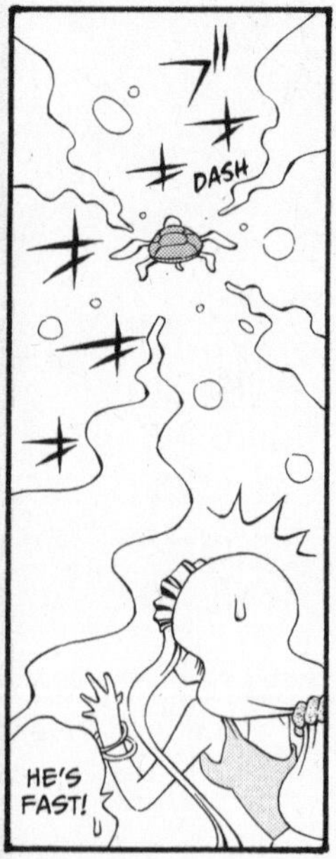
DASH
HE'S FAST!
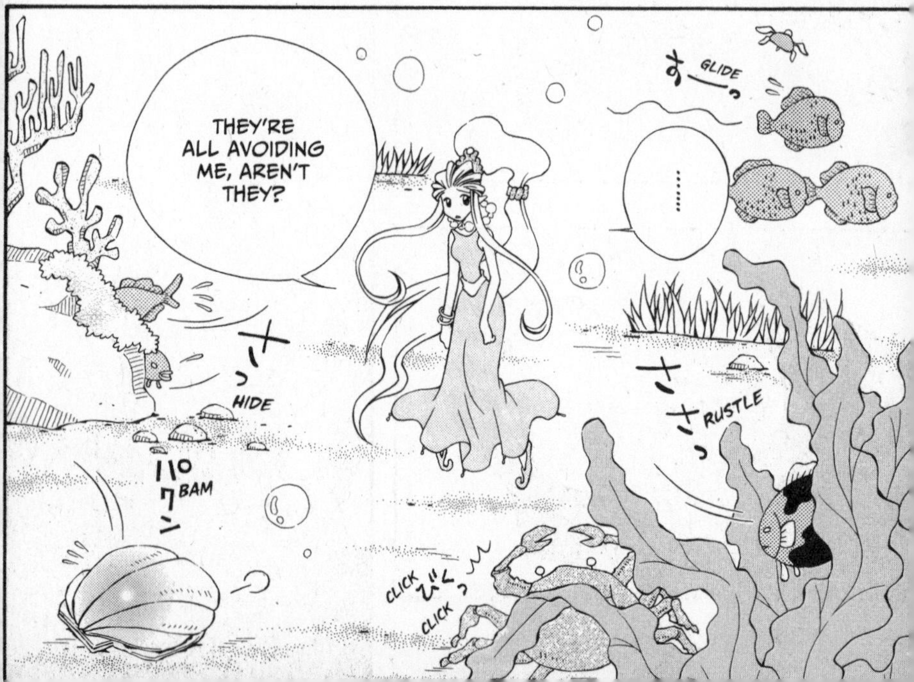
すーっ
GLIDE
……
THEY'RE ALL AVOIDING ME, AREN'T THEY?
ささっ
RUSTLE
さっ
HIDE
パクン
BAM
びくっ
CLICK
CLICK

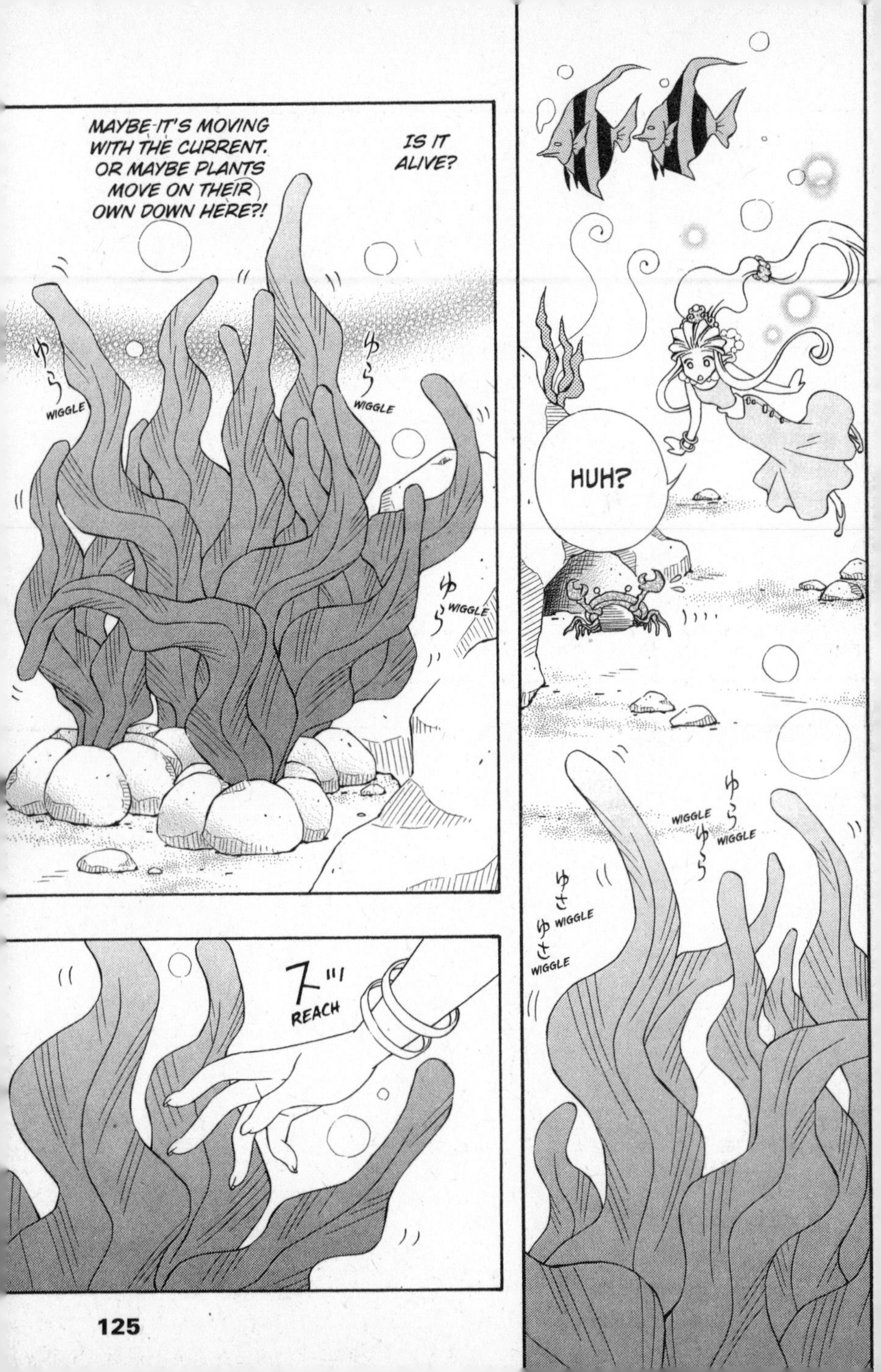
HUH?
ゆら WIGGLE
ゆら WIGGLE
ゆさ WIGGLE
ゆさ WIGGLE
IS IT ALIVE?
MAYBE IT'S MOVING WITH THE CURRENT. OR MAYBE PLANTS MOVE ON THEIR OWN DOWN HERE?!
ゆら WIGGLE
ゆら WIGGLE
ゆら WIGGLE
REACH

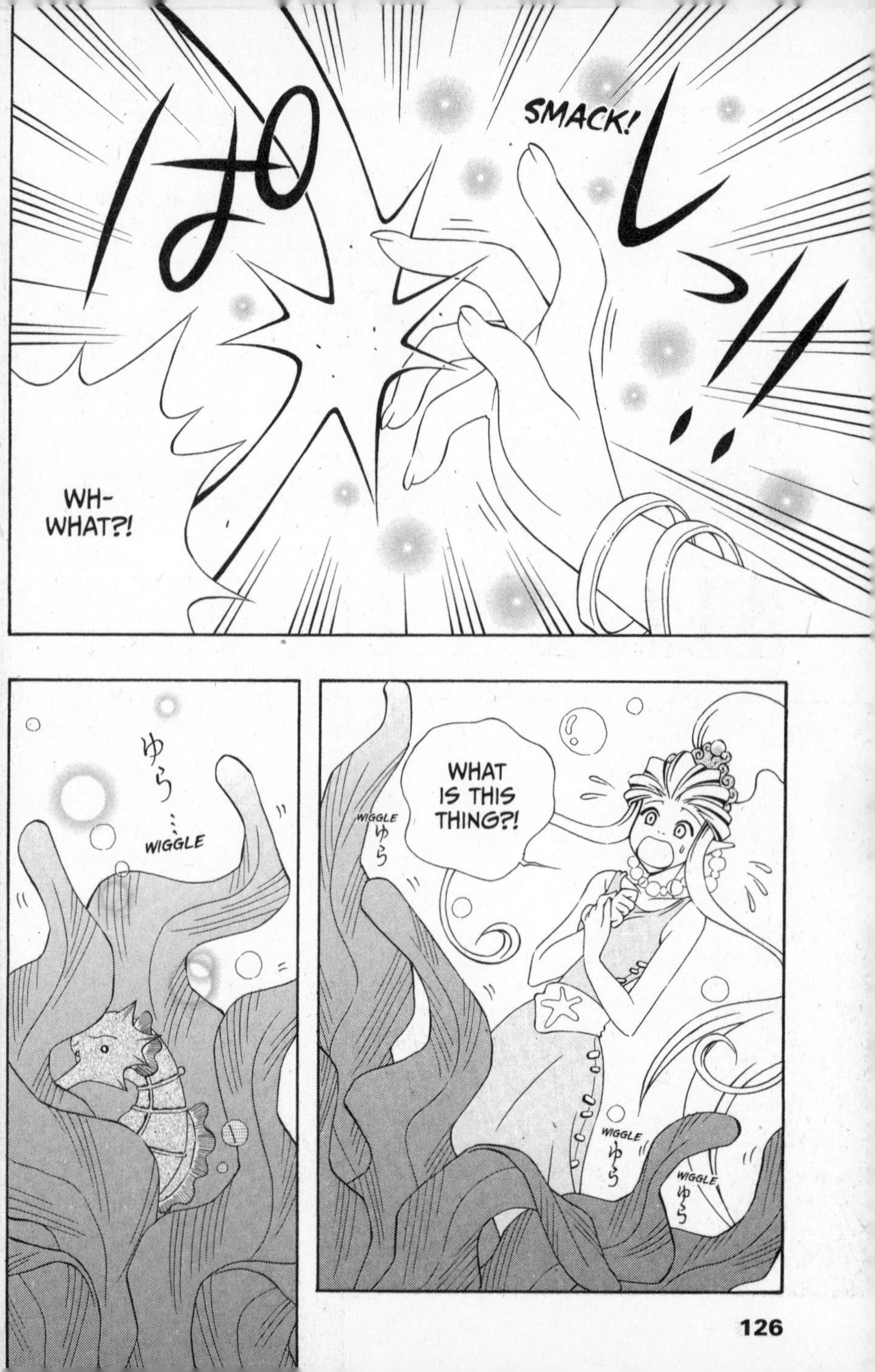
SMACK!
ぱしっ!!
WH-WHAT?!
WHAT IS THIS THING?!
WIGGLE ゆら
WIGGLE ゆら
WIGGLE ゆら
ゆら
WIGGLE

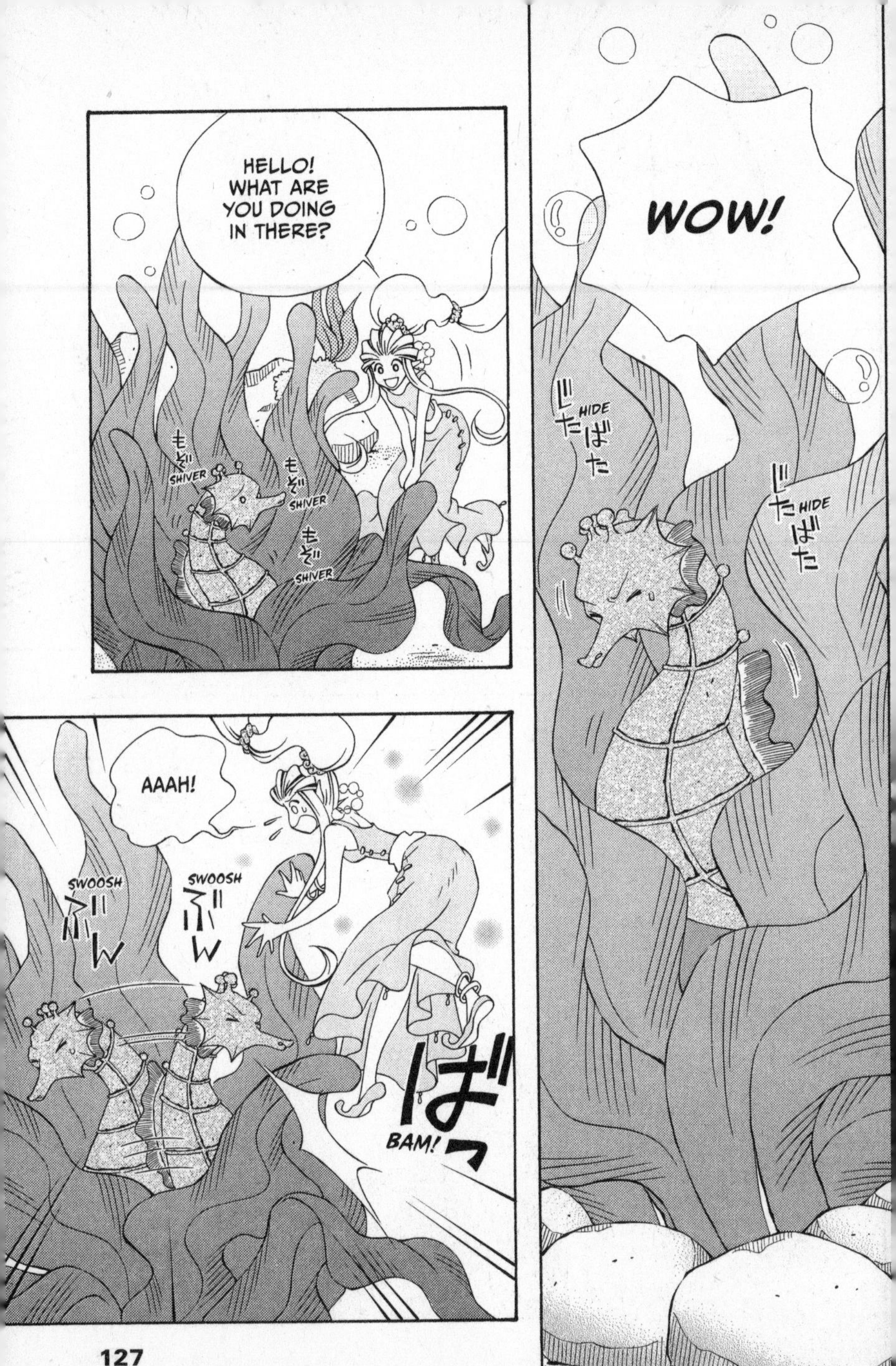
WOW!
じたばた HIDE
じたばた HIDE
HELLO! WHAT ARE YOU DOING IN THERE?
もぞ SHIVER
もぞ SHIVER
もぞ SHIVER
AAAH!
ぶぃ SWOOSH
ぶぃ SWOOSH
ばっ BAM!

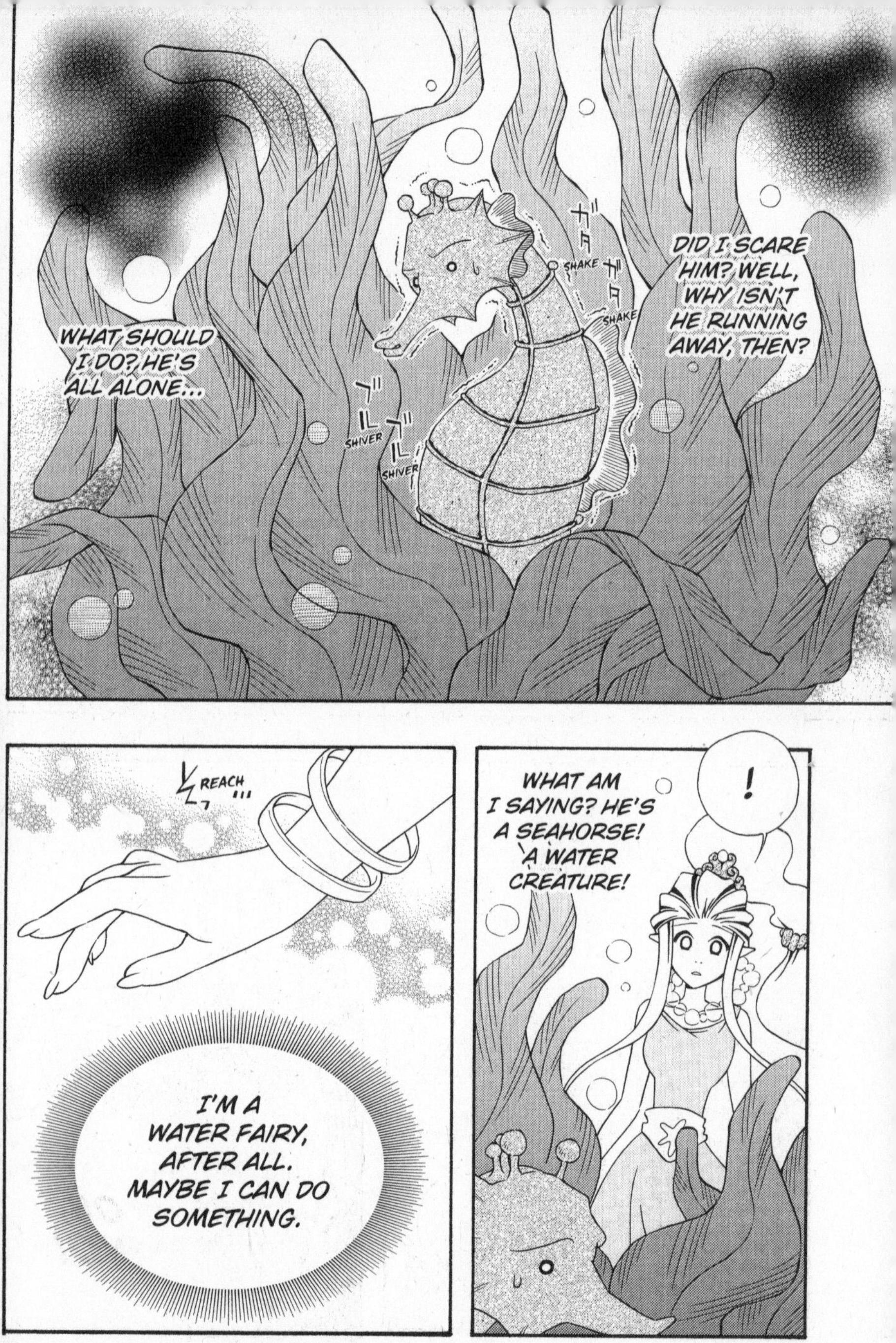
DID I SCARE HIM? WELL, WHY ISN'T HE RUNNING AWAY, THEN?
SHAKE
SHAKE
SHIVER
SHIVER
WHAT SHOULD I DO? HE'S ALL ALONE...
!
WHAT AM I SAYING? HE'S A SEAHORSE! A WATER CREATURE!
REACH...
I'M A WATER FAIRY, AFTER ALL. MAYBE I CAN DO SOMETHING.

HEY THERE! IS SOMETHING WRONG?

POOR THING! THAT'S WHY HE'S SHAKING!

DON'T WORRY, I'LL GET YOU OUT!

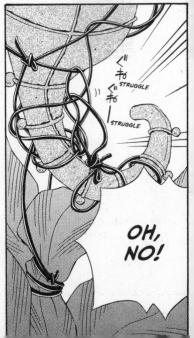

STRUGGLE

STRUGGLE

OH, NO!

JUST HANG ON, OKAY? I'M NOT LEAVING UNTIL YOU'RE FREE.

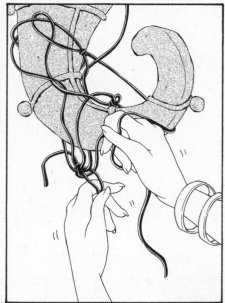

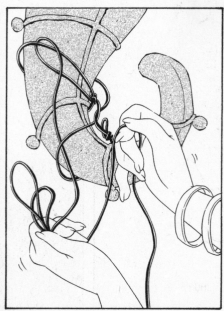

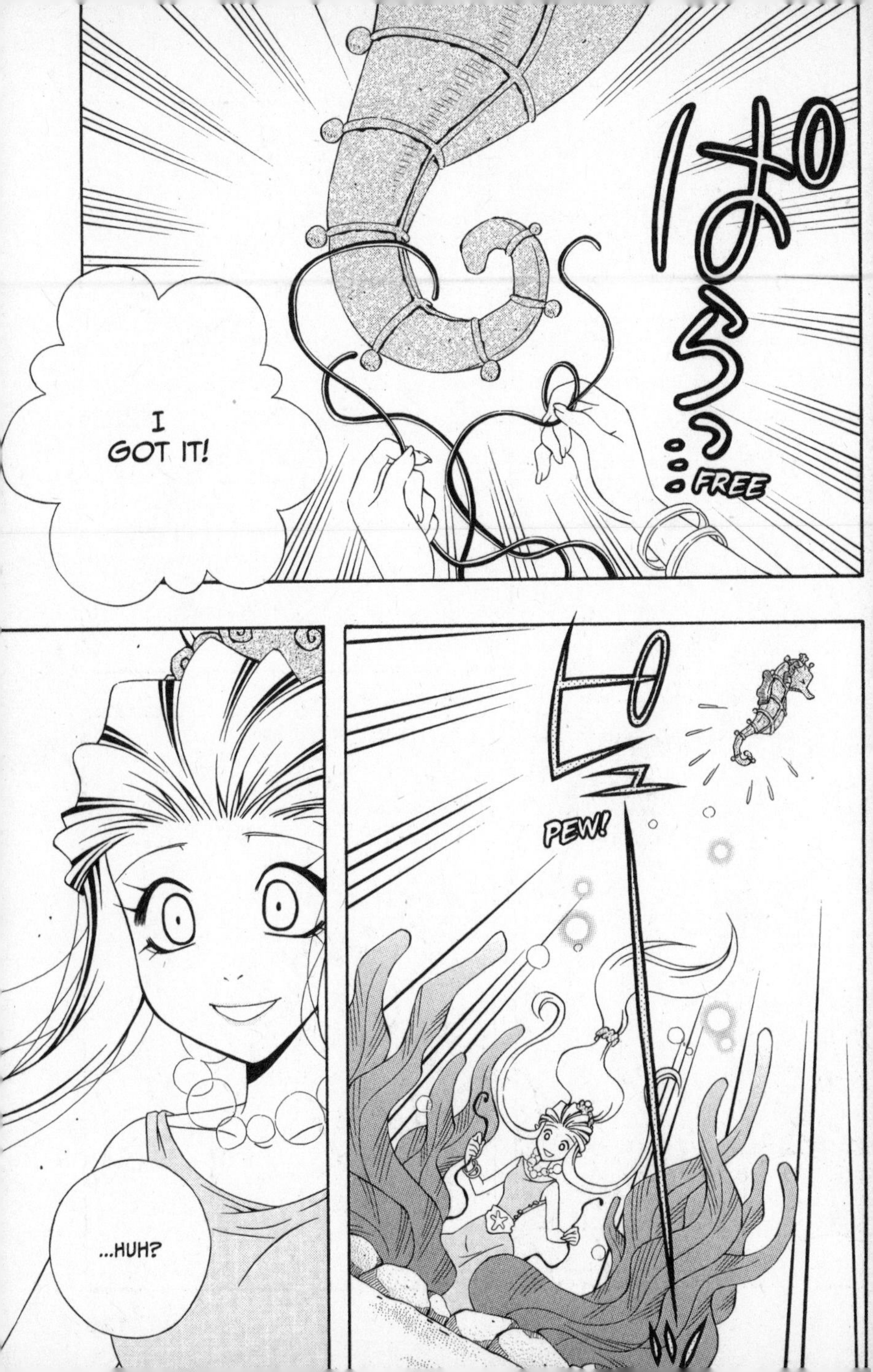
FREE
I GOT IT!
PEW!
...HUH?

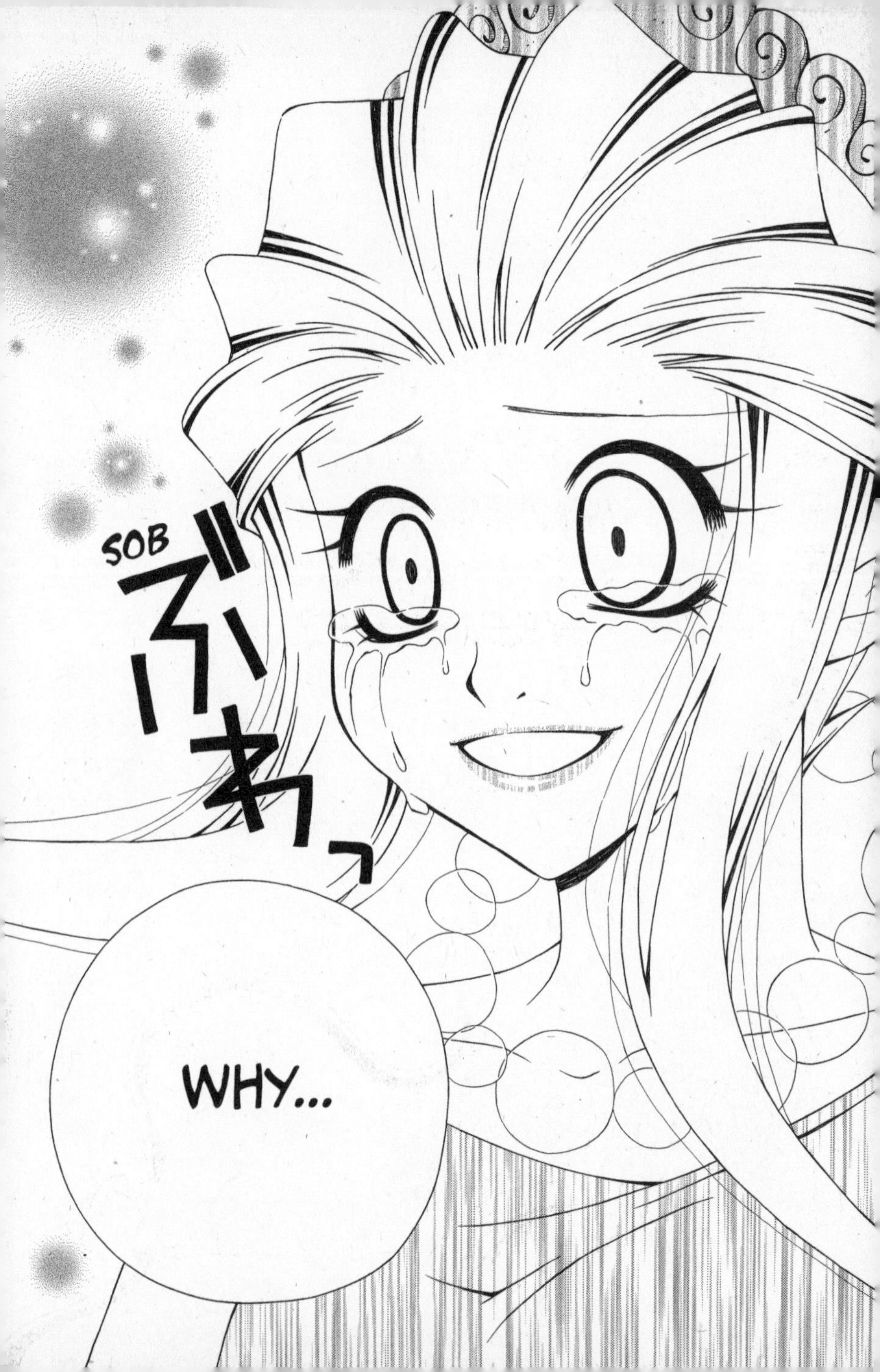
SOB
ヅびゃっ
WHY...

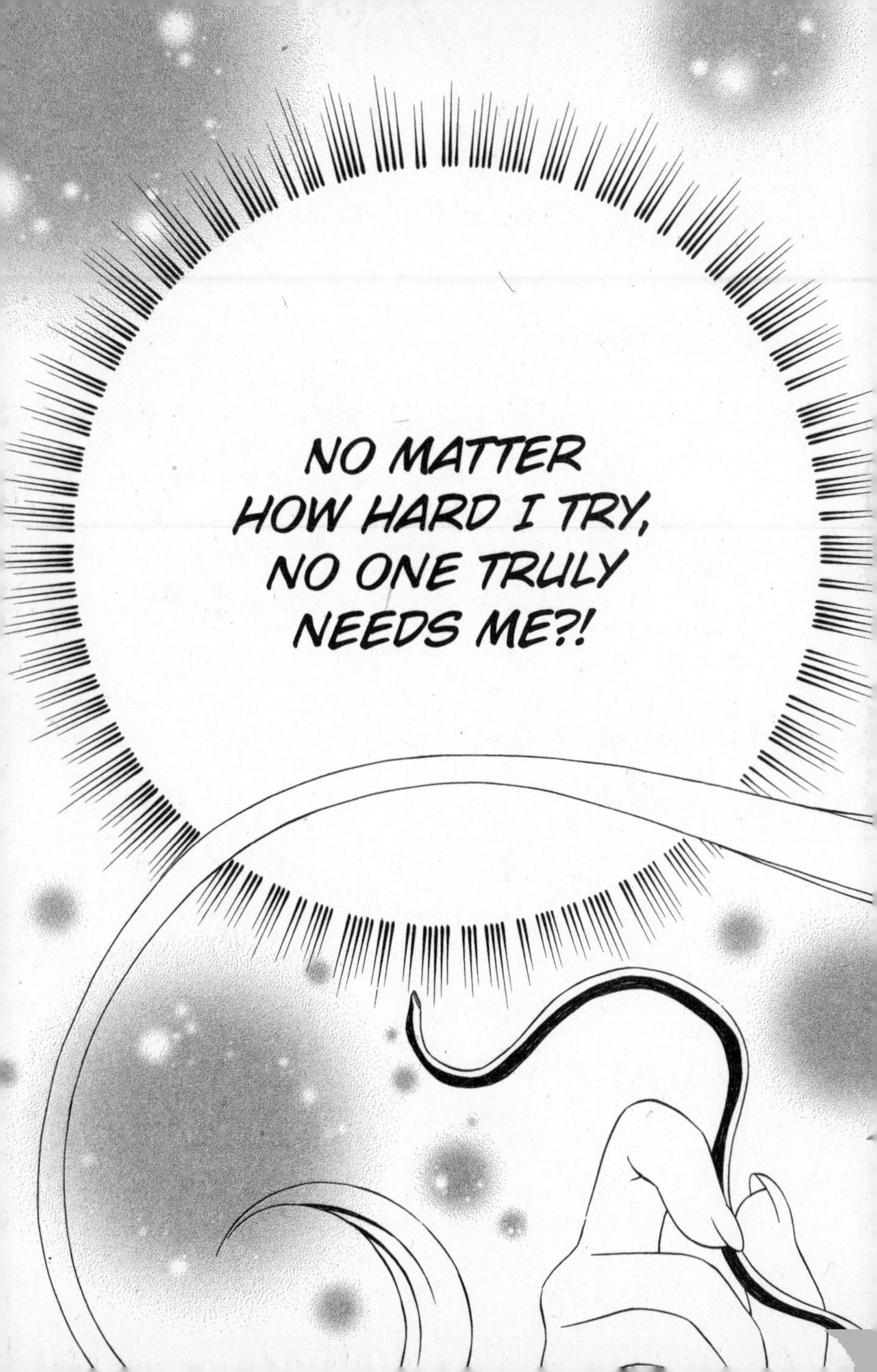
NO MATTER HOW HARD I TRY, NO ONE TRULY NEEDS ME?!

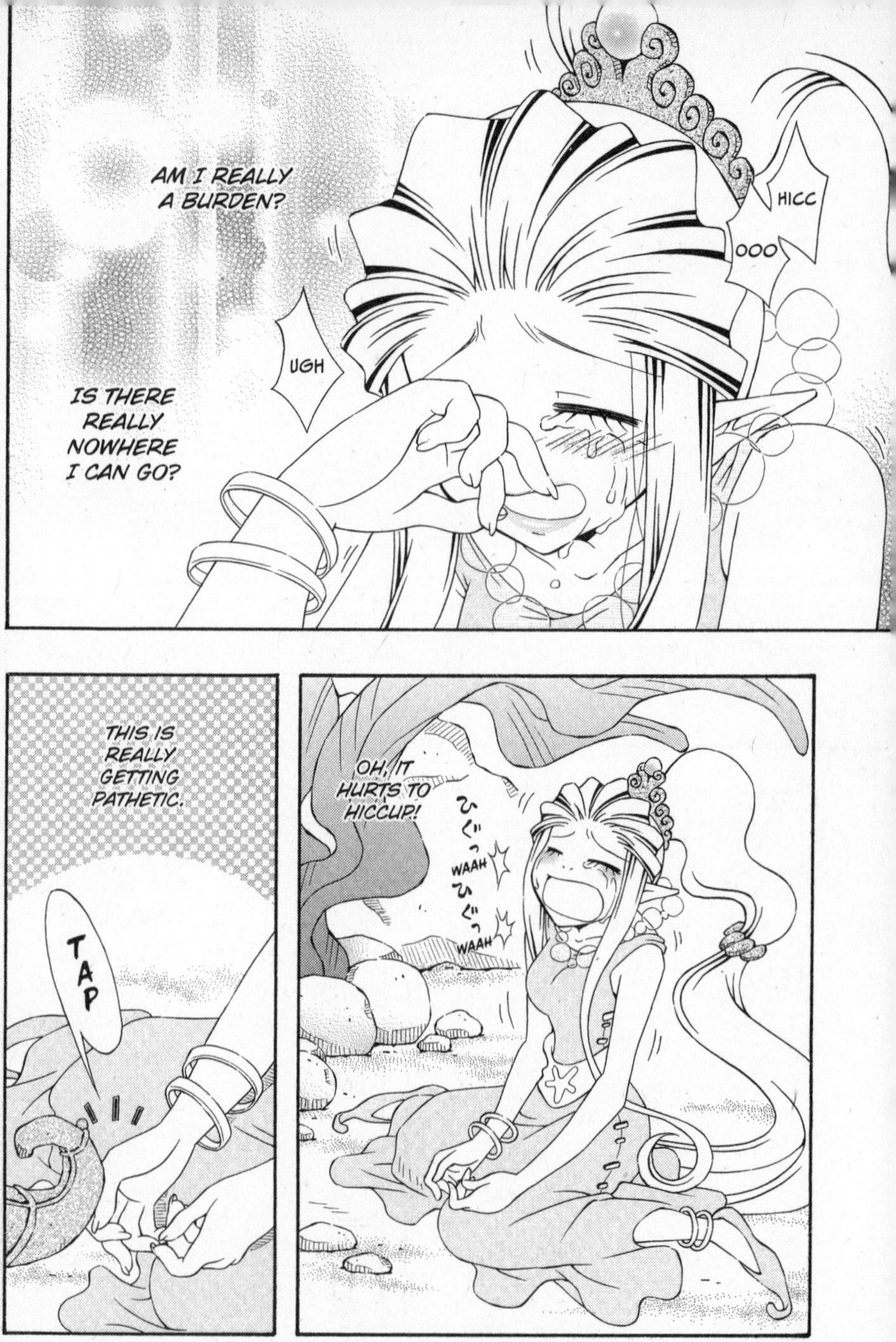
HICC
OOO
AM I REALLY A BURDEN?
UGH
IS THERE REALLY NOWHERE I CAN GO?
OH, IT HURTS TO HICCUP!
ひぐっ
WAAH
ひぐっ
WAAH
THIS IS REALLY GETTING PATHETIC.
TAP

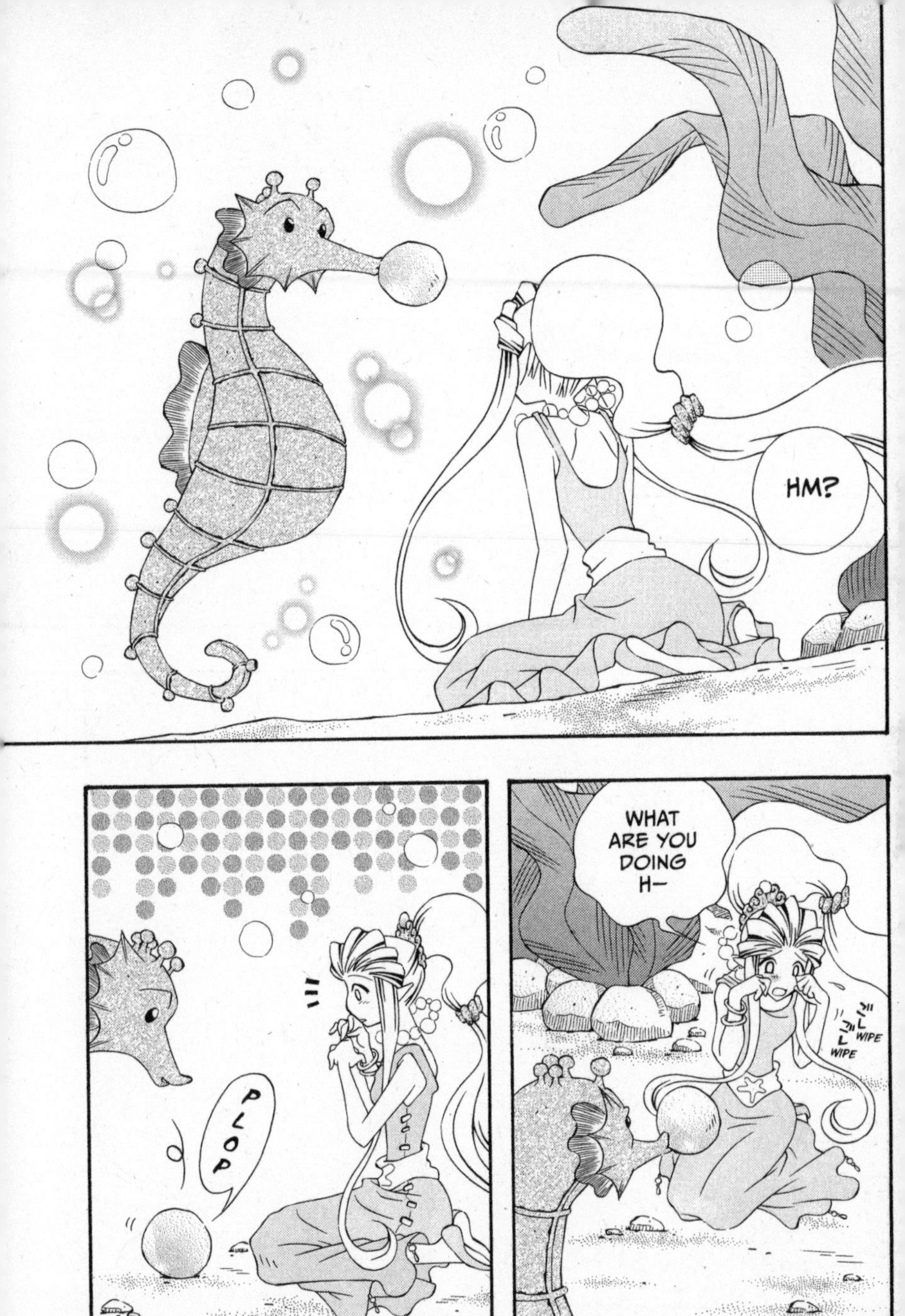
HM?
WHAT ARE YOU DOING H—
WIPE WIPE
PLOP

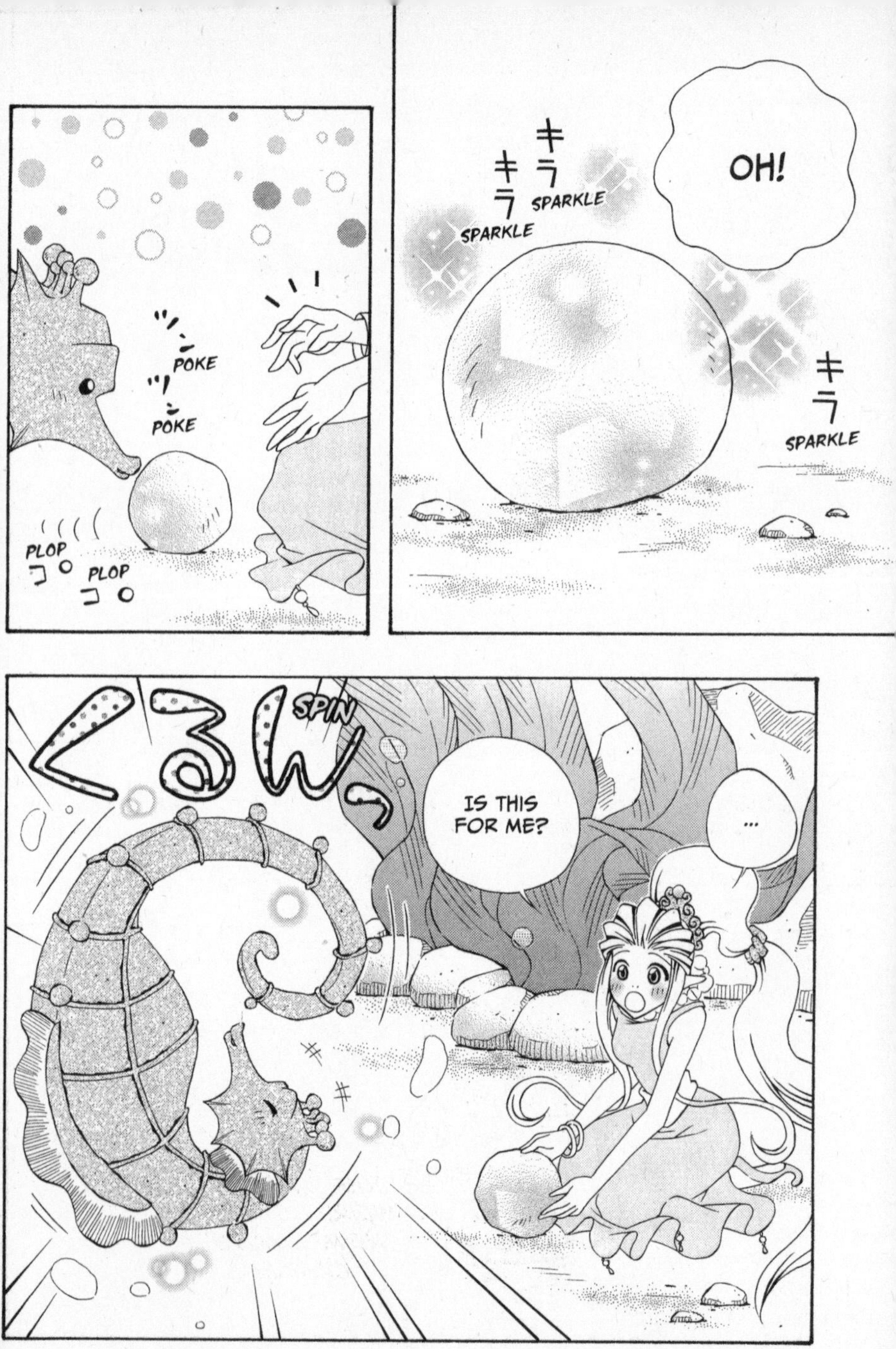
OH!
キラ
SPARKLE
キラ
SPARKLE
キラ
SPARKLE
POKE
POKE
PLOP
PLOP
くるん
SPIN
...
IS THIS FOR ME?

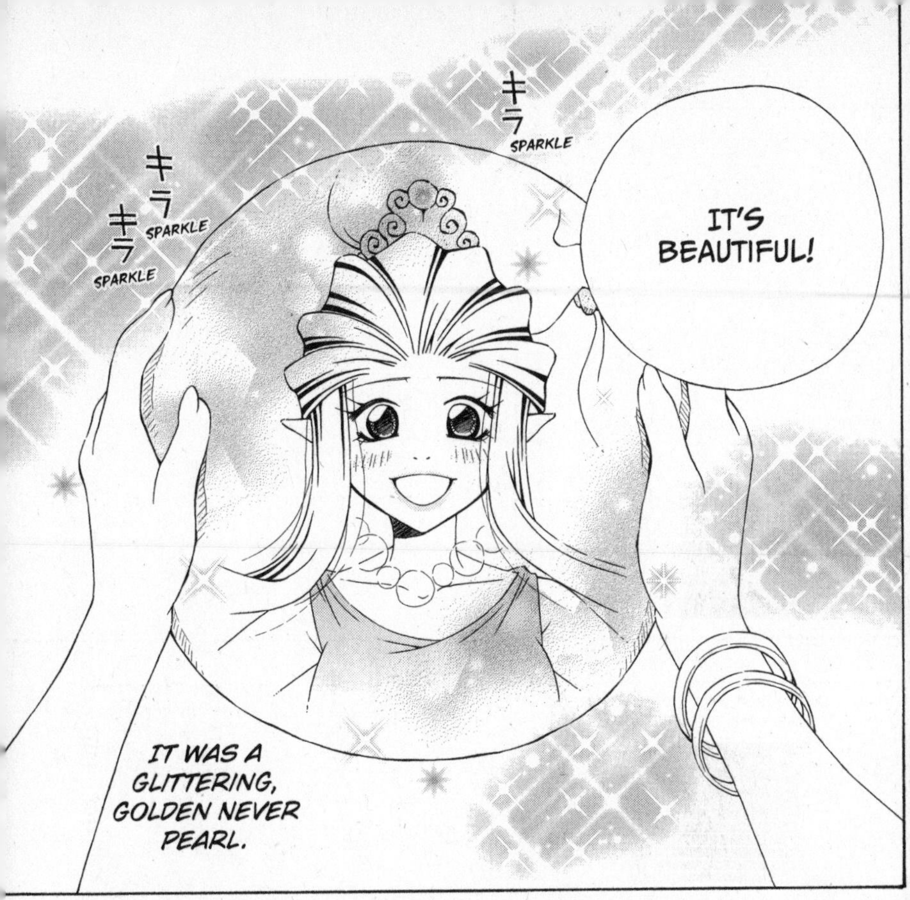
IT'S BEAUTIFUL!
キラ SPARKLE
キラ SPARKLE
キラ SPARKLE
IT WAS A GLITTERING, GOLDEN NEVER PEARL.

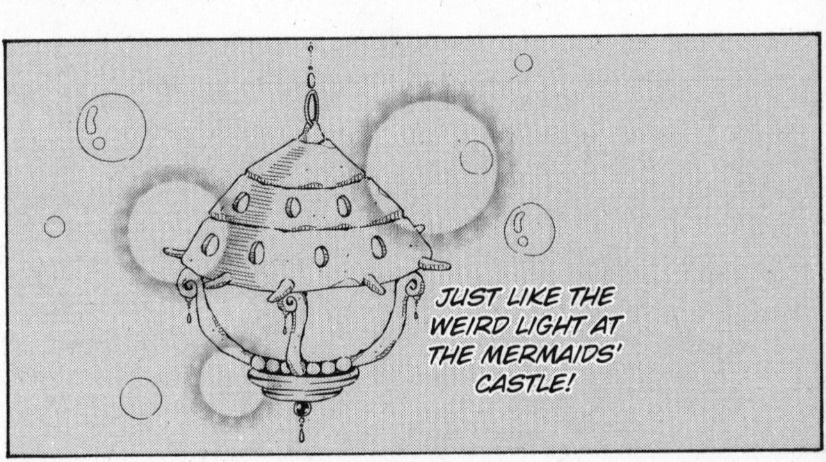
JUST LIKE THE WEIRD LIGHT AT THE MERMAIDS' CASTLE!

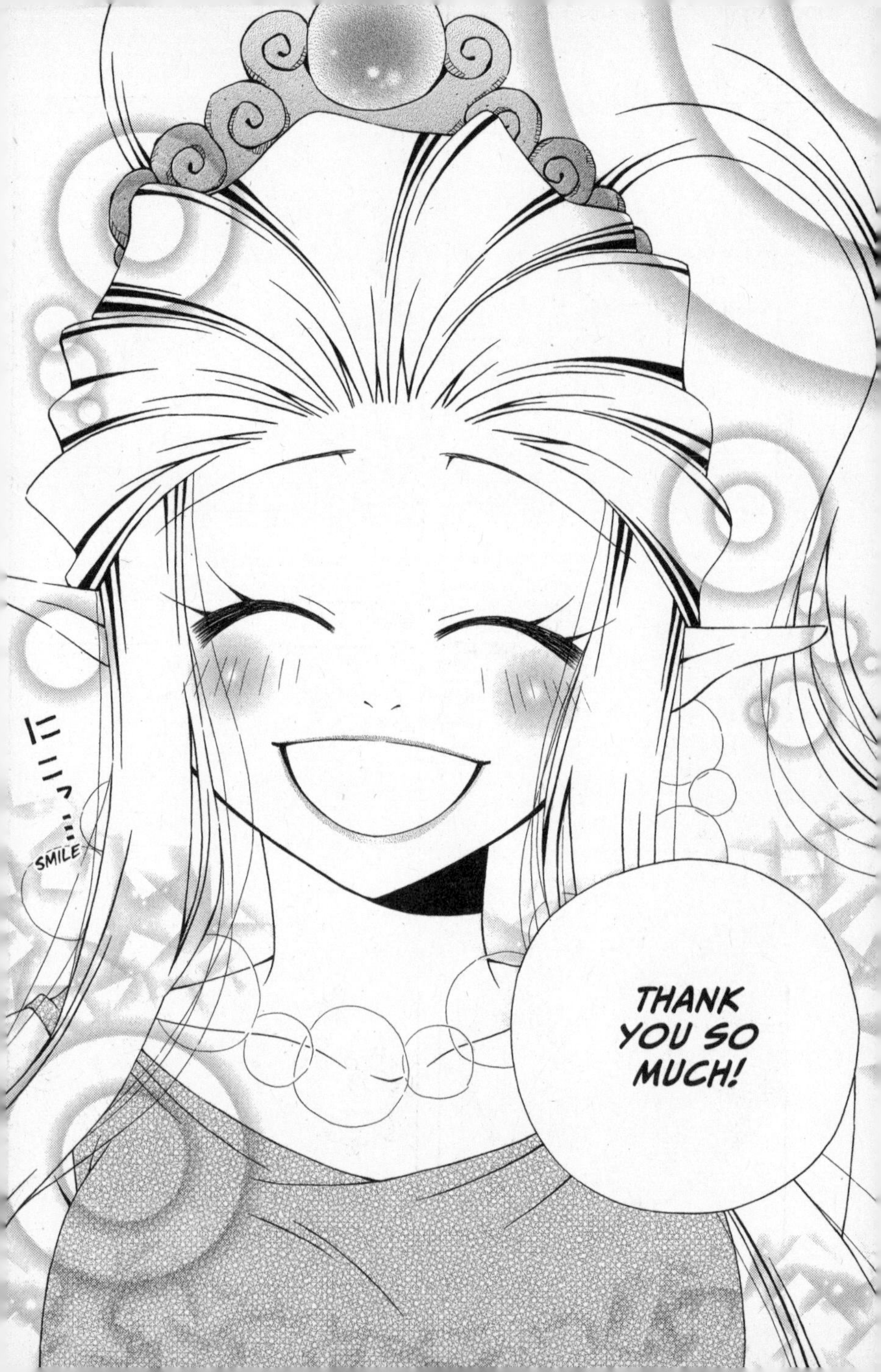
THANK YOU SO MUCH!
にこっ
SMILE

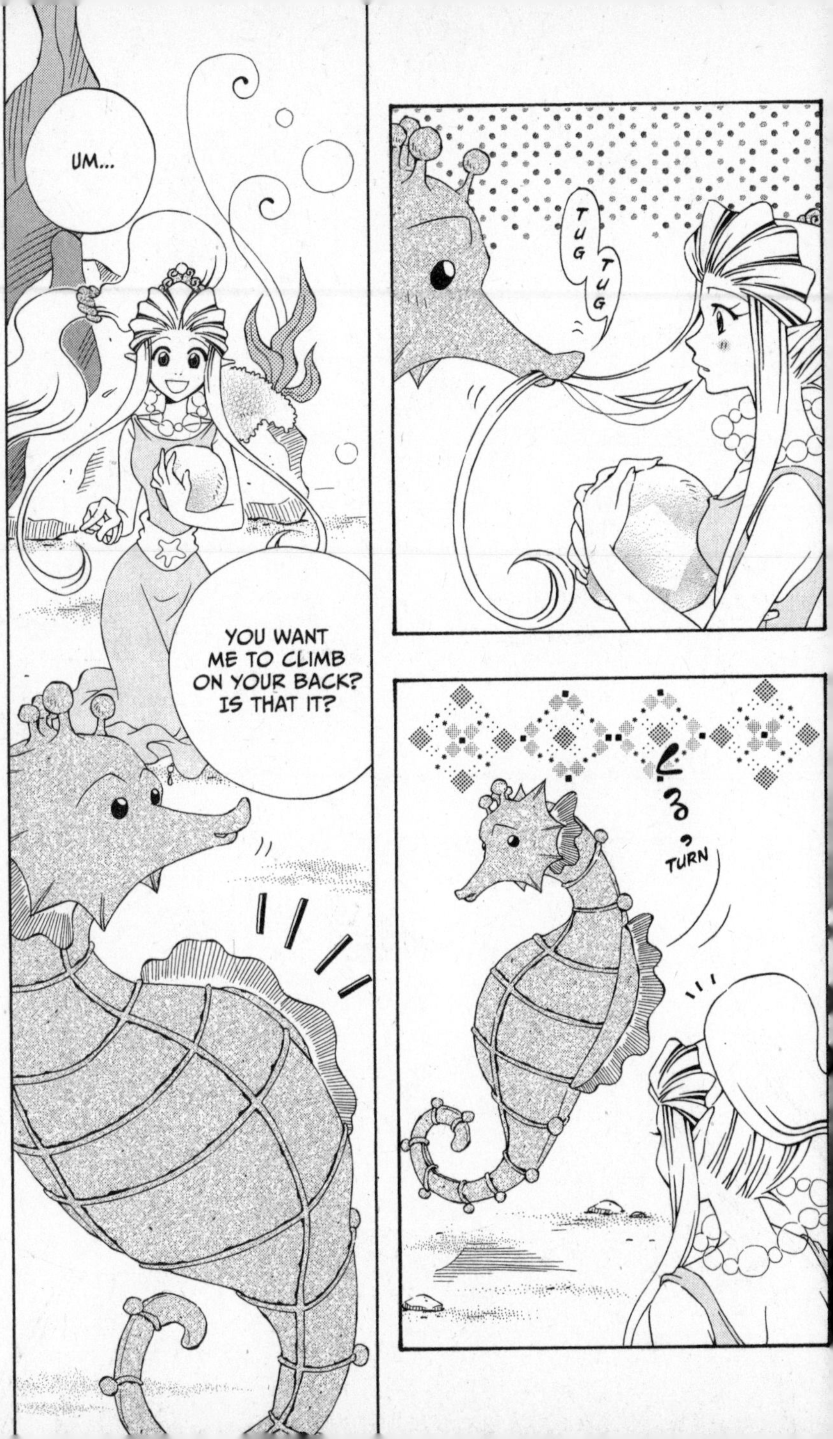
TUG TUG
くる
TURN
UM...
YOU WANT ME TO CLIMB ON YOUR BACK? IS THAT IT?

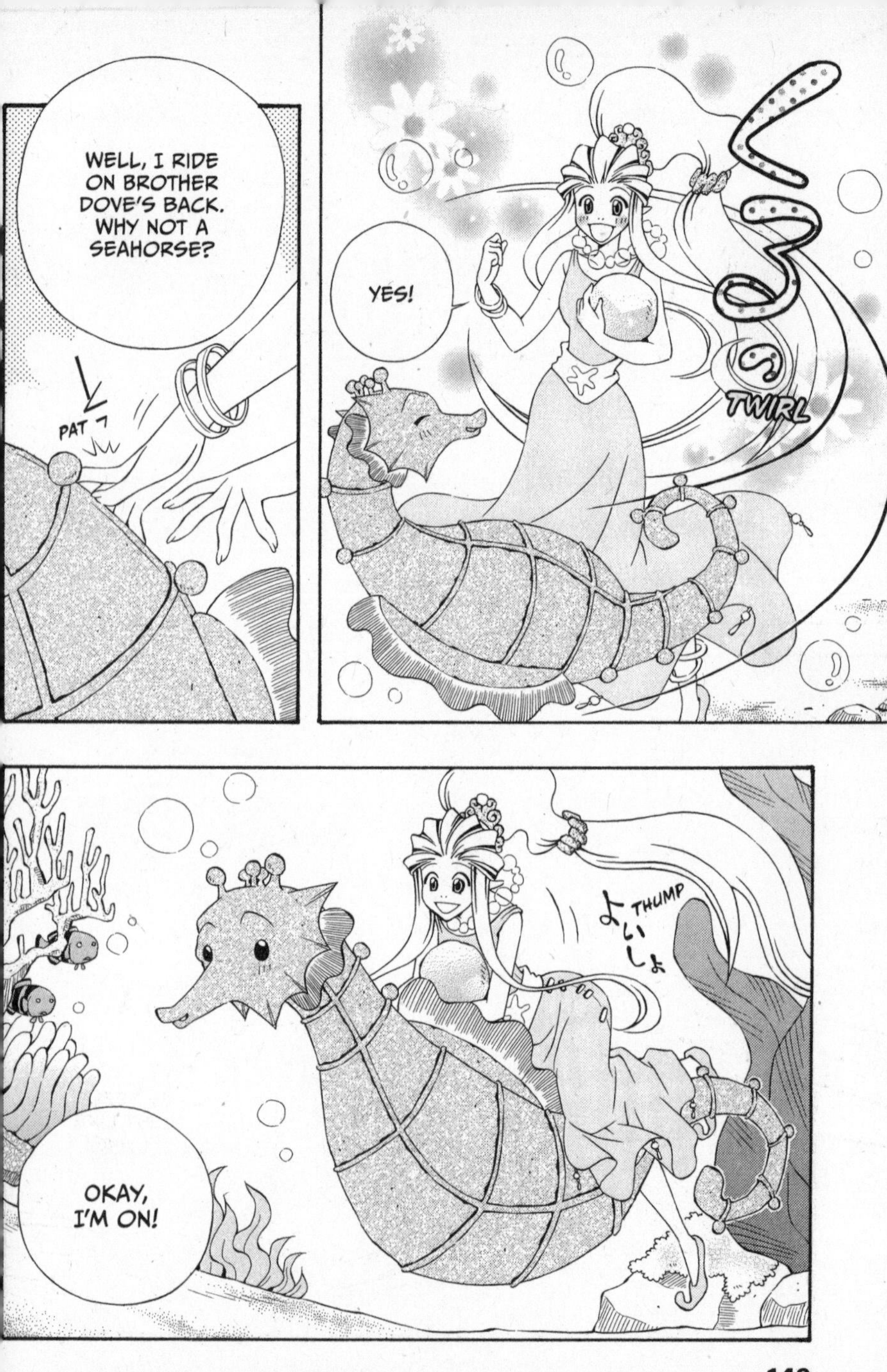
YES!
TWIRL
WELL, I RIDE ON BROTHER DOVE'S BACK. WHY NOT A SEAHORSE?
PAT
THUMP
よいしょ
OKAY, I'M ON!

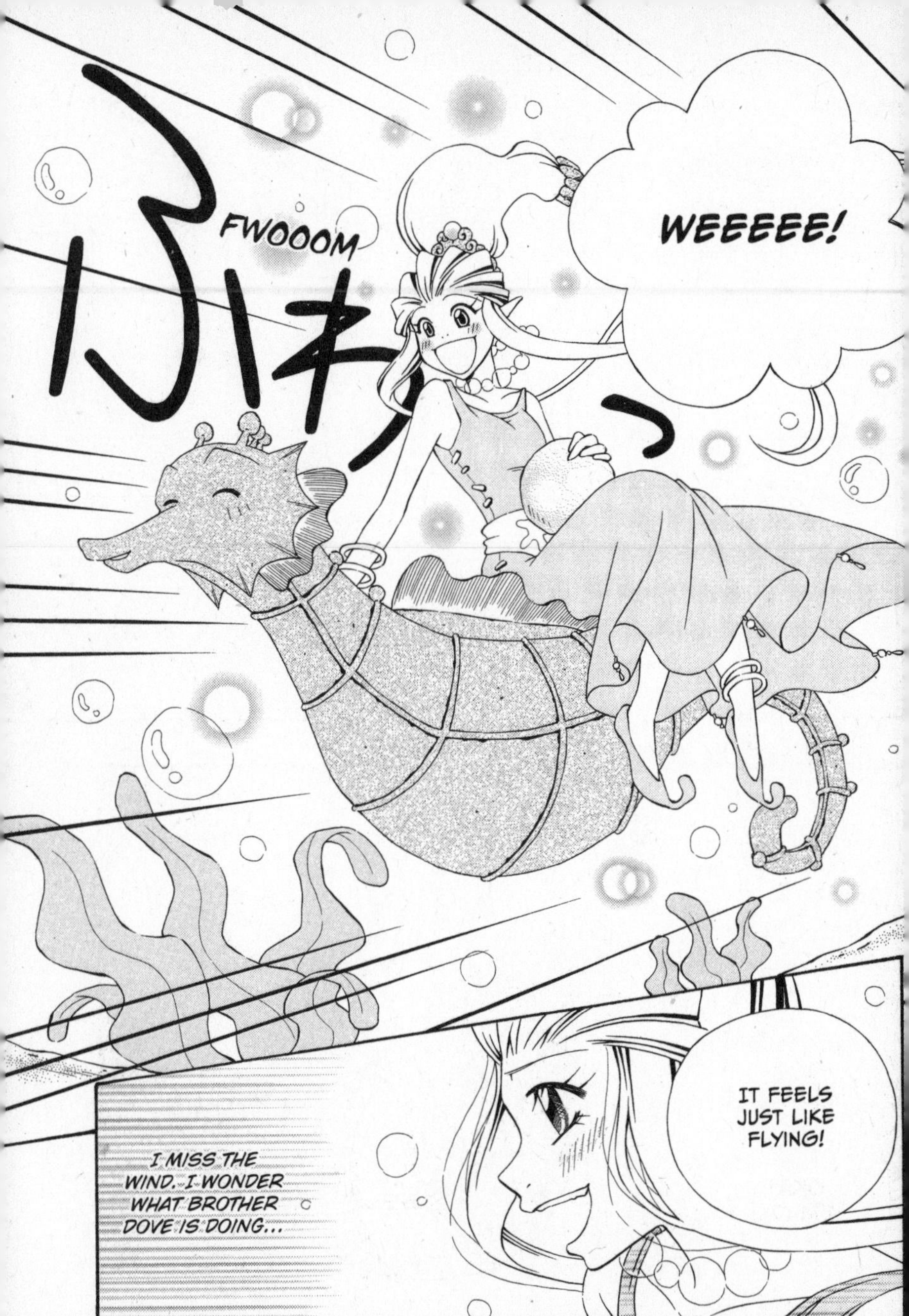
WEEEEE!
FWOOOM
IT FEELS JUST LIKE FLYING!
I MISS THE WIND. I WONDER WHAT BROTHER DOVE IS DOING...

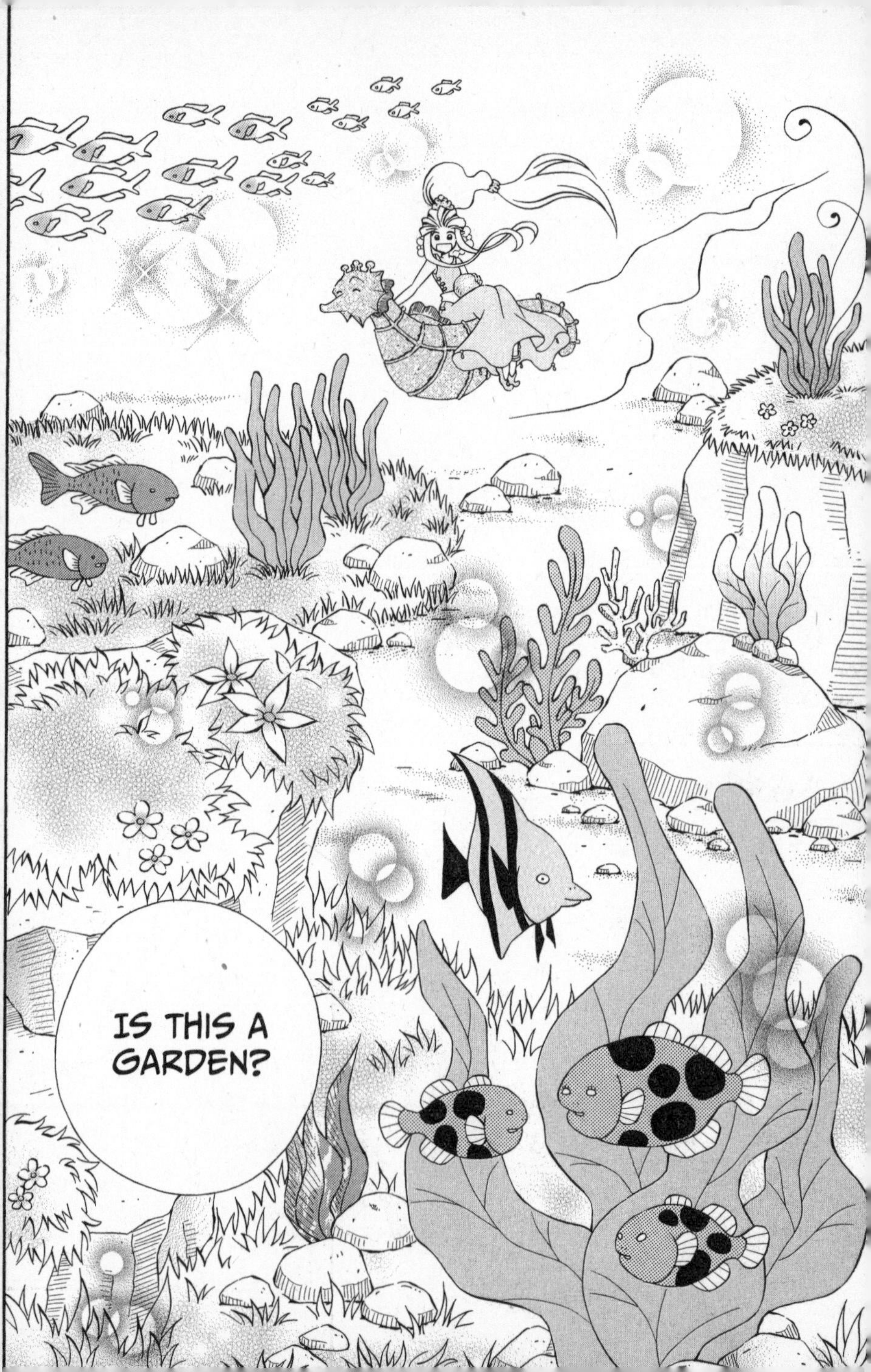
IS THIS A GARDEN?

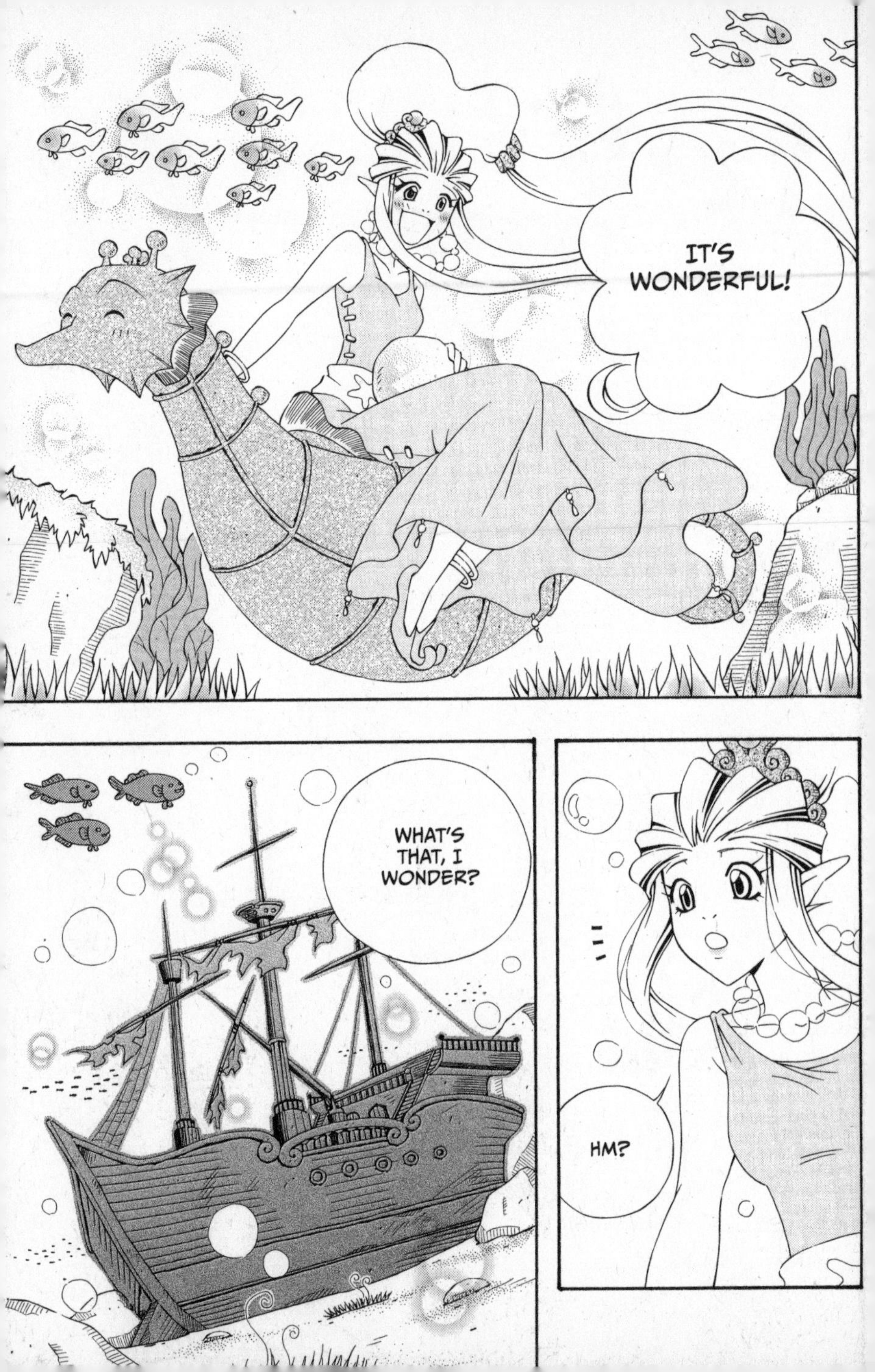
IT'S WONDERFUL!
HM?
WHAT'S THAT, I WONDER?

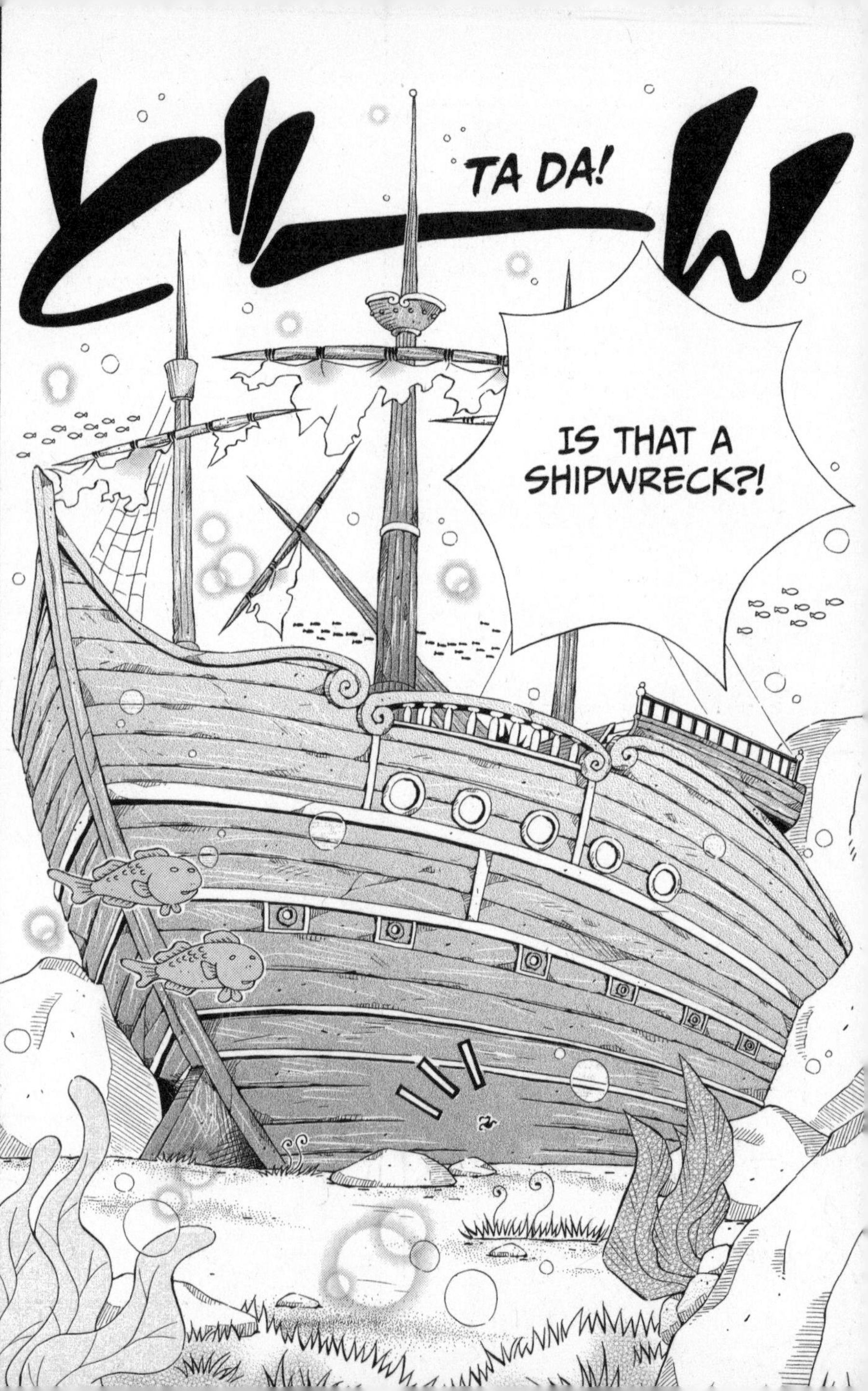
とりーん
TA DA!
IS THAT A SHIPWRECK?!

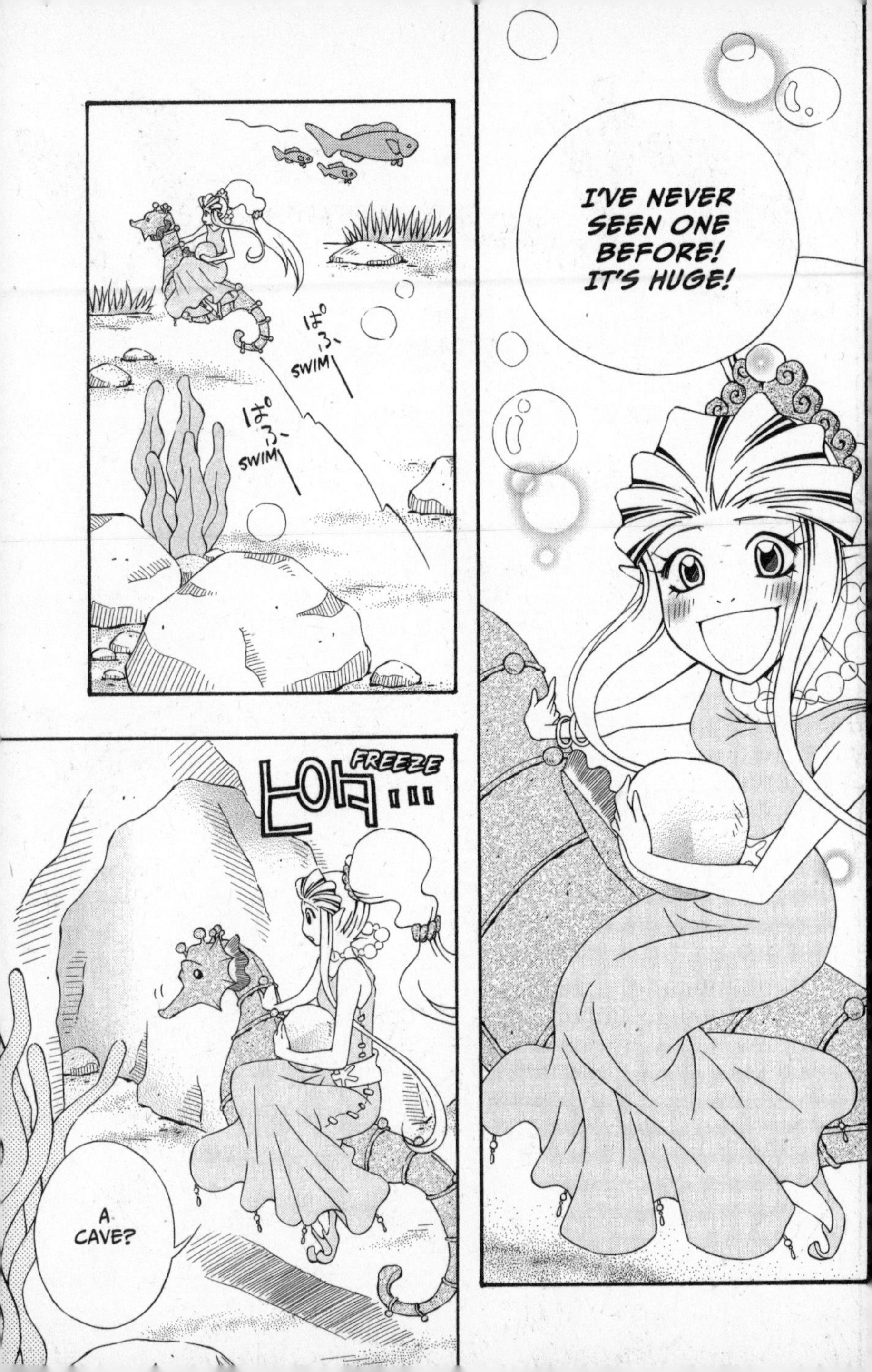

I'VE NEVER SEEN ONE BEFORE! IT'S HUGE!
ぱふ
SWIM
ぱふ
SWIM
FREEZE
A CAVE?

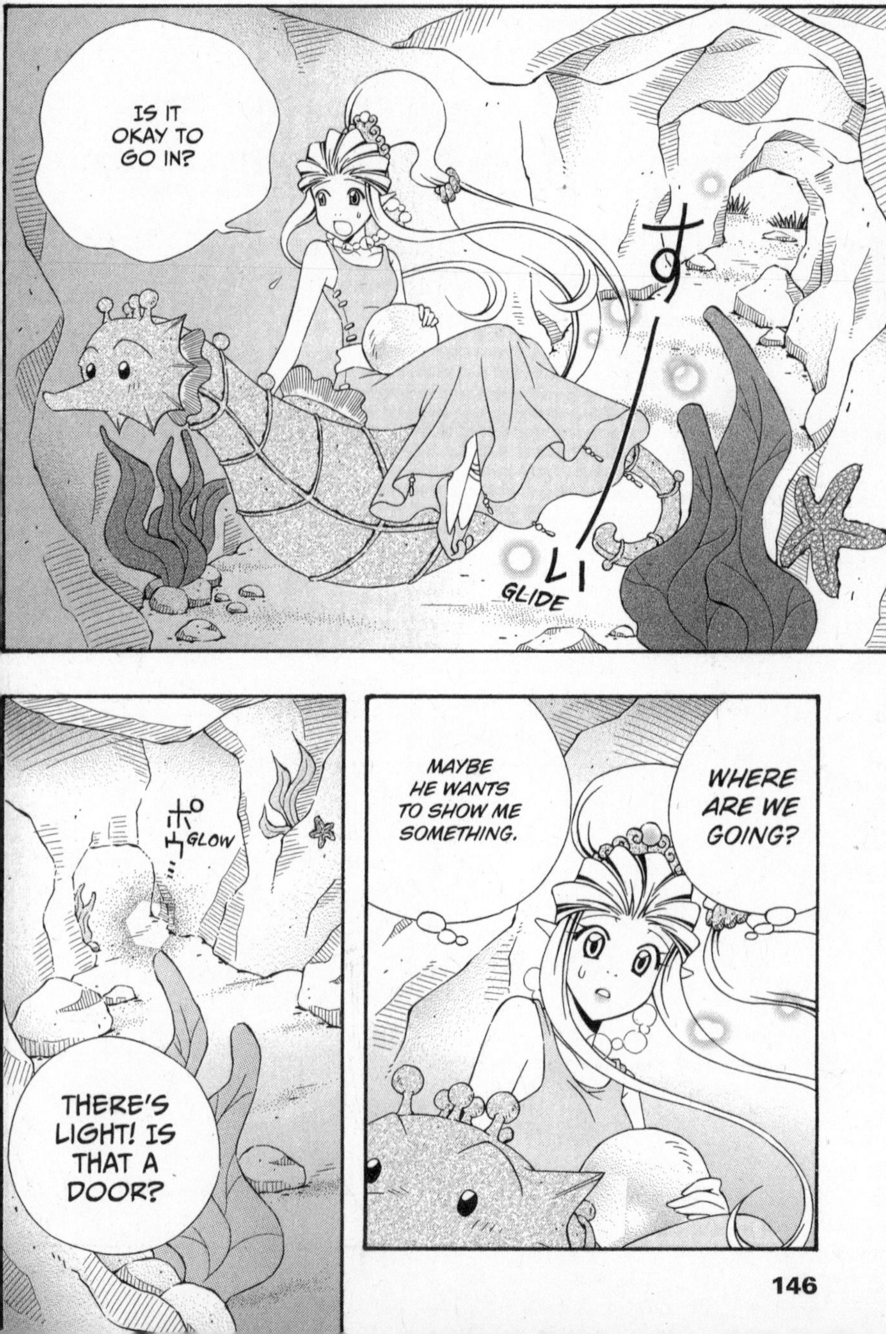
IS IT OKAY TO GO IN?
GLIDE
WHERE ARE WE GOING?
MAYBE HE WANTS TO SHOW ME SOMETHING.
GLOW
THERE'S LIGHT! IS THAT A DOOR?

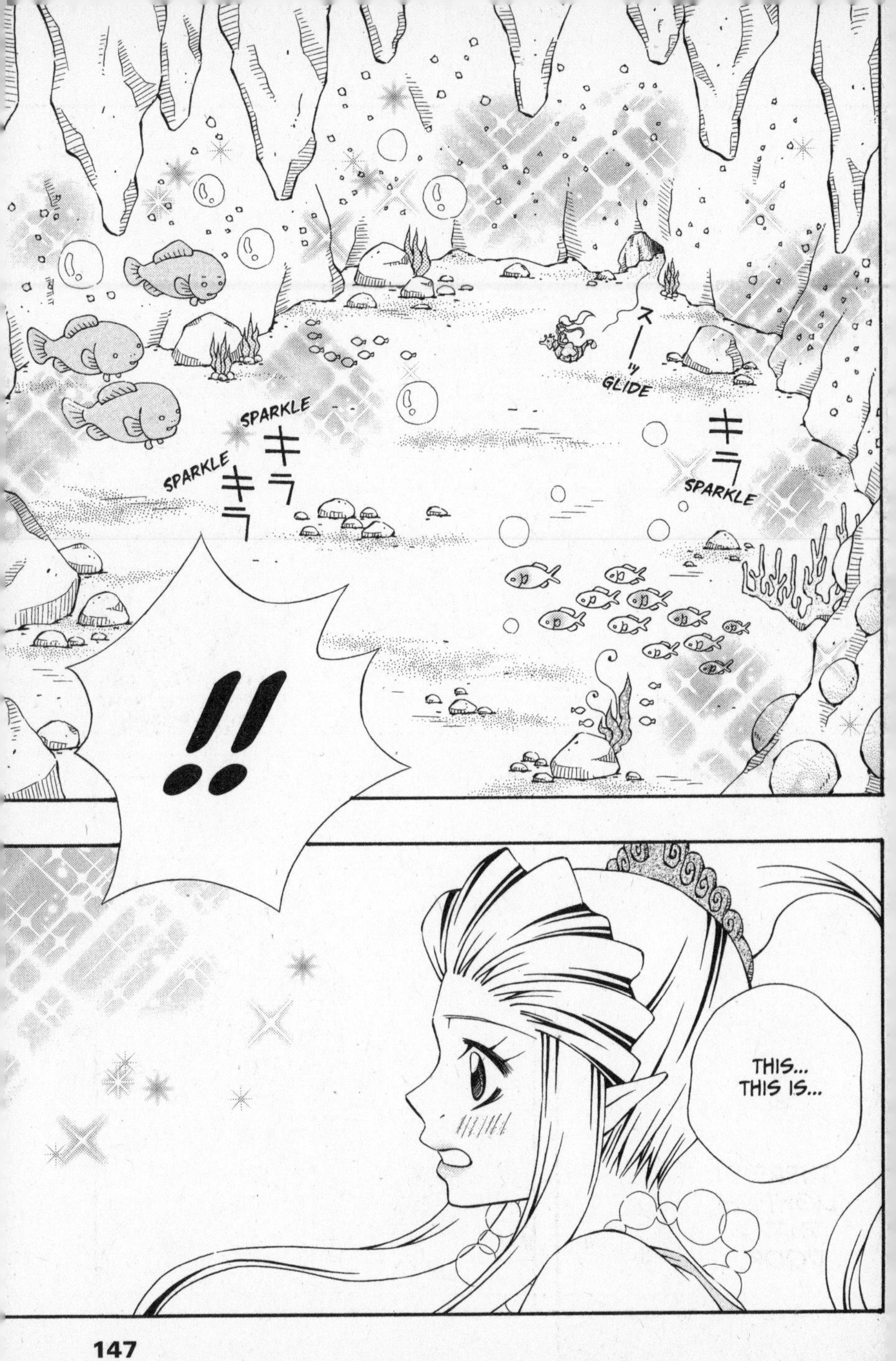

スーッ
GLIDE
キラ
SPARKLE
SPARKLE
キラ
SPARKLE
キラ
!!
THIS... THIS IS...

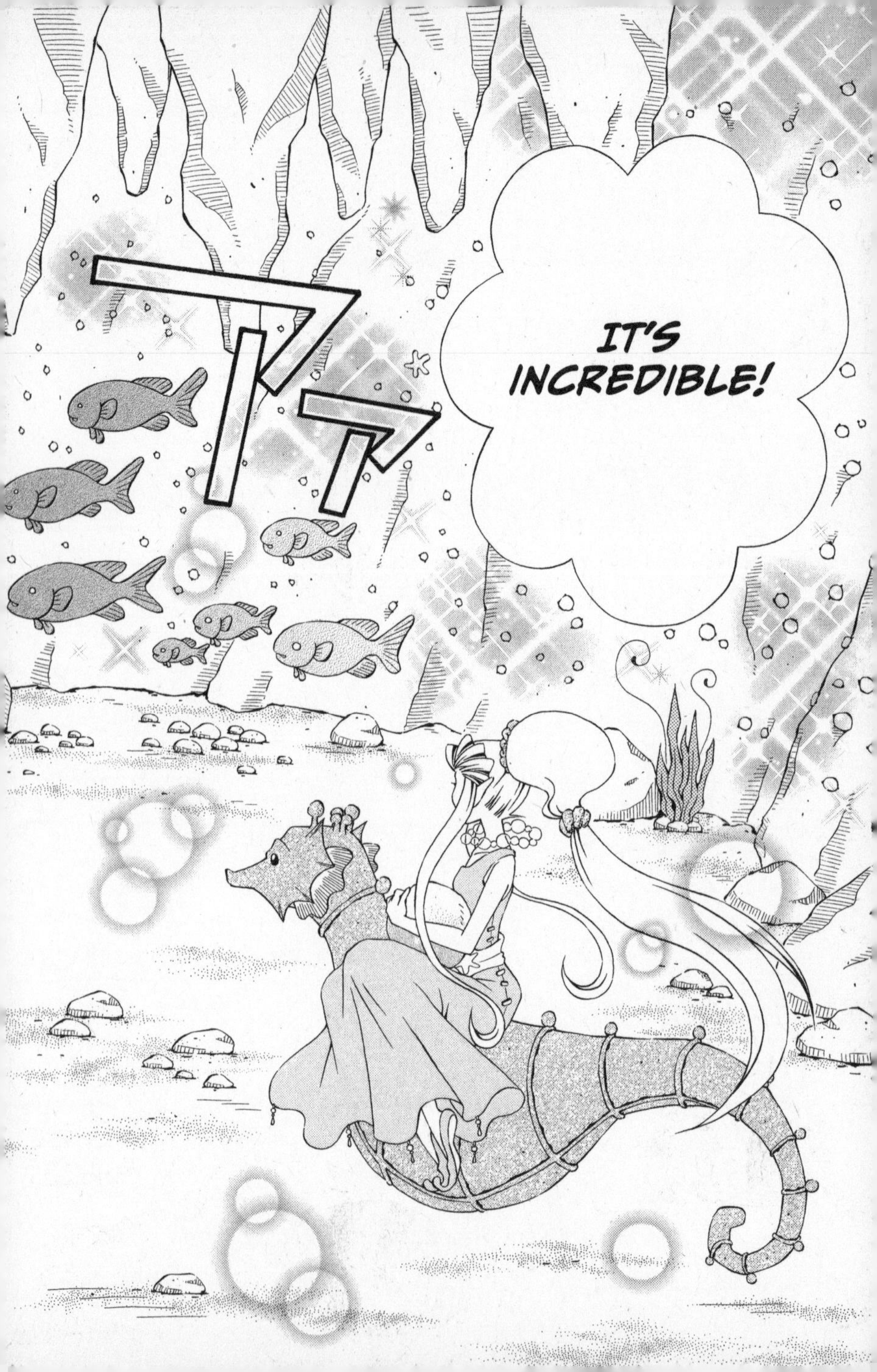
アア
IT'S INCREDIBLE!

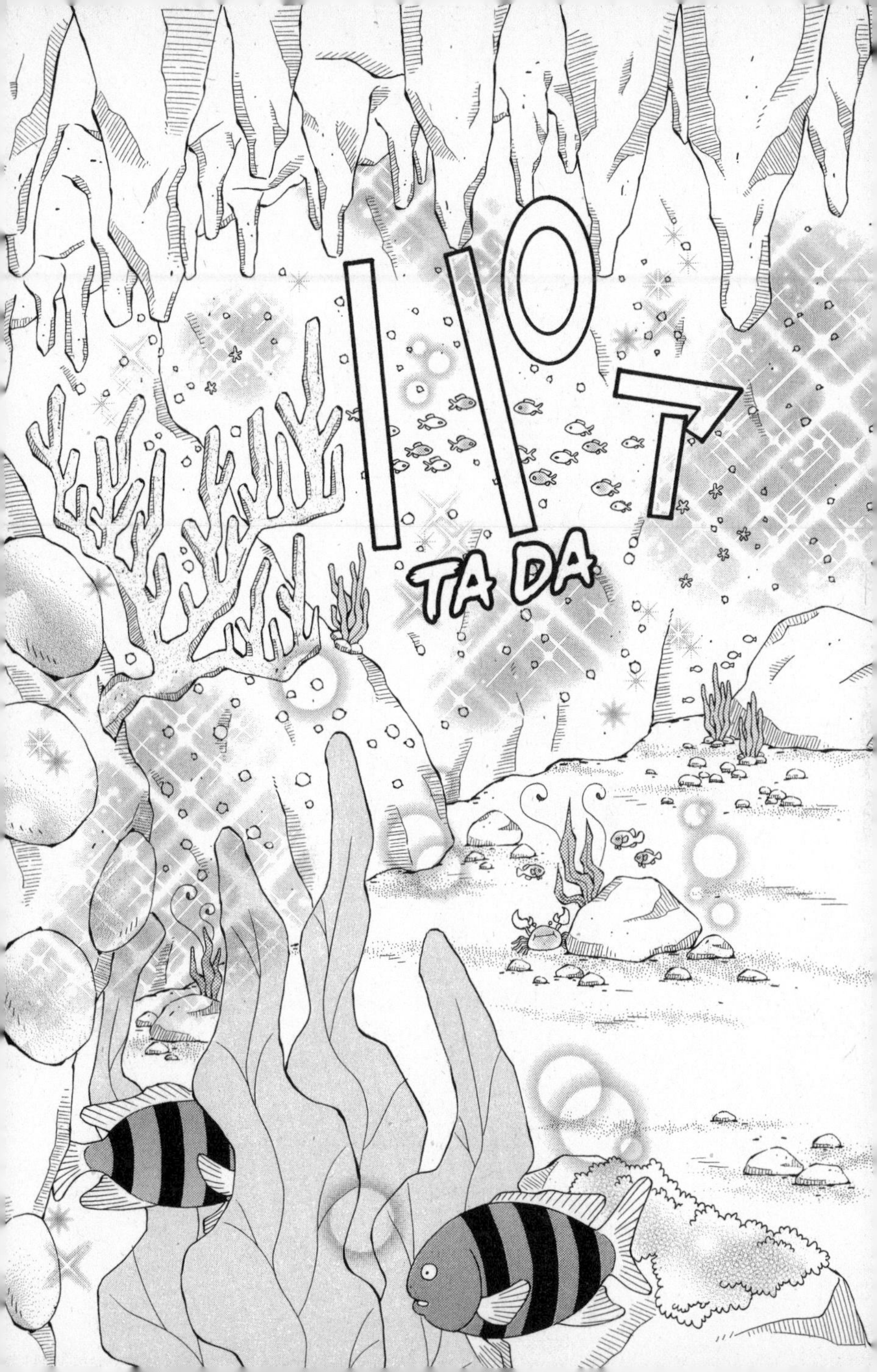
TA DA

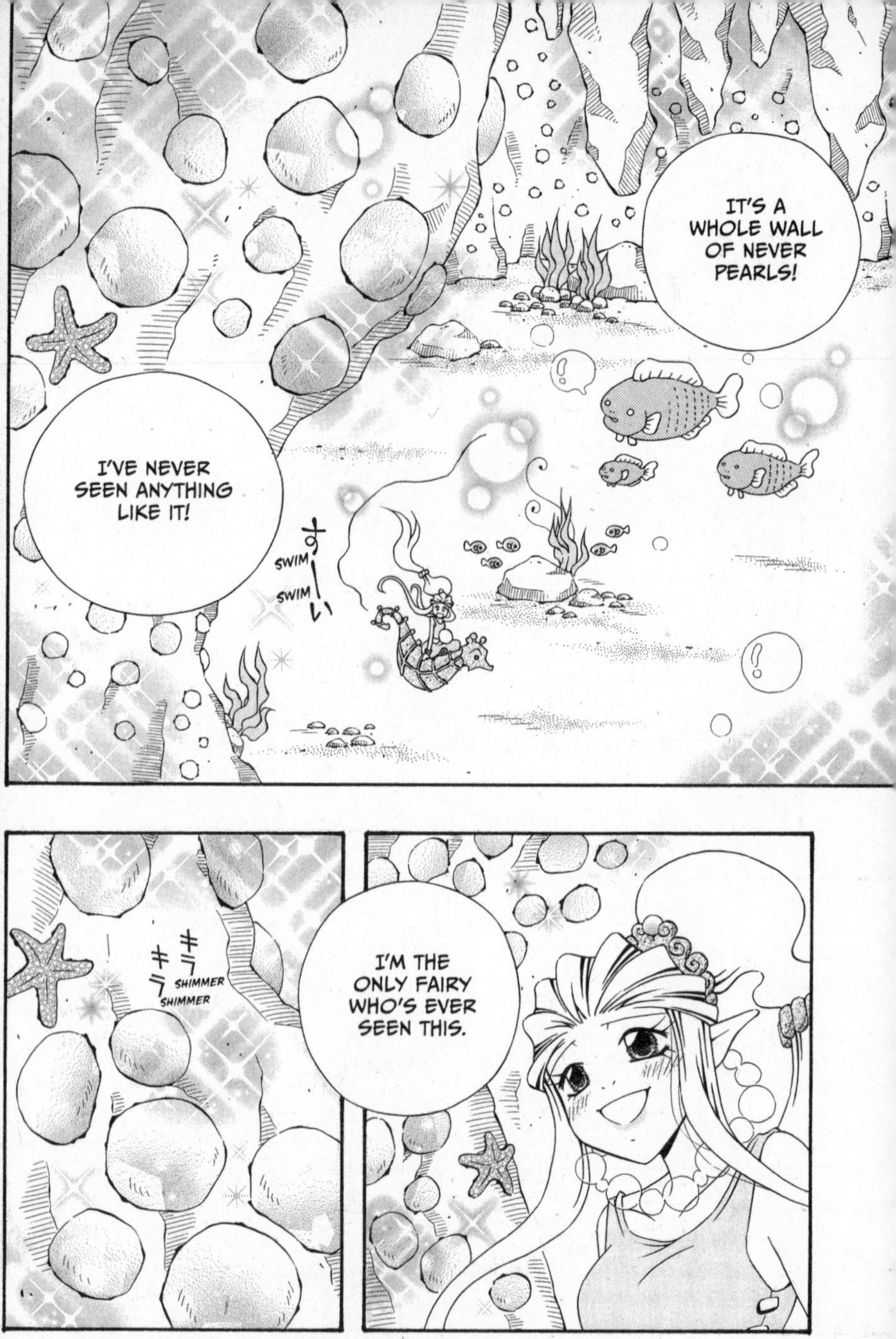
IT'S A WHOLE WALL OF NEVER PEARLS!
I'VE NEVER SEEN ANYTHING LIKE IT!
すーい
SWIM SWIM
I'M THE ONLY FAIRY WHO'S EVER SEEN THIS.
キラキラ
SHIMMER SHIMMER

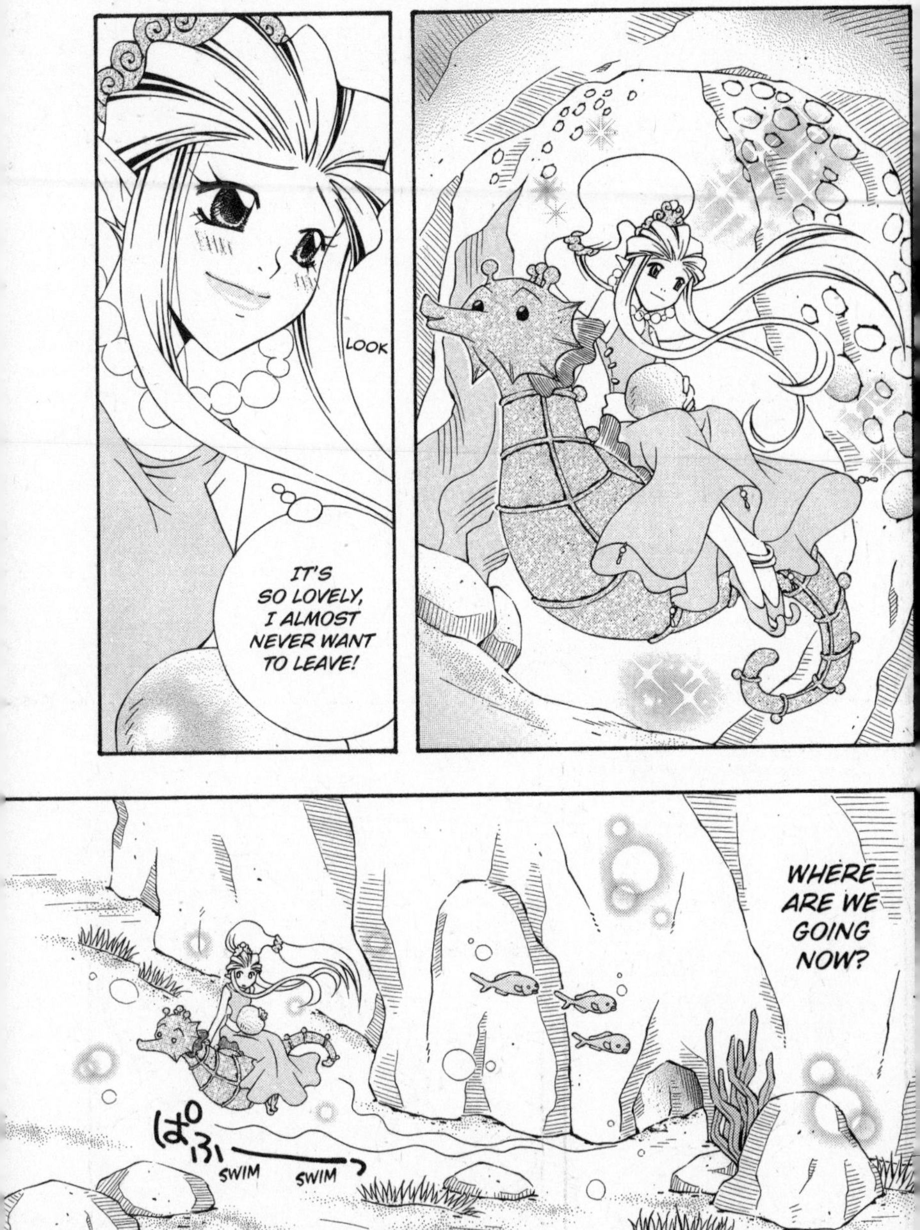
LOOK
IT'S SO LOVELY, I ALMOST NEVER WANT TO LEAVE!
WHERE ARE WE GOING NOW?
ぱふー
SWIM SWIM

WHERE ARE WE?
ぴょこっ
BOINK
ぴょこ
BOINK

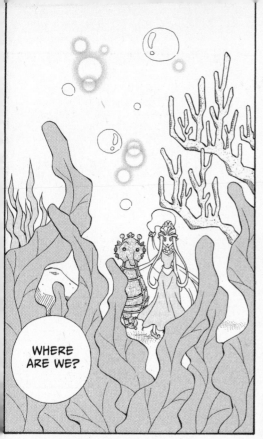

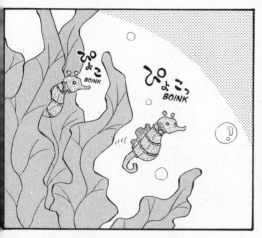

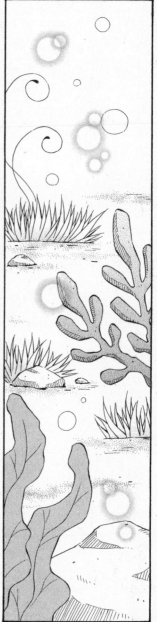

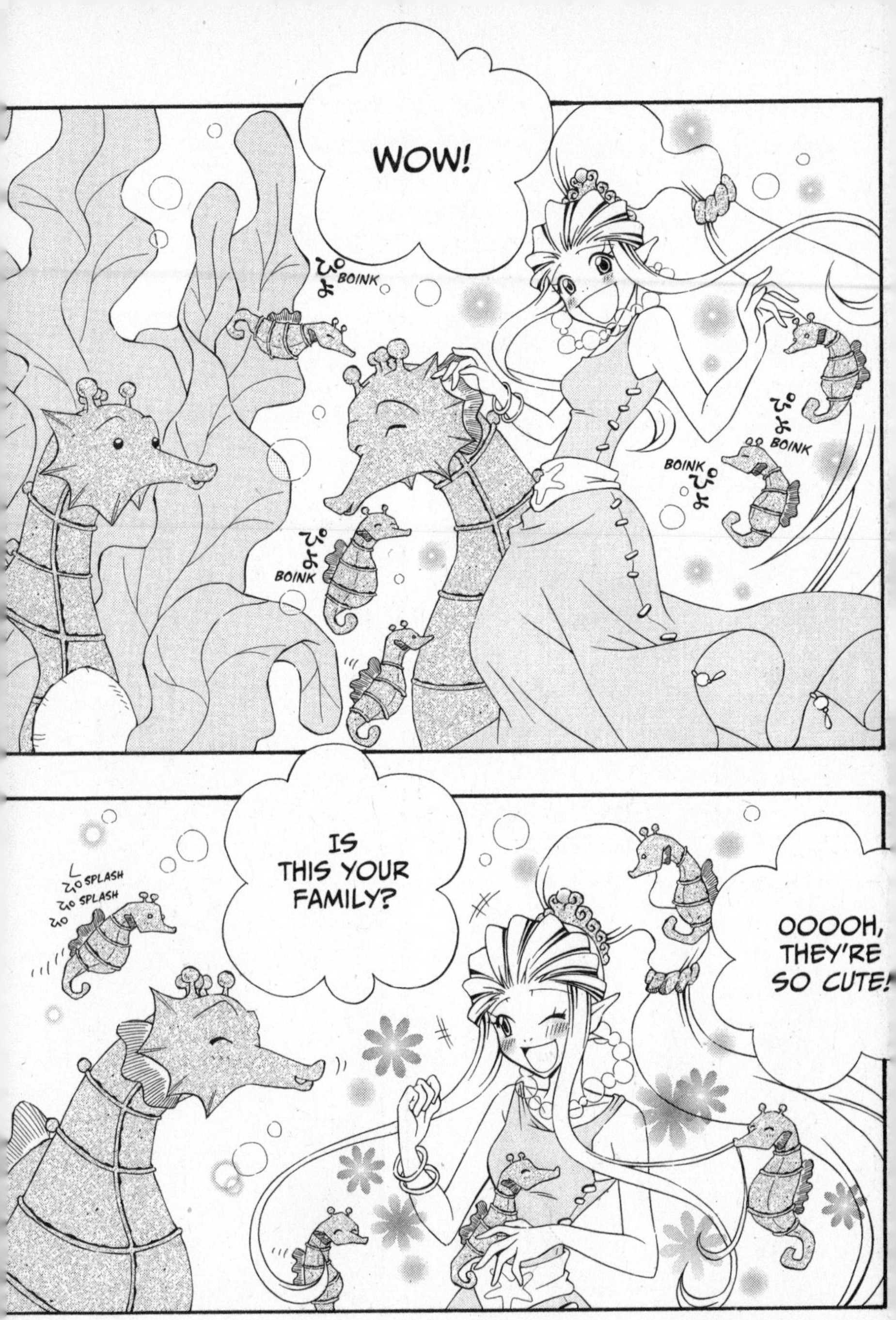
WOW!
ぴよ BOINK
ぴよ BOINK
BOINK ぴよ
ぴよ BOINK
OOOOH, THEY'RE SO CUTE!
IS THIS YOUR FAMILY?
SPLASH
SPLASH

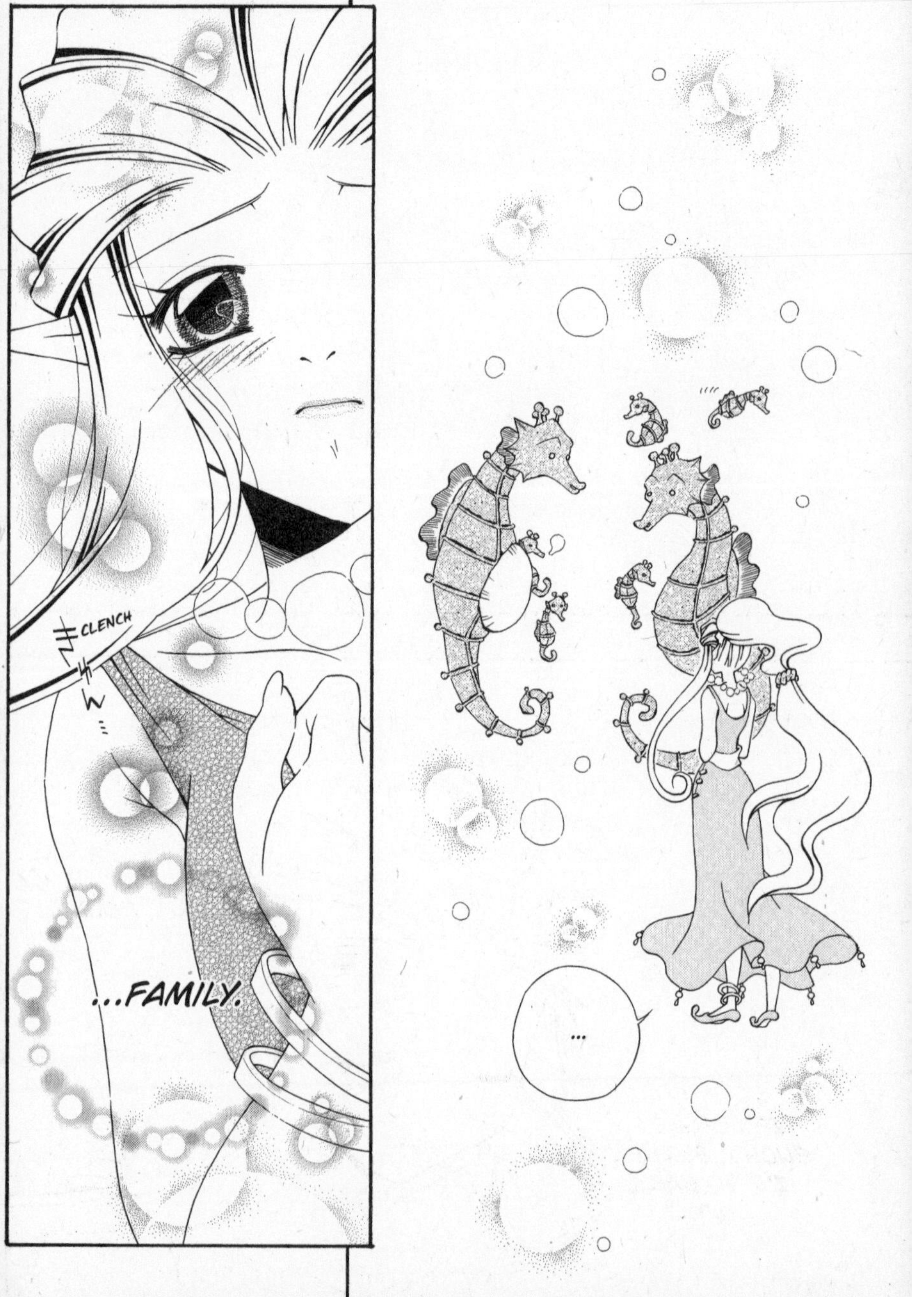
...
CLENCH
...FAMILY.

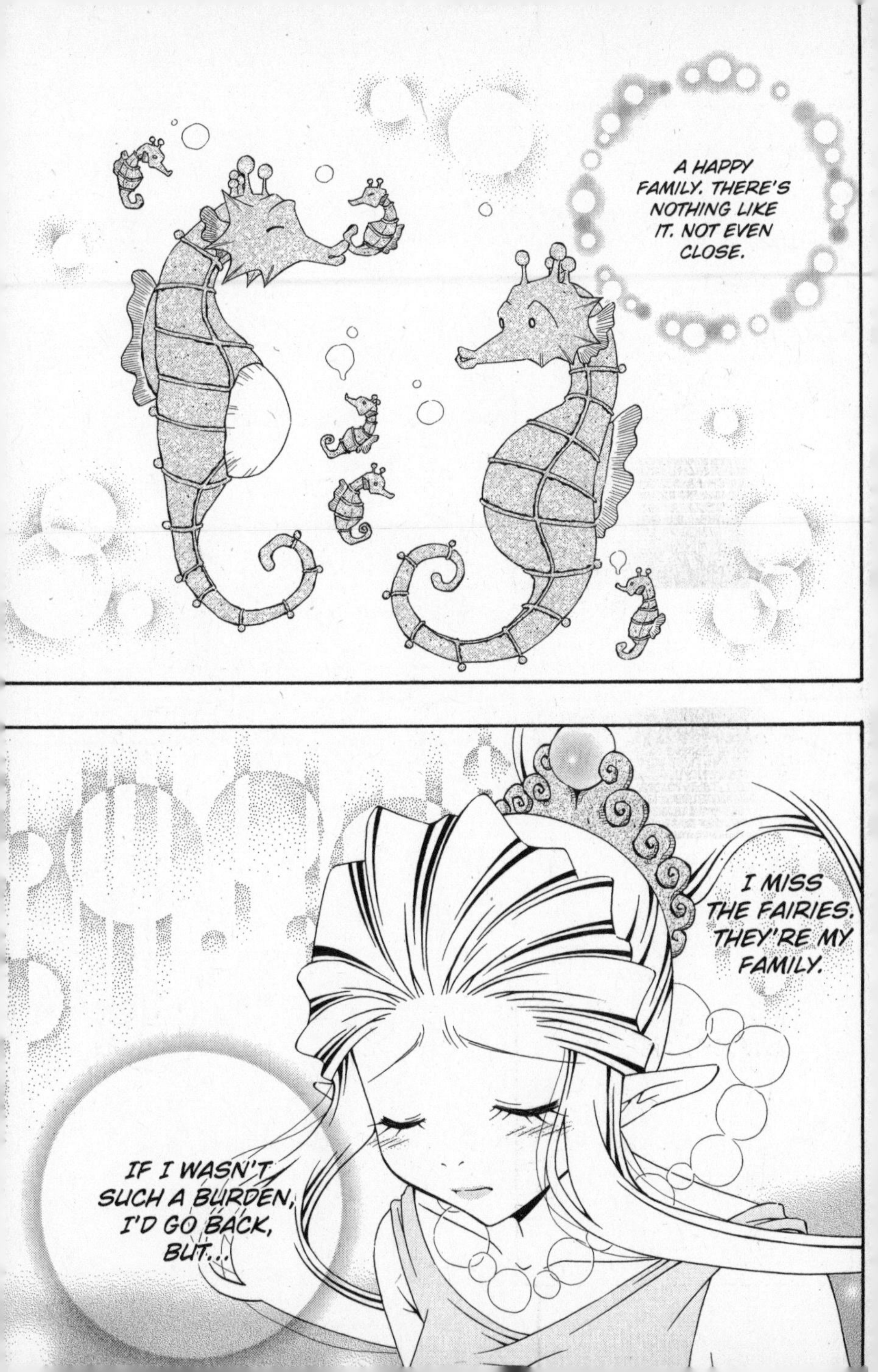
A HAPPY FAMILY. THERE'S NOTHING LIKE IT. NOT EVEN CLOSE.
I MISS THE FAIRIES. THEY'RE MY FAMILY.
IF I WASN'T SUCH A BURDEN, I'D GO BACK, BUT...

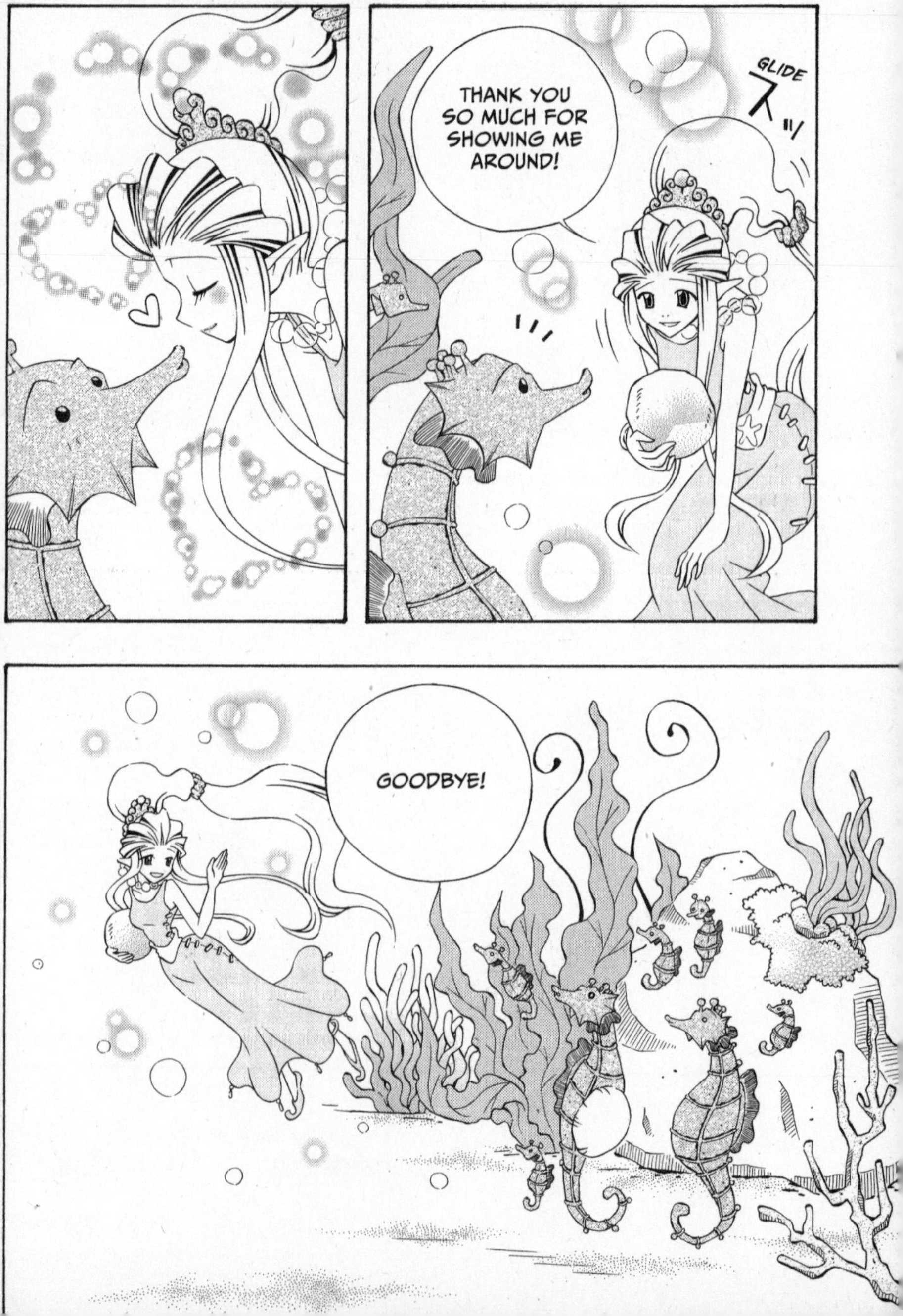
GLIDE
THANK YOU SO MUCH FOR SHOWING ME AROUND!
GOODBYE!

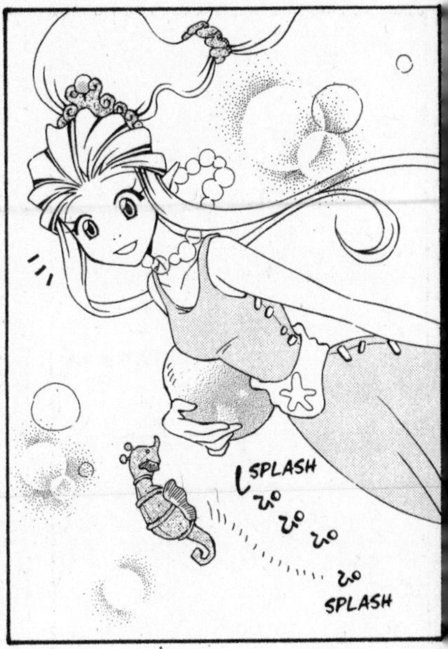
SPLASH
SPLASH

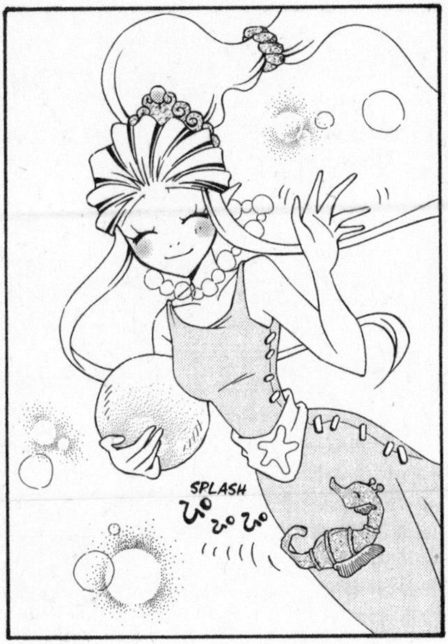
SPLASH

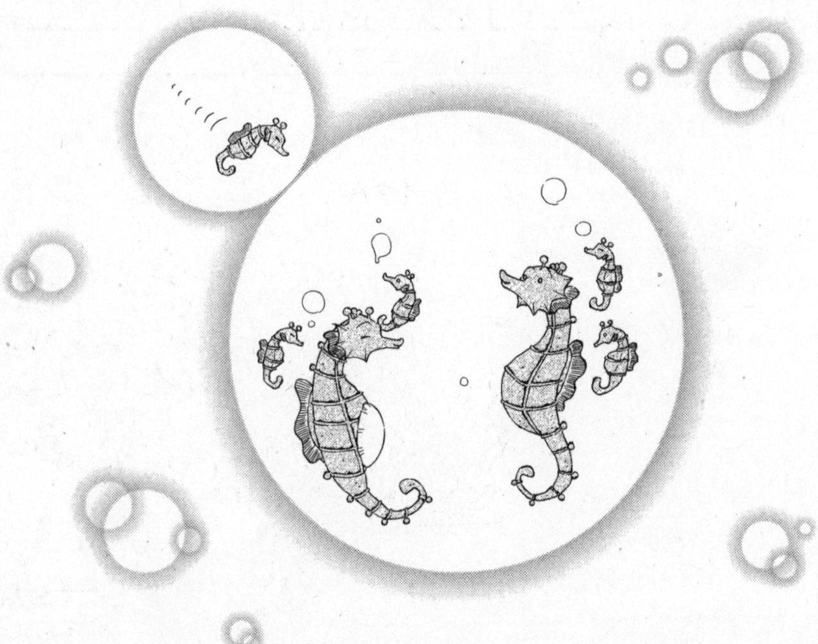

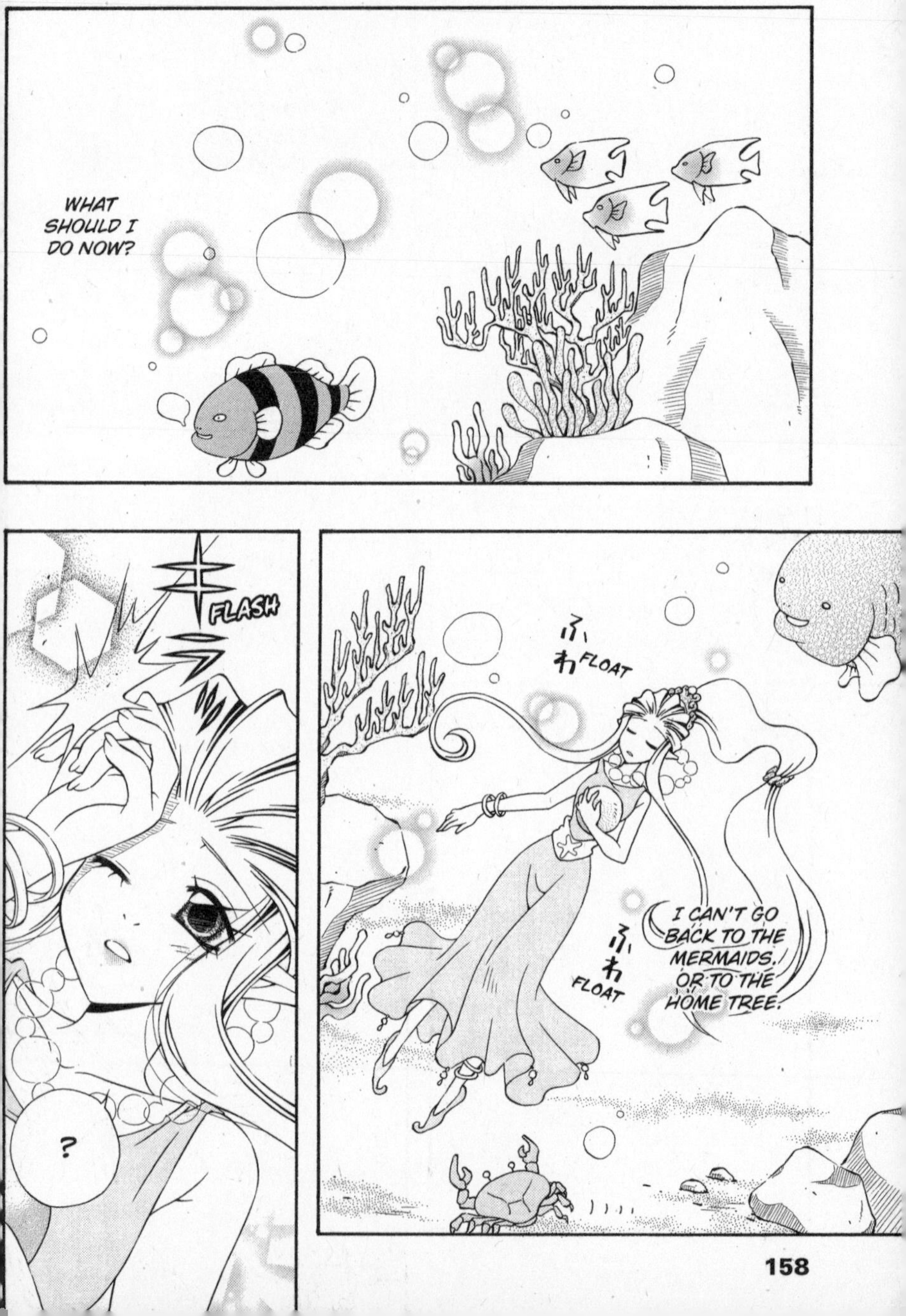
WHAT SHOULD I DO NOW?
ふわ FLOAT
ふわ FLOAT
I CAN'T GO BACK TO THE MERMAIDS. OR TO THE HOME TREE.
FLASH
?

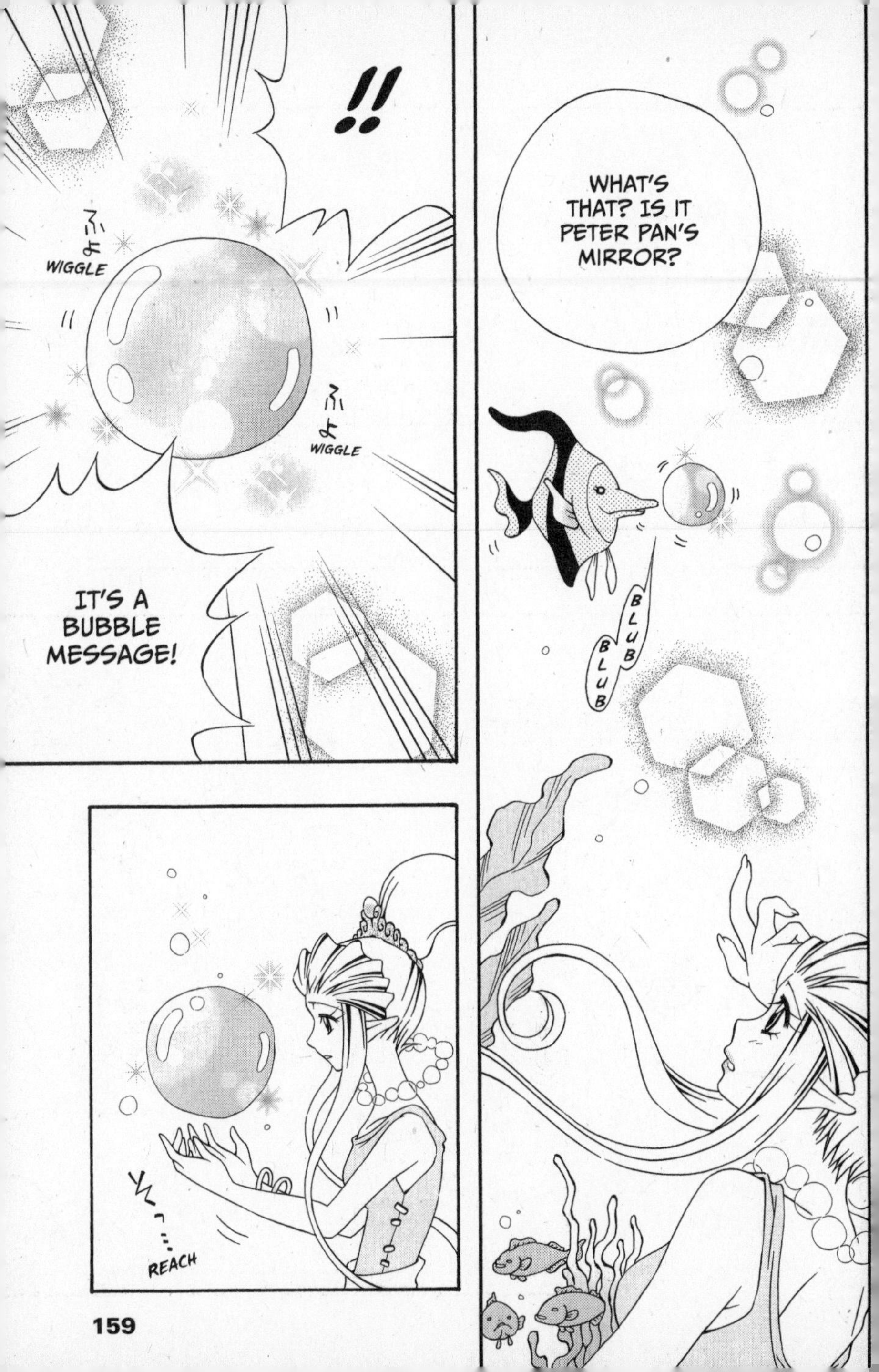
WHAT'S THAT? IS IT PETER PAN'S MIRROR?
BLUB BLUB
!!
ふよ
WIGGLE
ふよ
WIGGLE
IT'S A BUBBLE MESSAGE!
REACH

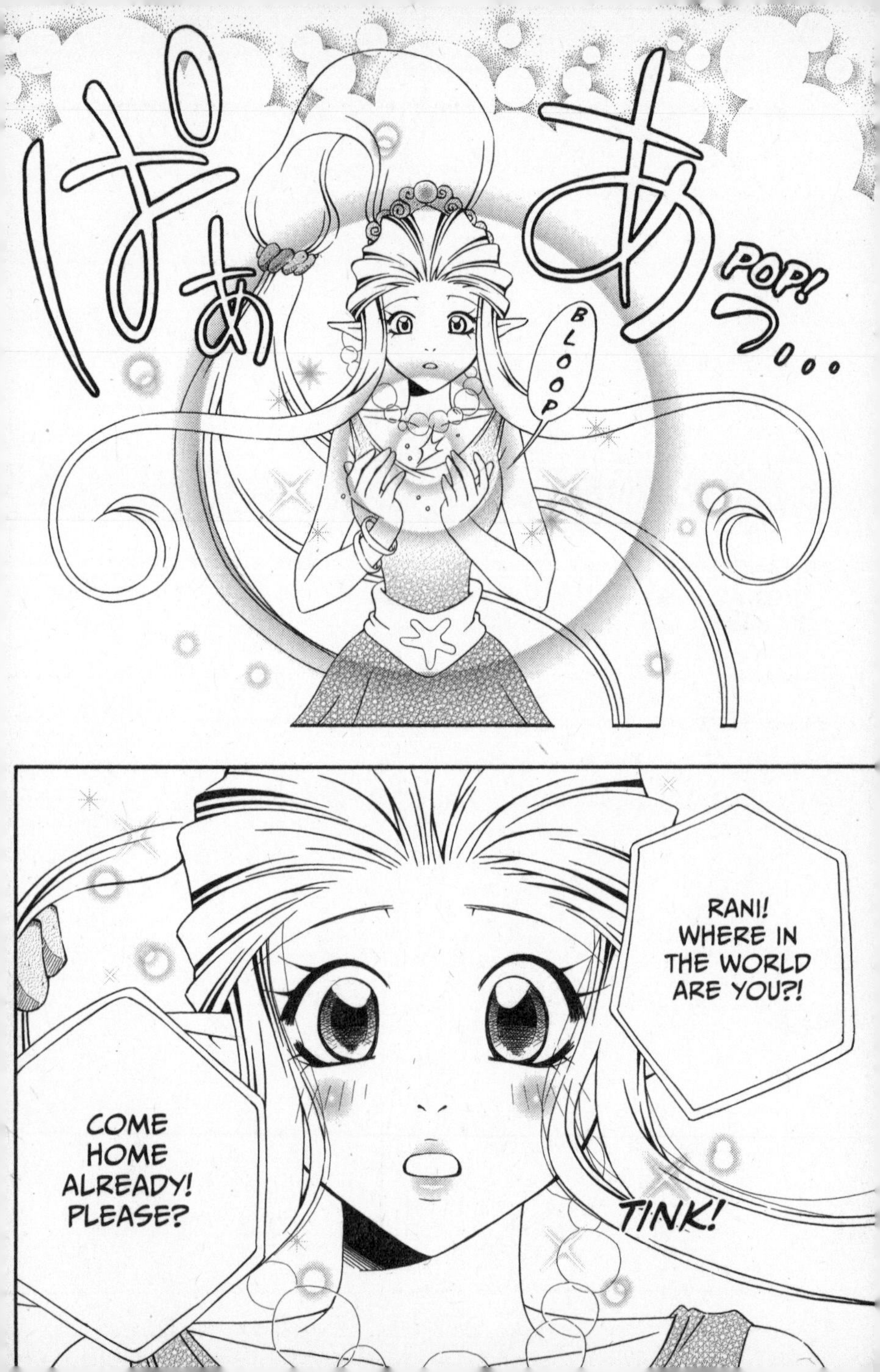
ぱぁあっ...
POP!
BLOOP
RANI! WHERE IN THE WORLD ARE YOU?!
TINK!
COME HOME ALREADY! PLEASE?

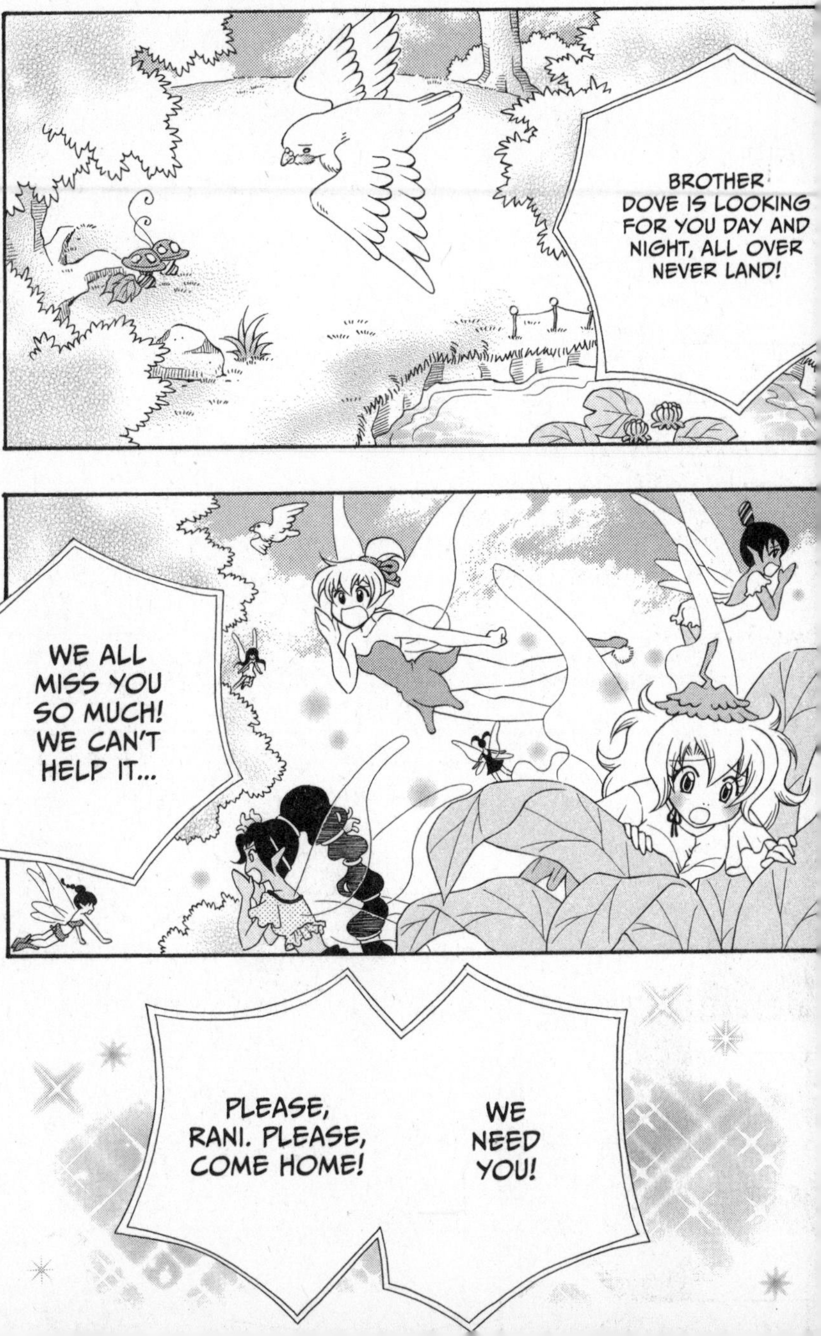
BROTHER DOVE IS LOOKING FOR YOU DAY AND NIGHT, ALL OVER NEVER LAND!
WE ALL MISS YOU SO MUCH! WE CAN'T HELP IT...
WE NEED YOU!
PLEASE, RANI. PLEASE, COME HOME!

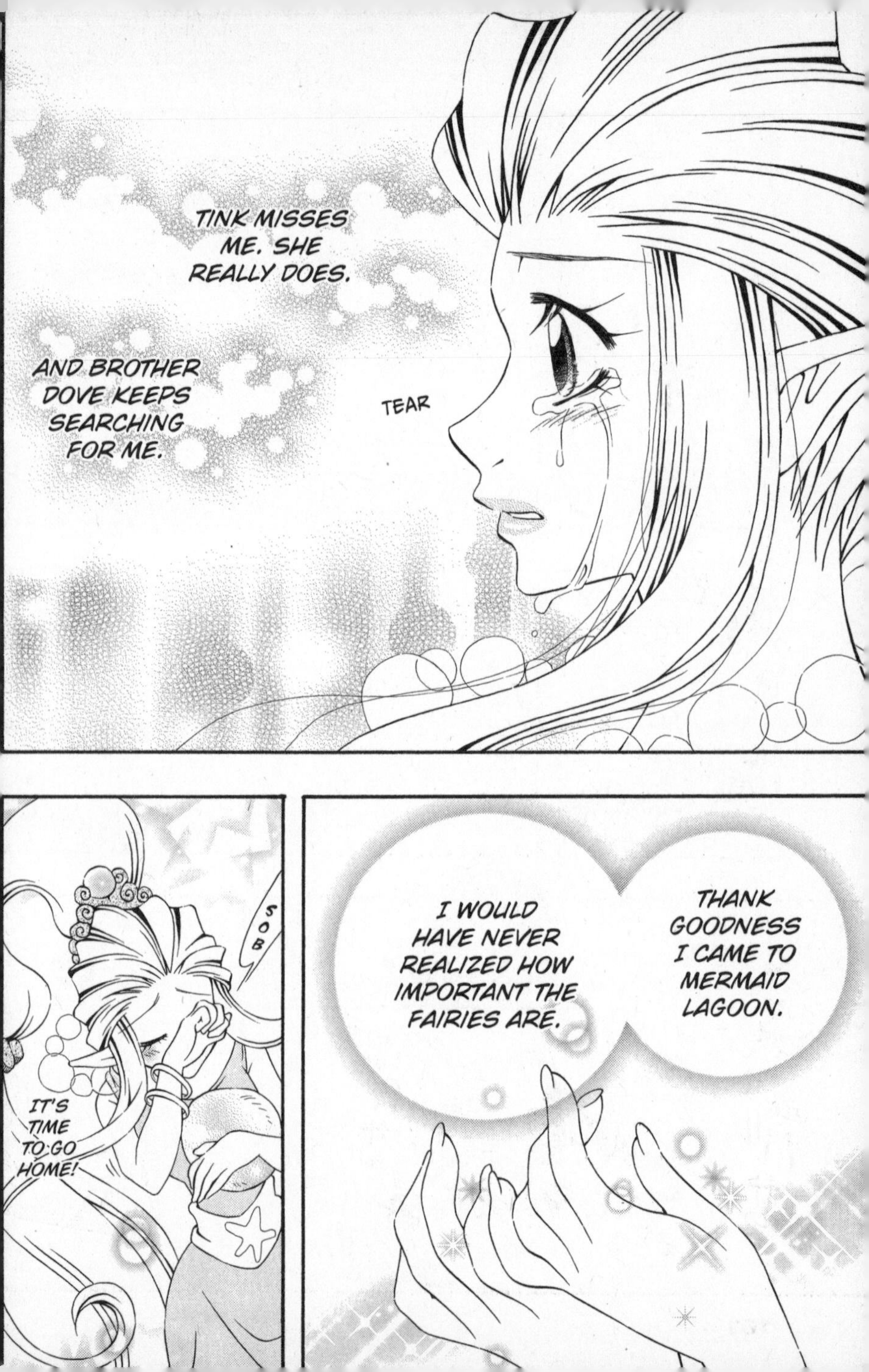
TINK MISSES ME. SHE REALLY DOES.
AND BROTHER DOVE KEEPS SEARCHING FOR ME.
TEAR
THANK GOODNESS I CAME TO MERMAID LAGOON.
I WOULD HAVE NEVER REALIZED HOW IMPORTANT THE FAIRIES ARE.
SOB
IT'S TIME TO GO HOME!

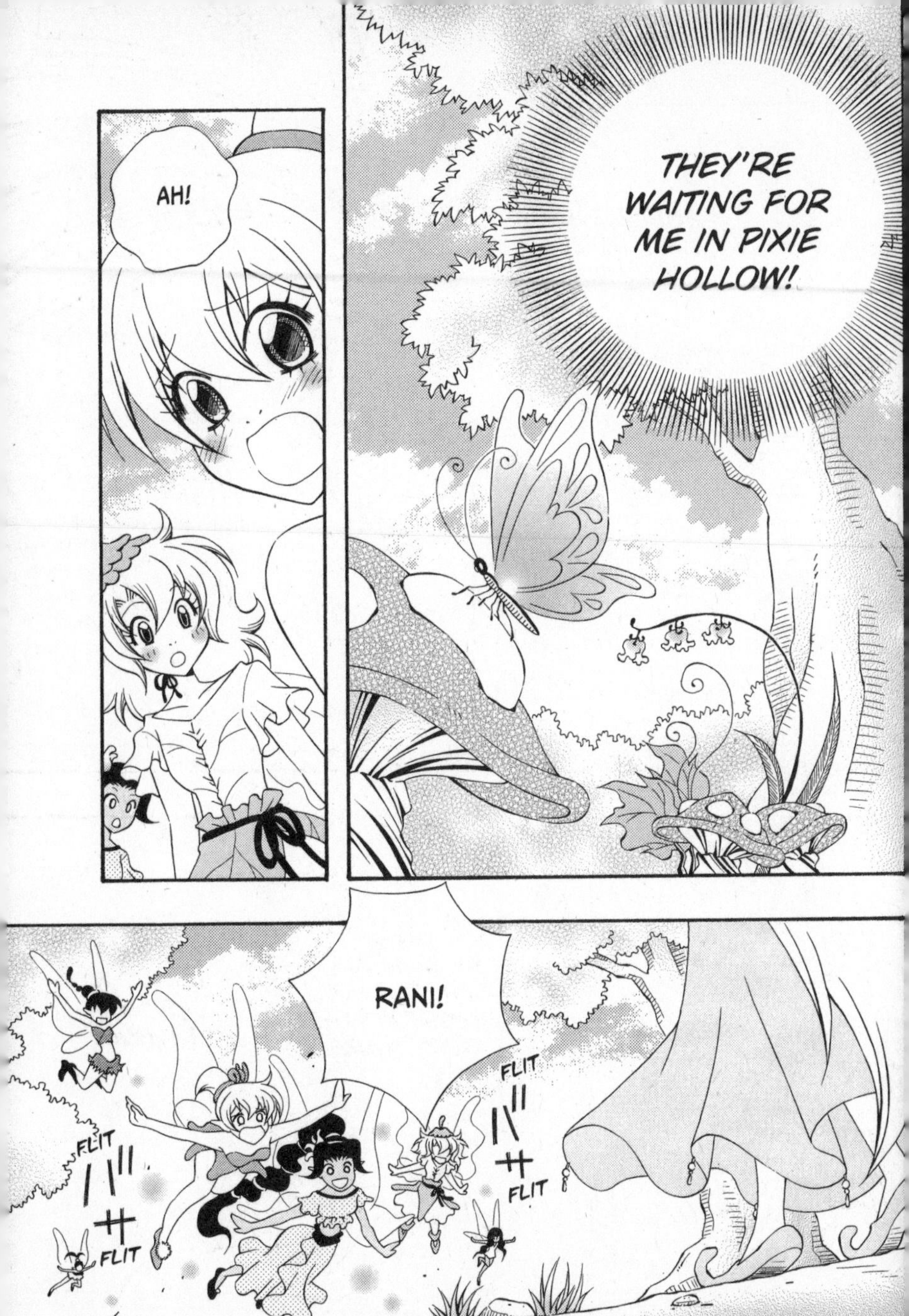
THEY'RE WAITING FOR ME IN PIXIE HOLLOW!
AH!
RANI!
FLIT
FLIT
FLIT
FLIT

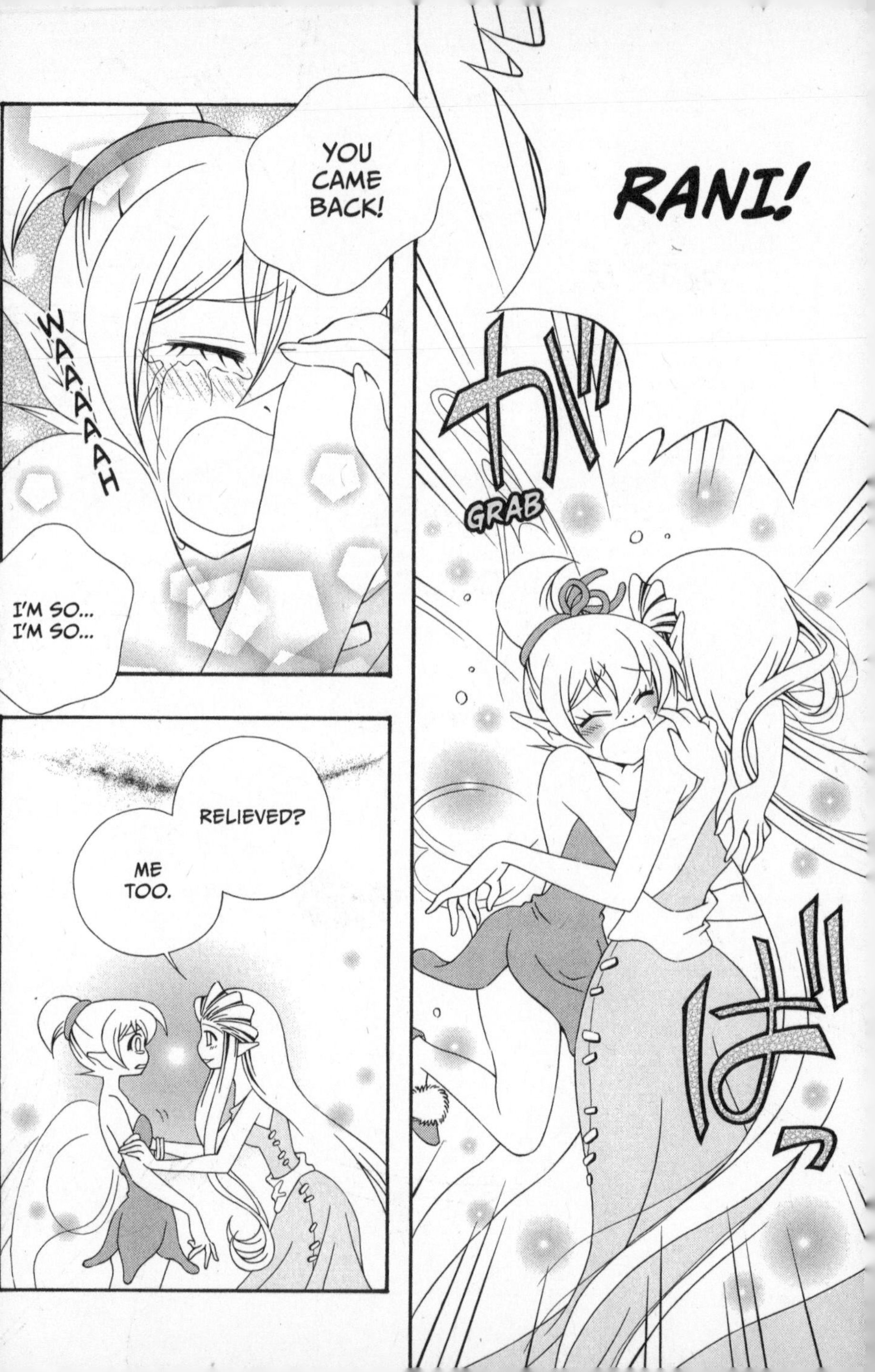
RANI!
GRAB
YOU CAME BACK!
WAAAAAAH
I'M SO...
I'M SO...
RELIEVED?
ME TOO.

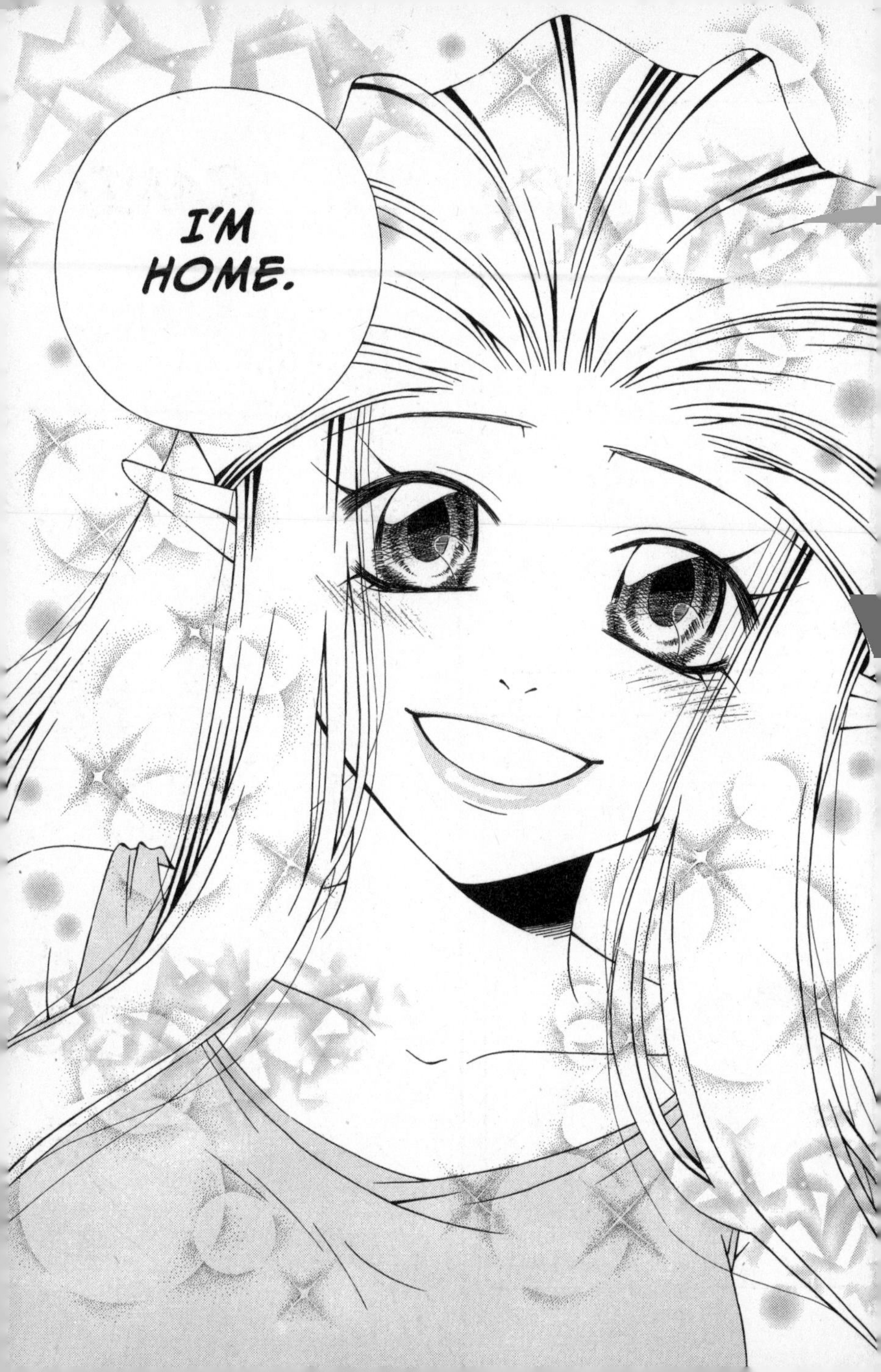
I'M HOME.

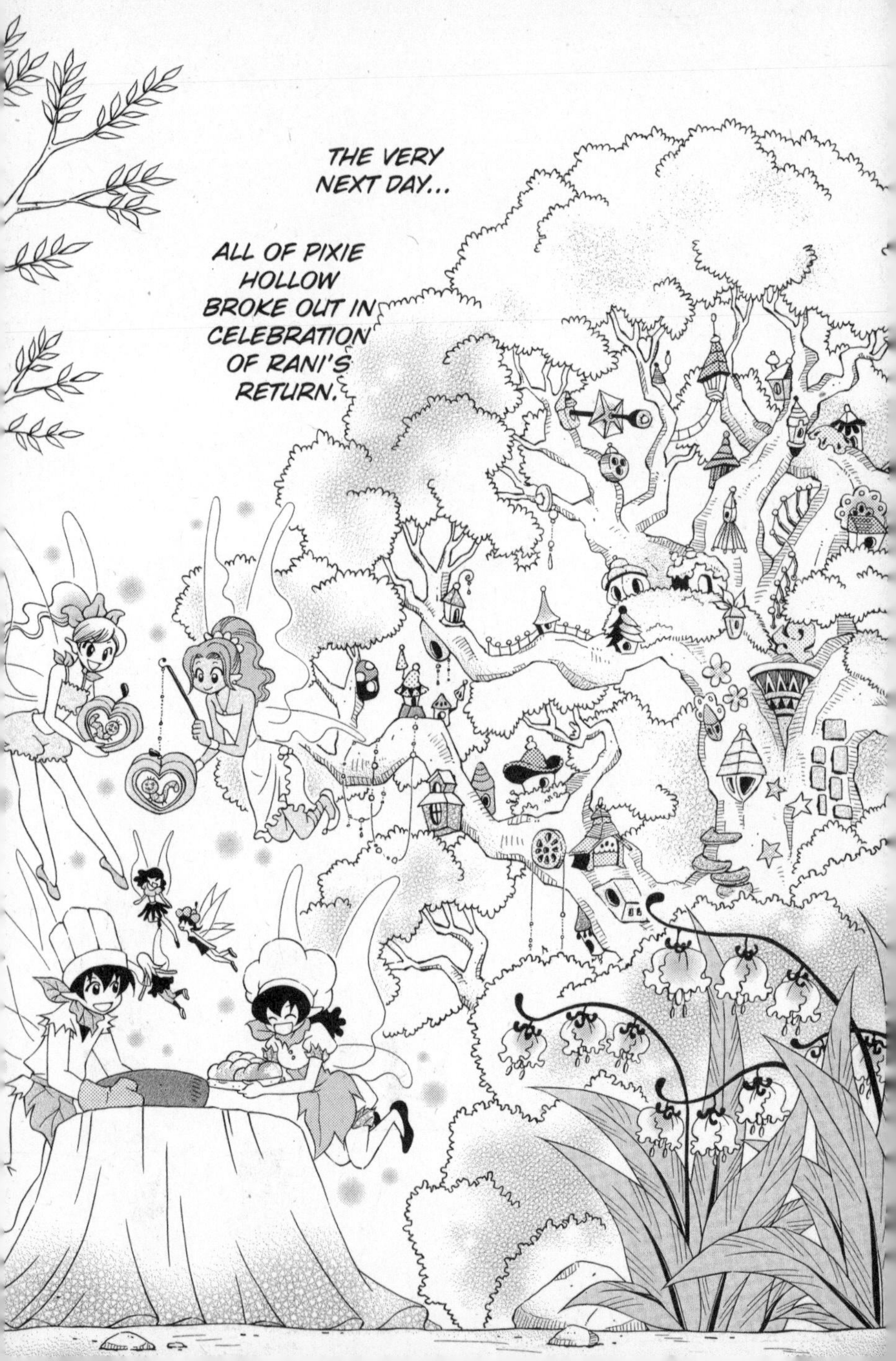
THE VERY NEXT DAY...
ALL OF PIXIE HOLLOW BROKE OUT IN CELEBRATION OF RANI'S RETURN.

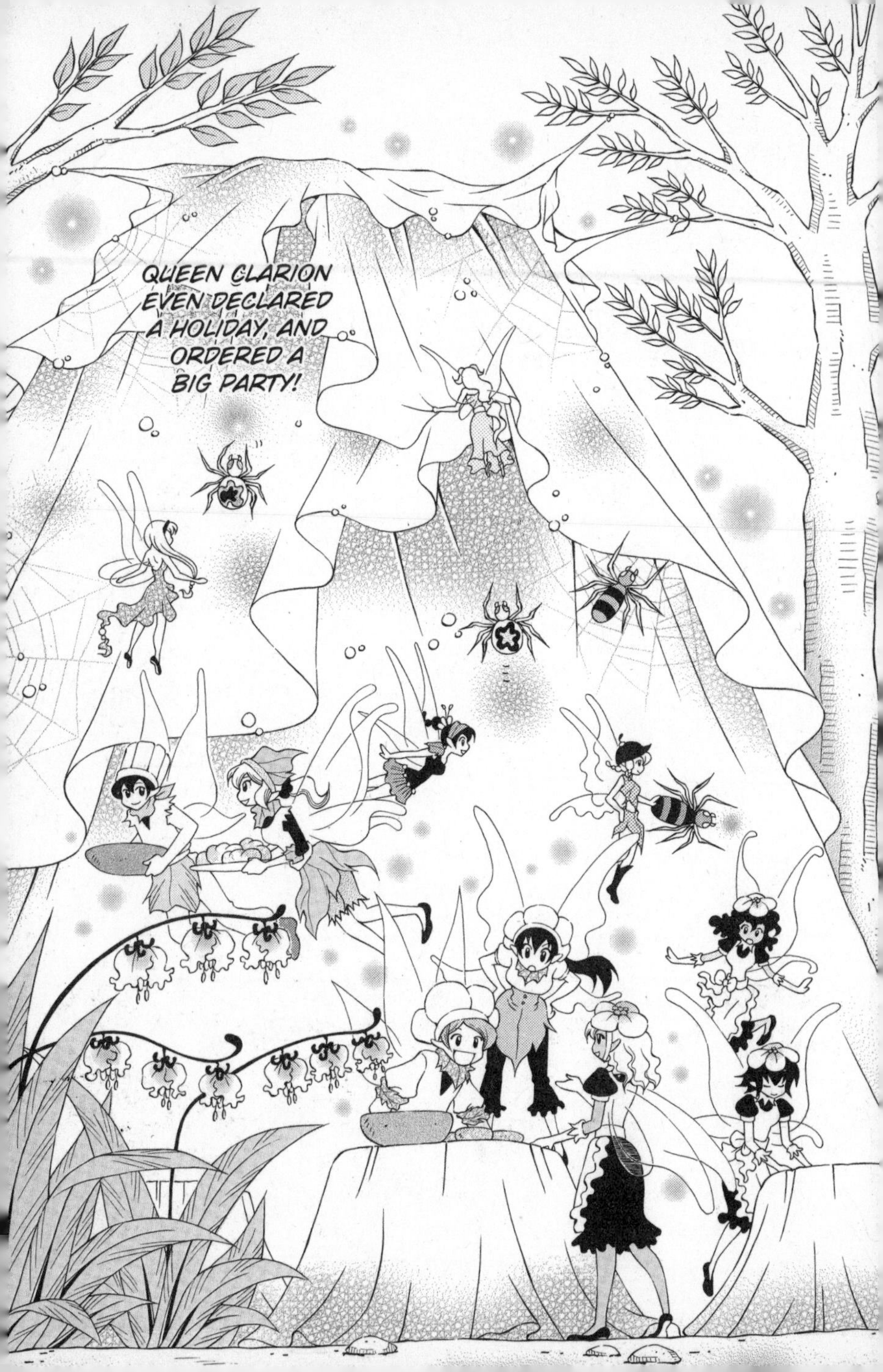
QUEEN CLARION EVEN DECLARED A HOLIDAY, AND ORDERED A BIG PARTY!

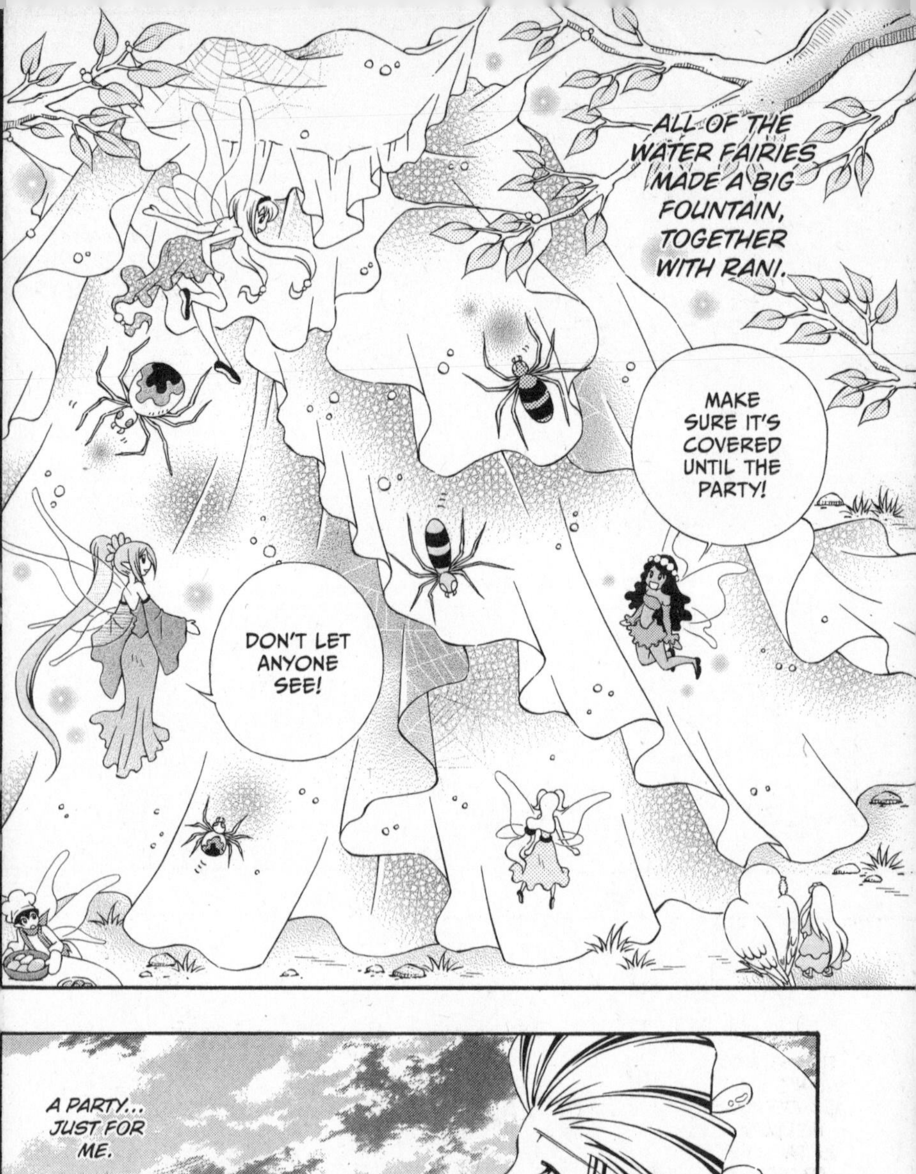
ALL OF THE WATER FAIRIES MADE A BIG FOUNTAIN, TOGETHER WITH RANI.
MAKE SURE IT'S COVERED UNTIL THE PARTY!
DON'T LET ANYONE SEE!

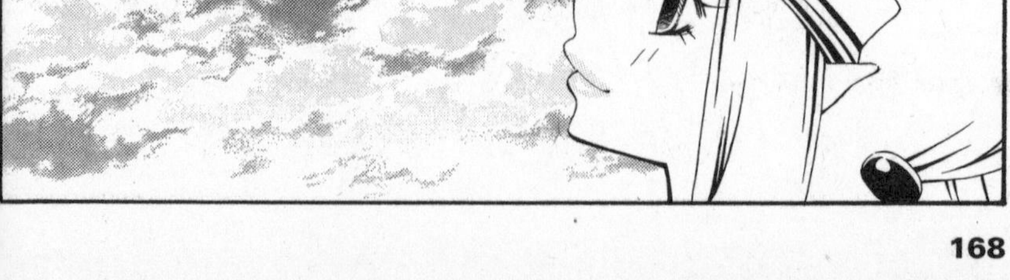
A PARTY... JUST FOR ME.

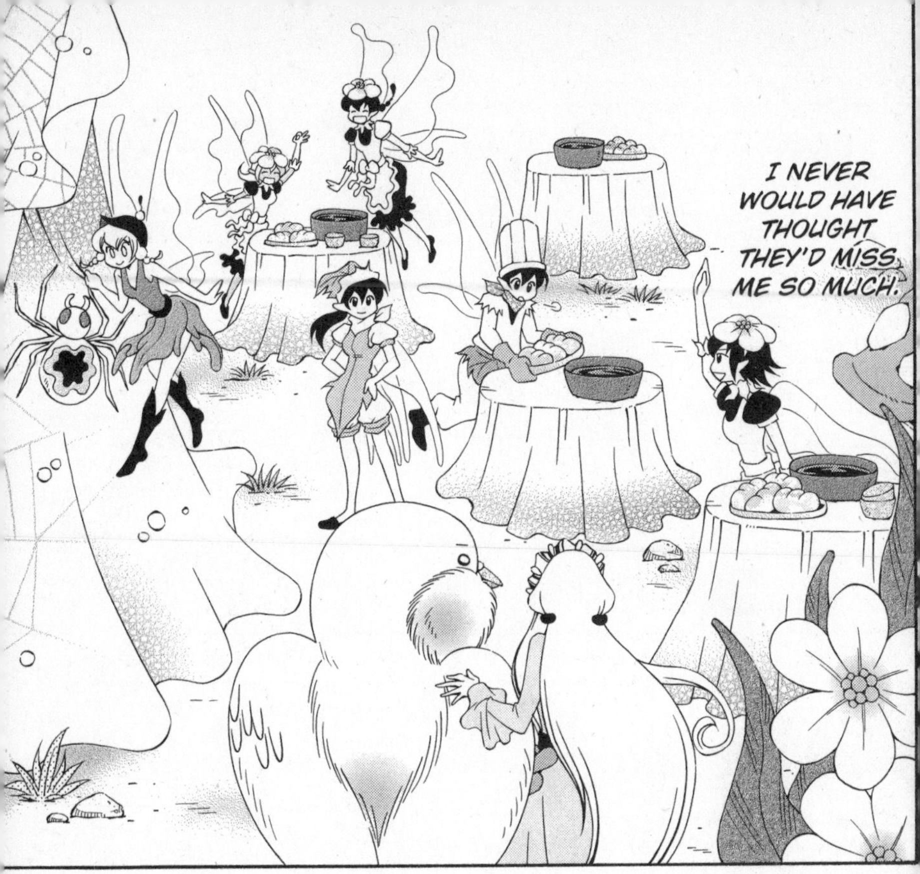
I NEVER WOULD HAVE THOUGHT THEY'D MISS ME SO MUCH.

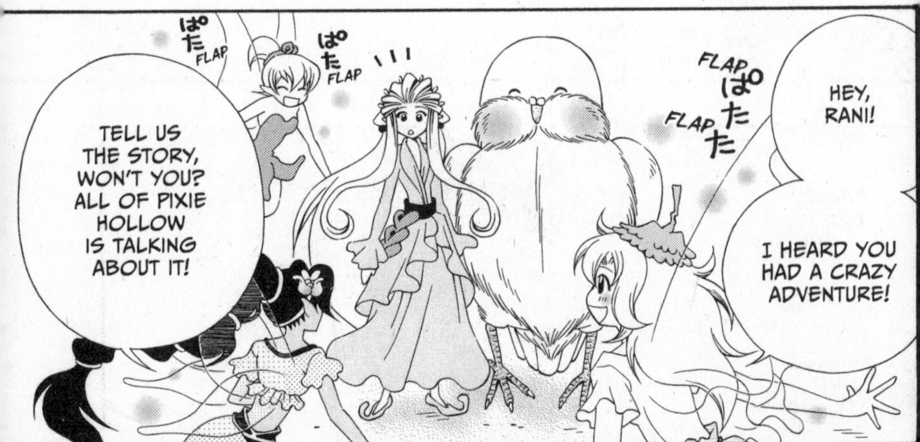
HEY, RANI!
I HEARD YOU HAD A CRAZY ADVENTURE!
ぱたた
FLAP FLAP
ぱた
FLAP
ぱた
FLAP
TELL US THE STORY, WON'T YOU? ALL OF PIXIE HOLLOW IS TALKING ABOUT IT!

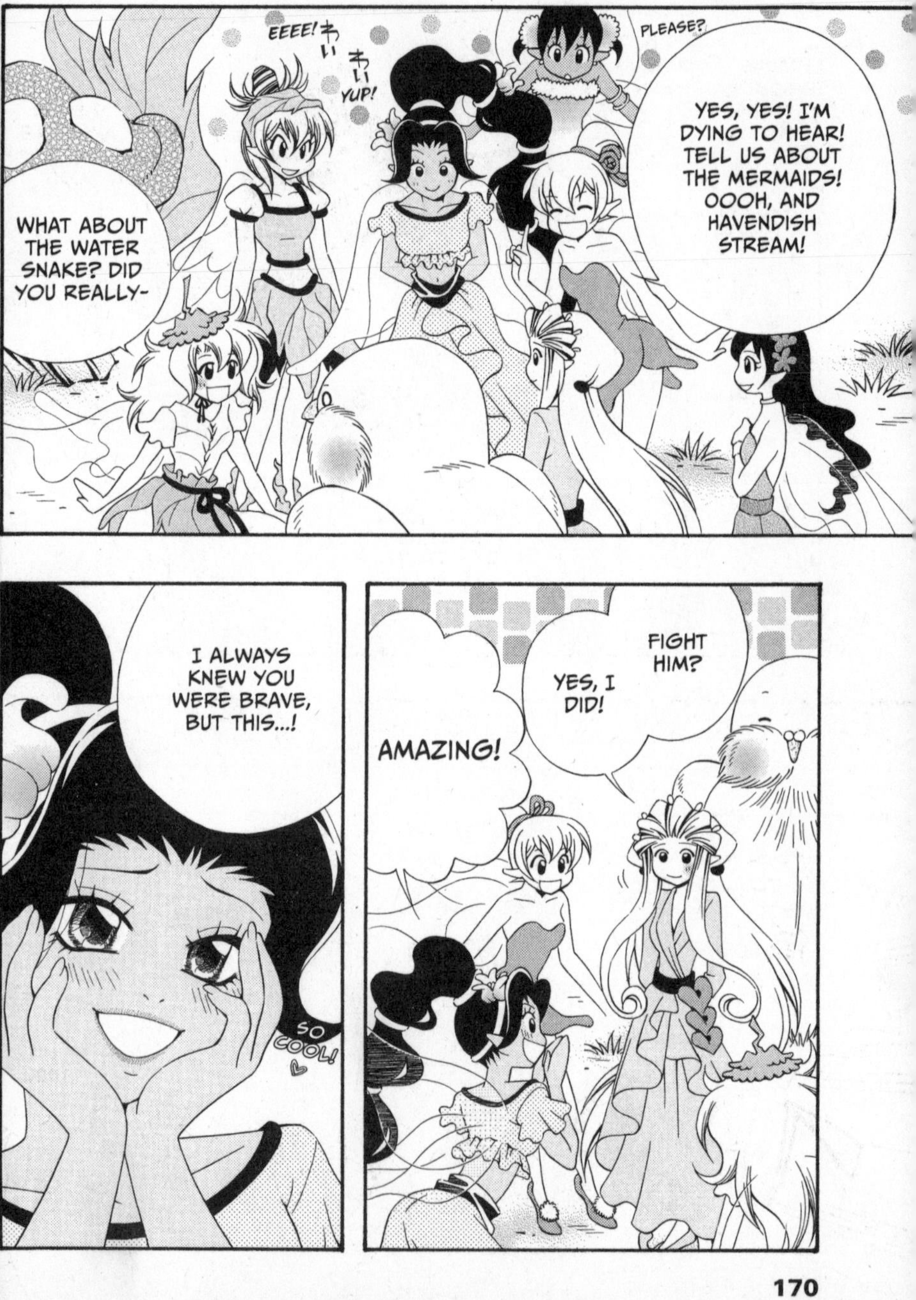
PLEASE?
YES, YES! I'M DYING TO HEAR! TELL US ABOUT THE MERMAIDS! OOOH, AND HAVENDISH STREAM!
わい
YUP!
EEEE! わい
WHAT ABOUT THE WATER SNAKE? DID YOU REALLY-
FIGHT HIM?
YES, I DID!
AMAZING!
I ALWAYS KNEW YOU WERE BRAVE, BUT THIS...!
SO COOL!

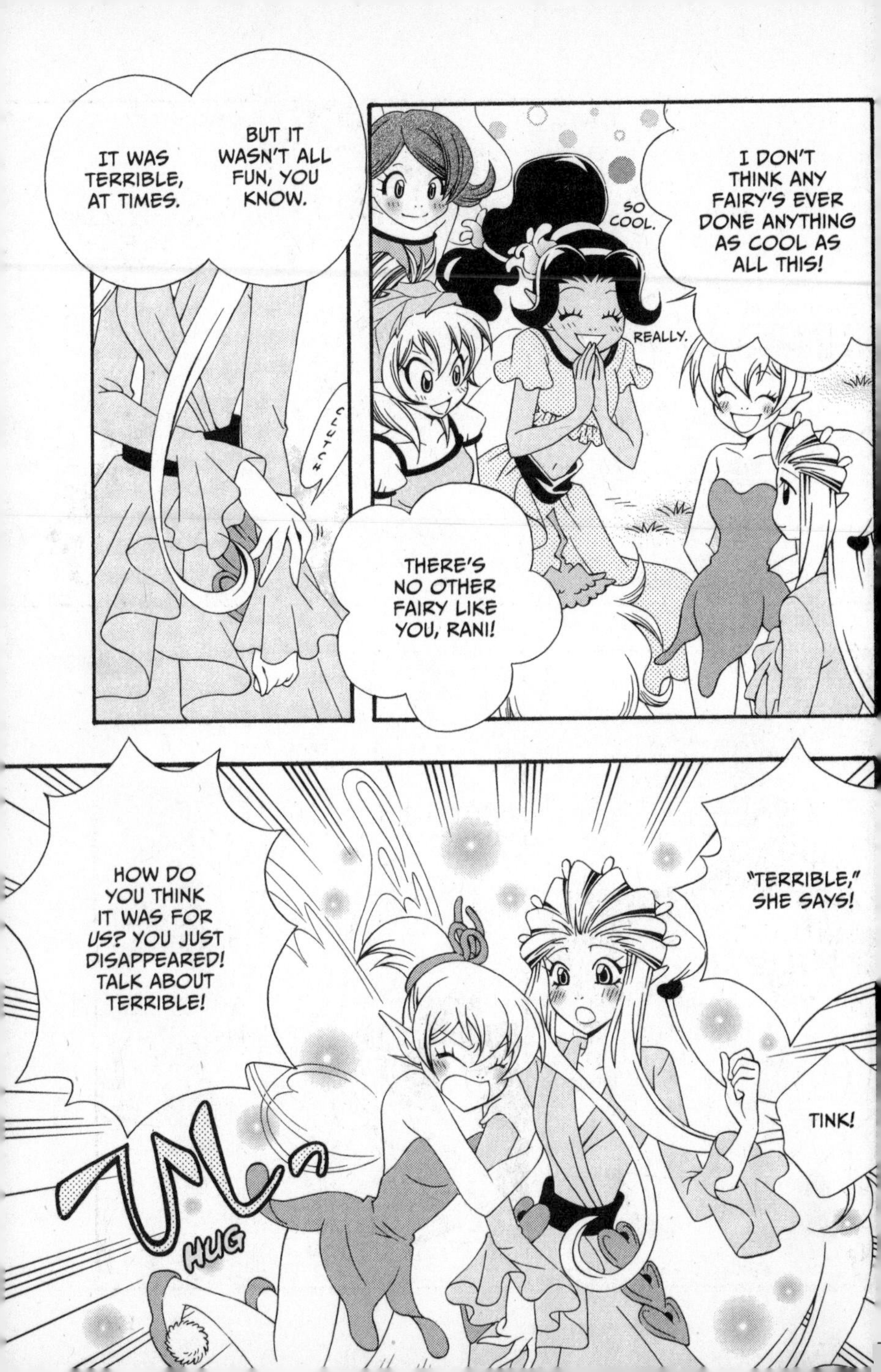
I DON'T THINK ANY FAIRY'S EVER DONE ANYTHING AS COOL AS ALL THIS!
SO COOL.
REALLY.
THERE'S NO OTHER FAIRY LIKE YOU, RANI!
BUT IT WASN'T ALL FUN, YOU KNOW.
IT WAS TERRIBLE, AT TIMES.
CLUTCH
"TERRIBLE," SHE SAYS!
TINK!
HOW DO YOU THINK IT WAS FOR *US*? YOU JUST DISAPPEARED! TALK ABOUT TERRIBLE!
HUG

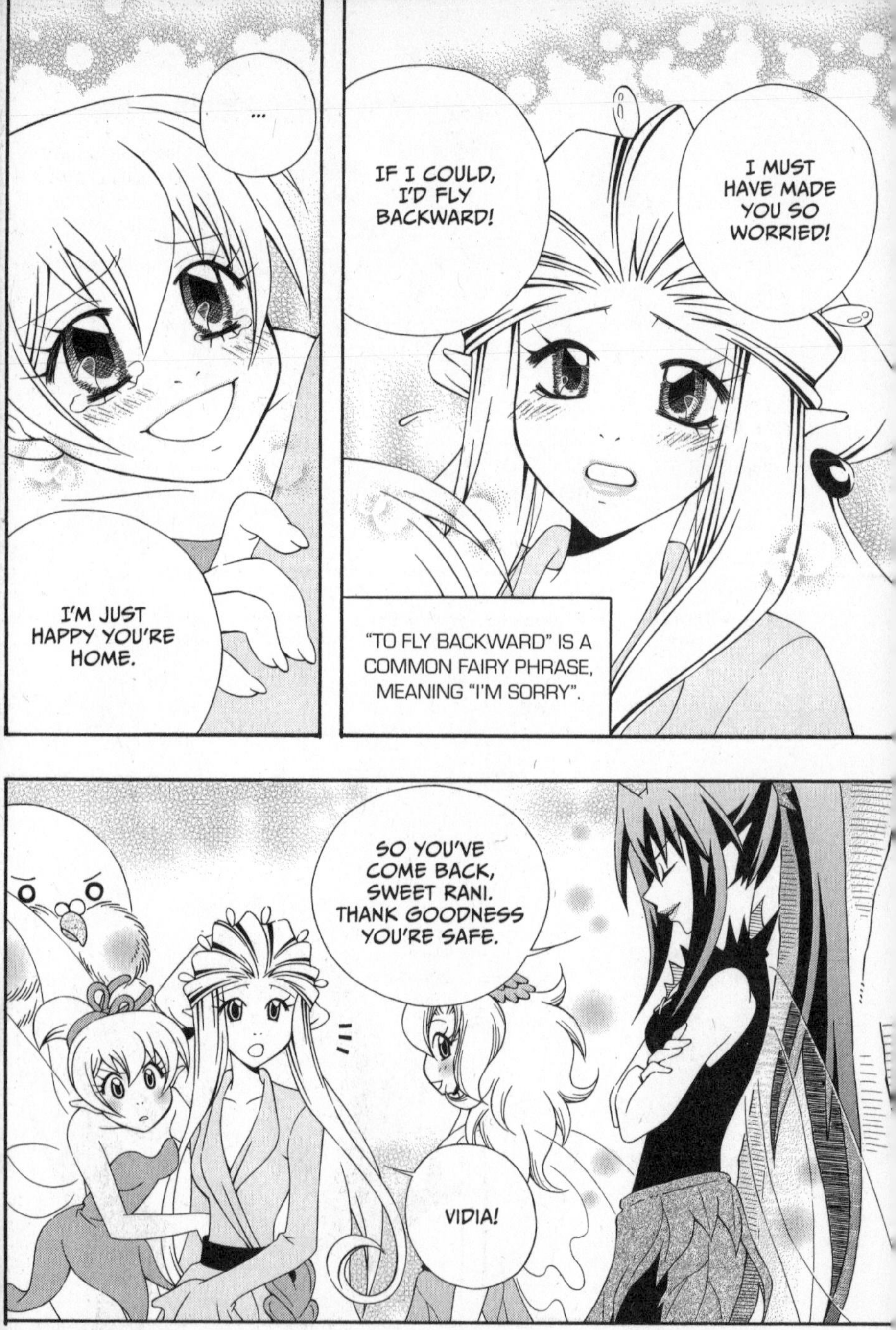
I MUST HAVE MADE YOU SO WORRIED!
IF I COULD, I'D FLY BACKWARD!
"TO FLY BACKWARD" IS A COMMON FAIRY PHRASE, MEANING "I'M SORRY".
...
I'M JUST HAPPY YOU'RE HOME.
SO YOU'VE COME BACK, SWEET RANI. THANK GOODNESS YOU'RE SAFE.
VIDIA!

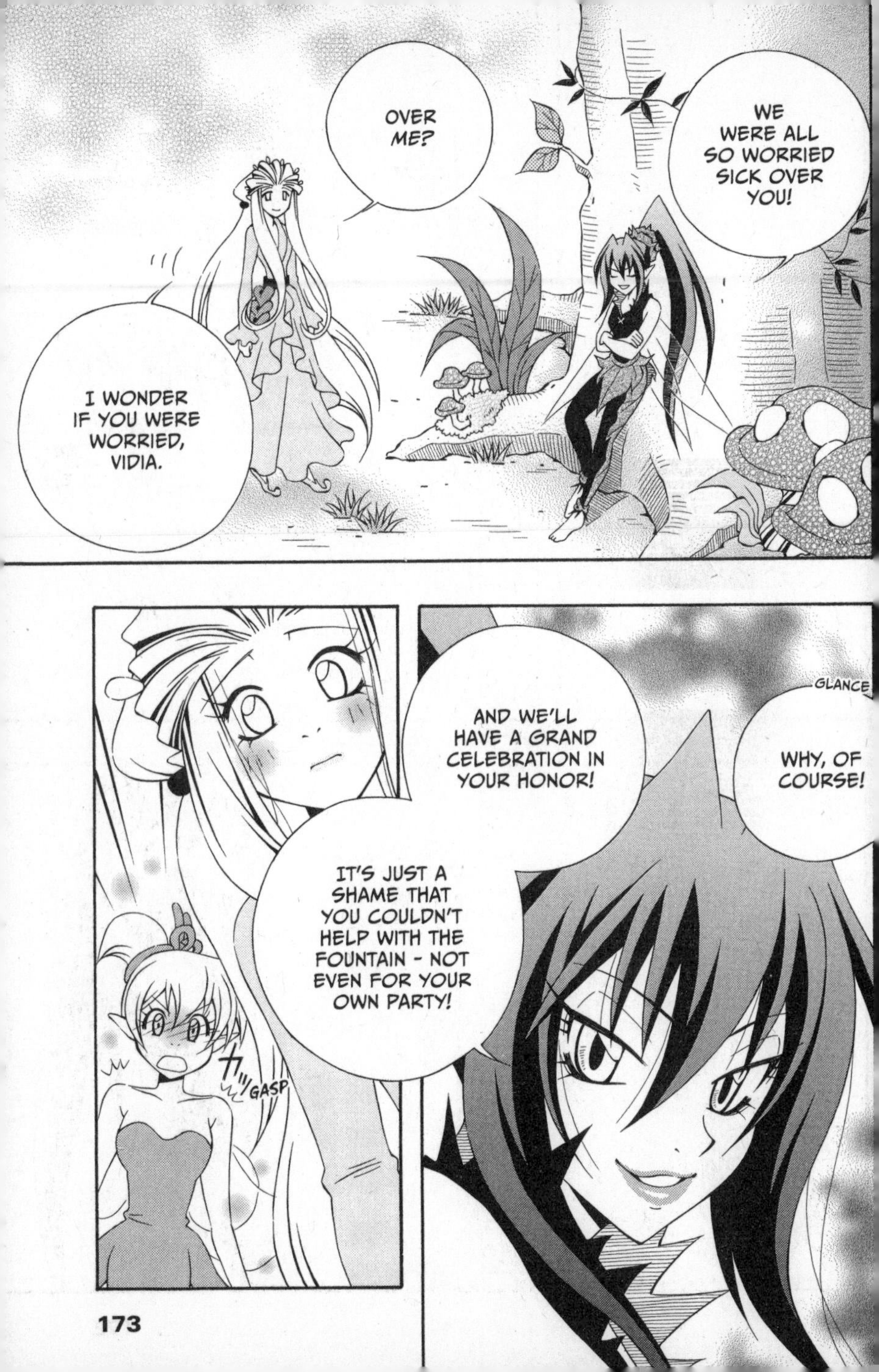
WE WERE ALL SO WORRIED SICK OVER YOU!
OVER ME?
I WONDER IF YOU WERE WORRIED, VIDIA.
GLANCE
WHY, OF COURSE!
AND WE'LL HAVE A GRAND CELEBRATION IN YOUR HONOR!
IT'S JUST A SHAME THAT YOU COULDN'T HELP WITH THE FOUNTAIN - NOT EVEN FOR YOUR OWN PARTY!
GASP

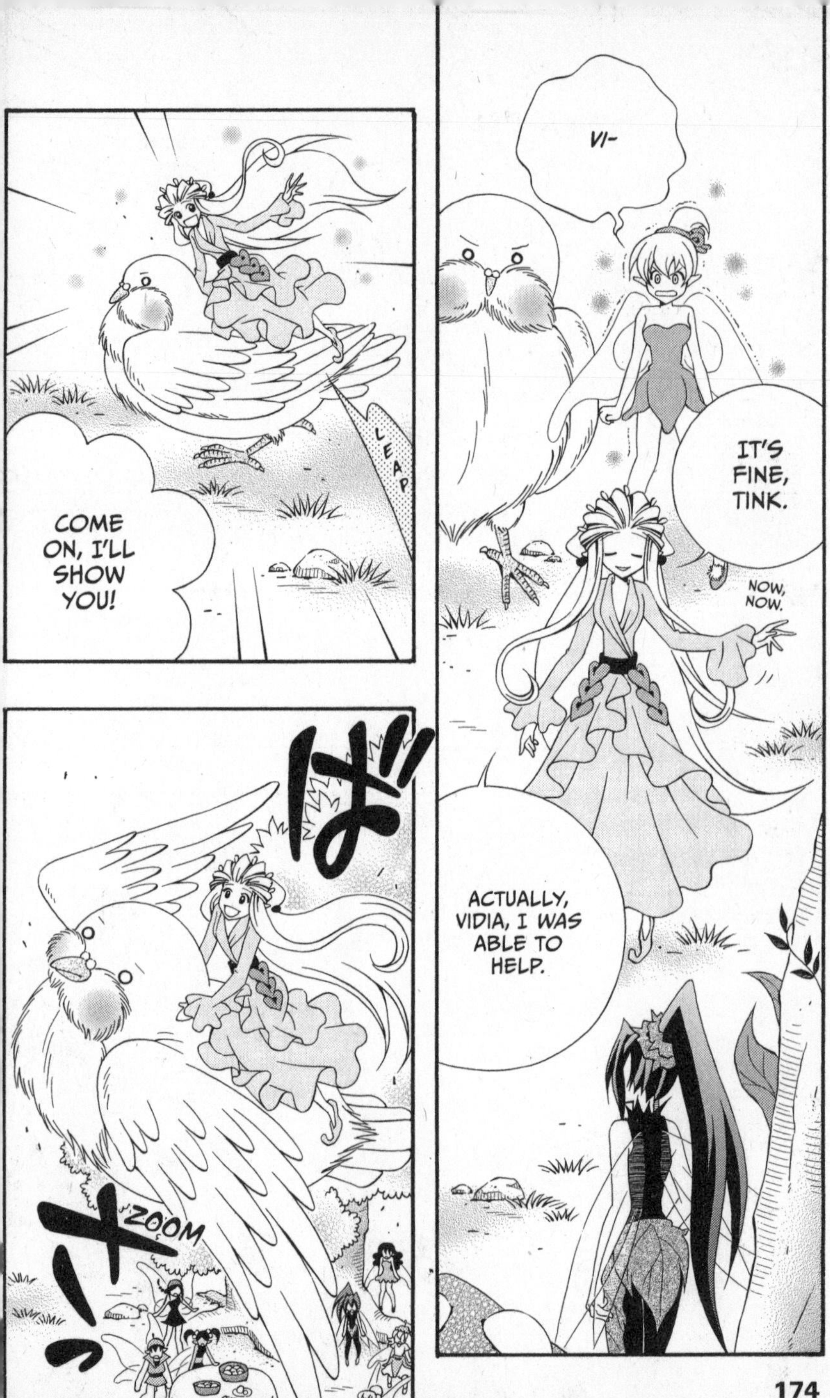
VI-
IT'S FINE, TINK.
NOW, NOW.
ACTUALLY, VIDIA, I WAS ABLE TO HELP.
COME ON, I'LL SHOW YOU!
LEAP
ば
ZOOM

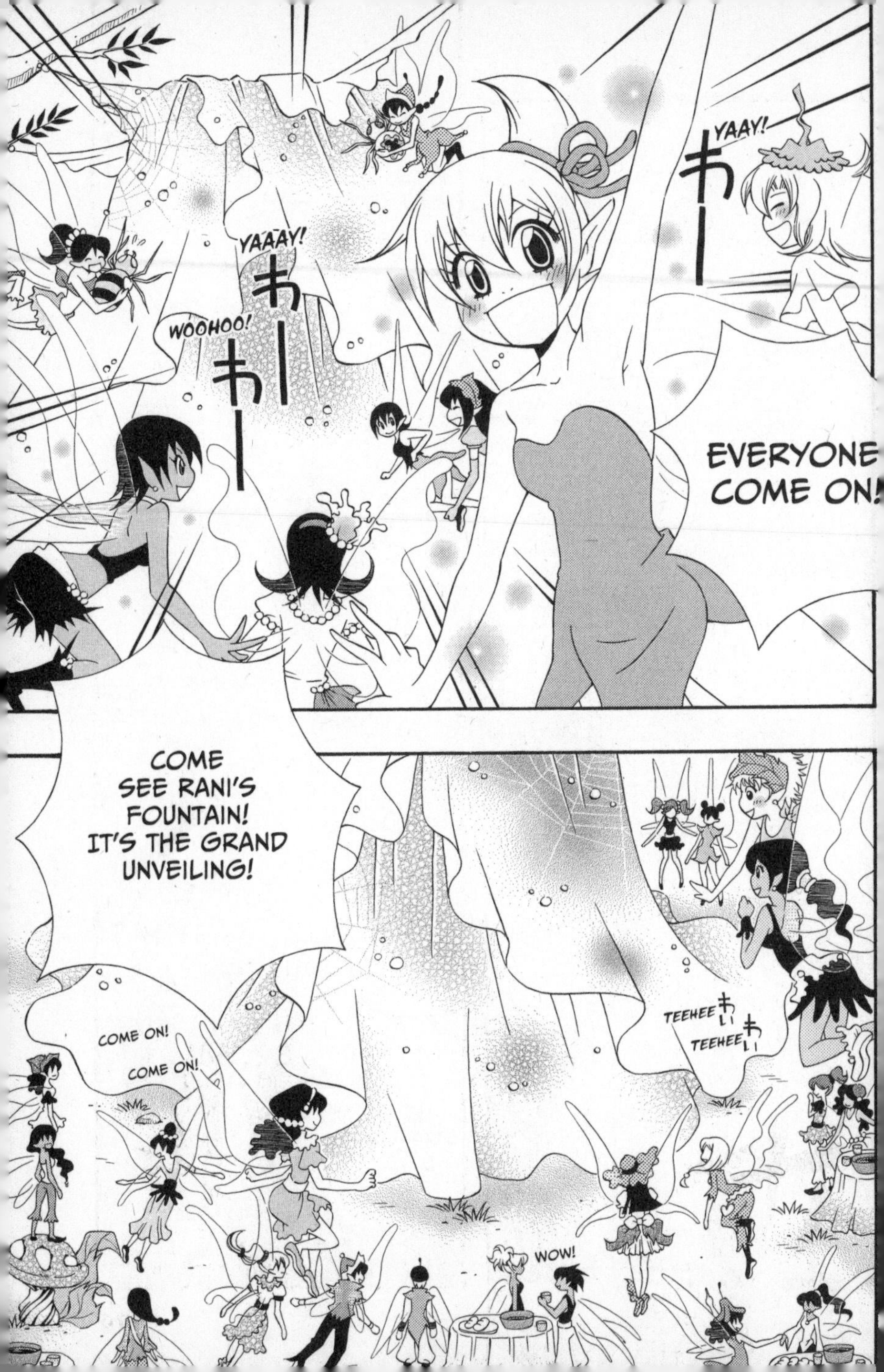

YAAY!
わー
EVERYONE COME ON!
YAAAY!
WOOHOO!
わーわー
COME SEE RANI'S FOUNTAIN! IT'S THE GRAND UNVEILING!
TEEHEE
TEEHEE
わいわい
COME ON!
COME ON!
WOW!

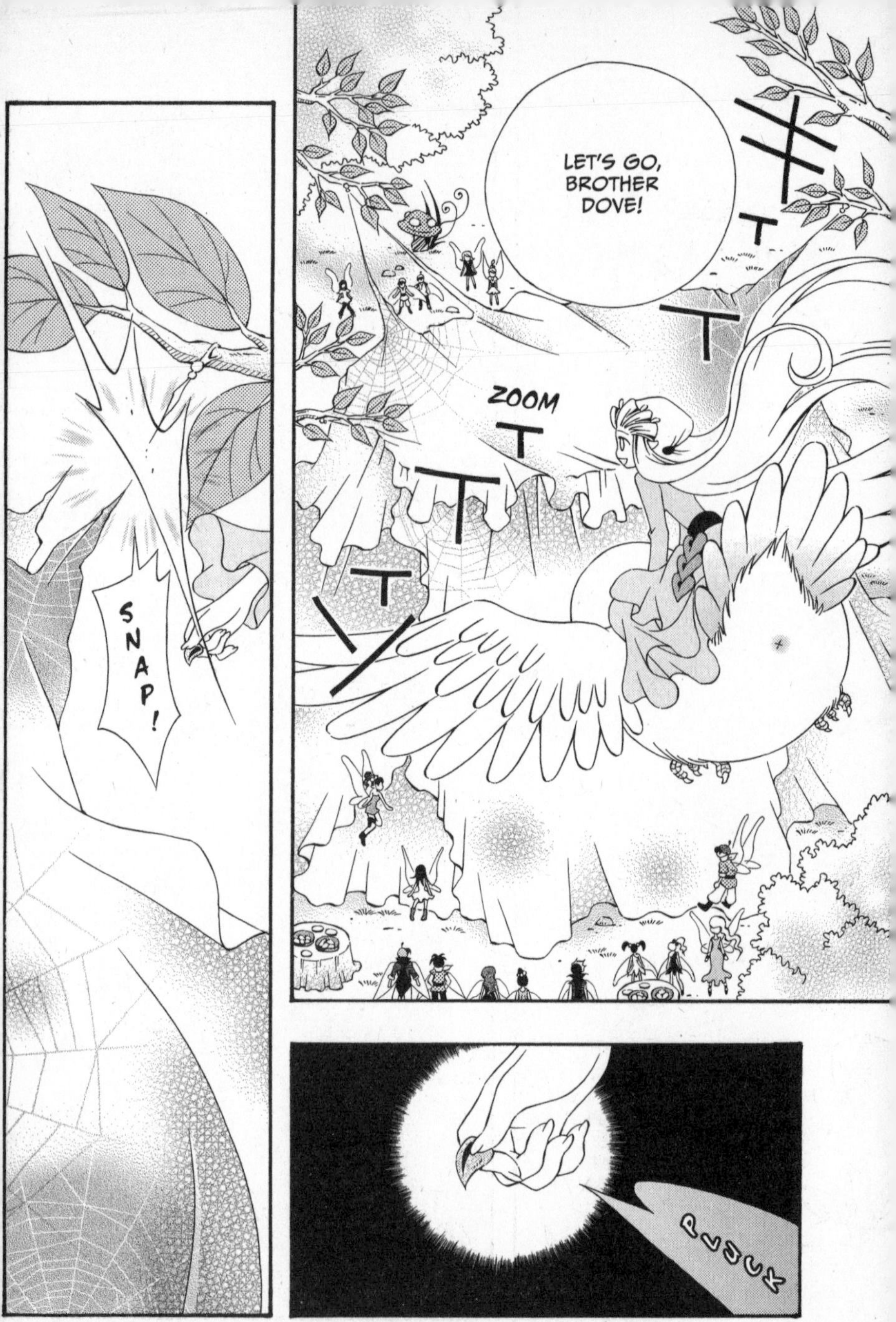
LET'S GO, BROTHER DOVE!
ZOOM
PLUCK
SNAP!

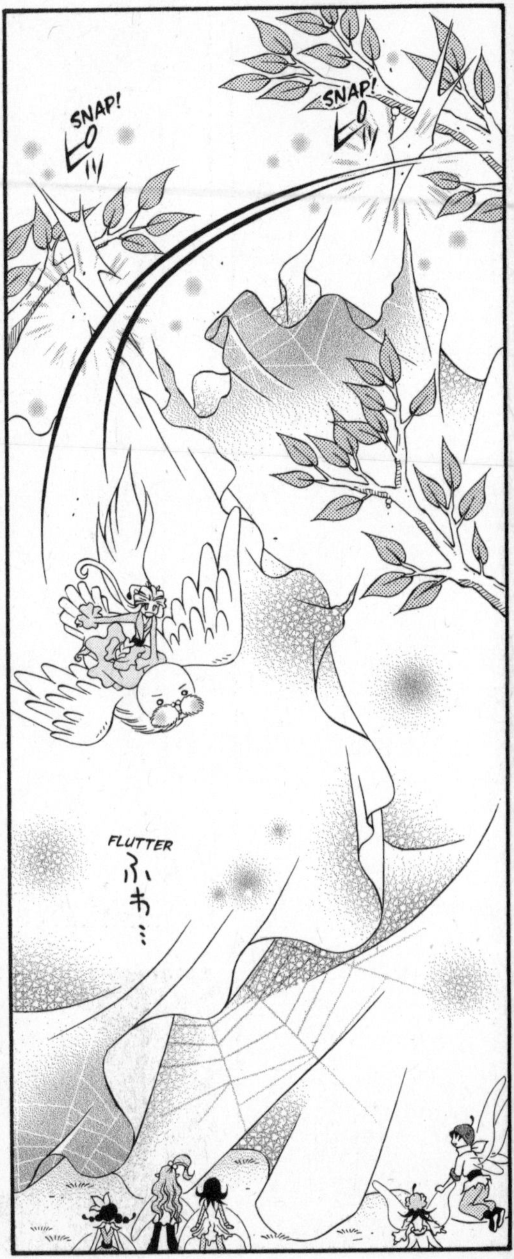
SNAP!
ピッ
SNAP!
ピッ
FLUTTER
ふわ…
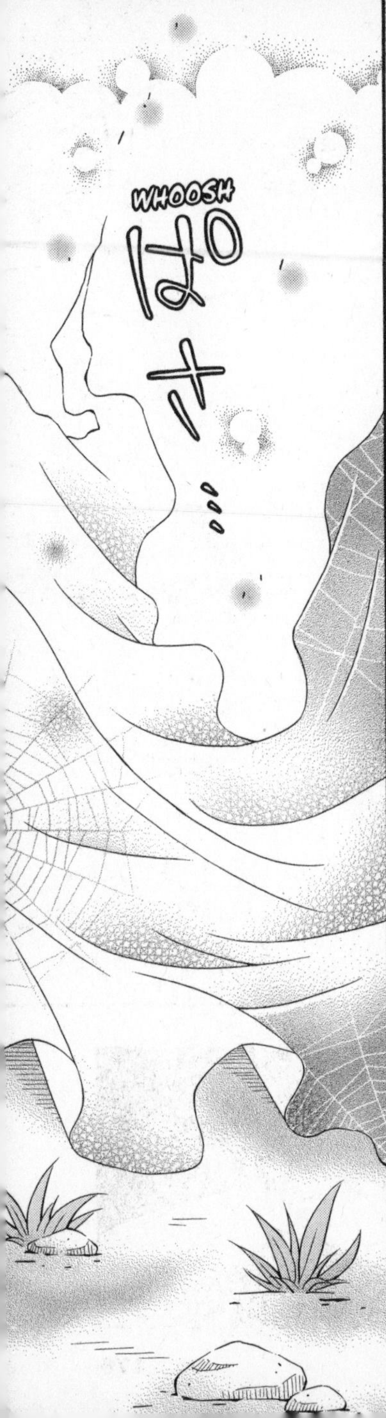
WHOOSH
ぱさ…

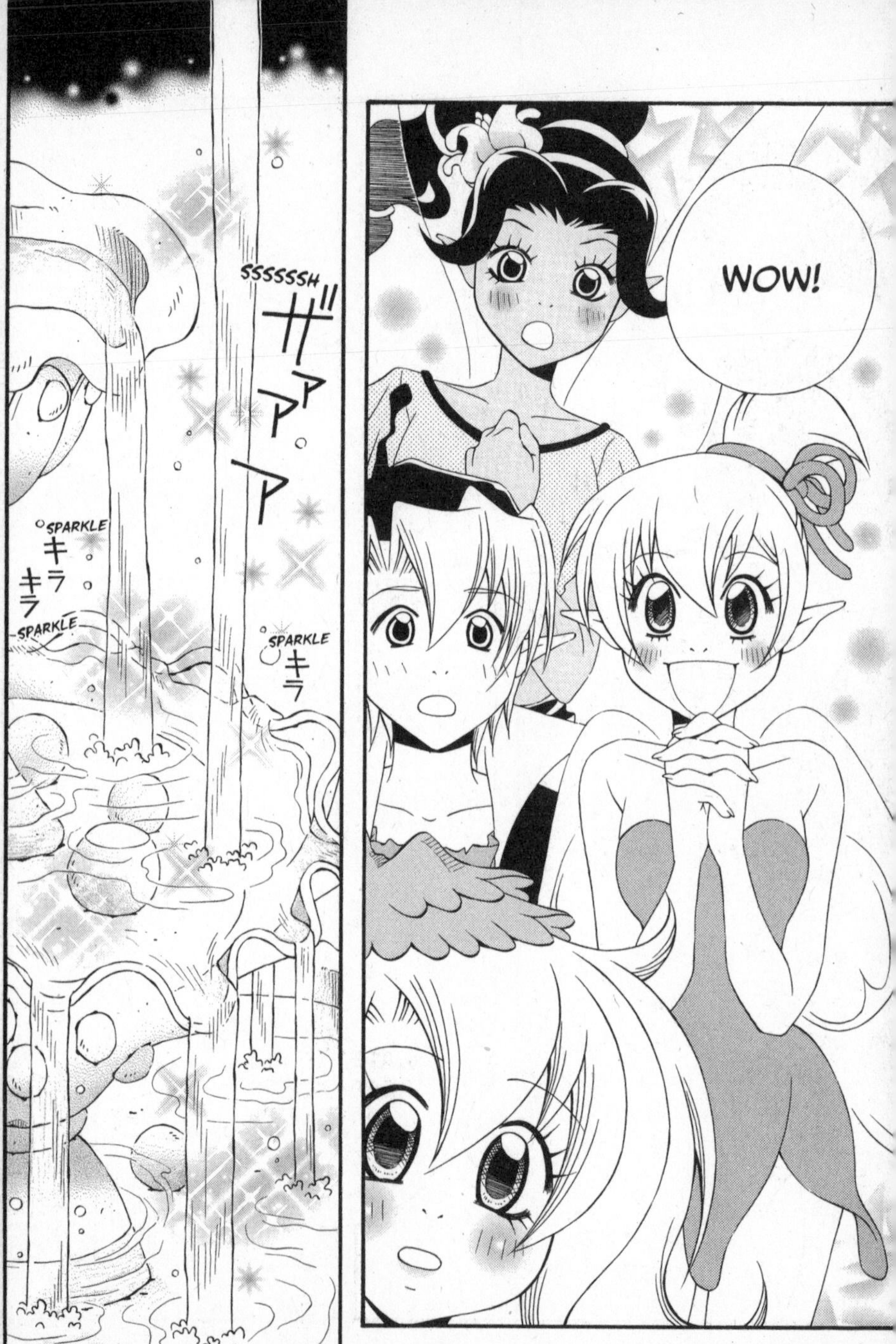
WOW!
SSSSSSH
ザアアア
SPARKLE
キラキラ
SPARKLE
SPARKLE
キラ

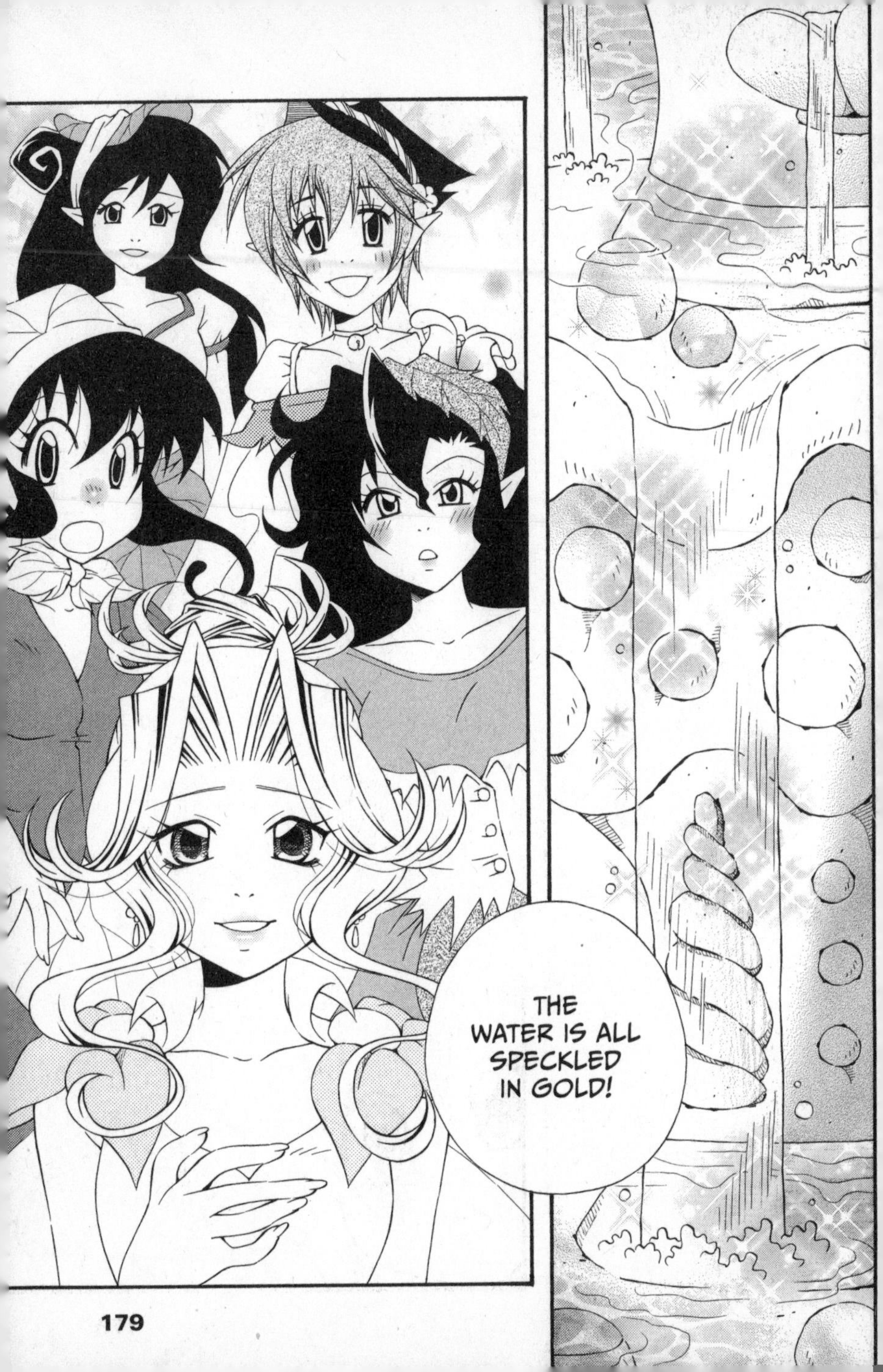
THE WATER IS ALL SPECKLED IN GOLD!

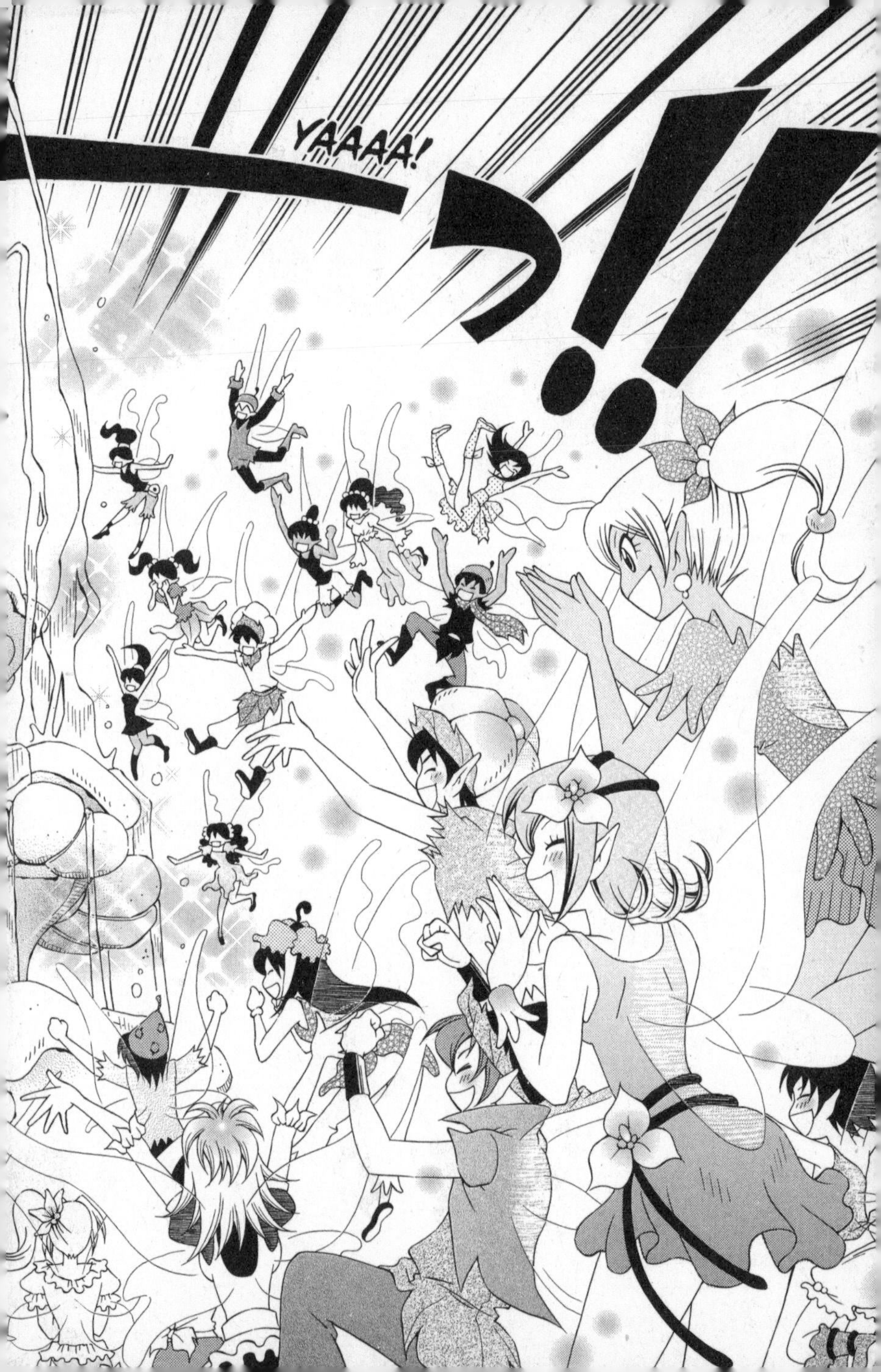
YAAAA!

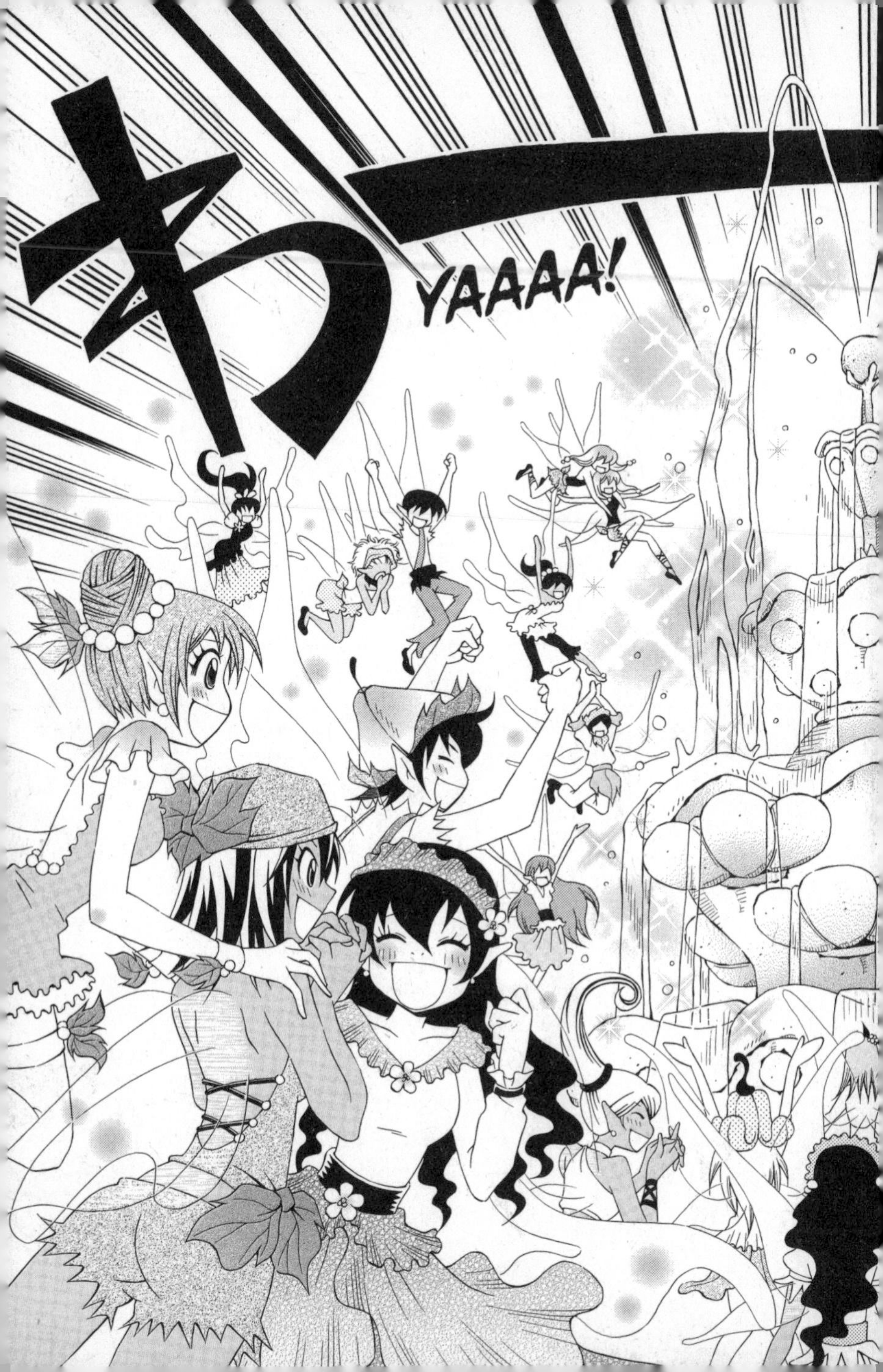
わー
YAAAA!

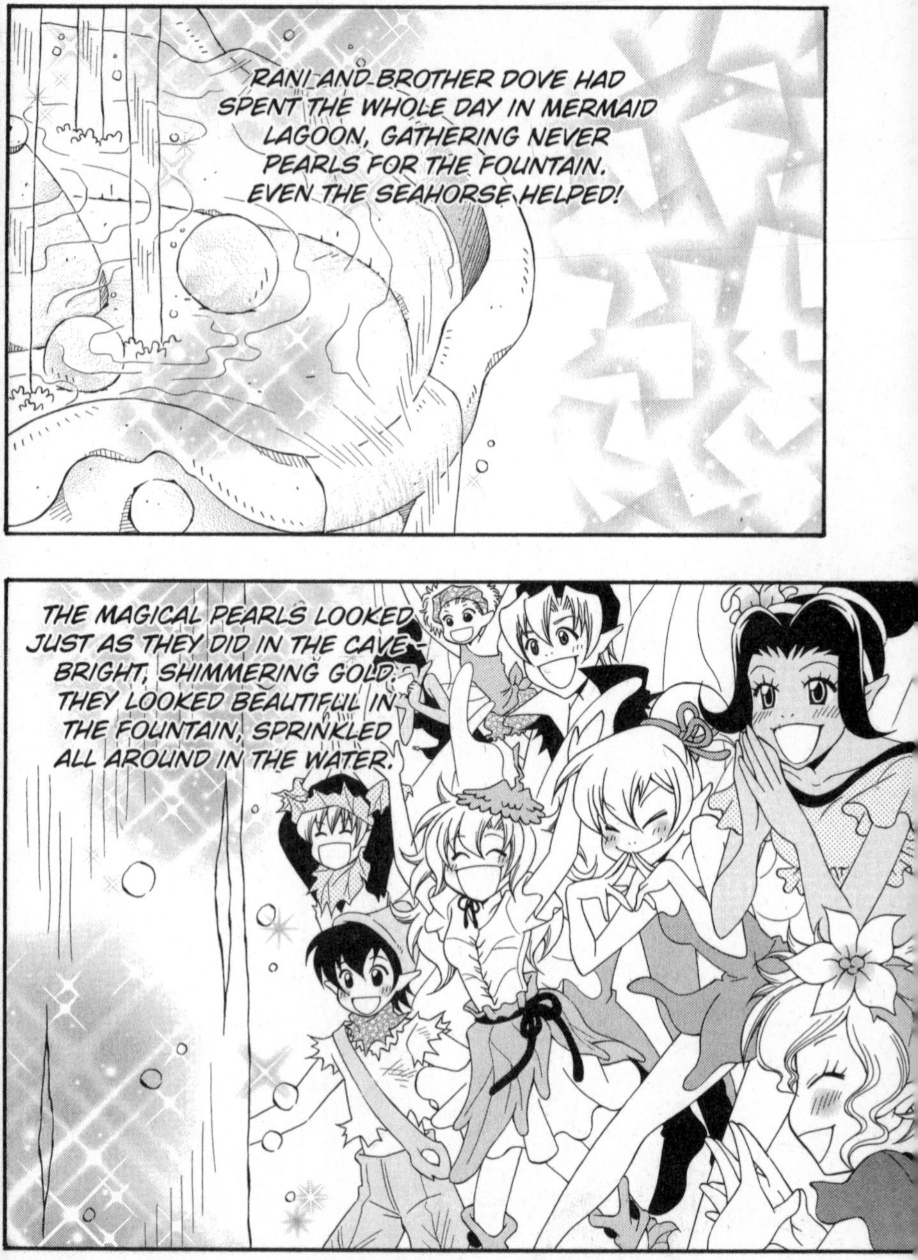
RANI AND BROTHER DOVE HAD SPENT THE WHOLE DAY IN MERMAID LAGOON, GATHERING NEVER PEARLS FOR THE FOUNTAIN. EVEN THE SEAHORSE HELPED!
THE MAGICAL PEARLS LOOKED JUST AS THEY DID IN THE CAVE - BRIGHT, SHIMMERING GOLD. THEY LOOKED BEAUTIFUL IN THE FOUNTAIN, SPRINKLED ALL AROUND IN THE WATER.

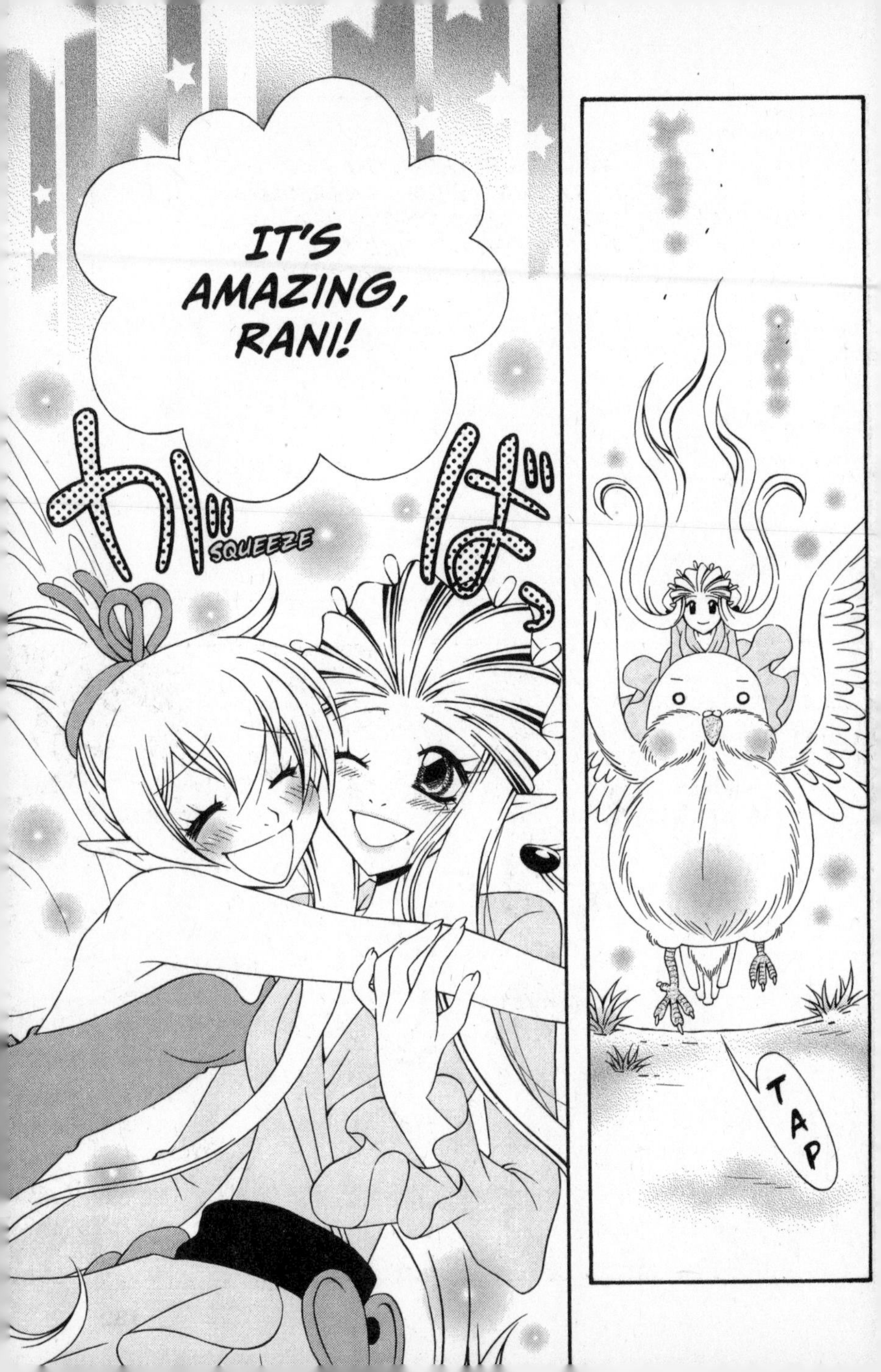
TAP
IT'S AMAZING, RANI!
がばっ
SQUEEZE

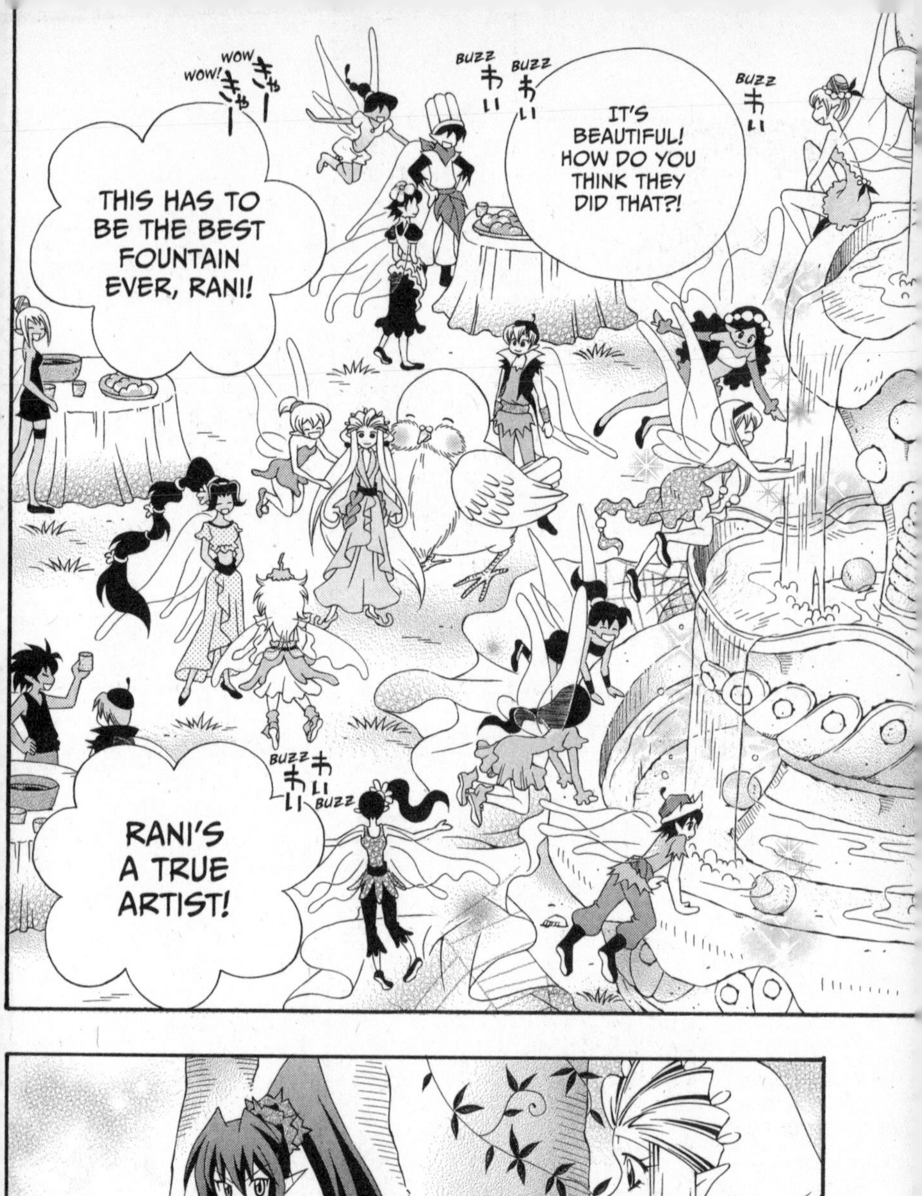
BUZZ わい
BUZZ わい
BUZZ わい
IT'S BEAUTIFUL! HOW DO YOU THINK THEY DID THAT?!
WOW きゃー
WOW! きゃー
THIS HAS TO BE THE BEST FOUNTAIN EVER, RANI!
BUZZ わい
BUZZ わい
RANI'S A TRUE ARTIST!
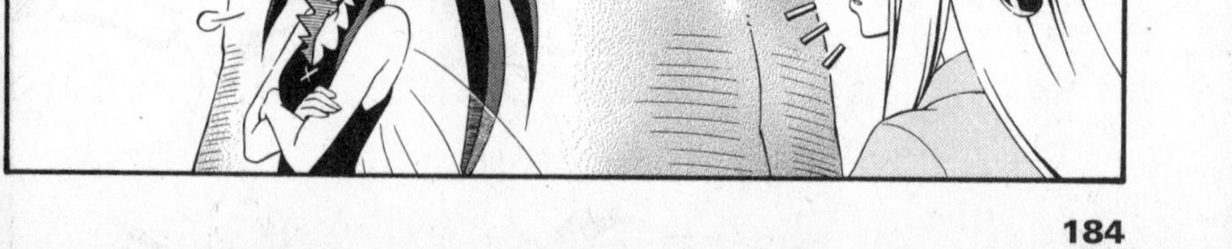

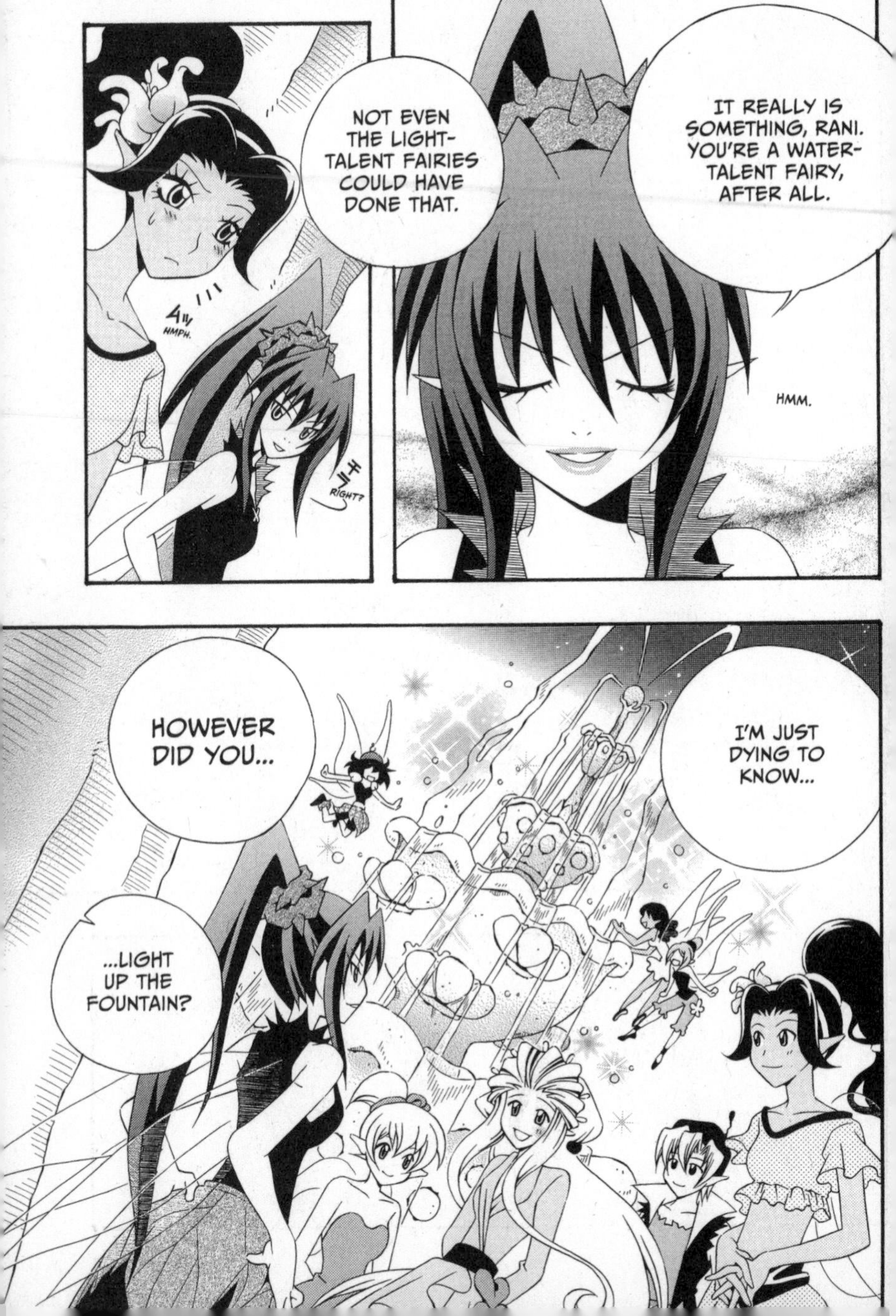
IT REALLY IS SOMETHING, RANI. YOU'RE A WATER-TALENT FAIRY, AFTER ALL.
HMM.
NOT EVEN THE LIGHT-TALENT FAIRIES COULD HAVE DONE THAT.
HMPH.
RIGHT?
I'M JUST DYING TO KNOW...
HOWEVER DID YOU...
...LIGHT UP THE FOUNTAIN?

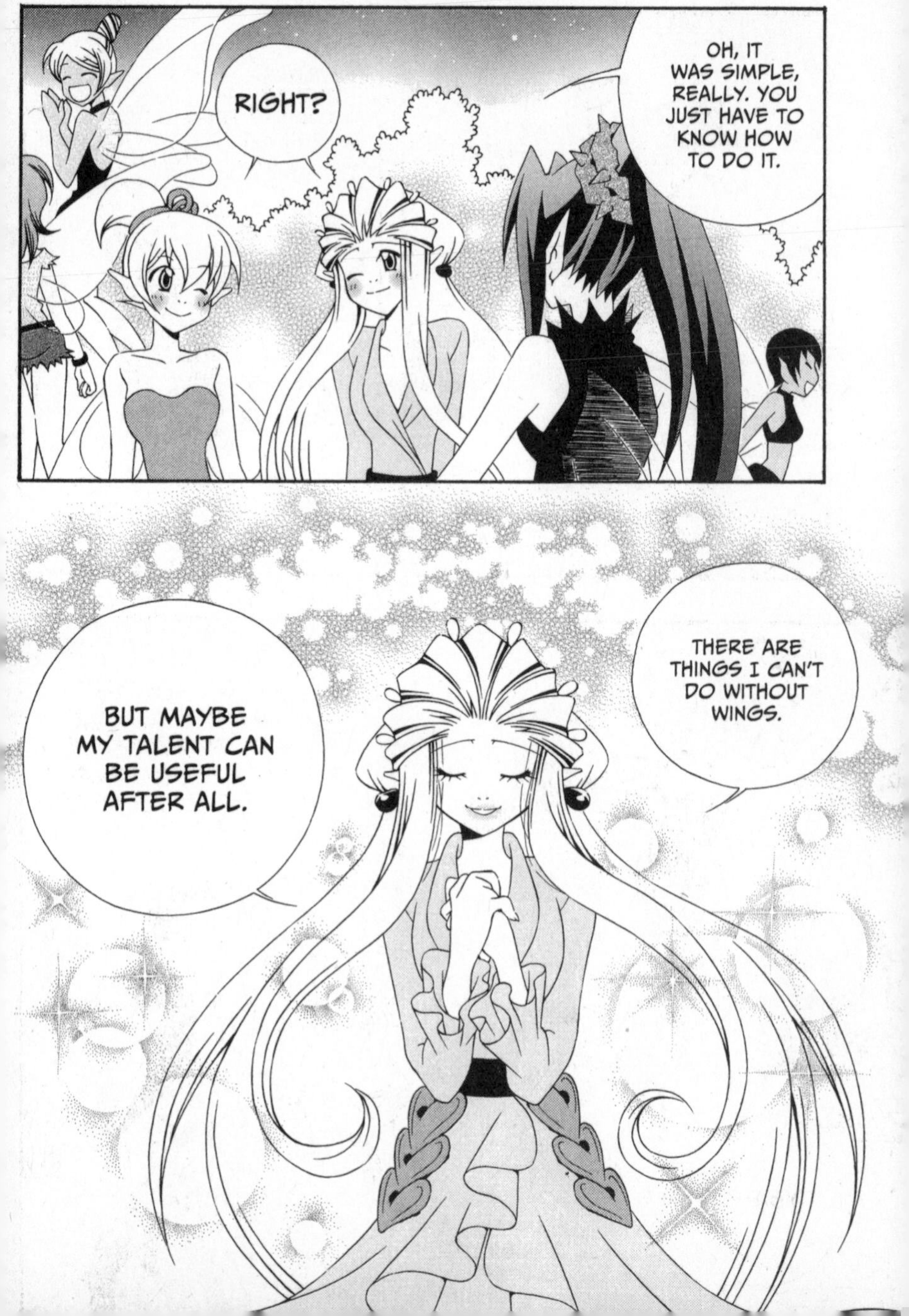
OH, IT WAS SIMPLE, REALLY. YOU JUST HAVE TO KNOW HOW TO DO IT.
RIGHT?
THERE ARE THINGS I CAN'T DO WITHOUT WINGS.
BUT MAYBE MY TALENT CAN BE USEFUL AFTER ALL.

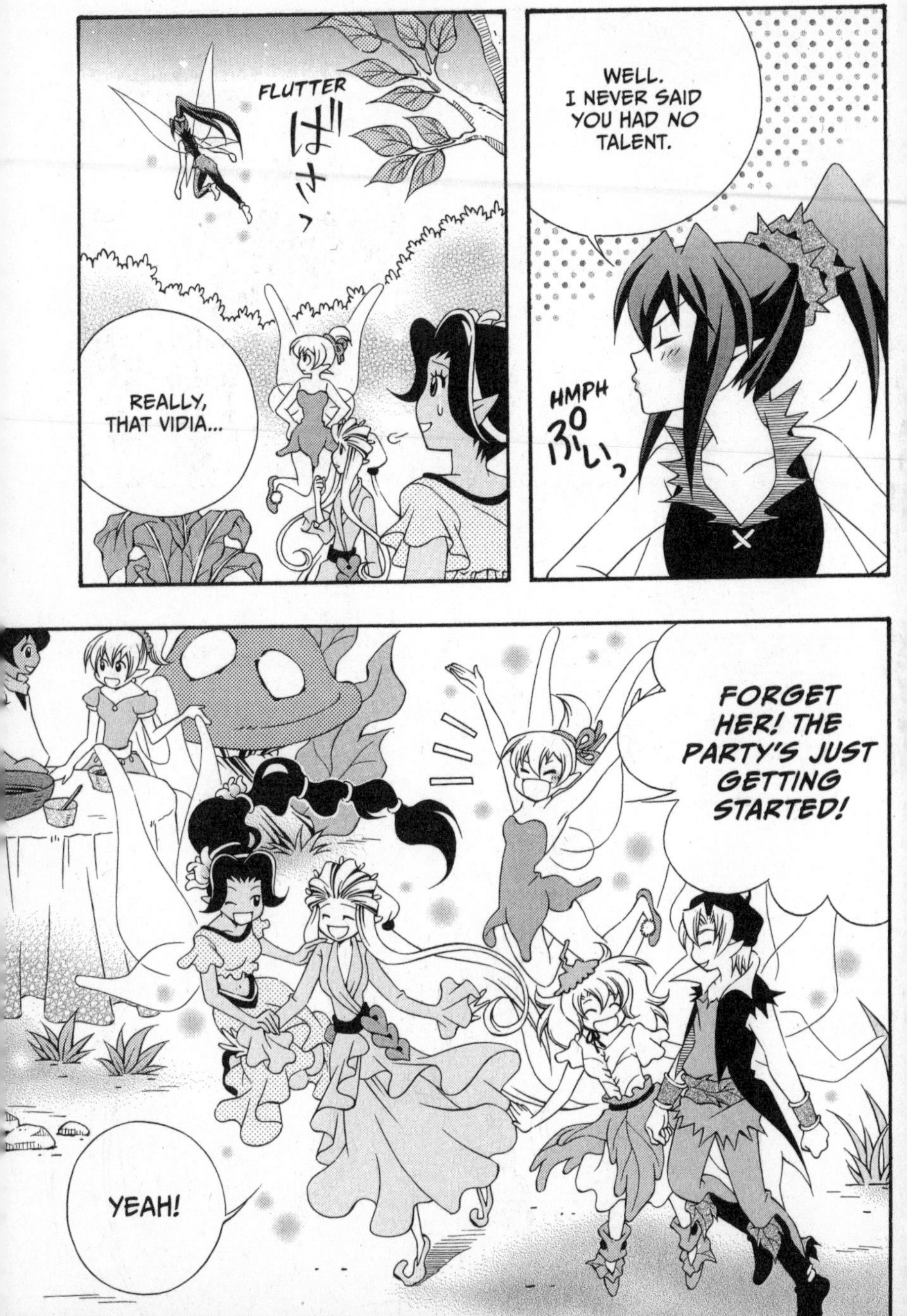
WELL. I NEVER SAID YOU HAD NO TALENT.
HMPH
ぷいっ
FLUTTER
ばさっ
REALLY, THAT VIDIA...
FORGET HER! THE PARTY'S JUST GETTING STARTED!
YEAH!

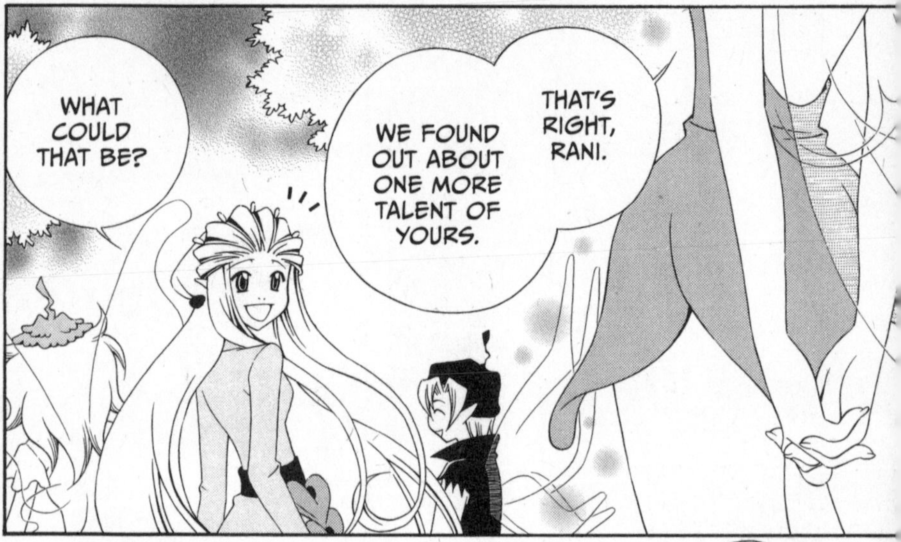
THAT'S RIGHT, RANI.
WE FOUND OUT ABOUT ONE MORE TALENT OF YOURS.
WHAT COULD THAT BE?

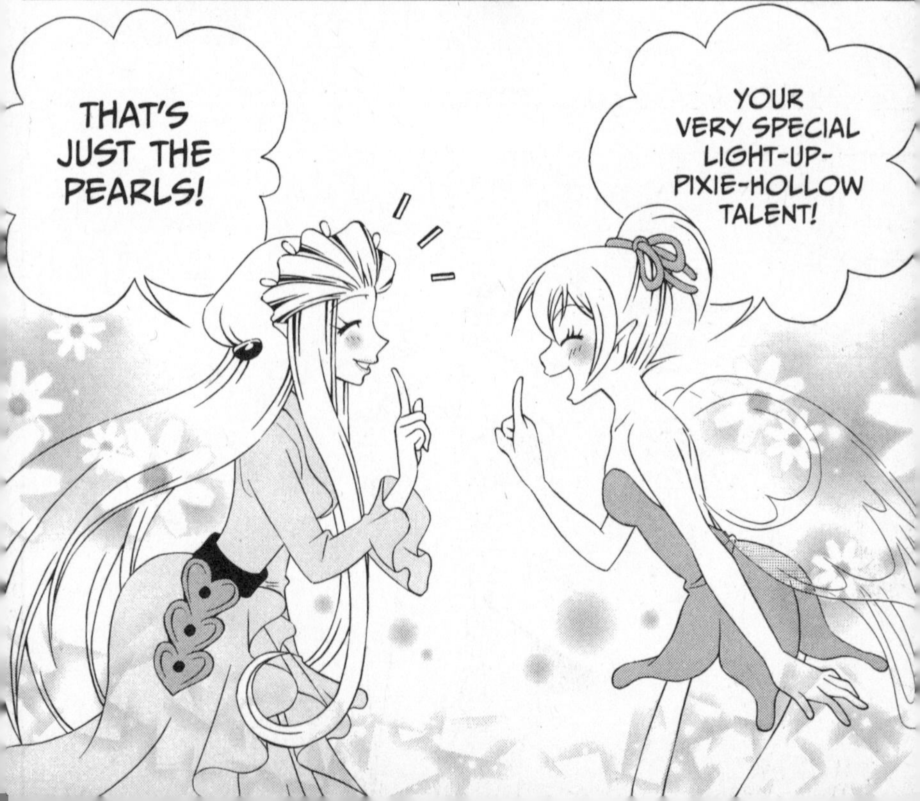
YOUR VERY SPECIAL LIGHT-UP-PIXIE-HOLLOW TALENT!
THAT'S JUST THE PEARLS!

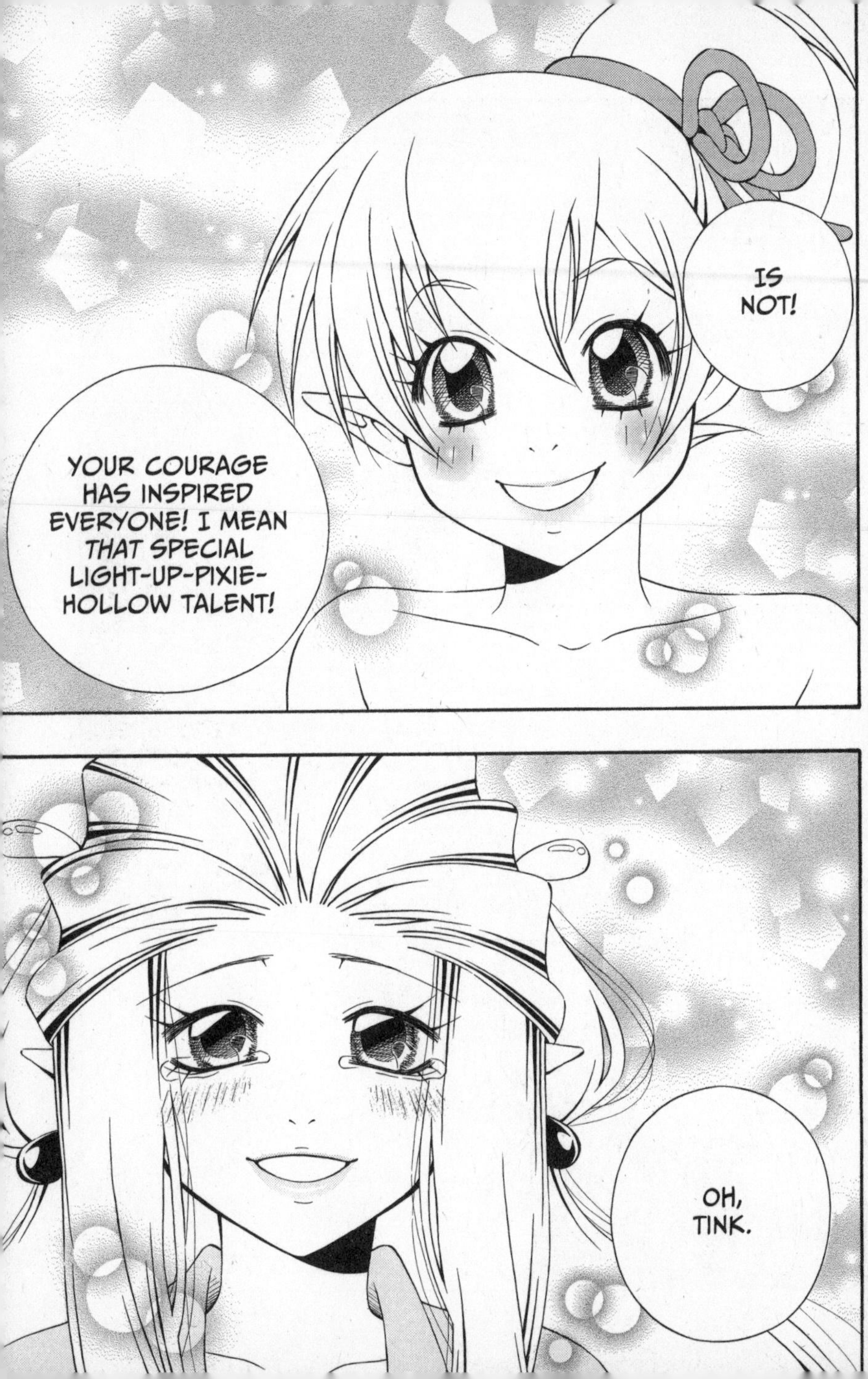
IS NOT!
YOUR COURAGE HAS INSPIRED EVERYONE! I MEAN *THAT* SPECIAL LIGHT-UP-PIXIE-HOLLOW TALENT!
OH, TINK.

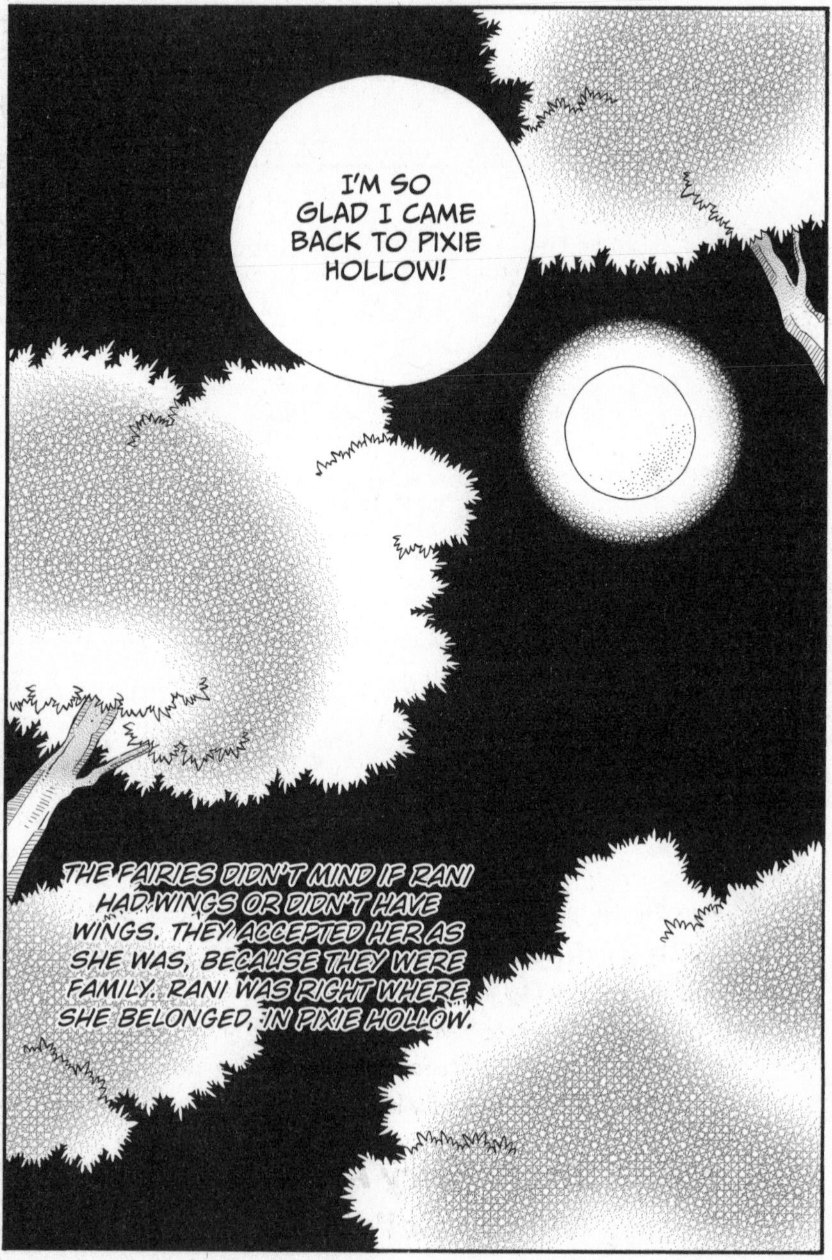
I'M SO GLAD I CAME BACK TO PIXIE HOLLOW!
THE FAIRIES DIDN'T MIND IF RANI HAD WINGS OR DIDN'T HAVE WINGS. THEY ACCEPTED HER AS SHE WAS, BECAUSE THEY WERE FAMILY. RANI WAS RIGHT WHERE SHE BELONGED, IN PIXIE HOLLOW.

In the next Disney Fairies Manga!

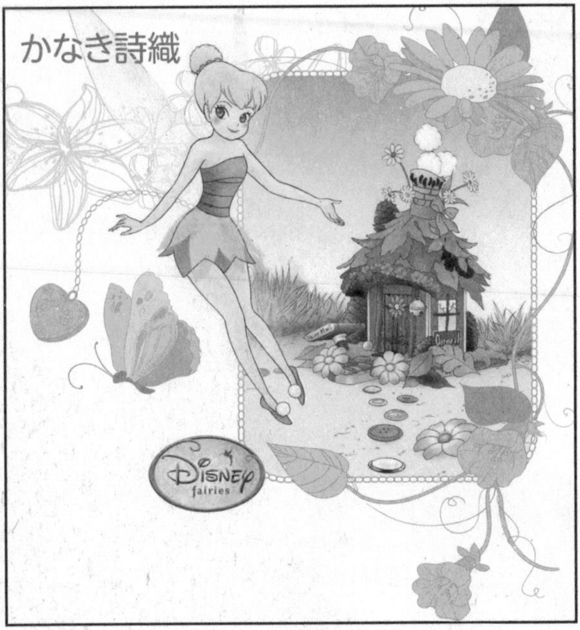
かなき詩織
Disney fairies

The Great Fairy Rescue

Every fairy attends the annual fairy camp on the mainland, and Tinker Bell is no different! When she finds out about the human family living nearby, her curiosity gets the better of her and she accidentally gets trapped in a tiny house made by a young girl named Lizzy. Now Vidia and the other fairies must come together to rescue Tink, before the humans discover her!

Add *The Great Fairy Rescue* to your Disney Manga Collection today!

LET'S COUNT TOGETHER!

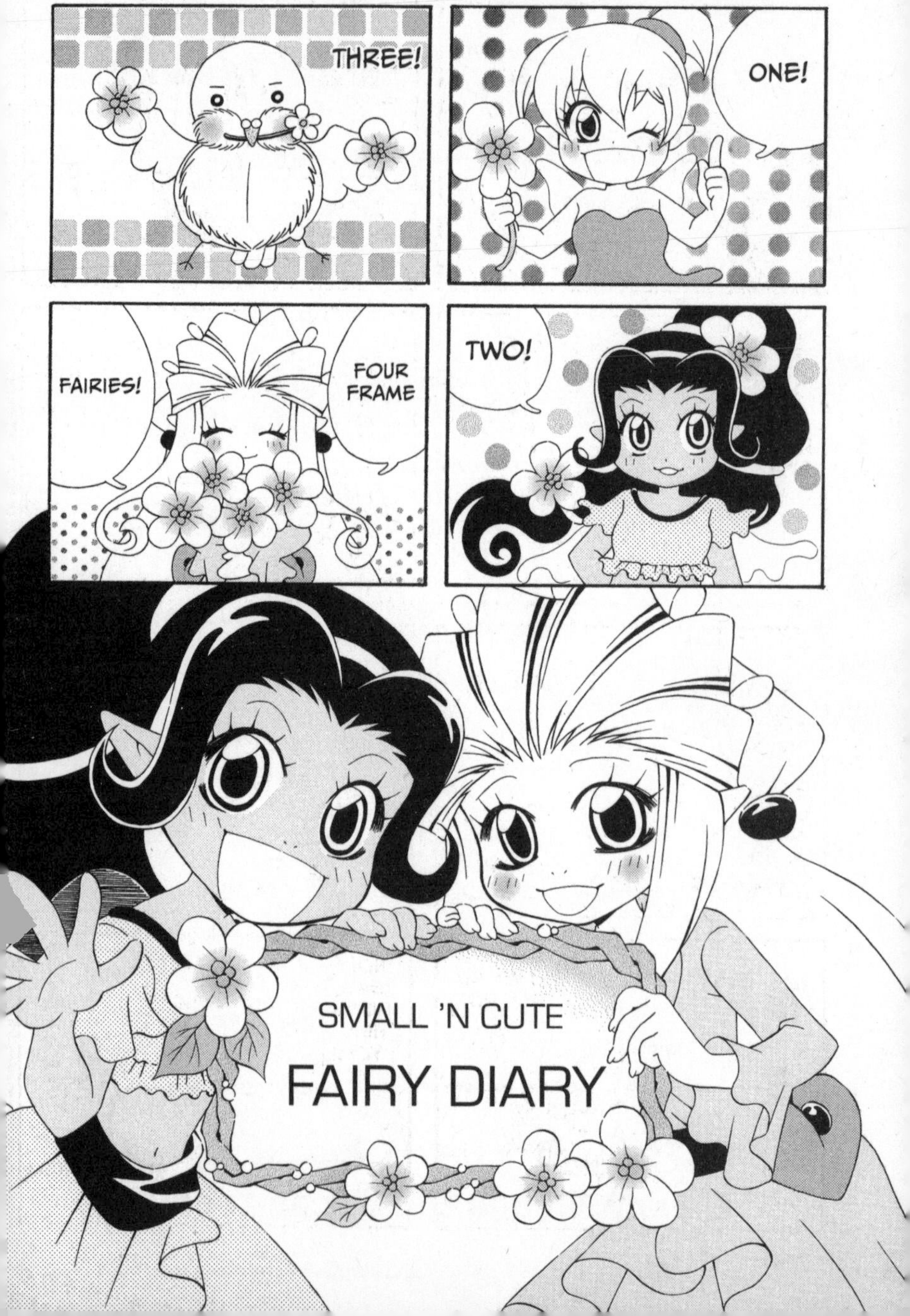
ONE!
TWO!
THREE!
FOUR FRAME
FAIRIES!
SMALL 'N CUTE
FAIRY DIARY

VIDIA'S CLOTHES

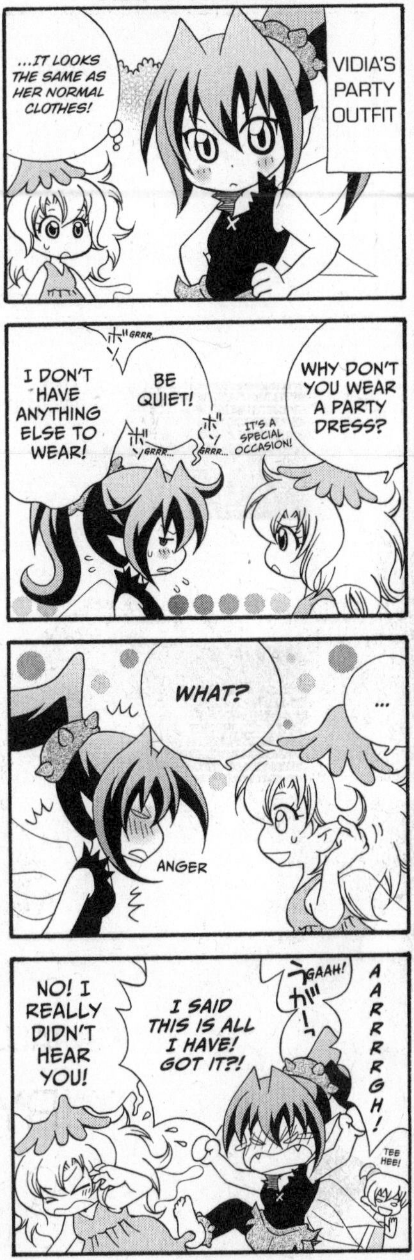
VIDIA'S PARTY OUTFIT
...IT LOOKS THE SAME AS HER NORMAL CLOTHES!
WHY DON'T YOU WEAR A PARTY DRESS?
IT'S A SPECIAL OCCASION!
ボッ GRRR...
BE QUIET!
ボッ GRRR...
I DON'T HAVE ANYTHING ELSE TO WEAR!
...
WHAT?
ANGER
AARRRGH!
うがーっ GAAH!
I SAID THIS IS ALL I HAVE! GOT IT?!
NO! I REALLY DIDN'T HEAR YOU!
TEE HEE!

I MADE A DRESS!

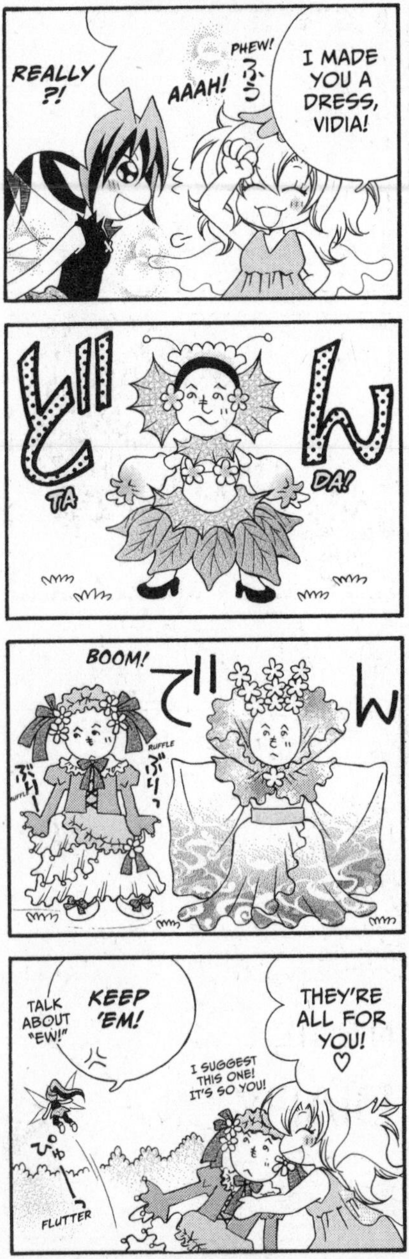
I MADE YOU A DRESS, VIDIA!
ふう PHEW!
AAAH!
REALLY ?!
どん
TA DA!
でん
BOOM!
ぶりっ RUFFLE
ぶりー RUFFLE
THEY'RE ALL FOR YOU! ♡
I SUGGEST THIS ONE! IT'S SO YOU!
KEEP 'EM!
TALK ABOUT "EW!"
ぴゅーっ FLUTTER

BROTHER DOVE

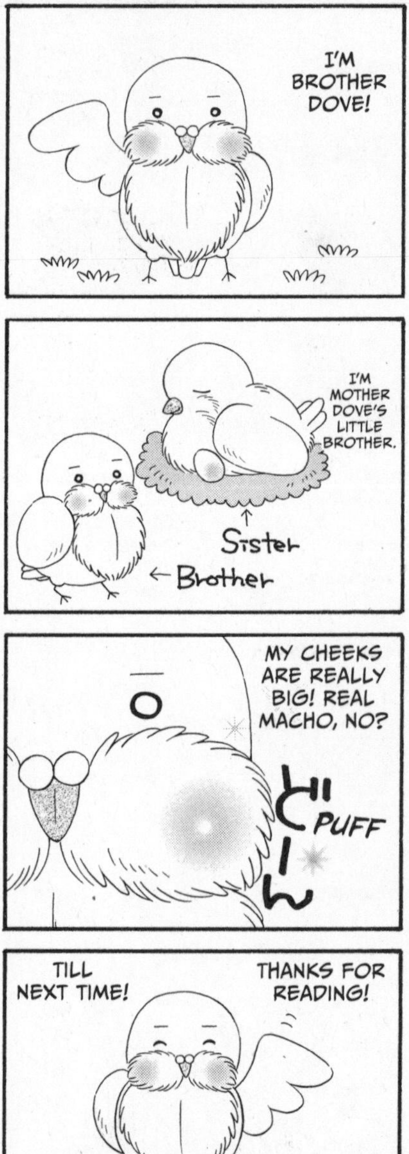
I'M BROTHER DOVE!
I'M MOTHER DOVE'S LITTLE BROTHER.
Sister
Brother
MY CHEEKS ARE REALLY BIG! REAL MACHO, NO?
どーん
PUFF
THANKS FOR READING!
TILL NEXT TIME!

MY FAVORITE THING

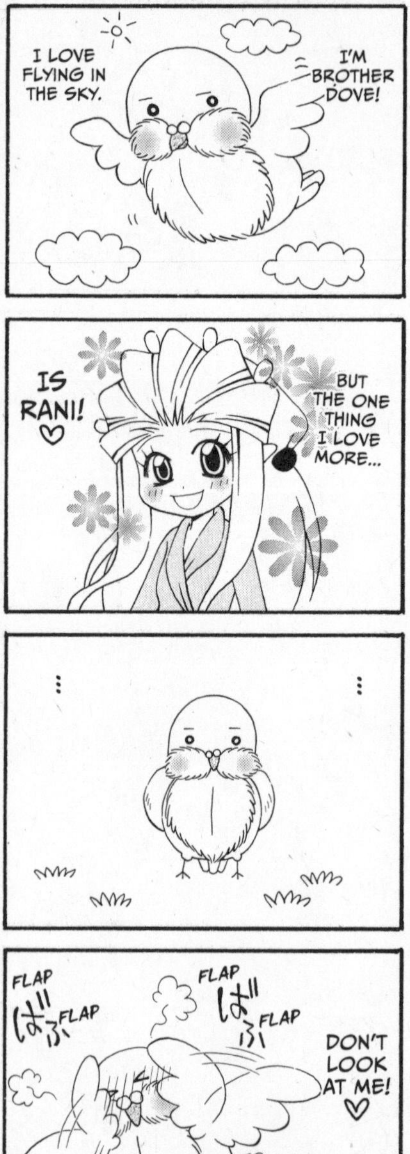
I'M BROTHER DOVE!
I LOVE FLYING IN THE SKY.
BUT THE ONE THING I LOVE MORE...
IS RANI! ♡
...
...
DON'T LOOK AT ME! ♡
FLAP ばふ FLAP
FLAP ばふ FLAP

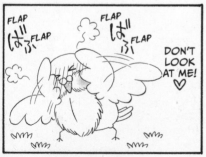

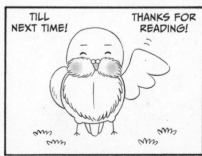

DID SHE HEAR?

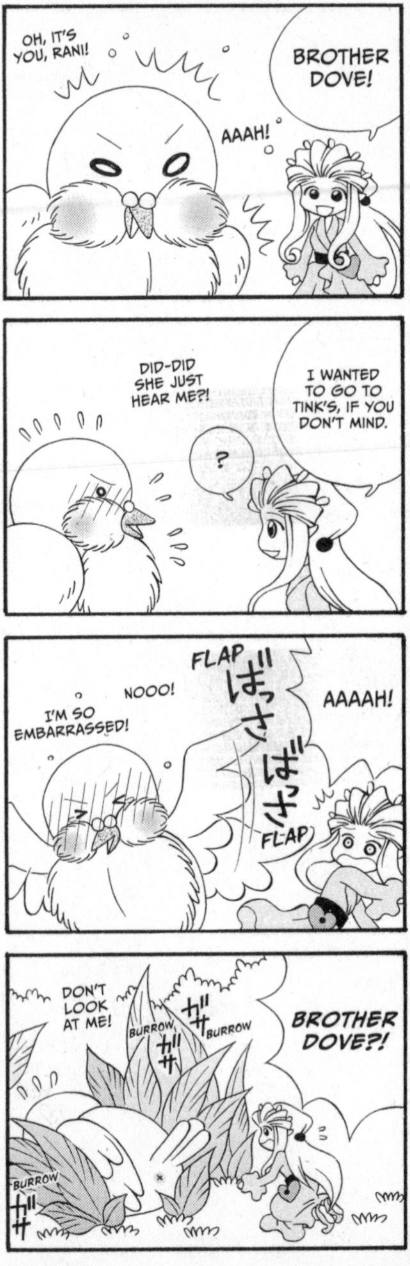
BROTHER DOVE!
OH, IT'S YOU, RANI!
AAAH!
I WANTED TO GO TO TINK'S, IF YOU DON'T MIND.
DID-DID SHE JUST HEAR ME?!
?
AAAAH!
FLAP
ばっさ
NOOO!
I'M SO EMBARRASSED!
ばっさ
FLAP
BROTHER DOVE?!
BURROW
ガサ
BURROW
ガサ
DON'T LOOK AT ME!
BURROW
ガサ

I LIKE BOTH!

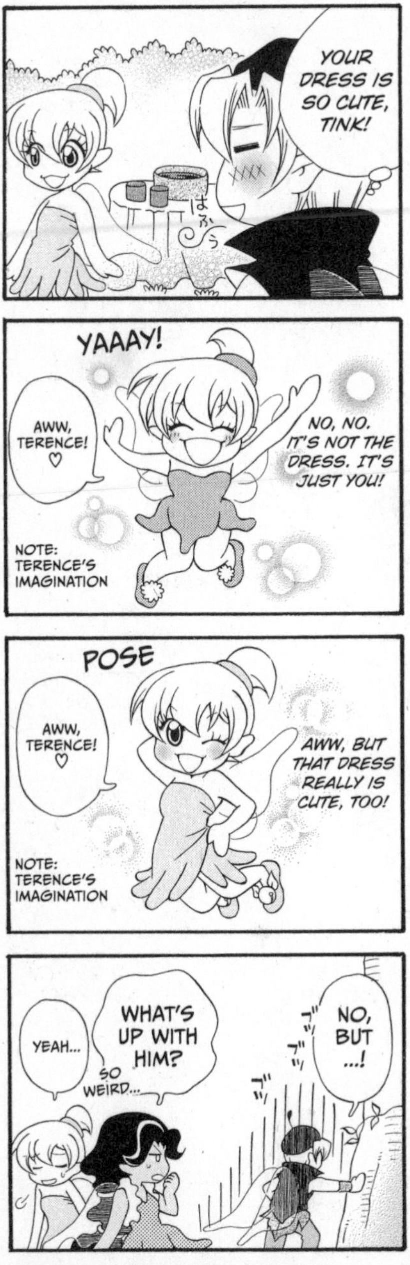
YOUR DRESS IS SO CUTE, TINK!
はふぅ
NO, NO. IT'S NOT THE DRESS. IT'S JUST YOU!
YAAAY!
AWW, TERENCE! ♡
NOTE: TERENCE'S IMAGINATION
AWW, BUT THAT DRESS REALLY IS CUTE, TOO!
POSE
AWW, TERENCE! ♡
NOTE: TERENCE'S IMAGINATION
NO, BUT ...!
WHAT'S UP WITH HIM?
YEAH...
SO WEIRD...

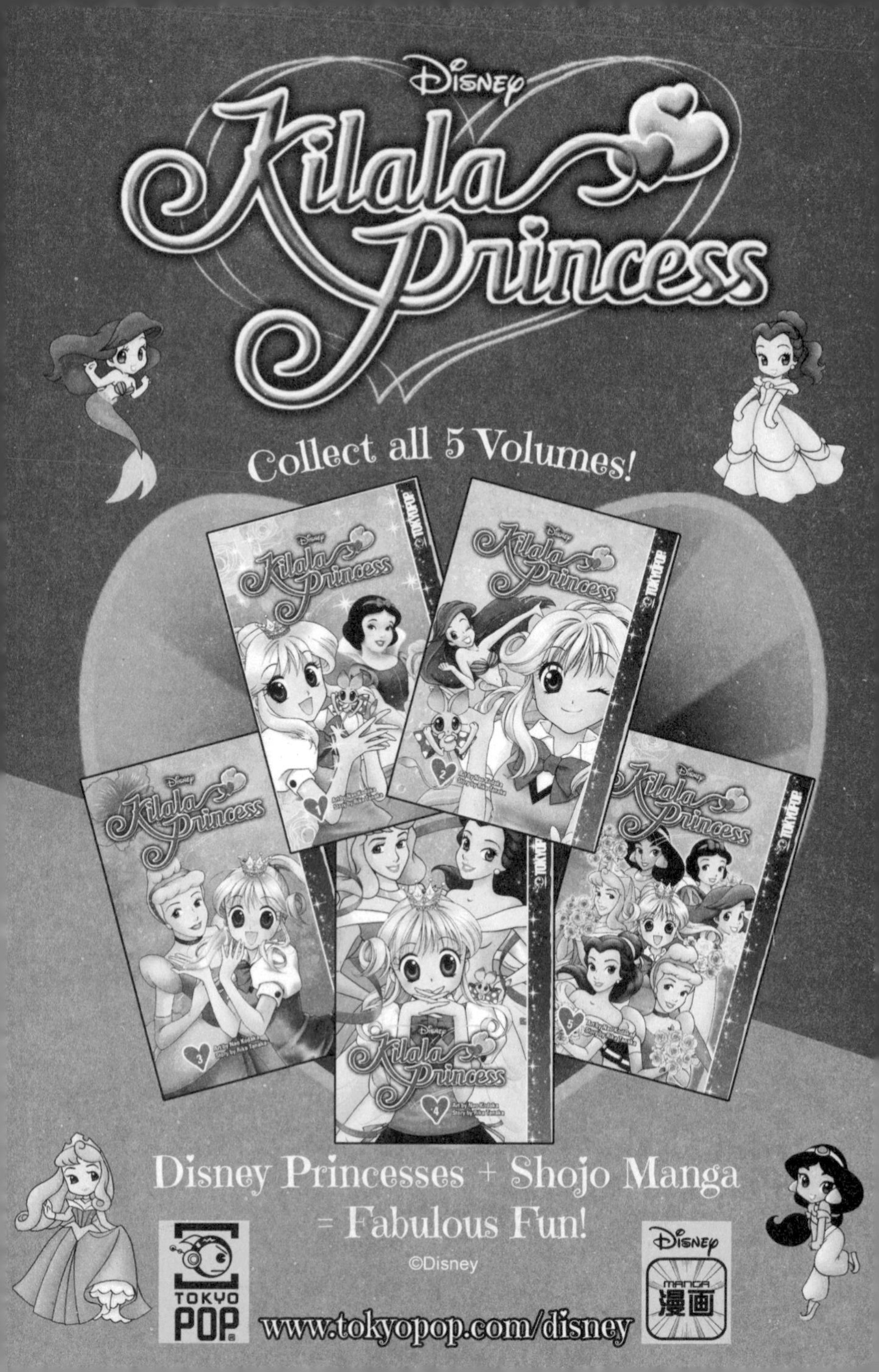
Disney
Kilala Princess
Collect all 5 Volumes!
Disney Princesses + Shojo Manga
= Fabulous Fun!
©Disney
TOKYO POP
www.tokyopop.com/disney
Disney
MANGA
漫画

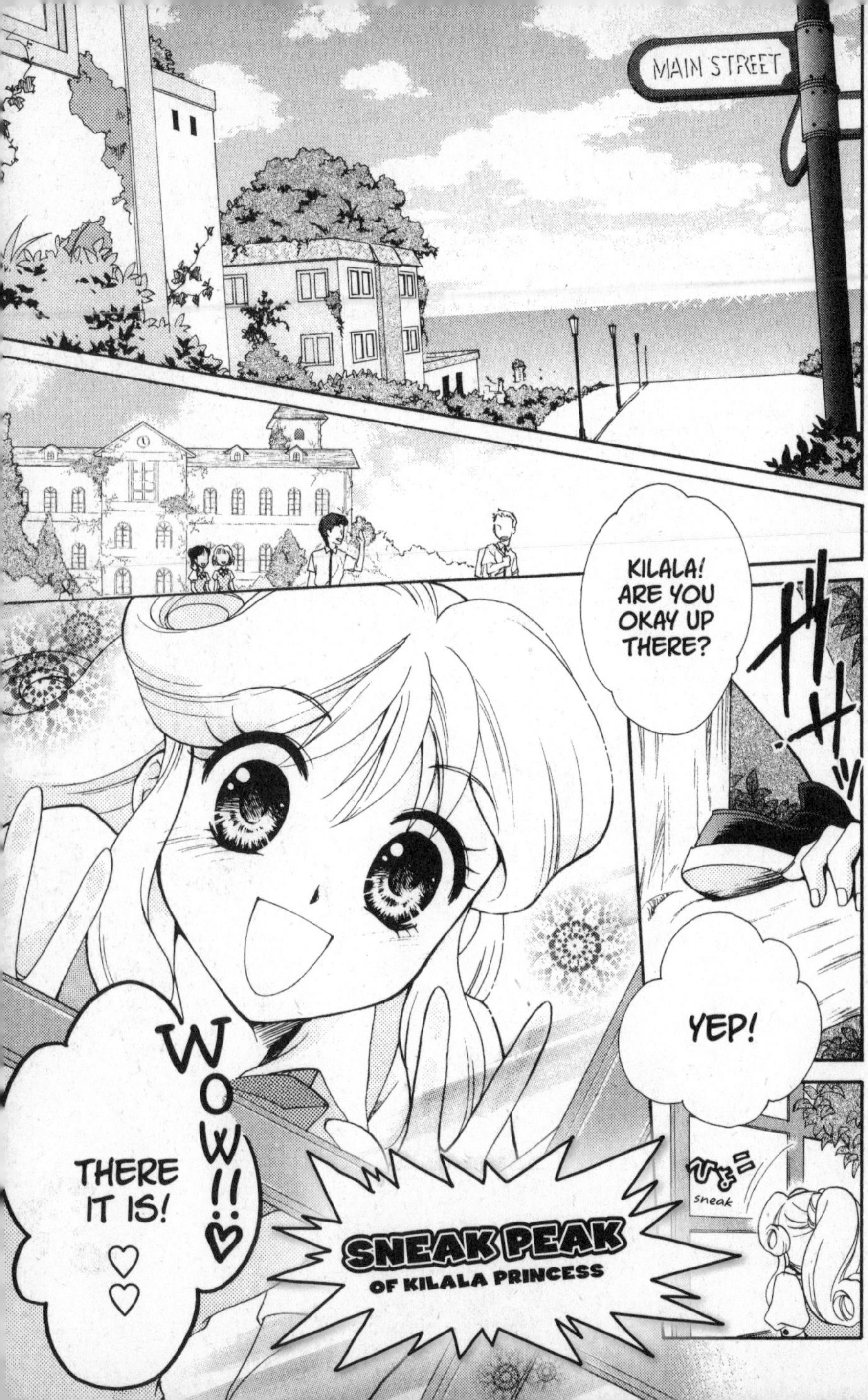
MAIN STREET
KILALA! ARE YOU OKAY UP THERE?
YEP!
sneak
WOW!! ♥
THERE IT IS! ♡ ♡
SNEAK PEAK
OF KILALA PRINCESS

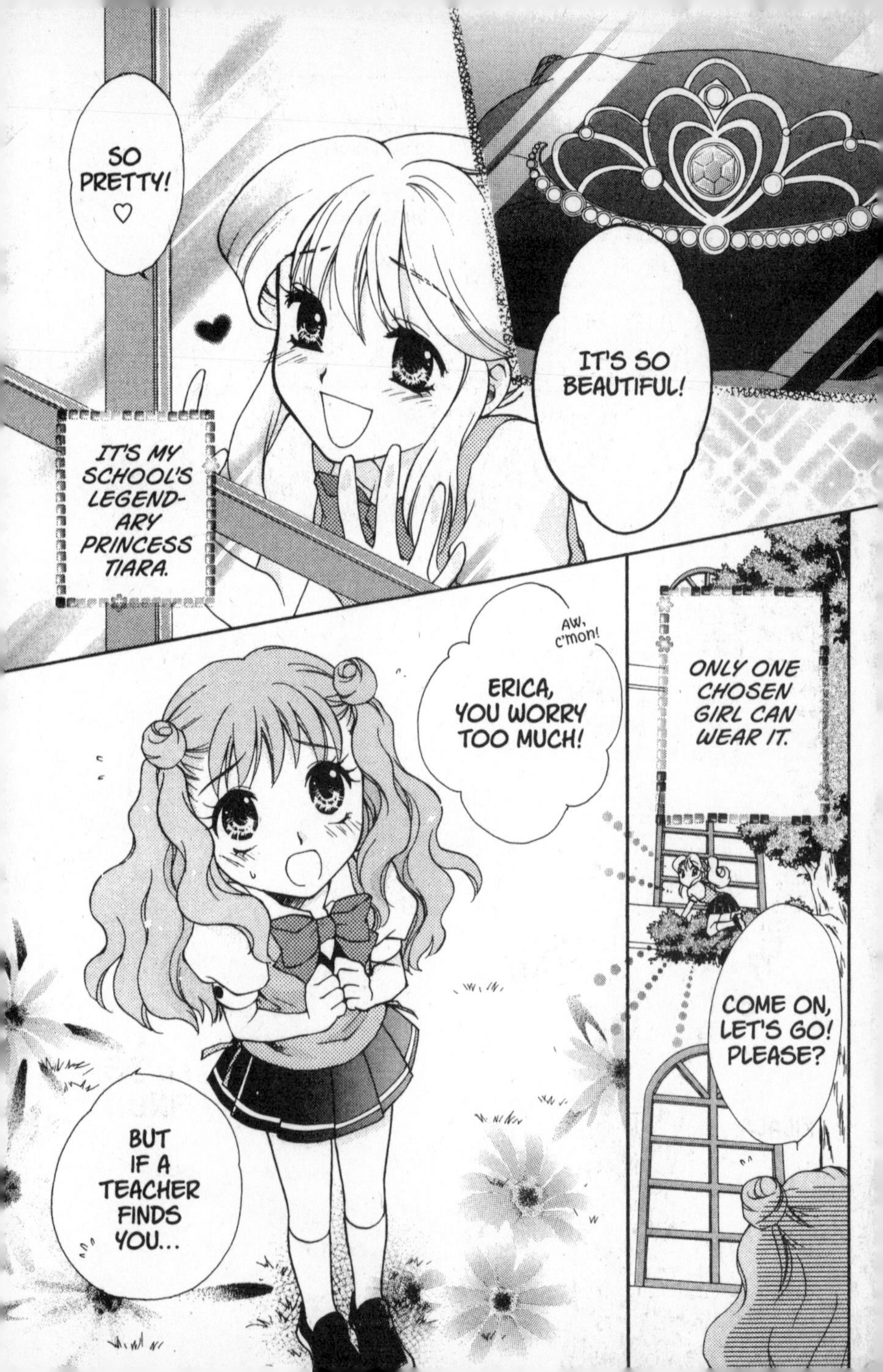
IT'S SO BEAUTIFUL!
SO PRETTY! ♡
IT'S MY SCHOOL'S LEGENDARY PRINCESS TIARA.
ONLY ONE CHOSEN GIRL CAN WEAR IT.
COME ON, LET'S GO! PLEASE?
BUT IF A TEACHER FINDS YOU...
AW, C'MON!
ERICA, YOU WORRY TOO MUCH!

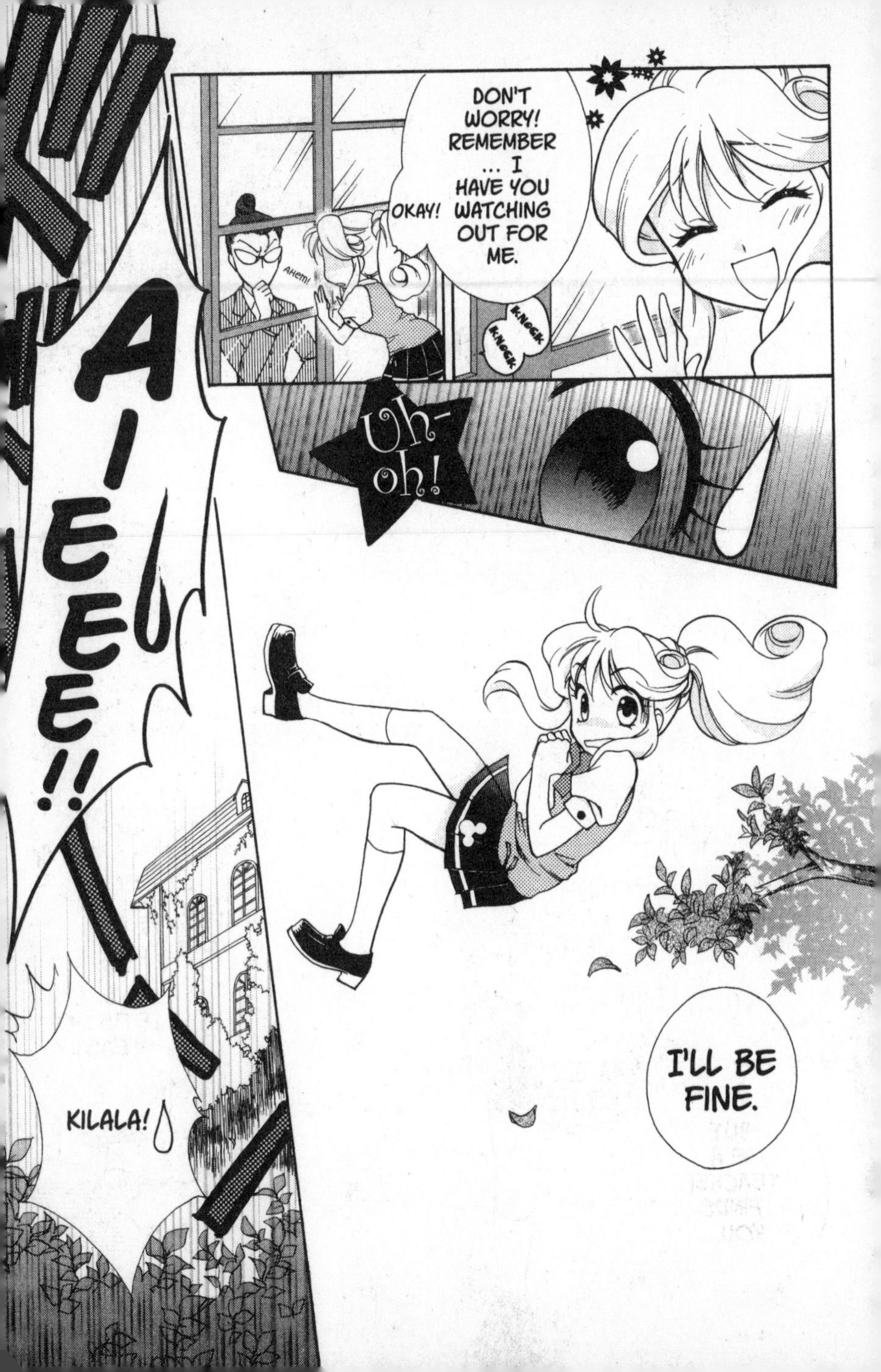
DON'T WORRY! REMEMBER ... I HAVE YOU WATCHING OUT FOR ME.
OKAY!
AHEM!
KNOCK KNOCK
Uh-oh!
I'LL BE FINE.
AIEEEE!!
KILALA!

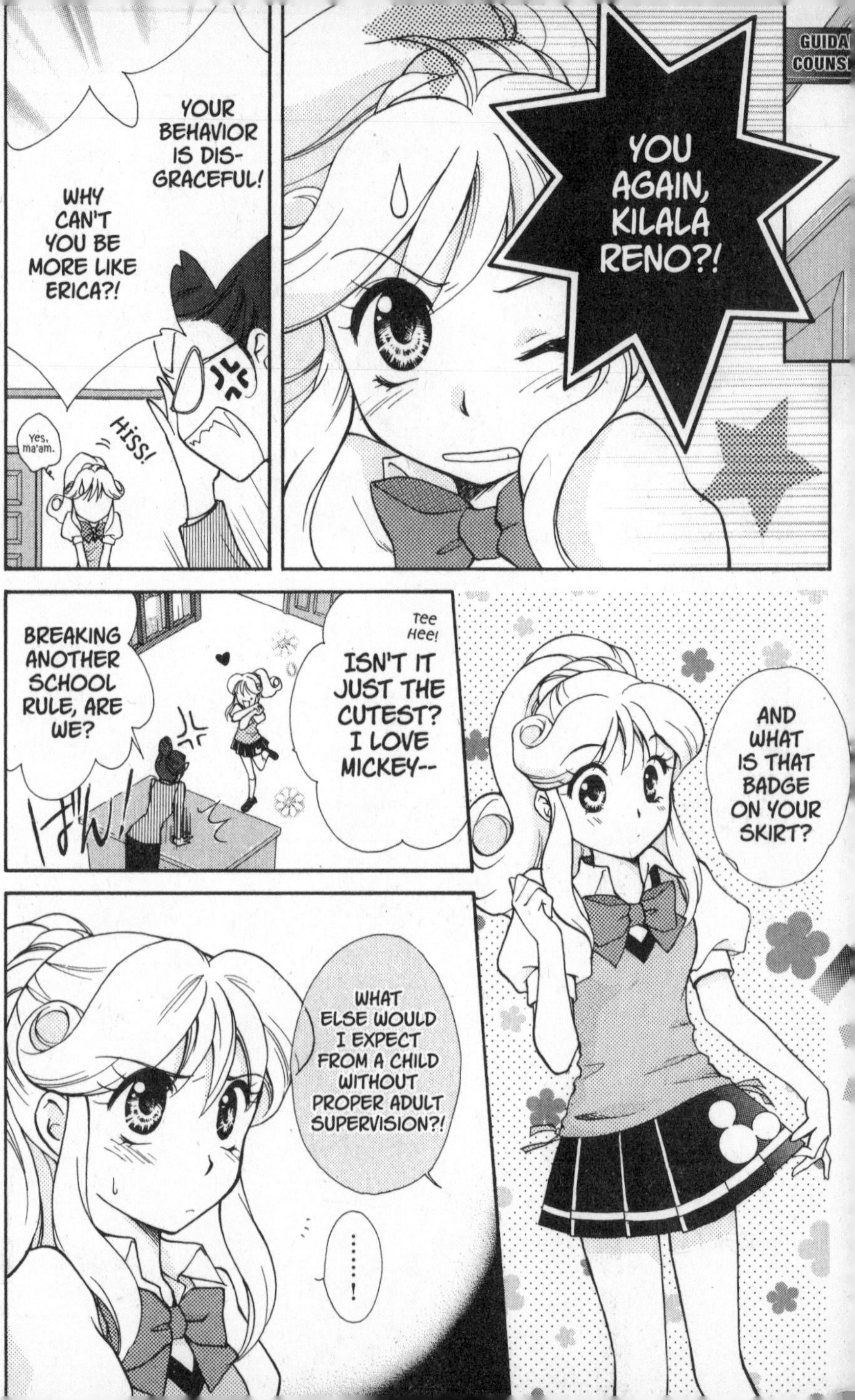
GUIDA
COUNS
YOU AGAIN, KILALA RENO?!
YOUR BEHAVIOR IS DIS-GRACEFUL!
WHY CAN'T YOU BE MORE LIKE ERICA?!
HISS!
Yes, ma'am.
AND WHAT IS THAT BADGE ON YOUR SKIRT?
Tee Hee!
ISN'T IT JUST THE CUTEST? I LOVE MICKEY--
BREAKING ANOTHER SCHOOL RULE, ARE WE?
ばん!
WHAT ELSE WOULD I EXPECT FROM A CHILD WITHOUT PROPER ADULT SUPERVISION?!
......!

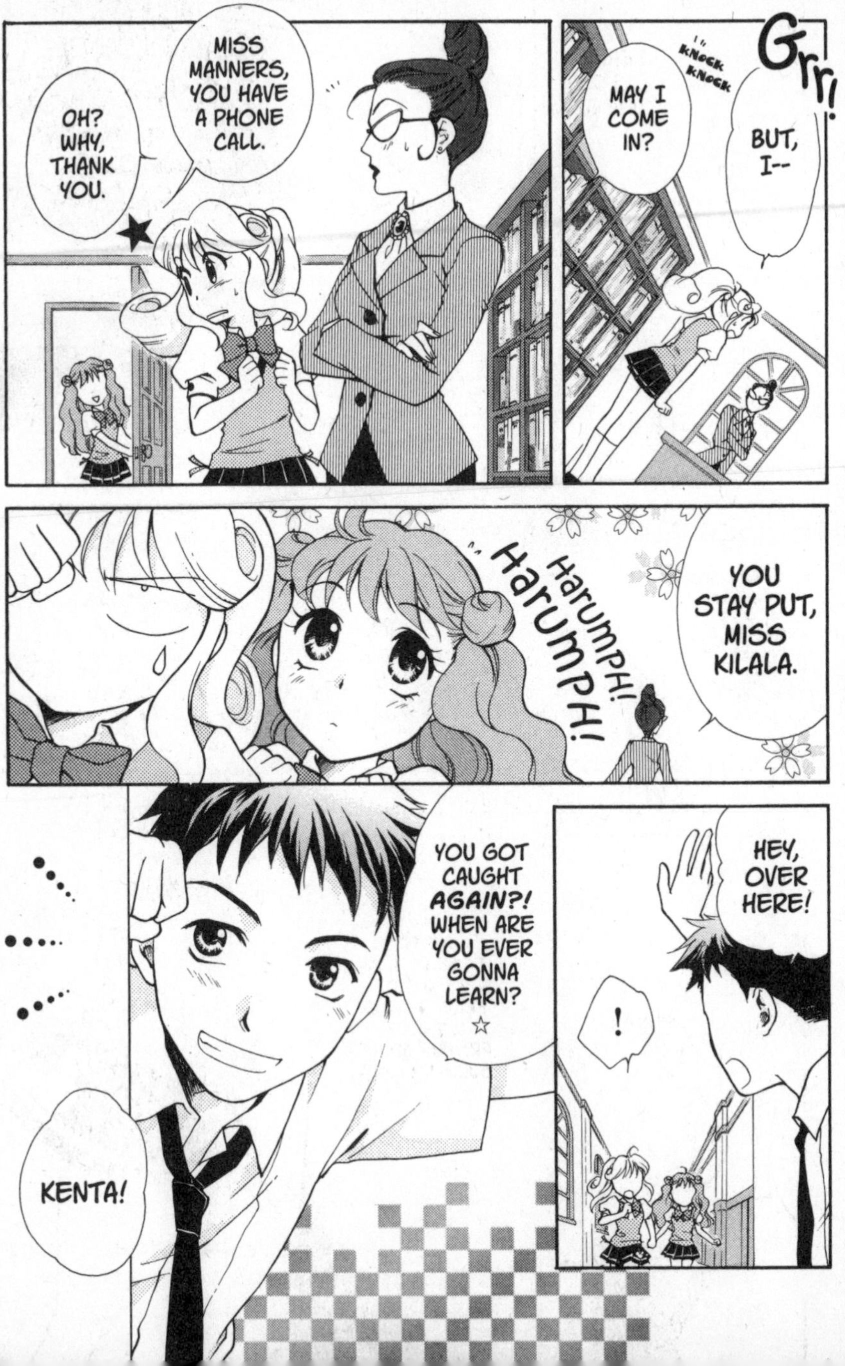

GRR!
BUT, I--
KNOCK KNOCK
MAY I COME IN?
MISS MANNERS, YOU HAVE A PHONE CALL.
OH? WHY, THANK YOU.
YOU STAY PUT, MISS KILALA.
HARUMPH! HARUMPH!
HEY, OVER HERE!
!
YOU GOT CAUGHT AGAIN?! WHEN ARE YOU EVER GONNA LEARN? ☆
KENTA!

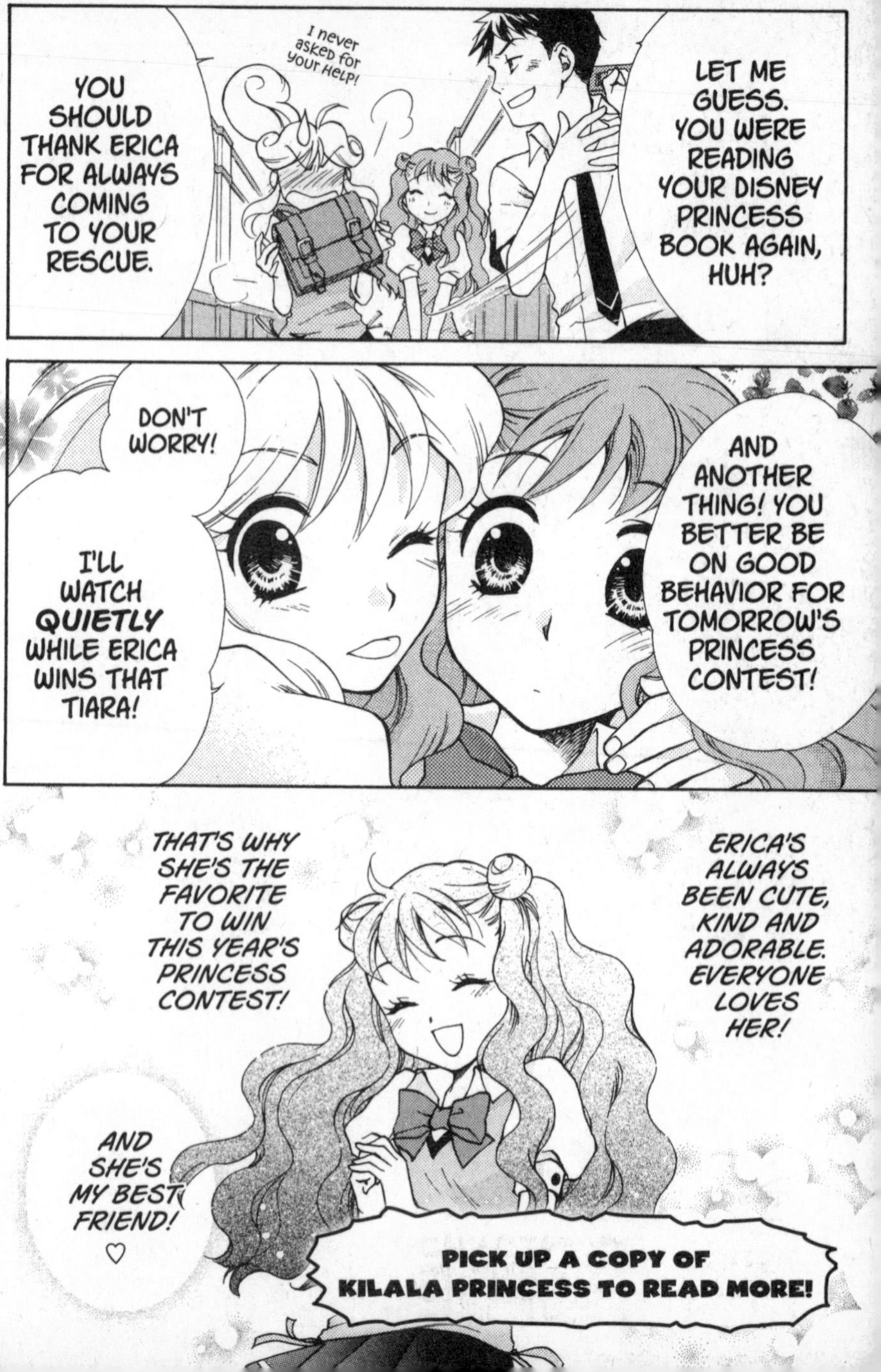
LET ME GUESS. YOU WERE READING YOUR DISNEY PRINCESS BOOK AGAIN, HUH?
I never asked for your help!
YOU SHOULD THANK ERICA FOR ALWAYS COMING TO YOUR RESCUE.
AND ANOTHER THING! YOU BETTER BE ON GOOD BEHAVIOR FOR TOMORROW'S PRINCESS CONTEST!
DON'T WORRY!
I'LL WATCH **QUIETLY** WHILE ERICA WINS THAT TIARA!
ERICA'S ALWAYS BEEN CUTE, KIND AND ADORABLE. EVERYONE LOVES HER!
THAT'S WHY SHE'S THE FAVORITE TO WIN THIS YEAR'S PRINCESS CONTEST!
AND SHE'S MY BEST FRIEND! ♡
PICK UP A COPY OF KILALA PRINCESS TO READ MORE!

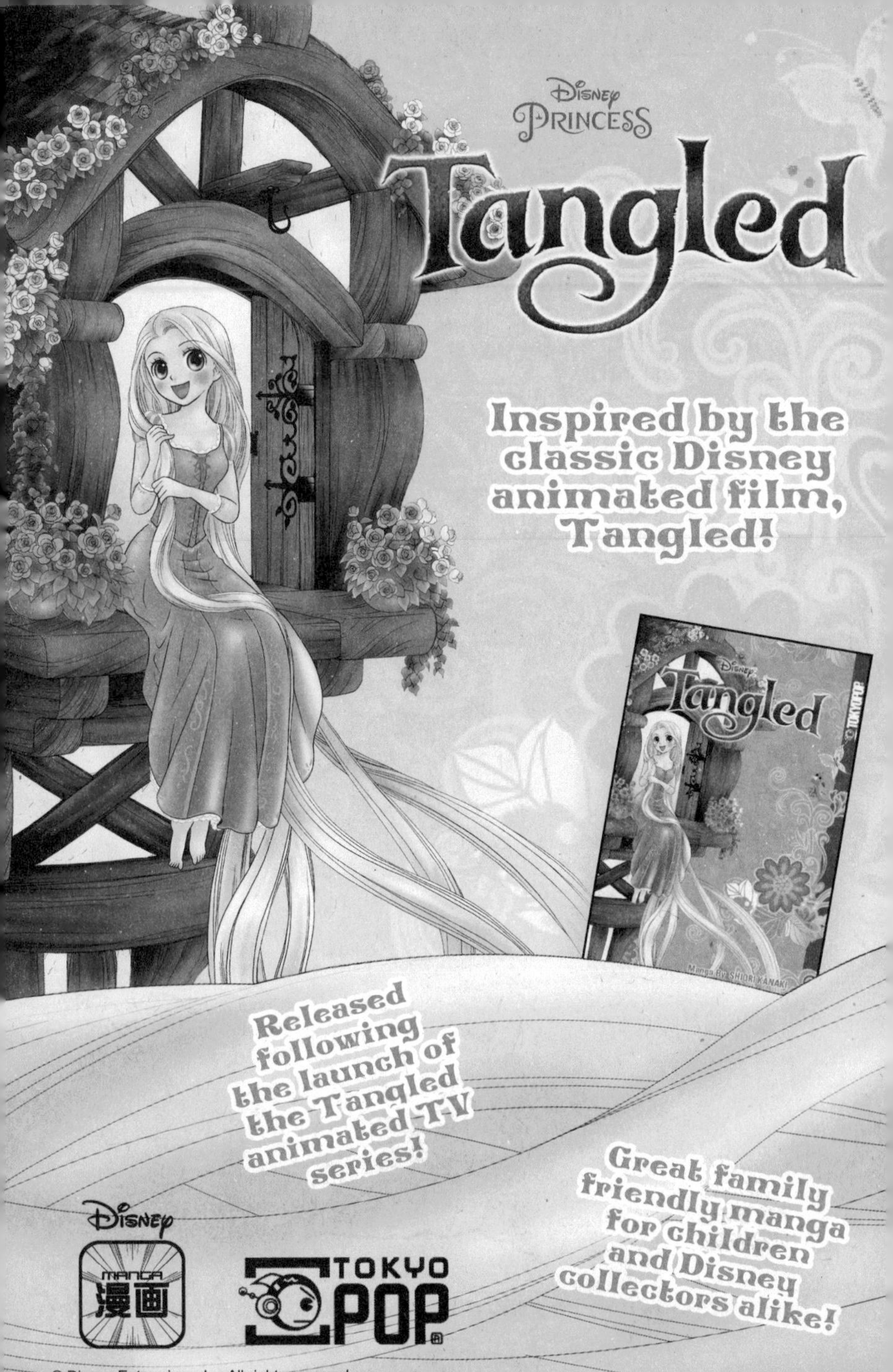
Disney PRINCESS
Tangled
Inspired by the classic Disney animated film, Tangled!
Disney
Tangled
TOKYOPOP
Manga By SHIORI KANAKI
Released following the launch of the Tangled the Tangled TV animated series!
Great family friendly manga for children and Disney collectors alike!
Disney
MANGA
漫画
TOKYO POP

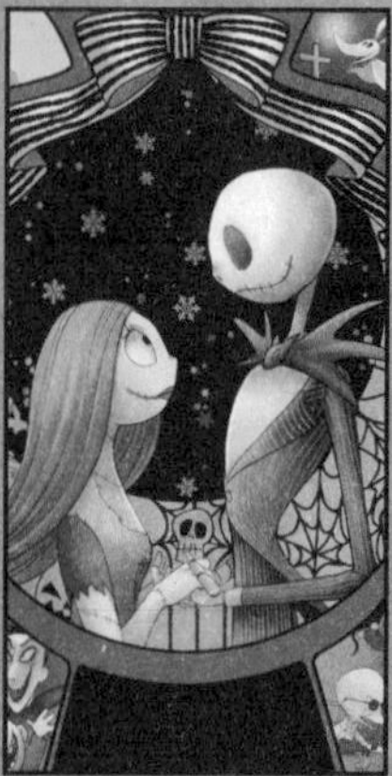
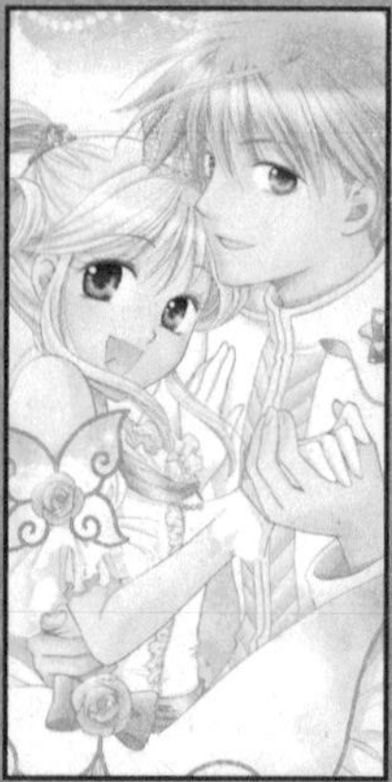
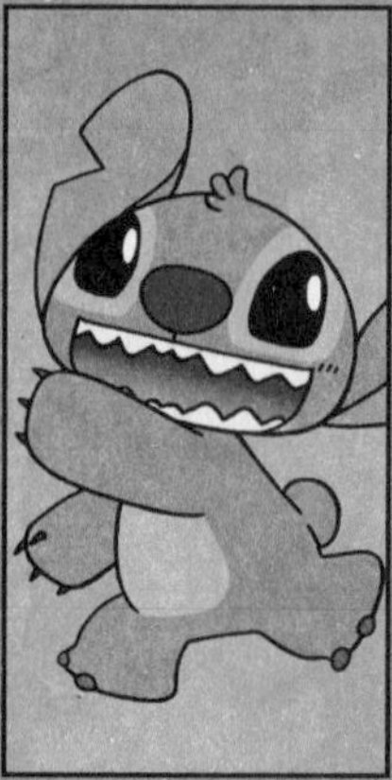
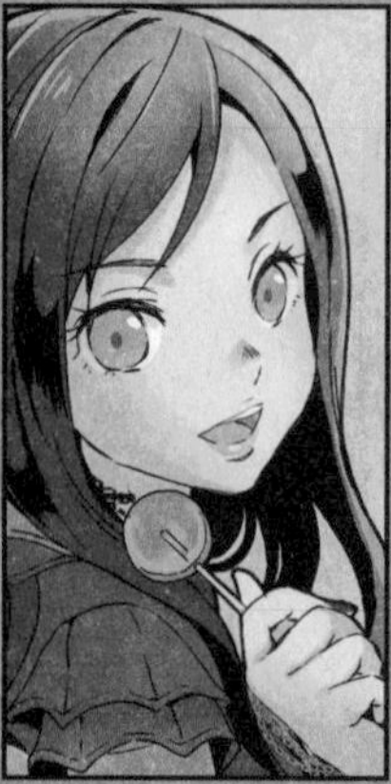
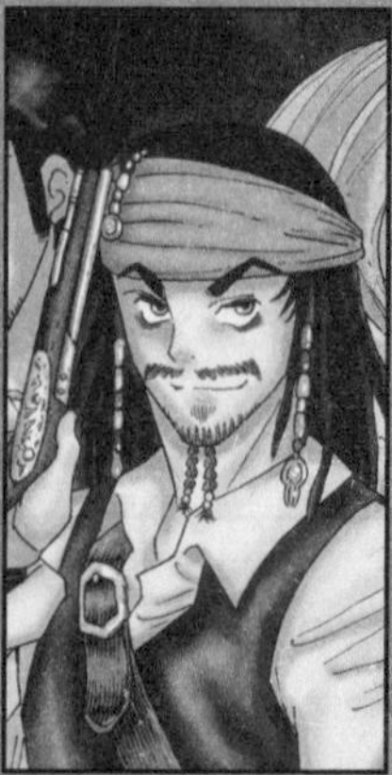
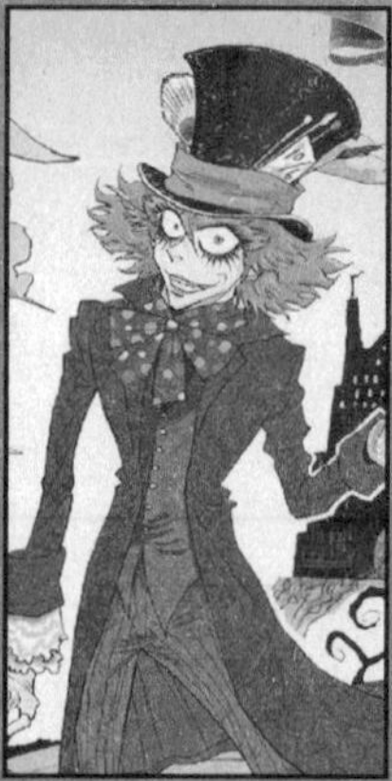
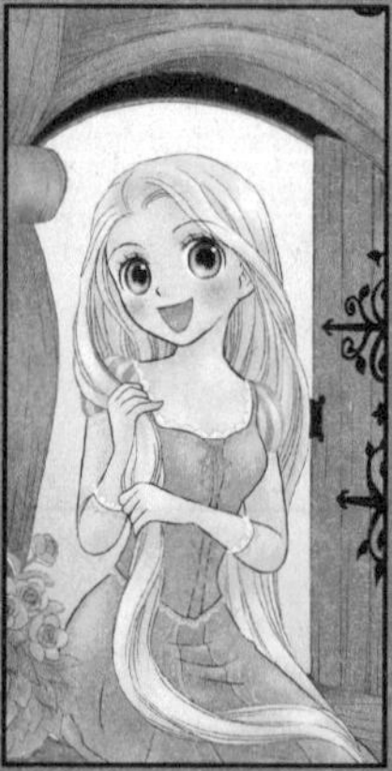
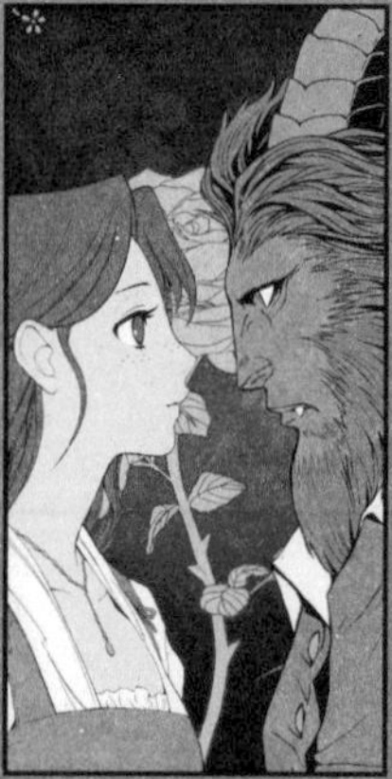
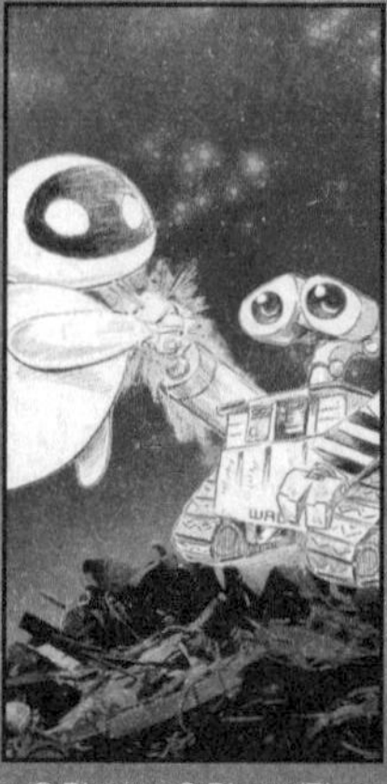
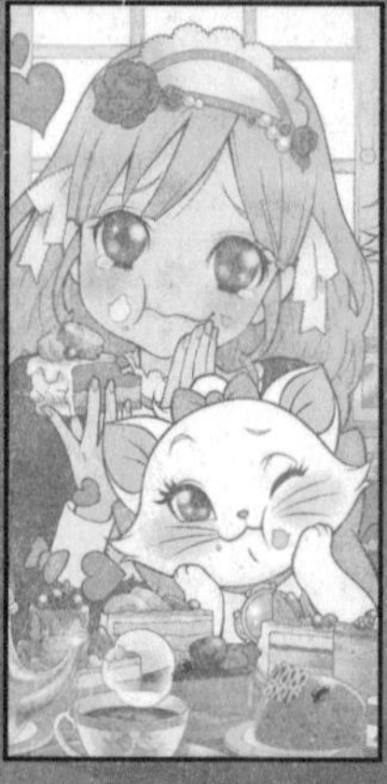
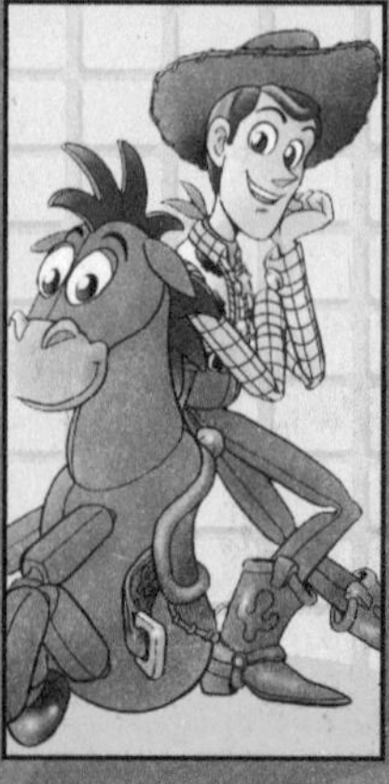
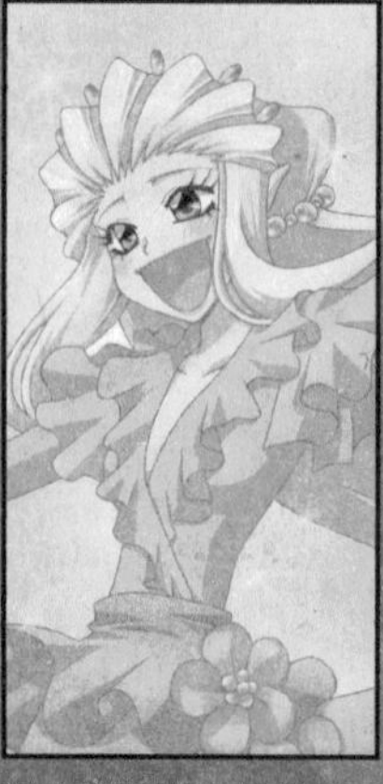

Add These Disney Manga to Your Collection Today!

SHOJO
- ☐ DISNEY BEAUTY AND THE BEAST
- ☐ DISNEY KILALA PRINCESS SERIES

FANTASY
- ☐ DISNEY DESCENDANTS SERIES
- ☐ DISNEY TANGLED
- ☐ DISNEY PRINCESS AND THE FROG
- ☐ DISNEY FAIRIES SERIES
- ☐ MIRIYA AND MARIE

KAWAII
- ☐ MAGICAL DANCE
- ☐ DISNEY STITCH! SERIES

PIXAR
- ☐ DISNEY • PIXAR TOY STORY
- ☐ DISNEY • PIXAR MONSTERS, INC.
- ☐ DISNEY • PIXAR WALL-E
- ☐ DISNEY • PIXAR FINDING NEMO

ADVENTURE
- ☐ DISNEY TIM BURTON'S THE NIGHTMARE BEFORE CHRISTMAS
- ☐ DISNEY ALICE IN WONDERLAND
- ☐ DISNEY PIRATES OF THE CARIBBEAN SERIES

TOKYO POP

Believing is Just the Beginning!

BY TOKYOPOP